Having previously worked as a journ̶ Caroline Dunford enjoyed many y̶ their personal life stories before taking the plunge and writing her own stories. She has now published almost thirty books in genres ranging from historical crime to thrillers and romance, including her much-loved Euphemia Martins mysteries and a series set around WWII featuring Euphemia's perceptive daughter Hope Stapleford. Caroline also teaches creative writing courses part-time at the University of Edinburgh.

HOPE
FOR
TOMORROW

CAROLINE DUNFORD

ACCENT

First published in 2022 by Headline Accent
An imprint of HEADLINE PUBLISHING GROUP

2

Cataloguing in Publication Data is available from the British Library

ISBN 978 1 4722 7667 4

Typeset in 10.5/13pt Bembo Std by Jouve (UK), Milton Keynes

Printed and bound in Great Britain by Clays Ltd, Elcograf S.p.A.

HEADLINE PUBLISHING GROUP
An Hachette UK Company
Carmelite House
50 Victoria Embankment
London EC4Y 0DZ

www.headline.co.uk
www.hachette.co.uk

To my loyal readers, without whom
none of this would exist

Acknowledgements

As ever, huge thanks go to
– my magnificent agent, Amy Collins, whose unwavering belief in me is ever uplifting
– my superb publisher Clare Foss
– my long suffering family
– the Schism Book Group: Tim, Andrew, Alba, et al.
– Fitzroy, who insisted on being included, and who still has a regular Friday diary

Author's Note

During World War Two, a great many pilots claimed to have seen both strange creatures on their planes mid-flight, and also balls of light. After the war, it was discovered that German fighter pilots independently reported the same phenomena. Air Chief Marshal Lord Hugh Dowding, who was largely responsible for the victory of the Battle of Britain, compiled a report for Churchill on the phenomena. To this day no one has ever been able to explain what pilots on both sides of the war saw.

Chapter One

Homecoming

'What do you mean it's about my father?' I asked.

Fitzroy kept his eye on the clouds ahead. He didn't immediately answer. The plane bumped again in the mild turbulence outside. The night was calm enough, but the small, light craft bucked at every air current. Involuntarily I groaned. The British double agent I had caught earlier in the day had managed to give me a whacking great thump on the head. His head had fared worse, but I had been barely conscious when my godfather, Fitzroy, had found me. He'd flown in unexpectedly, landing close to where I'd been fighting. By the careless way he'd left his aircraft without a backward glance, and by the strut of his walk, I'd known it was him. He mopped up the end of my adventure, taking most of the credit, more, I think, by habit than any malign design. Then he literally swept me off my feet to plonk me in the passenger seat of his aircraft.

'Head still sore, Hope?'

'What do you think,' I muttered between gritted teeth. 'I shouldn't be flying. You bullied that doctor into saying I could.'

'Hang on a mo, I think . . .' He let go of the controls and continued to steer with his knees while he reached over the seat behind him. The plane ducked and dived more than ever.

'Should you be doing that?' I managed to keep my voice level.

'Don't fuss,' came the muffled reply behind me. 'Just let me know if anything gets in the way.'

'What?'

'You know, like a bird or something. How's that dial doing, by

1

the way? The one that I couldn't get working. Give it a tap for me, will you?'

I leaned over and tapped at the dial that had troubled him earlier. 'Still nothing,' I said.

'Aha!' My godfather turned back round with a furry cap in his hand. He dumped it on my head, and took the controls in hand again. 'Keep your head warm,' he said. 'Should make it less sore with the altitude and whatnot. I say, I wonder if that's the altimeter. This dashboard isn't the one I'm used to.'

'Altitude?'

Fitzroy peered more closely along the dash. 'Oh, my mistake. That's this one.' He tapped another dial. 'Working perfectly.'

'You didn't know?'

'I fly more by instinct. That's how it was in the Great War. None of the luxuries pilots get nowadays. Parachutes. Hah!' He took his hands off the stick again and gestured around him. 'Practically like travelling by Pullman.'

'I wish you wouldn't keep taking your hands off the controls,' I said.

'Bah!' he said, varying his term of disdain slightly. 'Modern planes more or less fly themselves.' I could have sworn I heard him add 'thankfully' under his breath.

'Now, you were about to tell me about my father,' I said, settling the hat more firmly on my head. Annoyingly enough it did seem to be helping.

'Are you sure you don't want me to teach you about the stars? It's a glorious night. Clear as anything. You've got to take time, Hope, to appreciate the beauty around. If you concentrate solely on whatever disaster mankind is up to—'

'Like war?' I said sarcastically.

Fitzroy turned and gave me one of his most charming smiles. These are always quite blinding, especially as nowadays he's often all dour and stoic. 'Exactly, my dear god-daughter. Like war. If you only concentrate on that nonsense you'd go completely mad. Take the good moments that the good God sends you.'

2

Now I knew he was stalling. I don't remember Fitzroy ever going to church when he visited us at home. My father always said it was just as well. 'If he steps inside the building, Hope, he'll probably go up in a puff of smoke. Divine retribution for all his misdeeds.'

Of course, my father had said it with a smile on his face. When I was older, I became less sure he meant it as a joke, but my mother always laughed and agreed.

'My father,' I said. 'What's happening with my father?'

Fitzroy's shoulders heaved with another big sigh. 'You really won't be guided, will you?'

'What are you talking about?' I demanded.

'I'm sorry, my dear. It doesn't look as if he will pull through this time.'

I took a deep, unsteady breath. 'We've been here before and he's always made it. We shouldn't give up hope yet.'

'My dear girl, do you think your mother would consent to me – me! – flying you home if she didn't think this time it was serious. You know how she feels about my flying. She hates it almost as much as my driving.'

'More,' I said. 'She thinks you're a good driver.'

'Really?' said Fitzroy in a brighter voice. 'Well, that's nice to know.'

'But serious isn't the same as dying,' I said.

'I don't believe your mother could ever put the word dying and your father's name in the same sentence. Besides, Dunkirk—'

'Yes, I am terribly proud of him,' I said.

Fitzroy nodded. 'That's exactly how he would want you to remember him. Like that. Not as an invalid.'

'Do you mean he didn't think he would come back?' I said. I stared out into the darkness, following his gaze. 'Do you mean he wanted to die?'

'I think he'd had enough of putting your mother through the ups and downs. He hated the strain he put on her. Despite their arguments they are totally devoted to each other. I've always known

3

that.' Was it my imagination or did I hear a tone of regret there? 'But no, I don't think he went to die. He knew the risk, certainly, and I imagine he thought if he didn't come back, he'd have made one last difference in the world. It's certainly the way I would like to go. Doing something useful rather than lying around half dead.'

I inhaled sharply at this.

'Sorry, Hope,' said my godfather, 'that must have sounded insensitive. I don't mean your father lies around being an invalid all the time. In fact, in between his bouts of illness he's always been more than up to the job.'

'It's a pity he ever started doing the job,' I said.

'Please,' said Fitzroy. 'You're sounding like your mother. I never made Bertram do anything he didn't want to. And I knew absolutely nothing about him planning to go off in his friend's boat. He kept the whole thing under wraps. Even from me. Most impressive.'

There were a lot of things I could have said, but I was beginning, since I had come to work for him, to realise that my beloved godfather was not a man without faults. He might have been the hero of my childhood, but now as I entered into the shady world of espionage, I was learning he was far from infallible. Yes, he was hugely courageous, but he was also stunningly egotistical and sure of his own abilities. There was little point arguing with him on anything, unless you had a cast-iron case and a method of compelling his attention. It was fortunate he was intelligent and frequently worked things out for himself.

'Try and get some sleep,' he suggested. 'We'll be there sooner than you think, and whatever we find, you'll want to be as together as you can.' He looked round at me for longer than I found comfortable, and added, 'You look awful. What your mother is going to say—' He broke off, shaking his head. Then added, 'I did think your hand-to-hand combat was better than this. I'll have to see what we can do about it.'

I didn't even bother trying to defend my reputation but curled up as best I could and closed my eyes. I didn't think sleep was likely, but I also knew I wasn't up to any more conversation, especially with Fitzroy. When he was trying to be kind, it was always rather like an electric eel snuggling up to you. There was no way you were going to avoid being stung.

It felt as if I had barely closed my eyes when I heard Fitzroy softly repeating my name. I opened my eyes and looked at him. Even in the darkness I could see signs of fatigue written across his face. There were bags under his eyes, and a five o'clock shadow had sprouted on his normally clean-shaven jaw. He stared intently forward, his profile made rough granite by the shadows.

'Good, you're awake. Always best to be awake during a landing. If anything goes wrong you have a better chance of getting out.'

'Especially if you're the pilot,' I said sleepily.

Fitzroy gave a low crack of laughter. 'Especially then. Ready?'

I nodded. Though I wasn't entirely sure what I was meant to be ready for. Fitzroy pulled at a lever. Or rather struggled to pull it. 'Come on,' he muttered under his breath. 'Come on, damn it!'

'What is it?' I asked.

'Landing gear. Plane's been kept in a shocking state,' he grunted with effort. The lever gave and then came off in his hand. 'Ah,' said my godfather in quite a different tone. He fiddled with the lever. 'I wonder if I can reattach it. Hmm, sheared off, I fear. Be a sweetheart, Hope, and look to see if the light over there is on.' He indicated a rough area of the dashboard with a careless flick of a finger. My stomach wobbled a bit as I realised which light he was indicating. It had been helpfully labelled.

'No,' I said as calmly as I could. The landing gear had not been released. We were going to crash.

'Damn it,' said Fitzroy dispassionately. Then he half rose and stamped hard on the floor several times. 'And now?'

'No. I don't think it works like that. Are there any parachutes?'

'Hmm, what? No. Too low anyway,' said Fitzroy. He kicked the floor hard enough to make the little plane wobble. Astonishingly, the light in front of my eyes winked and then lit up.

5

'It's on!' I shouted.

Fitzroy winced and sat down. 'I'm right next to you, Hope. No need to raise your voice. Now let's hope that little bulb is telling the truth.' Then quite calmly he set about guiding the plane in.

It was my first chance to see White Orchards from the air, but I couldn't take my eyes off my godfather. There were no beads of sweat on his brow, and his forehead remained smooth and unworried. For the first time I wondered if he was more mad than courageous. Or if he simply had a death wish.

'Are we all right?' I asked.

He kept his eyes on the horizon as our descent continued. 'Of course,' he said. 'Your mother would have my liver if I crashed with you on board. And as I like a decent drop of claret that would be a great pity. But brace yourself just in case,' he added, almost as an afterthought.

Then with an almighty jolt we touched the ground. However, the plane seemed to have a different view of things than my godfather. Although the landing gear was clearly, and thankfully, down, the plane didn't seem to want to follow suit. Instead it bounced back up into the air. Fitzroy wrestled with the controls, and we bounced off the ground again.

'Bloody gravity,' he muttered. 'Never there when you need it.'

We bounced another four times before we stayed down, swinging in a fishtail, as he pulled up short of the courtyard gates. I found myself plastered to the door. Fitzroy raised an eyebrow at me, and offered his hand. He pulled me upright.

'Feeling better?' he asked.

'Feeling *safer* now we're down.'

'Don't let a bit of hopping worry you,' said Fitzroy. 'Any landing you walk away from is a good 'un. Now all we need to do is trundle right up to the front door.'

We had landed in the field in front of the house, rough grazing we kept for the sheep. Indeed, as he taxied through towards the house gates, more than one woolly face peered up at me, looking rather startled.

'Are you sure the wingspan will fit through the gates,' I said.

'I think so,' said Fitzroy, 'don't you?'

The question came out as a mildly curious one, and alarmed me further. Then, as we approached the gates, I saw two figures emerge from the house. One immediately began to run towards the plane, while the other held back.

It was still too dark for me to be sure who they were. I only knew neither of them was short enough to be my father. He must still be ailing. Fitzroy brought the plane to a stop. 'Out you hop,' he said, as he reached for the catch on his door. He disappeared in a flash, leaving me scrabbling with my door, and wondering how I was going to get down without jumping. I feared the top of my wounded head might pop off if I leapt down to the ground. Fitzroy's door flapped in the wind. He'd not bothered to shut it. I heard him say, 'Oh, my dear girl, I'm so sorry.' Then I heard a muffled sob. Turning back from the stubborn catch on my side, I saw the silhouette of him embracing a smaller figure, who could only be my mother. I pulled harder at the door, and finally it fell open.

Giles, our butler, stood on the ground in front holding out his hand. He was near enough that I could see how rigidly he was standing.

'We've put him in the library, Miss Hope,' he said, his voice thin and reedy instead of its normal bass tones. I realised he was trying not to weep.

'How long ago?' I asked.

'No more than an hour, miss,' said Giles. 'It was very peaceful. I don't believe . . .'

My composure cracked. I ran towards the house. I knew it was ridiculous, but I couldn't stop the thought that perhaps my father was sleeping, that he was resting, waiting for me, before he . . . before he . . . He wouldn't go without saying goodbye. I knew he would have waited for me. They had made a mistake. I would have known if he'd gone. I would have known.

I ran up the steps to the front entrance. There was a maid

sobbing in the hallway. I wanted to stop and tell her it was all right, that there had been a mistake, but I didn't have the time. My father was waiting for me. He was almost out of time, but he was waiting for me.

I flung open the library doors and stopped. My father was lying on top of a long table. Some kind of trestle from the outbuildings, I guessed. A light green linen cloth had been thrown over it, and a pillow of a similar hue placed under his head. Looking at it I recalled that it was one of a pair that used to be on the bench in the hall, and wondered what had happened to the other. My father wore one of his favourite brown check waistcoats. One of those hard-wearing country ones. But instead of a normal jacket he wore his favourite smoking silk. Two still-wrapped cigars peeped out from his front pocket. The fez Uncle Hans had given him, and which I'm sure he would have worn to bed if mother had let him, had been placed on his head. The fez was even older than I, and I could see the neat stitching of my mother's needle where she had darned and re-sewn the object she hated over and over again, because her husband loved it so much.

My throat tightened. I took one pace forward. His favourite brown brogues peeped out at the end of the blanket. The ones he always used for walking. Except now they no longer bore their usual coating of mud, but shone to a mirror-like finish. On the table beside his right hand were his reading glasses, neatly folded. Another step and I could see his face. It hadn't changed. It was the same old owlish face surrounded by his beard and his hair. Some- one had tidied the straight line of his moustache, but no one had shaved his side whiskers as my mother had threatened to on more than one occasion; she said he looked like a sheep.

He was still my father. My aged, white-haired, slightly – or perhaps in truth more than slightly – plump, kindly faced father. Unlike my mother, whose hair showed barely a trace of silver, my father's hair, still thick, was white and woolly like his beard. My mother teased him about looking like Father Time, but he always seemed to me more like Father Christmas on holiday.

8

I noticed then that on his left side someone had left a small pile of books. I walked around the table, not touching anything, and read the spines. *Alice in Wonderland*, *Ten Thousand Leagues Under the Sea*, *The Iliad*, and Charles Dickens' *A Christmas Carol*. Every Christmas Eve that I could remember he had read to me from that book. It was never officially Christmas for me until I heard the opening lines in his voice: '"Marley was dead; to begin with. There is no doubt whatever about that."'

I saw my tears splash onto the linen cloth and mark it before I realised I was crying, silently, endlessly, like I had the whole sea inside me trying to get out.

'Come and have a cup of tea, Miss Hope,' said Giles from the doorway. 'Get yourself warm.'

'The fire isn't lit in here,' I said stupidly. 'Won't he be cold? I can't leave him in the cold.'

I heard footsteps behind me, and then the tartan blanket we keep in the music room for when the winds sweep down across the Fens, unfurled above my father and descended around him. 'Do you want me to cover his face?' said Fitzroy.

'What if he wants to read? They put his glasses behind him.' My voice hitched on a sob.

'His eyes are closed,' said my godfather, 'and he's sleeping now. Let him rest.'

He placed a hand on my shoulder as he twitched the blanket over my father's face. 'Come away now, my dear. Giles won't be happy till you drink some of his wretched tea, but I have a flask in my pocket that will help make it more palatable.'

'I don't want to leave him,' I said, resisting the gentle pressure on my shoulder.

'My dear girl, do you think he would ever leave you? He'll always be with you, Hope. He loved you.'

Chapter Two

Things Carry On

I was exhausted and I don't believe my godfather was much better. I half drank, half drowned in the bowl of soup I was given to 'warm me up'. The three of us – my mother, Fitzroy and I – were in the dining room. Normally, for such an informal meal, we would have eaten in the library, but obviously not tonight. We gathered down one end of the large table, and my mother had the soup urn and bread placed on the table, before dismissing all the staff.

She rose to her feet to serve us, but Fitzroy took the ladle from her hand. 'I'll do this, Euphemia. You look all out.'

She sat and glanced up at him. 'You look awful.'

'Thank you. Hope is suffering from a mild concussion. None of us is at our best.'

The words 'especially my father' flickered across my mind, but I managed to keep them between my teeth. I realised I was so tired I was verging on hysteria.

'I think I'll just head up to bed,' I said.

'No,' said my godfather sharply, 'you will not.'

'I'll help in any way I can tomorrow,' I said, 'but I'm practically asleep on my feet.'

'I know, and you can escape to your bed as soon as you've finished your soup, and at least half of one roll.' He passed another bowl to my mother. 'And that goes for you too, Alice,' he said, using her code name. 'It's an order. I don't believe you've eaten all day.'

'I had breakfast,' my mother said meekly, and picked up her spoon. She hesitated and looked over at me. 'I am very grateful you're here, Hope. And you, Eric. I don't think I could have borne today if I didn't know you were on your way. I appreciate everything you both did to get here as soon as you could. Your father knew you were coming, Hope. He said he needed a little nap before you arrived . . .' She looked down into her soup.

Fitzroy, who had been serving himself, took his seat again and reached over to place a hand on her shoulder. 'I take it it was his heart?'

My mother nodded. She raised her head again and pressed her lips together to hold back the tears. She put a hand on top of my godfather's, and gave him a swift smile. 'Yes, that's what Dr Butcher thinks. The attack was early this morning. There had been no sign anything was wrong, and then . . . Afterwards, when he was resting, I think he knew. I said something about it being a near thing, and he didn't agree with me, but asked me if I knew where you were, Hope. Dr Butcher wasn't worried. We both knew that the hours afterwards are a dangerous time but, if anything, it looked as if your father had pulled through better than before.' She hesitated. 'I think I even berated him about this all being down to his love of sailing.'

Fitzroy removed his hand and began to calmly break his roll. 'He would have liked that,' he said. 'Bertram never felt better than when you were sparring with him.' He caught my eye. 'I don't mean arguing, Hope.'

'I know what you mean,' I said. And I did. Although I would have found it hard to put into words. My parents' relationship had always been a passionate one. They fought like cat and dog over politics. My father was far more of a socialist than my mother would have liked. My mother believed firmly in *noblesse oblige*, and always did her duty whatever the cost to herself. But that would turn in a moment into an exchange of affection. 'Father always wanted you to feel his equal, Mother,' I said. 'He treated you like—'

'A fellow combatant?' she said. 'We were always on the same

11

side, you know. We just differed in our methods at times. Your father hated that he couldn't keep up with me in the field, but he was strong enough to let me continue working for the Department without him. I don't think many men would have countenanced their wives doing that.'

'Especially with me being involved,' said Fitzroy with a smug little grin and, showing atrocious manners, he dunked his bread in his soup.

My mother smiled. 'He liked you in his way. He trusted you with me.'

'Yes,' said Fitzroy. 'I suppose he did.' He sounded as if he wanted to add something more, but stopped.

'I cannot believe he's gone,' my mother blurted out. She inhaled, her face creasing into a frown, her shoulders raised high as she physically tried to pull herself together. Then she stood. 'Please, finish your soup. I can't . . .'

She made to leave the room, but Fitzroy was quicker. Before she could reach the door, he was beside her and had pulled her into his arms. She gave a small cry, resisting him for a moment. I stood up, unsure what to do. But then all the rigidity left her body and she hid her face in his shoulder.

'Damn,' said Fitzroy. 'I knew I should have told Griffin to pack my mackintosh.'

'Wretched man,' said my mother through his shoulder. To my utter astonishment Fitzroy kissed the top of her head. I had never seen him display any physical affection to my mother.

'Sit down and finish your soup, Hope,' he said. 'I'm going to escort your mother to her room. I'll return shortly.'

'Shouldn't I—' I began, thinking I should be the one to go with her.

'No,' he said firmly.

When he returned some twenty minutes later, I was resting my head on the table and thinking about using the tines of a used fork to keep my eyes open. 'Ah, good, you've eaten something. You should get off to bed yourself.'

'Shouldn't I stay with Mother?'

Fitzroy shook his head. 'Perhaps if you two were closer, but I think Euphemia would feel she had to put on a brave face for you. Heaven knows she's going to have to do that over the coming days.'

'But not with you?'

'No, never with me. She knows she can be herself with me.'

I left him helping himself to another bowl of soup. Everything felt wrong. I paused in the doorway.

He looked up from his meal. 'What? You know I eat when I'm tired, and I am very, very tired. It's only going to be worse tomorrow.'

I nodded to him. It was hardly the platitude I wanted to hear, but he seemed in an odd mood, so I went off alone to my room. Sitting in the middle of my bed, waiting for me, was Fitz, the bear Fitzroy had bought for me as a baby. He was a large stuffed toy and made a suitable armful. So I picked him up, kicked off my shoes, and lay down on the bed. My eyes were full of painful sharpness. I pulled the bear close to my face, breathing in the scent of him that had always comforted me as a child, and cried silently into his fur.

I quickly discovered that when someone dies things get very busy. The next two days passed in a blur of activity. There was no more time to cry. Dr Butcher had signed the death certificate and the service in the local church had been arranged. Mother and I had to decide on the hymns. Fitzroy suggested 'For Those in Peril on the Sea' and had to quickly reassure my mother he was referring to my father's gallantry.

It wasn't long after breakfast that first day that everyone who lived locally or who had ever known us began to arrive to offer their condolences. Cook was kept busy producing sandwiches and cake at short notice. Fitzroy handed me paper and pen and told me to write up my last mission. 'Before you forget,' he said. 'Sorry, but it has to be done. And details, Hope. I want details.' I more than half presumed this was to keep me out of the way. Visitors from further afield arrived, and the staff had rooms to prepare and Mother had people to greet.

A couple of men in extremely smart suits came to present their condolences, but couldn't stay more than the night, and were extremely polite, and courteously distressed that we had to put them up for even that short amount of time. Fitzroy kept me as far away from these two as possible, even sending me luncheon where I sat in the morning room working over my report.

My godfather, who was a constant presence overseeing matters, had summoned both his major-domo, Griffin, and his dog, Jack, to his side. They both arrived very early the morning after us. Apparently, they had set off in Fitzroy's car late into the night. And Fitzroy never let anyone else drive his car. Ever. Also, he had more than an adequate supply of clothes on-site. A long time ago, he had become such a frequent visitor that part of the attic had been converted into rooms for him. However, both man and dog soon made their uses evident. Even though this Jack, around nine months old now, was more snappy than his predecessors, he followed their disposition in the adoration of my mother. I didn't even know she had met the puppy. But then Fitzroy didn't keep me apprised of his war work, so I could hardly expect he would brief me on what my mother was doing. I had assumed she was staying with my father permanently at White Orchards. But then, I was beginning to question many of my assumptions. The questions Cole, an agent who had also been trained by Fitzroy, had raised about my paternity now seemed ridiculous, and yet also more understandable from someone outside my odd little family. Fitzroy had always been an oddly constant presence in our house, due to my mother's work as an agent of the Crown, and the alacrity with which our servants obeyed him as he ordered various arrangements, made me realise how dominant in our affairs he must have seemed to any outsider. He rode roughshod over the disapproval of neighbours until they too had come to look on him as a fixture of White Orchards. I could see how Cole had made his mistake. Gossip had always followed my mother and her partner, but her distress at the death of my father was deep and sincere.

During those days my mother would stop in the middle of whatever she was doing, and simply look confused, as if she had suddenly remembered her loss. She would sit down in the nearest seat and within minutes the little bull terrier, Jack, would be in her lap, and she would absently fondle his ears. Our staff were similarly discomposed, but Griffin took charge there.

My mother received guests and checked or approved Griffin's endless lists. Fitzroy would have dealt with the lists, but my mother begged to be allowed to do something. 'I want to be so busy I can't think,' she said. A book of condolence appeared in the hall, and within the first day it was a third full with the names of tenants and neighbours.

When I finished my report and handed it over, I walked this way and that and got in everyone's way, trying to help. But they were far too kind to complain. Fitzroy threatened to make me write up more reports if I didn't find a proper use for myself. Clearly he had decided that being stern with me during my bereavement was best. It wasn't.

My mother constantly came up to me with an extra shawl in her hands, fearing I was too cold. She sent for Dr Butcher to check my concussion frequently. Griffin, himself once a local doctor, had checked me out as soon as he arrived, and told me not to do anything strenuous, and to rest as much as I could. Dr Butcher said exactly the same. Fitzroy came up to me every now and then, and handed me the end of a leash with Jack attached. 'Take him for a walk. It'll do you both good. Besides, this one hasn't got to know you well yet.' So Jack and I went for walks in the forest behind the house, and I managed every time to find my way back to the house without getting lost.

Fitzroy said we'd need to discuss matters after the funeral, and I would have to stay and hear the will read the day after that. Then he stalked off to do something somewhere. It was only after he'd gone that I realised he'd made it sound as if he wouldn't be here then. I had assumed we would return to duty together, not simply because it wasn't easy to travel around at this time, but because I was under his command.

Two hours before the service I caught both Fitzroy and my mother coming out of her writing room. It occurred to me then, rather like a damp squib of an epiphany, that her writing room was an intelligence station of sorts. 'How long has that been—?'

'Shhh!' said Mother. She was dressed for the funeral in a well-cut black dress that despite its sombreness gave her a certain chicness. 'I was going to talk to you about this after the funeral,' she said. 'Obviously, it will be yours now. Anything you're not cleared to see has been removed. And the only clean telephone line in the house is there.'

Fitzroy looked between us, frowning deeply. 'As you say, it's not something to be discussed here and now. There are a great many people milling around this house.'

My mother nodded. 'I'm afraid you have to clean it yourself. None of the maids and not even Giles is allowed in there.'

'But . . .'

Fitzroy took my mother's arm. 'Euphemia, you need to rest before the service. You know the reading is going to take a lot out of you.' He gave me a smiling nod, and led my mother firmly away. It was like going back to my childhood. There had been so many times when I had wanted to talk or play with my godfather and he had said he had to speak to my mother. I remembered all too clearly the Easter when I was desperate to go egg-hunting in the orchard, because I knew Cook had hidden eggs for me there. I was also as determined as an eight-year-old can be that I was going to go hunting with Fitzroy. My father had to break it to me that my godfather and mother had left late the night before on important business. I threw a tantrum – one of only three I threw during my childhood – and refused to go out with my father. I was sent to bed early without supper, but the next morning all the coloured eggs were there in a basket at the foot of my bed. Clearly my father had gone out and found them all by himself.

Remembering this, I found myself blinking back tears. How unthinkingly cruel I had been as a child. Regret has no purposeful function, but it can still cling and gnaw like a burr. Worse yet was the realisation that having lost my father, it appeared my mother's sorrow was now consuming Fitzroy's attention. Couldn't they see I too was struggling? I tried so hard not to feel jealous. My mother had lost her partner of so many years, but I had lost my father. However, it was obvious which of us Fitzroy believed most needed support. Cole's voice whispered again at the back of my mind. *They have always been lovers.* But even though I felt abandoned, I recognised the raw, primeval grief my mother carried with her. I knew that but for her strong will and practised composure, she would be on her knees howling like a dog. Perhaps Fitzroy knew that too, and was determined to help her stay strong. My mother is of a passionate nature. I buried my feelings deep down inside me, allowing them to coalesce into rocks and stones that dragged me down and slowed my steps.

When the time came for us to set out for the funeral service, I was deep in my sorrow. In the last few days I felt I had lived a year and a half. Dimly, I wondered if Germany was about to, or indeed even had, invaded Britain, while we were locked in our tragedy in the Fens. Perhaps that had been what my mother had been checking in her writing room. If the invasion had occurred I imagined Fitzroy would either have gone back to London or, as my mother had once suggested, tried to put me on a boat to somewhere the Nazis hadn't yet reached. Not that there were many options left.

The frost on the ground had thawed not long after our arrival. The water seeping back into the earth had left the lanes and byways a deep rich and creamy mud. At least we were far enough away from the swamp not to have that dreadful rotting smell. One of my father's projects late in his life had been to put in more drainage, and almost overnight the land around White Orchards had improved immensely. Still, we had more than our fair share of mud. After a quick consultation with Fitzroy, my mother decided the family would walk, and that no, Fitzroy could not bring Jack to the church. 'Too unpredictable,' she said, 'with everyone but us.' Fitzroy would have complained, but my mother said in a cool, firm voice, 'Today is not the day for him to bite the vicar.' Fitzroy's face reddened slightly, and whatever joke was between them made my mother lift the corners of her mouth almost imperceptively. It wasn't a smile exactly, but it was a crack in the iron calm she had outwardly portrayed until now.

I would like to write how wonderful and moving the service was. But the truth is it passed in a blur and was, for me, completely eclipsed by what came after it.

Chapter Three

Two Steps Forward, Three Steps Back

Everyone came back to the house. We had laid on a light luncheon, the first setting of which disappeared as if a horde of locusts had descended on it. Then everyone said they were only going to stay five minutes. All of them were still there at teatime, which sent our housekeeper Mrs Templeton into a terrible flurry. 'The goings-on, Miss Hope? I never thought to see Farmer Oates drink out of our best porcelain teacups. But your mother would have us put out the best! And the whisky-drinking going on in the billiard room. Mr Fitzroy's got upwards of twenty gentlemen in there finishing the master's best malt.'

'Fitzroy's getting drunk?' I said, offended and astonished.

'Oh no, dear. He's been rounding up the gentlemen who felt tea wasn't quite enough to toast your father and corralled them in one room. It's made things so much easier. Although I do worry about the billiard table.'

I put my hands lightly on her forearms. 'Don't worry, Mrs T. I'll see if I can find Mother or failing that Mr Griffin. As a last resort we can have Mr Fitzroy start to escort people from the building.'

'I don't want to be inhospitable – and it's the last thing your mother would want – but honestly, they've been here a good while, and what with the rationing they've eaten us out of house and home.'

'That's probably it,' I said. 'Stop laying out more sandwiches and cake, and I think you'll find the crowd will begin to thin.

This must be the most food a lot of them have seen since the war started.'

Mrs Templeton twisted her fingers together. 'If you think I should.'

'Yes,' I said firmly. 'You can't empty your entire pantry for the funeral party, and Father would have had a fit if he thought there was no cake left in the house.'

'If you say so, Miss Hope.' She fled as speedily as a pencil skirt would allow her down one of the servants' passages, well away from the baying crowd.

To be fair, things weren't out of control, but some of the men were a little merry. I peeked into the billiard room, trying to stay out of eyeline of the drinking posse. I couldn't see Fitzroy. I went through to the main drawing room. It was thick with people. Voices that had been kept low when they first arrived had now risen. People no longer talked in hushed whispers. They even laughed. Plates and glasses chinked. The air smelt of stale coffee and cheap cigarettes. A middle-aged woman, whose face looked vaguely familiar, waved at me. I drew my head back immediately. I doubted my mother could have been present. She would have politely, but implacably, chivvied the smokers to the courtyard.

The only place I could think where both of them could have remained hidden was the office attached to the morning room. I knocked briefly on the door and entered. My mother and Fitzroy both jumped. 'I thought you had locked that,' said my mother.

'I haven't slept in forty-eight hours,' said Fitzroy snappily. Then, 'Sorry, Alice.' He was leaning against the desk, with my mother seated in a captain's chair to one side. The room was lit only by a single oil lamp that hung from the ceiling. It cast shadows into the corners, and made the room seem less familiar. Alien somehow. Even the two of them were wrong. Fitzroy had his arms crossed, and was using his full height to lean over my mother. His eyes were lidded and his lips thin. My mother had her back pressed against the chair and her hands clenched in a knot in front of her. Her face was slightly flushed, and she was frowning heavily.

'Oh, for Heaven's sake, Hope, come in and close the bloody door,' said Fitzroy. 'This is a remote operational base. You can't let any Tom, Dick or Harry just wander in here.'

'I'm not happy about this,' said my mother. 'The timing is all wrong.'

'What's happened? Have we been invaded?'

Fitzroy gave a cold, short laugh. 'Hardly. I would have disturbed even your father's wake for that. But if you want an update, I think you'll find we are not going to be invaded. The country is set on a long hard path, but there is cause for hope.'

I looked at my mother, wondering if this had been what they were arguing about. 'He's right,' she said. 'It looks increasingly likely that invasion may not happen. It all depends on whether we can gain air superiority.'

'Of course we can!' said Fitzroy.

My mother shrugged. 'It's not impossible, but it will be far from easy.'

'And they can't bloody well invade without air superiority,' said Fitzroy triumphantly.

'Yes, but they can bomb us to hell and back while they try,' said my mother.

'Here?' I said.

'Unlikely,' said Fitzroy. 'But you will have to go back to London. After the will. You'll find orders at your flat. It'll be in one of the codes I taught you. You'll work it out.'

'Where will you be?'

'If you're asking as my subordinate, none of your damn business.' His face softened slightly. 'If you're asking as my god-daughter, I will be with your mother. I'd tell you more if I could.'

'You won't be in Germany?' I asked. My heart thumped loudly in my ears.

'Seeing as your mother never bothered to learn German,

21

'no.' He gave my mother a gimlet look. She returned his gaze, unaffected.

'Do you honestly think anything you might say to me today is going to upset me more than I am already?'

Fitzroy huffed into his moustache. 'I'm not trying to upset you. I'm only telling you what has to happen next. You must see I have no option and under the circumstances . . .'

My mother's head drooped. 'Yes, you're right. The timing is horrid.' She got up and embraced me gently. 'Nothing about today is what I would have wished,' she said. 'But please, Hope, understand, everything that has been done has been done out of love for you. Misguided or not. And what I am about to do, it's not how I would have wanted it to happen, but—' She broke off after a stern cough from my godfather.

On this very odd note, she released me and left the room. Fitzroy closed the door behind her. 'Are you all born in bloody barns up here?'

'As you doubtless know, my mother wasn't born here. She is, however, somewhat distracted.'

'Of course she damn well is. Her husband's dead.'

'He was also my father, and I wish you'd stop swearing at me.'

'Pah!' he said. 'Call this swearing? You'd hear worse in any bloody nursery.'

I took my mother's seat. 'It would help if you'd tell me what's going on.'

Fitzroy stood up and started pacing. He was careful not to look me in the eye. 'Your mother and I are about to leave. We both know what the will says, and have no reason to remain.'

'I don't follow.'

Fitzroy paused, mid-pace, and stared out the window, which was shuttered tight, at a view he couldn't see. 'Your father's will does not include your mother.'

'What do you mean?'

'Exactly what I said. Everything is left to you. Unconditionally.'

'How? Why? How do you know?'

'He asked me to witness it. I refused,' said Fitzroy keeping his back to me.

'He cut my mother out entirely? Why would he do that?'

Fitzroy clasped his hands behind his back, but remained facing the closed shutters. 'I've had quite a few years to think about that,' he said. 'And all I have ever come up with is two options, both of which are somewhat unsavoury.'

'Tell me.'

Fitzroy finally turned round, his face hard and expressionless. 'Are you sure you want to know? Think about it. If you believe me to be right, it is a black mark against your father's character. If you believe me to be wrong, it is a mark against mine.'

'Whichever way, everyone loses. I understand. But do you think it is beyond my ability to reason out what you are thinking, or even worse?'

'Very well. The two most likely reasons were firstly, to warn me that should anything happen to your father your mother would be left without money, home or status. Even if you were a child, she would be dependent on your good graces, through the guardian appointed for you. And as you and your mother have never been close, it would have doubtless made your mother's life difficult.'

'Who was to be my guardian?' I interrupted.

Fitzroy scowled. 'That was a second document I never saw. Obviously. Can I continue now? This is all very distasteful.'

I nodded.

'The second was to emphasise to me that Euphemia was totally dependant on him.' Fitzroy looked up at the ceiling. 'I don't think your father ever appreciated my assets. He believed the Department paid me very little, and there was no way I would be able to support your mother, if she chose to run off with me.'

'Good God!' I said.

'It should go without saying that your mother would never have abandoned your father, and that he even thought this lowered him, inexorably, in my esteem. We were civil to each other after that, for both your mother's and your sake, but any vestige of friendship, at least on my side, died that day.'

I sat for a moment thinking it through, being as dispassionate as I could. As if these were not the most important people in my life. 'You're suggesting my father wanted complete control over my mother – that he was genuinely afraid she might leave him?'

'It seems so.' He stopped pacing and returned to lean against the desk. 'I know this is not the time to speak of such things, but I am afraid, Hope, that in some ways your father was a fool. He underestimated your mother's character enormously.'

'I don't believe it. Not for one moment,' I said, rising to my feet.

'It doesn't matter what you believe,' said Fitzroy, becoming equally cold. 'The situation stands.'

'If any of this were true you would never have agreed to be my godfather.'

Fitzroy raised his eyebrows. 'That was a duty I bore to you, not to either of your parents. Now, if we can bring this unpleasant conversation to an end, I must check Griffin has remembered to pack everything.'

He stood up, but before he took so much as a step I said, with more force than I had intended, 'What did you do?'

He leaned back on the desk once more, his arms stretched out behind him, clearly ready to depart. 'I have already said. I refused to witness it.'

'That's not what I mean, and you know it,' I said. 'What did you do to make him believe you wanted to steal his wife?'

'I haven't the faintest idea,' said Fitzroy. 'In many ways your father's thoughts were unfathomable to me. I have always done everything in my power to protect your mother's reputation.'

'My mother had a flat in London.'

'Has.'

'That means she always had a place to go. Unless my father didn't know about that?'

Fitzroy went very still. In a low, and much more gentle voice, he said, 'Hope, all this happened a long time ago. I really think it is best that you let things be.'

'Besides, if you didn't tell my mother, how does she know she isn't in the will? Did you tell her today? That would be insensitive even for you.'

Fitzroy flinched. 'Hope, this isn't helping you or her.'

I went and stood against the door with my arms folded. 'I want the rest. All of it.'

Fitzroy stood up and turned to face me. 'My dear Hope,' he said in an indulgent voice, 'do you honestly think that you can prevent me from exiting this room, or anywhere, for that matter?'

'No,' I said. 'But I don't think you want to scrap with me today, of all days.'

'There would be no scrapping,' said Fitzroy. 'You would simply be moved.'

'And yet you're still here?'

'Yes, I bought the flat. I put it into your mother's name when I was confident that she would neither tell your father about it, nor could he legally take possession of it. I also arranged for her salary to be paid into a bank account that your father never knew about. He believed she worked only to do her duty to King and Country. Which, of course, she would have done.'

'But you wanted her to have an escape route? From my father?' I heard my voice rising.

Fitzroy sighed and shook his head. 'I knew you wouldn't understand. But try. I wanted your mother not to feel controlled. I wanted her to stay wherever she wanted because she chose to, not because she believed she had no choice. I actually thought it would help their marriage, and I believe it did.'

'So you and my mother were never . . . close?'

Fitzroy tilted his head on one side. 'What are you asking, Hope? I should think it has always been obvious that I care deeply for your mother. She has been my partner in the field for many years. We have faced death together on multiple occasions, and

I've lost count of the number of times we have risked our lives for each other.'

'I mean, do you love her? Are you, have you been, in an arrangement together?'

Fitzroy's face closed in on itself. He said nothing.

'Are you lovers?' I was almost shouting now.

Fitzroy stepped up to me, and bowing his head low, he put his hands on my shoulders. For a moment I thought he was going to speak, but I suddenly found myself manoeuvred to one side, and he was gone.

Chapter Four

Endings

I stayed in the office for a goodly length of time. There was a clock, so I knew when I left it was around 8 p.m., but as I hadn't looked at the time when I went in, I had no idea how long I had hidden there. I hadn't cried. Instead I'd sat in a sort of daze, turning things round and round in my head, but achieving nothing except a deeper and deeper sense of confusion and the beginning of a headache. If my godfather and my mother had not been lovers I had acted inexcusably. If they had been then my mother had acted inexcusably. My godfather would not be without blame, but his philandering had always been occasion for late-night quips. I had never thought before that his terminally bad behaviour would encroach on my world.

I waited for someone to be sent to find me. I knew I was being childish, petulant even, but if Fitzroy or my mother came, or even sent someone else, I would know I was forgiven for what I had said. I would know also that I had been wrong and that my foolish words had been no more than that. No one came.

Eventually, I gave up my wait. My stomach made me. I hadn't managed any of the funeral luncheon, and I'd done no more than peck at a piece of toast this morning. I may have mentioned I'm not one of those rail-thin girls. I have reasonable physical strength, more than most girls my age, and I have a healthy appetite to accompany it. So rather than shame, or regret, or even anger, I came out of hiding because I was hungry.

Immediately I noticed how quiet everything was. I went

through to the dining room to find the table cleared. The chairs, which had all been placed around the walls, were now neatly tucked under the table. In the hallway, the carpet looked brighter in some places, where the pile had been brushed and not smoothed down properly. The grandmother clock, which had been stopped when my father died, had not yet been restarted. The hall felt spectrally cold and quiet. There was no sign of Giles or any of the maids.

I had the queerest sensation of my stomach and heart separating. My stomach dropped as into a bottomless pit and my heart rose to beat a rapid tattoo in my throat. Sweat prickled my scalp and my palms. The edges of my vision began to turn black.

The front door burst open, and my mother, in coat and hat, came in. For a moment I didn't think my feet would move, but then I was running towards her and throwing my arms around her. My mother caught me in a light embrace, rocking slightly under the impact and dropping her handbag.

'Hope, whatever is wrong?'

'I thought everyone had left me,' I said, panting for air. 'I thought I was all alone.'

My mother set me slightly back from her, using much the same technique Fitzroy had. 'Did you fall asleep?' she asked with a slight smile. 'I thought you probably had. I told everyone not to wake you. You've been through so much recently. The guests are all gone.'

'Shall we go and have a cup of tea?' I said, trying to return her smile.

My mother gestured at her coat and fallen handbag. 'I'm afraid I do have to go, Hope. Fitzroy is taking me back with him.' I must have looked as horrified as I felt as my mother gave a tiny laugh and touched me briefly on the forearm. 'Oh, don't worry! We're not flying. I think he's chanced his luck in the air more than enough times this lifetime!'

'But it's dark, and you'll have no lights.'

'The moon isn't bad, and we can take it in turns to drive.

Which is another reason for me to go. He's absolutely shattered, poor man. I can at least help him get back to HQ. Besides, now I'm no longer caring for your father my place is in London. I can be of most use there.'

'But what about me?'

My mother frowned slightly. 'Eric said you would be travelling down after the will.' Clearly he had not told her about our argument.

'I thought you were angry with me,' I said.

My mother gave a small shake of her head. 'I can't think why I would be,' she said. Then she adopted a practical tone. 'I would get things signed over to McArthur for the duration if I were you. He's an excellent factor and too old to be called up. We should be able to keep our people supplied with food at least. Mrs Templeton has been leading an army of female volunteers. We might even get a couple of land girls for the fields. But you can leave all that to her and McArthur. Merry and Sam might ask you if you'll allow them to open up the old hospital again. I'd rather hoped it wouldn't be needed, but if you have no objection, I'd let it happen. The pair of them can run it efficiently enough, and Merry can write to me about acquiring provisions or monies she needs. If I'm not involved with that I can hand it on to whoever is. I'd stay to hear the will, but your father mentioned to me . . .' she paused fractionally, 'your father mentioned to me that we should leave the estate to you. He knew I'd be off to the war, and he thought – well, I don't know quite what he thought, but I had no objection. I know you love this place, Hope, and that you'll make sure all our people are all right – or as much as anyone can be during this dreadful time.' She stopped. 'Goodness, I am running on. It's not like you to let me. Is something wrong? We'll see each other very soon, I'm sure. After all, we all work for the same department.'

'Yes,' I said stupidly.

'That reminds me.' She bent down to pick up her bag. She fished around inside it, and then pulled out a rail warrant, which she passed to me. 'It's valid for the next three days,' she said. 'Eric asks you use it as soon as possible, and says orders will be awaiting you at your flat.'

'I see,' I said. 'So as soon as I've seen the lawyer—'

'As soon as you feel well enough. You must return to duty as soon as you are able, but I, not Fitzroy, insist you get Sam Butcher to sign you off as ready for work. If he says you need more time, you take it. Call me on the office line and I'll arrange your absence. The operator will put the call through to wherever they've billeted me.'

She raised a hand to my face and touched my cheek lightly. 'I am awfully proud of you, you know, Hope. I know we haven't been that close – well, for a while – but maybe with us both in London we can manage to grab some time to . . . well, get to know one another again. And after the war, we'll have a chance to start again.'

'That sounds good,' I said.

My mother smiled properly for the first time since I'd arrived home. 'Then I'd better hurry up down to London and sort them all out,' she said.

'Where is Fitzroy?'

'In the car. He sends his love. You know how he refuses to do goodbyes.'

I nodded. My mother turned and, linking her arm through mine, began to walk back to the door. 'I came back to leave the rail warrant. I hoped I'd catch you. I'm glad I did. It didn't seem right to leave without seeing you.'

I wanted to ask her the same questions I had asked Fitzroy, but the words would not come. I had already driven Fitzroy from me, and I was not willing to lose the last member of my family. But this was one of the longest, most pleasant speeches I would remember my mother giving me for a long time. I couldn't help but notice she seemed lighter, and said as much.

She stopped by the door. I could see Fitzroy sitting in the car outside. He gave me a curt nod, and picked up something and started to read. Whatever it was it soon had him scowling fiercely. My mother touched my wrist lightly, acquiring my attention. Then she followed my gaze. 'Oh dear, he can get in a dreadful mood if he's made to wait before an off – whether it be a car journey, a mission, or even going into dinner.'

'He won't be cross with you today, will he?'

My mother shook her head. 'He's never – well, hardly ever – cross with me. Usually, he's most cross with himself.' She gave a slight smile. 'I understand him better than most. He's a good man, Eric. Although for Heaven's sake don't repeat that. He'd worry about his reputation. When we were younger, he was very much the maverick. I think now, he's adjusting to being more of an authoritative and omniscient senior officer. Or that's what he likes to think, dear man.'

I was listening as well as watching her closely. I could hear the affection in her voice, and her facial muscles were relaxed when she spoke of him, but it was hardly a lover-like ardour.

My mother, who had lapsed into silence, gave herself a small physical shake, like an otter getting rid of the last water when it exits the stream. 'But to answer your implied question, Hope. When you care for an invalid for as long as I have, even one you dearly love – maybe more so – and you see their daily discomforts and indignities, there is an initial relief that they are suffering no more. And, I suppose, to be utterly honest with myself, there is a feeling of freedom in being finally released from the sickroom.' She suddenly took both my hands in hers. 'I'm going to start missing him dreadfully in a few days, but I haven't been able to sleep through a whole night for years. His attacks nearly always came when he had retired for the night. I have no idea why. But after he decided he wanted a bedroom downstairs, I used to lie awake listening to every creak and strain the wretched house made, thinking it was him falling out of bed having an attack.'

'You didn't sleep—'

'Not in the same room. It was very much the done thing not to do that when we were young – and there was the snoring.' She

31

gave a small laugh. 'On a bad night he could rival a train. Besides, he wanted to be alone, Hope. He could keep up the facade to me during the day that he was getting better, and let it down when he was alone. We did an awful lot of pretending between the pair of us, even though we both knew we were pretending. There, I suppose that's a marriage for you. Anyway, I intend to be very busy with war work, so busy that my grief will have few occasions to arise. I know it will. But I want to take it in as small pieces as I can. Otherwise, I am very much afraid it might rise up and overwhelm me. So, please, Hope, if I seem less than heartbroken, understand, it's simply my way of carrying on. I can't spend the rest of my life weeping, can I?'

'No, of course not,' I said. Though at the time it felt as if I would spend the rest of mine crying on the inside.

My mother took a long look along and around the hall. 'This was the first part of White Orchards I ever saw, it's fitting it's the last. I remember coming back here at the end of our honeymoon. Goodness, that was a night. I got news the same night I had to go on a mission. Your father was not well pleased. But we worked everything out in the end.' She nodded to herself. 'I'll miss the people here, but I won't miss the house, I'm afraid. I'm glad it's going to someone who will love it.'

'You didn't like living here?'

'Not particularly. Your father loved it, and it had its moments. The people too became important to us. But no, I would have lived in London if I could have done. I grew up in the countryside, and I spent much of my childhood wishing to escape it.'

'I didn't know,' I said. 'I didn't know you disliked it quite that much.'

'Oh, it was fine. It was the best place to bring you up. I had so many enemies by then, from my work, that we needed to keep you somewhere remote. Somewhere we could control. The city would have been too dangerous.'

'I didn't know,' I said again, stupidly. 'Is that why you didn't have any more children?'

32

'No, that's something different. Another time. I am beginning to feel rather tired, and I won't be any help to Fitzroy if I can't share the driving. I hope you don't mind if Griffin packs up a few of my things to send on. I won't take anything that belongs to the house. Only a few things that were gifts to me.'

'You can take whatever you want, Mama,' I said, using my childhood name for her without thinking. 'This is your home.'

My mother shook her head. 'It's yours now, Hope. Don't worry, darling, I really don't mind a bit. Of course, if you invite me, I'll still visit.'

'But where will you go?'

'Fitzroy tells me he's told you I have a London flat. One of his properties actually, but he likes to pretend it's mine, so there's that. I expect to be billeted where I will be of most use. You can get me through our exchange, same as ever. I'm always on the other end of the telephone for you.'

She stopped, her eyes flickered. 'I am getting the distinct impression that your godfather is within a moment of leaning on the horn.'

She reached over and kissed me on the cheek, then releasing my hands, she walked through the door and ran lightly down the steps to the waiting car. Fitzroy got out to open the car door for her. I was too far away to hear their conversation, but he brightened noticeably at her approach and he was no longer frowning. I thought he might wave to me. I held my hand up. But he didn't look back at the house, just got behind the wheel, reversed quickly and was away down the driveway in what felt like a moment. I watched until the car went out of sight.

Chapter Five

Plus Ça Change

The days following my mother's departure seemed long and tiring. In fact very little happened. The lawyer came and read the will. Both Fitzroy and my mother had been wrong. My father left the estate to Mother and me jointly, but with the proviso that Mother could hand the whole thing over to me to manage, on the understanding she always had a home here.

Fitzroy had misjudged my father completely. I realised with a growing anxiety that my father had meant to threaten my godfather only. The whole story about the will was an attempt to force Fitzroy to behave as the gentleman he always claimed not to be. I should have known, Fitzroy should have known, that my father cherished my mother, and would never have allowed her to come to harm in any way. He would certainly never have dispossessed her of a home and an income. It was Fitzroy he disliked and distrusted. The question that remained was simply, had my mother been strong-willed enough to resist any lures my godfather had thrown out to her?

Giles was gifted a cottage and a pension, but asked to be allowed to continue working in the house. 'I need to be useful, Miss Hope,' he said. I could not refuse him. Although I made Mrs Templeton promise that she would ensure he carried out lighter and lighter duties. She too was given a cottage for life and the promise of a generous stipend on retirement. None of the servants were forgotten, and various books and other trinkets were left to people who would appreciate them.

The only shock was the last item. My mother's friend, Aunt Merry, to her astonishment and embarrassment, was left the mills my father had inherited from his elder brother, a man who had died before I was born. My father spoke of him infrequently and when he did it was with considerable dislike. However, this legacy represented a small fortune. It came with the caveat that the mill community must continue on the current lines of operation. It transpired my father had installed a school, a doctor and a cottage hospital, and ways for the workers to better themselves and their offspring if they chose. There were social amenities and extremely high standards of safety. It had kept the business going when so many other mills had closed. I had never heard of it before, and thus had no anticipation of inheriting it. My godfather had given me a trust fund, the size of which he had forbidden me to tell my parents. I had more than enough. The bequest surprised, even bemused me a little, but I had no jealousy. Running the mills and the mill community sounded like an onerous and time-consuming task. I had other things I wanted to do.

After the will reading, at a sherry reception at the house, Dr Butcher sought me out. 'Your mother wanted me to check how you were doing,' he said. 'How's the headache? Any blurred vision? Appetite all right?'

I nodded. 'I feel fine, thank you, doctor.'

He smiled. 'Excellent. Apart from looking rather pale, you seem in good health to me. That's youth for you. A bit slimmer than last time I saw you, but healthy nonetheless. Make sure you eat enough to keep your strength up.' He cleared his throat. 'It was enormously kind of your father to leave me the Dickens, but I feel I should offer it to you. I know how you loved that story.'

I smiled. 'He left me another copy, doctor. You are perfectly welcome to yours.'

'Oh, that's a weight off my mind. I say, Hope. I suppose I should say Miss Stapleford now you're the landowner—'

'Please don't,' I said. 'Hope is perfectly fine.'

'All right – Hope, it is. Anyway, my dear, would you mind having a quick word with Merry. She's feeling rather bad about things.'

Merry wasn't feeling bad. She was mortified. 'I feel I have stolen part of your inheritance,' she said when I sought her out. She was standing as far into the corner as possible.

'Aunt Merry,' I said, 'I have no interest at all in the mills other than to see they are run well by my father's successor. I have another position to fill.'

'Family business,' said Merry in undertones. 'I wouldn't wonder if Fitzroy and your mother want you to get out after the war ends. I know they never wanted you involved in all that stuff.'

'You knew?' I asked. 'Were you involved?'

'A tiny bit,' said Merry. 'I used to get caught up in Euphemia's adventures when we were both young – and, of course, it wasn't long before your godfather came on the scene, and . . . Well, Euphemia has a natural talent for certain things. Even someone like me could see that. Then I married Merrit, and I had Michael just after Merrit went off to war. I wasn't in a place to be involved, and well, they didn't want people like me joining. I mean the Department. Although Fitzroy and Euphemia were never highhanded.' She sighed. 'Good times, before the Great War. Your mother and I had a lot of fun together.' She took a deep breath. 'Does she know about what was in the will? Is she angry about it? I can't understand why he would do this,' she continued. 'Is what the lawyer said really all anyone knows? That I should apply to Euphemia for further explanation?'

I shrugged helplessly. 'I don't know anything about it, Aunt Merry. It's a good thing for Michael, isn't it? You said he was unsure what to do when the war is over.'

'I'll write to him, of course,' she said. 'He was posted overseas, but he couldn't tell me where he was going. Could you?'

'I can ask my godfather to enquire,' I said, 'but I can't make any promises.'

At this point the first person to leave, the factor McArthur, came up to me and offered his condolences, yet again. I reminded

36

him of our appointment the next morning with the lawyer, so I could sign off the relevant papers for him to take care of the estate.

'Are you sure you want to do that, Miss Hope? Only, with us turning so much of the land over to food, I reckon you count as a farmer. That's a reserved occupation. You could stay here for the duration.'

I told a small lie and said I had already got my papers. 'Besides, I will be of far more use than I might be here. I love this estate, Mr McArthur, but you are the one who runs it.'

'Not for ever, Miss Hope. I had thought to hand it over to young Michael Merrit – the factoring, that is. But seems like he'll have other things on his plate when he comes back from the war.' He paused, and I could see he was waiting for a comment on Merry and her son's inheritance. I liked McArthur, so I didn't snap at him, as I might have anyone else. I told myself his comment was merely curiosity.

'If he decides to take up the mill management, I expect he will excel. Merry tells me he did very well at university.'

McArthur nodded. 'It was good of your father to send him.'

I shrugged. 'He was older than me, so we never got to know one another, but I believe he showed great promise from an early age. My father would have hated to see that wasted. And, of course, Merry was my mother's best friend.'

'Aye, that she was,' said McArthur. 'Your mother would ask her up to the big house all the time. Less so after Michael was born.'

'I expect she was busy with her baby,' I said. 'I really must say goodbye to the Framtons. They came such a long way to be here, and their son is away in the Army too.'

As I extricated myself from my factor, I had the oddest feeling he was trying to tell me something. It was only later when I was seeing the last guest off the premises that it struck me, rather like a missile to the head, what he had been implying.

I closed the door behind them. 'Good grief,' I said aloud, 'does everyone round here put two and two together and make five?'

'I couldn't tell you, Miss Hope,' said Giles, who I hadn't realised was standing behind me. Of course he would have been hovering in the background. He was extremely territorial about the door. A fact that Fitzroy exploited ruthlessly by always trying to sneak up to the house and let himself in. 'If you could tell me what you are referring to I might be able to help, miss.'

I turned and smiled up at him. His shoulders stooped very slightly now with age, but I would always have to crane my neck to see his face at close quarters. 'You know how it is at funerals, Giles. Everyone wants to tie up the loose ends of the deceased's life. They either ask or imply things to try and get at the truth.'

'Very acute, Miss Hope,' said Giles, 'but with respect, truth and White Orchards do not sit comfortably. It was often your parents' duty to obscure the truth, and it became somewhat of a habit for them to obscure their own lives.' He coughed. 'I hope you do not feel I am speaking out of turn.'

'Of course not,' I said. 'I suppose my parents, for all their good work on the estate, were private people. Reserved while outgoing. I hadn't thought of it like that.'

'Your mother's habit of coming and going raised a lot of questions when she first married your father. Your father took the line it was no one's business but his own what she was doing. Of course, I couldn't have worked here all those years without coming to the conclusion that, surprising as it was, your mother was in the service of, shall we say, another authority than her marriage. I never discussed it with any of the other staff of course. But as you say, people will put two and two together and become a victim of their own inferior mathematical capabilities.'

'I imagine Mrs T suspects.'

'If she does, she has the good sense not to comment to me or anyone else.'

'A house full of secrets.'

'This is somewhat distasteful,' Giles said, 'but I believe there is something I should tell you. Would you be willing to step into my pantry?'

'Goodness,' I said. 'I haven't been in there since I was a child.'

'I believe you will find it not much changed.' Giles led the way. The pantry, as we called it, was his sitting room. A bright room that I recall my grandmother exclaiming was far too good for a servant. One large window faced out over the Fens, and there was a good-sized hearth with a slate mantel. Red leather wingback chairs, worn smooth with age, and moulded to the human form, stood either side of the fireplace. Giles gestured to me to take a seat. 'It's about your godmother,' he said. 'Mrs Merrit.'

'So McArthur *was* implying what I thought,' I said. 'He was suggesting Michael was my half-sibling. What a cheek!'

Giles' cheeks tinged with red. 'I did wonder if something of that might happen when I heard the will. It's all most distressing. Would you like another sherry, Miss Hope? There is some left, and I did procure the very best for your father.'

I swallowed involuntarily at the thought of that sticky nastiness. 'I'm fine, Giles, but you go right ahead.'

He did, and took longer about it than I expected. Giles was having trouble coming to the point. I decided to help him along. 'I take it there is no truth in that rumour. In fact, I felt it was rather rude of McArthur.'

'Presumptuous, certainly,' said Giles, taking his seat again. 'But I'm afraid it was more a reflection on Merry Merrit's character than your father's.' He took a long swig from the tiny glass. 'Michael was born not long after Merrit joined up for the Great War, and while he was away. People remember Merry being alone with the child, and they recall her bringing her sister to help her. Michael is the image of his father, but not everyone has the memory for faces that I do. A requirement of a good butler, Miss Hope.'

'I have to say that I don't remember him. Did I ever meet him?' Giles shook his head.

I stood up. 'Thank you for clearing that up for me. I've a few last-minute things to do before I catch the train.'

Giles glanced at the clock on the mantel. 'You still have adequate time, and it's not Michael I wanted to talk about, but his sister.'

'His sister?'

'Merry had another child while her husband was away at war. There is no question of her being Merrit's child.'

'But—'

'Merry sent her away. The disgrace was too much. Your mother would have stood by her, but Merry felt it was unfair on the child to grow up with everyone knowing she was a bastard. Of course there's been a lot of water under the bridge since then, but Mr Stapleford deciding to leave Merry the mills has raised questions again.'

'I assume then it wasn't my father's?'

'No, of course not. As I understand it, Merry worked from a very young age in your grandfather's household. Although your father and siblings were sent away to school they still grew up alongside Merry. From the tales your father told she was the one bright light in a rather difficult house. In those days she was extremely cheerful. I presume you realise her name is actually Mary?'

'I'd never thought about it.'

'In some senses I think your father thought of her as a younger sibling. There was never so much as a whisper of romance between them. As you know, your father was completely devoted to your mother – until his last breath.'

'I see,' I said. 'This is rather a lot to take in. Merry has asked me to find out about Michael. I'll have to face her knowing all this.'

'I have the strong impression that Merry always regretted giving the baby up.' Giles coughed discreetly as only a butler who has been betrayed into demonstrating emotion can. He added in a much more formal tone, 'I hear she and Dr Butcher might be opening up the hospital again.'

'I'd prefer that it wasn't needed,' I said, straightening my skirt. 'But, of course, if it is, we must do so.'

It was only when I was on the train to London that I realised I had not asked who the father of Merry's child was. If it wasn't my father, then who? Oh heavens, I thought, please let it not be Fitzroy. I could hear his voice in my head asking if I was going to accuse him of fathering every bastard child in the kingdom. I actually felt a shiver run down my spine, a feeling I had previously only read about in books. I knew my godfather would never harm me, but he could be damned intimidating when he chose, and he was currently my commanding officer. I'd already mortally offended him once.

I had been unaware that beyond my parents and Fitzroy anyone knew about the association between White Orchards and the British Intelligence Services. I had, it appeared, been far too naive.

My parents may have thought they kept their private lives separate, but this had only added fuel to the fire, and gossip had clearly run rife. I wouldn't have heard it as a child, but I wondered what my parents had known. It seemed I was not the only one who had questions around their parentage.

I snoozed on the long train journey. The ordeal of my father's funeral had slowed my recovery from my injuries. I felt washed out and empty. I didn't even have the energy to grieve any more. I wondered how my mother was doing, and whether she had found solace in her work. Hopefully, I would see her soon, and perhaps we would even have a chance to exchange some truths. I would have to tell her what I had said to Fitzroy and hope she could straighten it out. I would have to hope she would also forgive me for what I had said. It was all very unpleasant.

The train pulled to a halt, and I reached up to take down my one bag. Fitzroy had had a second lieutenant (regular army) uniform sent up for me, so everyone around kept smiling at me, and opening doors.

I stepped out of the carriage onto a platform crowded with men in uniform, their wives or girlfriends, and various children. The sheer number of people in the tiny space was breathtaking after the wilds of the Fens. I inhaled deeply, fumes, smoke and the scents of humanity, in its best and its worst. Home. My other

41

home. I loved London, and I was so glad to be back and more than ready to do my bit.

I slung my kitbag over my shoulder and set off for a bus stop to catch a bus to take me to the flat. My shoulders were light, and my step brisk. I could attend to personal things another time.

Chapter Six

Doing One's Bit

The flat wasn't how I'd left it. It had been cleaned, tidied and smelled of bleach. I opened a window and went through to dump my kitbag in my room. I hung on to the parcel Mrs T had given me. My bed had hospital corners. On impulse I looked into Bernie's room. My recently married best friend's room remained a mess, with many of her things scattered out of drawers or draped across her wardrobe door. If you didn't know her you might think the room had been ransacked. There was milk, eggs, two rashers of bacon and three sausages in the fridge. A fresh loaf of bread stood on the side. I unwrapped my parcel and discovered I had been given another six eggs, all wrapped individually in newspaper. Five, amazingly, had survived. There was a large truckle of our home-made cheese and a cherry cake. Whatever happened next, it seemed unlikely I would starve.

My orders were in an envelope in the oven. I assumed it was someone's idea of a joke. I was to report as soon as I got back to the Department office by the Bakerloo line. An address was given. I went hunting for tea, and found the ends of a packet behind a pile of plates. Bernie had obviously put this away. I missed her. I decided as soon as I reported for duty, my first night off I would get a message to Bernie somehow, past her officious husband, and we would go for cocktails.

I hoped she was happy in her marriage. Although it seemed unlikely. Last time I'd seen her she'd been in hospital after some kind of accident. It had seemed suspiciously like her husband had been at fault. But I had learned recently how very much people like to gossip, and how poisonous rumours could be. If Bernie could tell me with her own lips that everything was fine, then I would make an effort to get to know her husband. After all, we were in the same line. He was in naval intelligence. Although when I'd asked Fitzroy exactly what this was, he merely barked with laughter and said it was an oxymoron. Of all the services he has least time for it was the Navy. I have no idea why.

I curled up on the settee with my tea. A light evening breeze drifted in through the window. I knew there were new blackout rules. The necessary curtains had been installed in the flat while I was away. However, it was still unnaturally light outside. All the same I got up again and went to close the window.

It was as well I had put down my tea. I was almost at the window when a man vaulted through and went for me. I dived to the side, and rolled away, coming up in a fighting stance. The room was empty. I ran from room to room, but there was no one else in the flat. Slowly I came back and locked the window. What the hell had that been? Was I seeing ghosts? Or . . .

I checked around the flat one last time, ensuring the door was double-locked. Then deciding I must be overtired I went to bed, setting the alarm for an early hour.

I jumped on the back of a bus just moving away from a stop. The pole was cold beneath my hands, and I stumbled slightly as I landed on the open backplate. The ticket inspector, a short, white-haired man, nodded at me to go in, and seeing my uniform didn't ask for my fare.

The bus journey was much like any other. I picked my way over the shoes and legs in my way. All the older women sat up straight, clasped the handles of their bag and pressed it into their stomachs, which invariably made their legs lift and stick out. I smiled as I tried hard not to kick anyone as I sought a seat.

It never failed to astound me that people could be so unaware of their limbs. A couple of gentlemen, if that term could be applied, lounged over two separate bench seats. I caught a whiff of tobacco from them over a smell of stale sweat. I sat next to an older woman who was knitting a blue, beribboned jacket that was so small it had to be for a newborn. What a time to come into the world, I thought, as I stared past her and out through the window.

The London streets had changed in the very short time I had been away. I didn't see a single pane of glass that wasn't taped over with an X. The hastily hemmed blackout curtains peeked at the edges of windows. The people were all much the same, except now, all of them, without exception, had a cardboard box strung over their shoulders. The dreaded gas masks. I'd been carrying one for a while. I'd even got into the habit of remembering to pick it up when I left somewhere, rather than leaving some poor soul to chase after me with it. However, since I had the first assay of trying to get the thing on, I had left it in the box. They were unpleasant things. The straps caught in your hair, and they smelled like the inside of a much-used rubber glove, coupled with an odd, almost diesel-like aroma. It was dehumanising and frightening to see others wear one. It meant you feared for an attack, but also because, even though it only obscured the face, it somehow shut each of us off from each other into a nasty little personal world. The small windows for the eyes obscured the view of everything around us. But much as I hated them, the minute a siren sounded I would be shoving mine over my face.

I now spotted brick shelters at the ends of some streets. Square structures, built of new bricks, and to my eye, rather small, were meant to house the locals in the case of an air raid. I couldn't imagine if I had the choice between being in one of these or under my stairs in a multi-storey house that I'd go into the brick shed. They didn't look to me like they could survive a bomb blast. Or what I imagined a bomb blast might be like. I would have to ask Fitzroy his opinion. Perhaps they were meant for people who were caught out in the street when the sirens went rather than local people. Of course, no one knew when the bombs might fall. At White Orchards the discussion was generally on the side of most of them being dropped on London, but whether that would be by day or night, no one seemed able to decide.

I experienced a sharp jab in my side. 'Excuse us, ducks. This is me stop,' said the old woman. I stood up to let her out. She smiled at me and shuffled off. I realised she must have poked me with her knitting needle. What a cheek!

Fortunately, I arrived at my stop before any other of the passengers could molest me. I stepped off the bus, excitement bubbling inside me. This would be my first proper job for the Department. I hoped that whatever I was asked to do, I could do it well, and it would make my father proud of me.

I marched smartly up to the front desk, my gas mask bouncing on my hip. A woman around my mother's age guarded the entrance. Her blond hair was a shade too yellow, and she had large victory rolls. Her yellow and pink dress had clearly been home-made from a pattern. A row of bright blue paste gems hung around her neck. Even without the ruby lipstick she was distinctive. An aroma of violets emanated from her person. She tore her gaze away from the ledger in front of her and turned her attention to me. Her eyes were blue, sharp, and not without humour. On either side of her stood armed guards. Here, then, was Cerberus. Then she did something most surprising. She saluted. Without thinking, I returned the salute.

Cerberus smiled at me, showing pretty, regular teeth. Obviously she had been brought up in a good household. 'You must be Fitzroy's protégée. You look so like your mother. It certainly explains your high security clearance. I imagine secrets are in your blood.'

'Oh, did you know them, Mrs——?'

'Dotty. The senior folks here call me Dotty. But I guess you get to do that too. A sort of historical precedence – or privilege.'

'Thank you,' I said.

'And I shall call you Hope. At least until you get a code name. I assume Fitzroy hasn't given you one yet?'

I shook my head.

46

'Let's hope it's not something like Dormouse.' She laughed loudly at her own joke. 'Your mother being Alice,' she said.

I could imagine Dormouse might be one of the names Fitzroy would be liable to use for me in the near future.

'Right, love. Through the door on the right, down the stairs and you'll find everything you need.'

I nodded my thanks and headed towards the door. My head was spinning with the idea that people knew my mother and Fitzroy when they were younger. From what I had gathered, reading between the stories – which from my mother were self-deprecating, and from Fitzroy were fantastic, self-glorifying and always funny – they were highly regarded. Fitzroy had said my mother was the first successful female full agent. It sounded as if people would be expecting big things of me.

However, as I trotted down the stairs, I heard a familiar noise. My fears were confirmed when I pushed open the big fire door. Four pairs of eyes looked up and took me in from my curls to my shoes. Four young women, none of them above twenty-five, sat behind typewriters. Fingers stopped moving, and hands hovered over keyboards. None of them were in uniform.

'Goodness,' said a curvy, curly blonde young woman. 'An officer.'

Another girl got up. She was tall, slender and moved with the grace of a dancer. Her vowels when she spoke were lethally sharp. 'I am Sammi with an i. That was Flossie. And that's Harriet and that's Edith. Harriet's the red.' The last two were clearly twins, with short brown hair cut in the pudding-bowl style. They dressed similarly, but with one in red and the other in green. They reminded me of dolls. Perhaps it was their neatness, but they seemed less than real. They both regarded me with big brown eyes that had the apparent vacancy of the cows in the field at home.

Sammi shook my hand firmly. 'Thank God you've come to join us. We are simply run off our fingertips. There's hardly any-one with a clearance high enough to work here. Harriet, Edith, bring over the new typewriter and set up her desk, please.' She must have seen the reaction on my face. 'I'm sort of in charge here, because you know, my grandfather. Harriet and Edith have eidetic memories. They're sort of kept here until they're needed. They're more or less another carbon, but in human form. As for Flossie,' she turned round and indicated the blonde girl, 'no one really understands why she's here, but as I said, we are so short-staffed no one has complained.'

'Hello,' I said.

The twins had brought over my desk. 'Have a seat,' said Sammi. 'Files over there. Ins. Outs. I call the breaks. Morning and afternoon we get twenty minutes and forty minutes for luncheon. If you need the loo, try to wait until the breaks. It's disturbing with everyone coming and going.' She pointed to the corner. 'Loos through that door, and a little kitchen. We take it in turns to make tea or coffee for the breaks. Not me, of course, because of my grandfather, you know.'

I didn't, but it didn't seem wise to say so. 'Does anyone else work here? Anyone who comes to supervise perhaps?'

Sammi shook her head. 'No, all the files come down the little slope over there.' She pointed at a letterbox with a sack beneath it on the far wall. 'They come in there, and whoever is on sorting puts them in the INs in the proper order. Then when we've finished we put them in the OUTs, that tray there. Everything is collected after we leave at four thirty p.m. sharp. By the way, we start at seven forty-five a.m. precisely. I don't suppose anyone told you.'

'No,' I said. 'What if there's a rush on something?'

'We don't do rushes,' said Sammi in a tone of strong disapproval. 'Now, sit yourself down. Edith has put a file out for you. You'll work out where everything else is. We need to get a march on. Tally-ho, girls!'

She sat down and began to type very fast. The other girls joined in immediately. The twins, fascinatingly, worked in unison. I picked up the file I'd been left and loaded up the machine.

This has to be some kind of a test, I thought. There's no way I would be sent to a typing pool again. Then I read the opening line of the first file: *Committee XX*. It contained the minutes of a special meeting that analysed what information was to be released to which department, and even which minister. I dearly hoped that Fitzroy would not ask me about this work. It was clearly of very high clearance.

It was only when I was halfway down the first page that I came across the comments made by Colonel Fitzroy who, it transpired, sat on the committee. Somehow I doubted there could be more than one. Although this made me less concerned about betraying high-level secrets between departments, it made less sense of my presence here.

I carried on reading and typing. The work was increasingly interesting and informative. Perhaps my godfather was trying to give me a quick update on what was happening?

Then it struck me. One of these girls must be passing on information to the enemy. I couldn't think why else I could be here. Clearly, my mission was to seek out the traitor. It was hardly the kind of thing to be put in writing. My godfather expected me to use my own initiative, and that I would do.

Chapter Seven

Old Comrades

The days fell all too quickly into a routine. I got up far too early, ate a slice of toast, caught the bus and typed all day. I went to the cinema with Flossie twice. She had no conversation beyond make-up and men. She read all the magazine stories about film stars, and desperately wanted to go to the United States. She fancied herself as a star of the screen. But apart from her ability to remember the measurements of starlets, which she was trying unsuccessfully to match, and her speed at typing, there seemed to be little else to her. In the breaks at the office, she began bringing in a tailor's tape measure and getting us to confirm her measurements. The red twin began keeping a record of her achievements. Even this had a dull familiar pattern. Flossie got thinner and thinner during the week, but when she came back on Monday she would be back to her original size and it would all begin again. Around this time, she developed a new interest in crash diets, and I stopped listening.

Red and Green both rebuffed any friendly overtures from me. 'They have to be awfully careful,' Sammi told me during a coffee break. 'Apparently, remembering everything means that one day they fill up and go mad. At least that's what some boffin has told them. Anyway, they don't do anything much except the work. They have to keep their input to a minimum. Saving themselves for the war effort.'

'Gosh,' I said, 'that seems rather harsh. I mean, no books, no films?'

'No parties and no dinners,' said Sammi. 'Anyway, I've noticed you've been trying to get to know people. I dare say compared to where you might have worked before, we're a bit of an odd lot. Why not come to dinner with me and my people? My grandfather won't be there, but it would be a relief from the monotony of it all.'

I had now been there two weeks and I still had no idea who this famous grandfather was, and I had let that go on far too long. There was no way I could now ask her. I did try and pump Flossie for information, but she said she had no idea.

'But you always nod when she talks about him!' I protested.

'So do you. The twins will know, but they never talk unless it's necessary.'

The dinner at Sammi's proved to be highly genteel. She introduced her parents, who were distinguished fifty-somethings, only as 'the mater' and 'the pater'. As no one had told me the surname of anyone in her tiny office, this forced me to call them 'sir' and 'ma'am' all evening. Her mother had dressed for dinner in a long green silk gown, and her father was in evening dress. Sammi wore a strappy crimson number. I, who hadn't been told quite how formal this was to be, was wearing a neat, black cocktail dress. It wasn't quite the thing for the elegant table laid out for dinner, but should that air-raid siren finally sound, I would be better at running.

Sadly, it was sherry, and not cocktails before dinner. 'I'm afraid I'm not quite dressed for the occasion,' I said to Mater.

'Oh, there is no need to worry, my dear. We all do our best. There is a war on after all. Incidentally, Cook says thank you for the eggs.'

'Eggs?' said Pater.

'A hospitality gift,' I said. 'Instead of wine or flowers. I didn't know if you drank wine, or which you might like, and flowers somehow don't seem right at this time. So I opted for eggs.'

Her father wore heavy black glasses. 'They're not black market, are they?' he said. Then, rather sweetly, he tried to give me an intimidating look over his glasses. After growing up with my godfather, it was rather like seeing a fluffy old cat, clawless and toothless, try to intimidate you.

'Not at all,' I said. 'I had too many. Our housekeeper gave me some to bring down with me, and there were far too many for me alone.'

'Your housekeeper,' said Mater, her voice losing some of its chill. 'So your parents kept up White Orchards?'

'Well,' I said, 'I have the land now. My father died recently, you see. We do have several tenant farmers, as well as the village. It's quite the community.'

'Oh, one of the more northern estates,' said the Pater, nodding. 'I'm not so knowledgeable about them. Very much a London man.'

'Yes,' I said, struggling for something else to say. 'I enjoyed my season very much.'

'You were a debutante?' said Sammi. 'I was to be this year. Who are you engaged to?'

'I'm not,' I said. 'Not everyone comes out of the season engaged. Although many do. I'm not ready to settle down yet.'

'Bit of an heiress, hmm?' said Pater.

'I am so sorry about your father,' said Mater, looking very like Mother used to when she wanted to step on my father's toe. 'As are we all. Was it expected? I heard about your mother, naturally, from my father, but I don't believe her husband ever worked for him.'

I could hardly say it had been expected since before I was born, so I said, 'He had been ill a number of years. May I ask who your father was?' I said, curiosity overcoming my fear of looking stupid. If I didn't ask now I might never know.

'Colonel Morley, Julian,' said Mater. 'I'm the daughter from his first wife. We try not to talk about his second.'

I remembered the name Morley, vaguely. My mother had mentioned it, but I couldn't remember Fitzroy ever doing so.

'And your poor mother?' continued Mater.

'She's down here too. I haven't seen her yet. She's on the hush-hush side of things.'

'Back in harness again! Good for the old gal!' said Pater, laughing.

'I'm not sure she ever left,' I said, somewhat stung at the way he referred to my mother. I immediately regretted what I had said. It was too much information in these times. Pater raised an eyebrow at me, but before he spoke the gong rang for dinner.

'Only a family party,' explained Mater. Her husband was looking at this watch. The doorbell rang. Not long after I heard two male voices in the hall. Both of them sounding a little merry.

'Damn that brother of mine,' said the Pater. 'Late, and it sounds as if he has led Wilfred into his bad ways. You need to rein that young man in, Samantha. He needs to know where he stands now before you marry. Your mother was perfectly clear on what she expected and we've had a fine marriage.'

'I expect he was only being polite. He must have run into Uncle Ralph on the way here.'

Two men in evening dress came through the drawing-room doors. One was tall and thin, with an overlarge Adam's apple, and what even the fondest parent would have described as a face like a bewildered trout. When I first set eyes on Wilfred, Sammi's betrothed, I could only assume he came with either a title or a large amount of money. I overheard him speak to Sammi in a sort of weaselly voice, 'S-s-sorry, S-s-sam, old girl. Couldn't get away from your Uncle Ralph. You look ever so topping tonight.' If ever there was someone who would come last in the lists of handsome young men, it was this one.

The mater flapped around urging her husband to get drinks for young Wilfred. Her husband told her curtly to 'ring for the butler' and he wasn't some kind of 'cocktail waiter'.

'Fascinating, isn't it,' said Uncle Ralph, who looked far too young to be anyone's uncle, sidling up to me. He didn't smell of alcohol, but faintly of good cigars and even better cologne. It was the one my godfather used. He was of average height, and had that look that some men can cultivate that means they could be anything from twenty-eight to forty-two years of age. It's a rather dull, worthy sort of a look, that makes you think they wear tweed in their leisure time. Only the whole persona was somewhat spoilt by the glint in this eye. I knew the type – mischievous.

His light brown hair was short and well cut, and he sported a neat moustache, but was otherwise clean shaven. His eyes were of an intense blue and sparkled with intelligence as well as mischief. It took me no more than a few seconds to sum him up. I had known his type from my cradle. I grinned at him. 'I take it Sammi and Wilfred are engaged. I don't think I have ever met Wilfred.'

'Ah, Wilfred Grimthorp. His father owns a manufacturing company, and Wilfred stands to inherit a fortune. Better yet, his father isn't putting him into the business, which having endured the young man's company for half an hour, I think is very wise.'

'You don't like him?'

'I doubt there's a bad bone in his body. I also doubt there is a brain cell in his head. Pity all that money couldn't buy him a chin, isn't it?' He swiped a couple of cocktails from the butler as he entered the family throng with refreshments. 'We seem to have been forgotten. I expect these will be nice enough. My brother generally keeps a good cellar. In case the father-in-law drops round – you know.'

'Colonel Morley.'

Uncle Ralph spluttered a bit over his drink, laughing. 'I rather think young Sammi has been told not to boast about her connections, and this is her idea of a compromise. He was a Colonel Morley. Quite a big thing in the last war.'

I almost commented on my mother's association then stopped. It was all too easy to talk to 'Uncle Ralph' unguarded and the cocktail had proved a lot stronger than I'd expected and gone straight to my head.

He took another sip, and then tilted his head on one side. 'They've almost finished their fussing so we'd better make this quick. You clocked me the moment I walked in the door, didn't you? And you've suddenly realised you shouldn't mention how you know Morley. The fact you're working with Sammi tells me your security clearance is high. So are you actually MI and if so can you tell me which department?'

'I don't know,' I said hesitantly.

'If you're MI or if you can tell me? I'm with the Special Operations Executive.'

I frowned.

'Oh, I'd rather you didn't pass it around, but we're in the process of trying to gather support. So if you've got any connections . . .'

'I don't recognise the name.'

'It's new and very hush-hush. A sort of field trip for auxies,' he laughed. 'Not that I expect you to understand that.'

'I trained with the auxies,' I said. I had the pleasure of seeing his eyebrows shoot up to his hairline, and then the gong sounded for dinner. Of course, by the time we'd sat down I realised what an idiotic thing it was to say. I was still grieving and all over the place. At least Sammi's parents seemed to know my mother. I had no idea if Ralph would too. He was much younger than his brother, and while he was clearly in the business of espionage now, I didn't get the faintest smell of it off Sammi's parents. My best guess was that Pater had moved into politics or become some kind of diplomat. If Ralph didn't know my antecedents I wasn't going to tell him.

As the guest of honour, I had the privilege of sitting between Pater, whose name I still didn't know, and Wilfred, who I quickly discovered, due to his overbite, drooled. He was a pretty repulsive chap all round. Mater and Pater sat at either end of the shortened table in the rather dark, wood-panelled room. The dining table was lit with single candles rather than the usual candelabras. I presumed this was more to do with the blackout than parsimony. But then they were marrying off their daughter to a drooling dolt.

Sammi sat across from me, and Ralph was between her and her mother. All rather well sorted for such a small gathering. My mother would have approved. Pater embarked on his soup, which was brown and tasted brown. It may have been an unhappy attempt at Windsor soup. He stopped once, mid bowl, to say, 'So, you work with Sammi. Don't suppose you can talk about that, huh?'

'Not really, sir,' I said politely. I was attempting to peer through the gloom and espy some salt. I was desperate for flavour of some kind.

'Th-th-there isn't any,' said a voice quietly beside me. 'Salt, that is. It's a bit of a muddy puddle, isn't it?'

'Oh dear,' I said. 'Does it show that I dislike it.'

'N-no,' said Wilfred. 'You're putting on a damn fine show. Better than I am. I'm ever so sorry, but I didn't get your name.'

'I'm Hope Stapleford,' I said, turning in my seat to offer my hand.

'Better not,' said Wilfred. 'Sammi's pater might get in a bit of a huff if I suggest anything isn't utterly tickerty-boo. Always trying to show me what's the thing. My family is in trade. Wouldn't give me the time of day if I didn't have an inheritance.' He stopped, and even in the gloom, I could see the edge of his blush. 'Not that he's a bad fellow. I don't mean that. Just of his class, I suppose. And Sammi's mater couldn't be nicer. I've nothing to complain about.'

'Except the soup,' I said.

'Well, that was between you and me, if you don't mind, Miss Stapleford. Be rather rude to suggest to one's host . . . even I know that.'

'So why did you say anything?'

'Well, I thought you looked a bit lost. Sammi's pater isn't interested in young women, which I suppose is a blessing to his wife, but it looked like it might be a bit of a bore for you. He likes talking man to man. Unfortunately.'

'Unfortunately?'

'I'm not very good at speaking man to man. Even my father calls me a bit of a pussy cat.'

'Well, you're not stuttering now,' I said.

'Yes, but it's dark and you're nice, and forgive me if I'm wrong, but you're not someone important I'm meant to impress, are you? I-I m-mean, I'm sure you're important to some people . . .'

'It's fine, Wilfred. I totally understand what you mean. I think I'm here to make up the numbers.'

Wilfred shook his head. 'No, that's Ralph. He doesn't like me either, but both Sammi's mater and pater disapprove of him. At least I have her mother on my side.'

'And what about Sammi?' I asked.

'Isn't she glorious,' said Wilfred. 'I drank a whole bottle of Scotch to get up the courage to ask her.'

'Well, it worked.'

Wilfred shook his head. 'No, it didn't. I passed out and when I woke up I was dreadfully . . . well, untidy. My man kept me in bed. Sammi called up and came round to see me when she heard I was ailing. Well, by that time I knew it was never going to happen . . .'

The footman took away my soup plate. 'Ah, so you grew up in the Fens? Bit wet, wasn't it?' said Sammi's father. Across the table I saw her nodding, encouraging us to converse. It was all very annoying as I wanted to hear the rest of Wilfred's story and I wanted to talk to Ralph. I adjusted my face to what I hoped was a charming smile. 'Yes, but it can be quite beautiful. Especially at sunrise and sunset.'

'Any good hunting?'

'We're not a hunting family,' I said.

The man gave me a look as if I'd stated my intention of running naked in the street, but he recovered himself. 'Ah, well, your father was a bit of an invalid, wasn't he? Can't blame the man.'

Having made his comment, the conversational ball bounced away from us and out the door. Wilfred had come under fire from Sammi's mother, whose voice had grown a bit staccato as she asked him a series of questions to which the young man made muffled and stuttering noises in response.

The fish course arrived. It was white and contained some fish bones. We were offered a few green beans and a potato to accompany it. I smiled up at the footman as I used the tongs to take the vegetables. I didn't drop one. And then, I suddenly thought I should have done. I had a nasty feeling Wilfred was unlikely to be good with tongs.

As the waiter served, and all eyes followed the paltry dishes, Ralph gave me an old auxie sign that signalled he wanted to speak to me alone. I looked him straight in the eye, and crooked my left finger. It was an old signal meaning 'Delay. Enemy present.' I thought I saw a muscle twitch in his cheek.

He was so like my godfather it was uncanny. But now I looked again, I was certain he was far too young to have worked in the Great War. There might be a chance I had stumbled on someone in intelligence who didn't know my godfather, and wouldn't think of me as some kind of adjunct to him. Mater and Pater knew Mother, but they hadn't mentioned Fitzroy, and I wasn't going to be the one to do so.

Sammi couldn't talk to me, being on the opposite side on the table, and her attempts to prompt her father into life were failing. He was far more concerned with having his wine glass topped up. But just when she looked frustrated enough to scream, or at least incur her parents' wrath by speaking across the table, Ralph distracted her with some story. When she stopped trying to prod her father into speech I realised how very tense I had become. I am disinclined to confrontation – especially verbal confrontation – and the position of being at a dinner table with various people I neither knew well nor was interested in learning more about, was increasingly wearing.

The fish was removed, and meat in gravy was placed in front of me. 'Oh Lord,' said Wilfred from beside me. 'I thought we'd got past the tong-ing.'

I looked round quite sharply, and followed his gaze towards the procession of three servants bringing three heaped mounds of vegetables on silver platters.

'When the waiter offers me the platters I can do yours at the same time. If we look as if we are deep in conversation, then no one will interrupt. Now, you were telling me about how you were hung-over, and Sammi came to see you.'

He nodded vigorously. 'You see, I hadn't mentioned to Sammi how I felt. I mean, I knew her when we were little. Her family's country estate and mine are right next to each other. Of course they've been on theirs for hundreds of years, and Pops only bought his when he married my mother. But we were too little at the time to know much about it. We happened to meet in an overlap when we were both on our ponies. We were very keen equestrians, and we got on like strawberries and cream. I mean, our grooms let us meet up to ride, and I showed her how to climb a tree. It was so much easier to be with Sammi than with any of the boys of my age. She never teased me about my stutter . . .'

'Potato, madam?' I started slightly at being called madam, but helped myself and without pausing in motion or conversation did the same for Wilfred.

'So why couldn't you tell her later?'

The servant moved on. Really, for wartime this family had too many servants. 'That was when we were little. She had freckles, a stubby nose, and scabs on her knees. She's different now.'

'She's beautiful,' I said.

'A goddess,' said Wilfred. 'Whereas I have never shown much promise in the looks stakes.'

I didn't contradict him, but I did serve his peas. Gratitude blossomed across his fishy face. 'So anyway, I had a terrible hangover, and I wasn't thinking straight, so for once I did say what I was thinking. I told her the whole miserable tale, and said I quite understood she wouldn't want me. I said I would be civil but keep my distance, but at least she would now understand the fault was with me.'

'And what did she say?'

'N-n-nothing,' said Wilfred, turning crimson. 'She kissed me. Turns out despite my poor physical showing, she thought I had a good heart. Not saying she's right, but I'm going to do my darnedest to be the best husband she could ever want. If all else fails I can buy her whatever she wants.'

I thought about kissing his trout-like face. 'I think she loves you very much, Wilfred,' I said. I couldn't explain it any other way. I doubted even the most gold-digging young woman wouldn't voluntarily press their lips to such an unfortunate and sloppy specimen.

Wilfred positively glowed with delight. It made him look almost human.

I finished by giving him some carrots, and left him happily munching away in sheer contentment. Against all the odds this weird young man had found his love match in a beautiful woman.

I looked over at Sammi, who scowled back at me. I frowned. She continued to scowl for the rest of the meal, while Wilfred, apart from the occasional comment about how wonderful Sammi was, entertained himself by noshing down on the main course (which might have been duck or shoe leather), and imbibing a rather alcoholic syllabub that formed the final course.

The ladies retired to take tea, and Sammi's mother asked me a lot of rather impertinent questions about White Orchards. I ended up answering politely, but in less and less detail. Sammi pointedly ignored me as much as she could without drawing her mother's ire. Fortunately the gentlemen joined us very quickly. I was eager to get away, and when Ralph said, 'I really must be going. I have another engagement tonight,' I stood up and said, 'Actually, it's been a wonderful evening, but we have work early in the morning. Thank you so much for inviting me.'

'I'll get Simmons to call you a cab,' said Sammi's mother. I thanked her, and followed Sammi to get my coat.

'Wilfred is awfully nice,' I said.

'Isn't he?' said Sammi, in a voice like ice, but Ralph appeared in the hall, behatted and carrying his cane before any more could be said. He tipped his hat to us, and left without waiting for the door to be opened for him. Then Simmons returned to tell me he had managed to hail a cab. I said goodbye to the still rather frosty Sammi, and got into the cab.

'Don't squeal,' said the man waiting for me in the backseat.

Chapter Eight

Soup, Champagne and Taxis

'I never squeal,' I responded in what was my iciest voice. 'Who the hell are you?' It was a wonder he could hear me over the thumping of my heart, which sounded in my ears like the kettle drums from the National Orchestra.

'Why, Uncle Ralph, of course.' He leaned out of the shadows into the light.

'Yes, well, I knew that. But what are you and what are you doing in my cab?' I said, doing my best to let my voice thaw only a little.

'Going wherever you are going, so we can have a little chat,' he said. 'I thought you saw my signal.'

'You have a message for me. That seems doubtful.'

'It was the closest I could think of,' he said, smiling and spreading his hands wide in a gesture of harmlessness. I wasn't fooled.

''Scuse me,' said the cabbie, opening the little glass partition between us. 'You are on the clock. If you could give me an address, and could you have your matrimonial private-like at home?'

'We're not married,' I said indignantly to the cabbie. Then to Ralph, 'You can ring me up tomorrow. It's late.'

Ralph nodded. 'Yes, it is a bit late. Hotel or nightclub? I assume we're going for cocktails.'

'I'm going home,' I said.

'Well, all right. I generally like a meal first, or even a drink, but there is a war going on. Back to your place it is. I'm afraid I'm not carrying a toothbrush. I hope you have a spare.'

'You are not coming home with me!'

'No?' said Ralph. 'I thought it sounded a bit quick off the mark. Cold feet? I expect your mother tried to bring you up well. It's not nice to go leading blokes on. Cocktails first, that's what we need. The Black Cat, driver, and don't spare the horses.'

'Right you are, guv'nor,' said the cabbie, and snapped the little glass back in place.

I reached forward to open it again, but Ralph caught me by the waist, and pulled me back in the seat beside him.

'You're totally wasted in Sammi's department, aren't you? Bored to tears. I might be able to offer you something more interesting.'

'In a nightclub?' I said. 'I don't think so.'

'Where else were you going flouncing along in that little black cocktail dress?'

'I'm in mourning,' I said. It would be easier not to make a scene. I'd get out when the cab stopped and hail another taxi. He could hardly kidnap me in the street.

'What for? Your sense of adventure?'

'No, my father.'

He started to laugh. Then stopped. 'Are you serious?'

'Yes,' I said, and to my great alarm I felt a sudden desire to burst into tears. I shoved my feelings aside. However, something of what I felt must have shown in my face.

'Oh, I'm sorry, Hope,' he said, and released his hold around my waist. 'I thought you were wearing black merely to be stylish. I didn't realise you were in mourning.'

'Why should you?' I said, attempting to meet him halfway. 'I don't know what you think I'm like but, even on a good day, I'm not the sort of girl who goes to a nightclub.'

He blinked and frowned. 'Honestly, you're what, twenty-three?'

'Twenty-two,' I said. Inside I heaved a sigh of relief. He might have realised I had some training in espionage, but he didn't appear to be connecting me with anyone. Of course my mother had her code name, and my father was never in the business after

I was born. It could be that he was reacting simply to me as me. That in itself was a reason not to throw him out of the cab, so I added, 'I got permission to go to university early.'

'Did you? What did you read?'

'Mathematics.'

'Well, that's really thrown me. That's not how I pegged you at all. And I'm usually good at figuring people out.'

'As has been evidenced by your endeavours tonight.'

'Mea culpa,' said Ralph. 'I didn't actually think you were the kind of girl who usually went nightclubbing—'

'Or invited strange men back to her flat,' I added.

'Oh, a flat,' said Ralph, his eyes suddenly twinkling. 'No landlady then?'

I ignored him and looked out of the window. I knew his type hated being ignored. Playing it very coolly would keep his interest. Not that I wanted his romantic interest . . . but still, he was right, I was sad and bored to tears.

The night had swallowed London whole. I remembered how lit up it had been during my debutante season. As if the city was permanently dressed up for Christmas. Cars zooming back and forth, with young people singing and waving their bottles in the air. Although, that side of things I didn't miss. It was more the life of the place. There were still people around, but they crept rather than walked, as if they were mice waiting for the cat to pounce. The season, for all it had involved a murder or two, had been mostly full of laughter and joy. London now was a city of darkness and fear.

I became aware Ralph had fallen silent. He was trying to make up his mind about me. If I tried to give him the shove now, he'd be utterly convinced it was the last thing he wanted. But I couldn't help myself and said, 'When we get there I'll let you out and ask the cabbie to take me home.'

'That would make me feel like a dreadful cad,' he said.

'If the shoe fits.'

'Ouch! How about coming in for one drink. No, better yet,

we'll be right next to Toby's Soup Kitchen. Come and have a bowl of decent soup with me, and then I'll take you home, and behave completely like a gentleman.'

'Can you do that?'

'If I have to,' he said. His teeth flashed white in the darkness as he smiled.

'A soup kitchen?'

'Oh no, not like that. Toby had this idea that people in the nightclub like to get some nibbles, so he opened a soup bar outside. Very open, respectable kind of place. Bowl of soup and a hot roll. No dark corners and perfectly clean.'

I had to admit that after the terrible dinner, I was hungry.

'All right,' I said. 'But if—'

Ralph put his hands up. 'Word of a rogue!'

When we drew up at the nightclub Ralph paid, and tipped the cabbie enough to make him doff his cap. Then, taking my elbow, he led me across the road and through a dark little doorway. Once inside he carefully closed the door and then pulled across the inside curtain. Light dazzled me, and I had to blink several times before the blur disappeared. Before us lay a brightly lit café. It had a number of tables with Formica tops and those wooden chairs with the brightly coloured cushions that look much more comfortable than they are. There were a few couples in evening dress. Capes and fur stoles were thrown incongruously across empty chairs. At the back of the café was a long counter. Ralph led me to a table, out of the draught from the door, and told me he'd be back in a moment. Then he disappeared towards the counter.

I looked around. The windows and doors were covered with thick blackout blinds. The lights might be bright but the walls were painted a cheery yellow. I couldn't help but notice two things: everything had wipeable surfaces, and the people were all intoxicated. One of the members of a group of six in the corner was even waving a champagne bottle around.

Ralph came back carrying two glasses and an opened bottle of champagne. 'Soup's just coming. I chose tomato for you. I mean, everyone likes tomato, don't they? In the same way everyone drinks champagne. You do drink champagne, don't you?' He filled my glass and sat down.

'Yes, I do,' I said, making no motion to pick up the glass. Although I couldn't help noticing the label of the bottle showed it was one of my favourites. 'I take it this place supplies alcohol as well as soup?'

'Cocaine, too, I believe,' said Ralph taking a sip. 'All the slightly sozzled nightclubber could want. Very up to the minute.'

'And you know the owner?' I hadn't taken off my coat, and at the mention of cocaine, I had slipped my hand through my bag and was about to leave.

'Don't worry, never touch the stuff myself,' said Ralph. 'One of my best assets believe it or not is my brain.' He tapped the side of his head. 'Not going to mess with prime material, am I?'

I looked pointedly at the champagne.

'Hardly counts,' said Ralph. 'Been drinking it at my mother's knee since birth. Or some such. Drink up! A glass or two of the good stuff can hardly hurt you. The stuff my brother served tonight could have been a weapon of war, it was so rough. Besides, I asked for two rolls each, so there'll be plenty of food to soak it up.'

Then he gave a very ordinary smile. If it had been one of dazzling charm or charisma, I would have probably left, but this was a chummy smile. The kind of smile someone gives you when they are genuinely pleased to see you. It wasn't flirtatious in the slightest. In retrospect I understood he played it perfectly, but at the time I was simply hungry and thirsty. I also foolishly thought I was in control. The truth was, I wasn't used to meeting other spies, only civilians. And the latter are remarkably easy to manipulate. Besides, in the flat I only had some stale bread and the last of the cheese truckle, which was growing distinctly hard and rubbery. I picked up my drink.

The soup arrived not long after. It was excellent and the rolls freshly baked. 'Tell me about this place?' I said.

'I had hoped you'd ask me about my enigmatic self.'

'I'm more interested in the soup.'

He winced and gave me a wry smile. 'Toby and I were up at Oxford together. Tobias, Viscount Uxbridge. Nice chap. Always trying to come up with schemes to save the family home, which is an unhappy combination of Tudor, Elizabethan, mice and dry rot. I think he should sell up and let some landlord make it into modern flats. I mean, I'm all for respecting the family homestead, but there's only so much wrack and ruin a man can fix. Especially if he's as good at business as Toby.'

'Hasn't he joined up?'

'Flat feet. He's an air-raid warden and down for fire training too.'

'Ah.'

'No, whatever else Toby is, he isn't a coward or a conshie. Just a bloody awful businessman. This place has potential, but letting his girlfriend – a denizen of the deep as far as I am concerned, but mentioned in Debrett's, which is all his family care about – sell cocaine is a non-starter. I say, you were hungry, weren't you?'

By now I had finished off the soup, the two rolls, and a couple of glasses without thinking. Ralph had kept topping up my glass. He hadn't been sly about it, but I had been too intent on quelling my appetite to object. I realised now, as I swallowed my last mouthful, that this had been a mistake. The wine at Sammi's parents, tonight might have been rough, but it had also been strong.

'I need to go home,' I said.

'But the evening is only beginning!'

'It must be past midnight, and I have to work tomorrow. In the fish tank.'

'What sort of stuff do you have to type up?' he asked.

'All sorts,' I said. 'Nothing that would interest you.'

'Secret-type stuff? Can you tell me a secret, Hope?' He waggled his eyebrows at me. 'Go on, I'd be terribly impressed.'

'Don't be an idiot,' I said. 'I can't tell you a thing no matter how much champagne you pour down my neck.'

'I may have poured, but you drank it,' said Ralph. 'But yes, I'm pleased to hear you have nothing to tell me.'

'Is this some kind of test? What right do you have to test me?'

'It's nice to know the future of the country is in safe hands.'

'I should bloody well report you,' I said.

'Please don't,' said Ralph. 'It was a very half-hearted attempt to get information from you. But I did have to try. I can't put you forward unless I have some degree of assurance in your integrity.'

'Well, then it's an awful test and it tells you nothing,' I said. 'You're an idiot. I'm going home.' I got up and found that my legs seemed to be in two minds about where they wanted to be. 'Home,' I said to them commandingly, and promptly sat back down again. 'Put me forward for what?' I said, trying to pretend that I felt fine.

'My goodness, young lady, are you drunk?' said Ralph.

'Mildly spiffy. I mean stiffy. I mean squiffy. Oh, Lord! I am drunk.'

'As a trout in a river,' said Ralph. 'Sorry, old girl, I didn't realise.'

'Sammi's father's wine was both vile and highly intoxicating. Better for a paraffin heater than drinking. Oh, why is my head . . .'

At this point I put my head down on the table.

'We definitely need to get you home. Where do you live?'

'Can't tell you,' I murmured to the table, 'you might be—'

'An enemy agent?'

'A cad.'

'No, I'm more of a bounder,' said Ralph. He came round to my side of the table and helped me stand, keeping an arm round my waist.

After that it became something of a blur.

Chapter Nine

New Horizons

To my relief I woke up in my own bed alone. I did seem to have thrashed around a bit, and I was only wearing my pants. Gingerly, I sat up. My stomach and head both objected strenuously. I wanted to vomit, and my normal-sized head had become an enormous glass bowl that threatened to shatter at any moment. I groaned and looked at my bedside clock. I was so late I would probably be up on some kind of charge. How I would by charged, by whom and for what, it was currently beyond me to process. All I had taken in was that I was in big trouble. Then I heard a noise from somewhere in the flat.

Not again.

This time I would not wait for discovery. I got up carefully, so as not to smash my glass head, and as quietly as possible, tied a dressing gown tightly around me, and crept to the door. I opened the door an inch, and the smell of bacon rushed up my olfactory senses. The contents of my stomach decided to rush up to greet it. Instead of sneaking through the hallway and tackling the villain I bolted to the bathroom and was copiously sick in the loo. If the rotter tried to tackle me now I would reorientate myself in his direction. What was it about my flat that invited intruders? Had this place once belonged to Fitzroy? No doubt people broke into his home all the time, and he found it jolly good fun defenestrating them. My stomach spasmed again. Oh, but this was nasty. However had Sammi survived to adulthood? As much as I could, I kept alert for anyone entering the bathroom. Although with the sounds and smells I was making, I thought I could probably scare off an entire German platoon.

Finally, it was over, and I sat on the floor, mopping my forehead with a towel. Using the basin as leverage I rose to regard myself in the mirror. My hair stuck up in strange directions. My skin was deathly pale with little beads of sweat. Around my eyes someone had painted dark circles, and these were dull with misery. My memory tugged at me. Had I drunk that much at Sammi's house?

Still, I looked frightful enough to put any would-be intruder at a disadvantage. I opened the bathroom with a sudden wrench, and this time I smelled coffee.

'My last intruder didn't make me coffee,' I said loudly, striding forth from the bathroom. It was horribly bright. My eyes insisted on staying half closed, and I was fine with that. My hearing didn't appear to be affected. 'Nice of you to let me finish in there before we fight.'

'You don't look as if you're in any state to fight,' said a well-educated male voice, 'but I'm game if you are.'

My eyes flew open. Sammi's Uncle Ralph stood in the middle of my open kitchen. On the hob was a pan filled with fried eggs and bacon. Toast had popped up from the machine, and the coffee was burbling away to itself.

Gradually, in bits and pieces the evening came back to me. 'Oh God,' I said and collapsed down onto the settee, my face buried in my hands.

'Well, I have to say, this is not normally how young women of my acquaintance generally greet me after a night of passion. Especially if I've made one of my special breakfasts.'

That brought my head up with snap. 'We didn't, did we?'

'I shall try not to take your expression of extreme horror personally,' said Ralph. 'No, of course we didn't. You were as drunk as a mouse at the bottom of a cider barrel. I don't take advantage of young ladies.' He gave a grin. 'You were awfully tempting. You started out so angry at me, but by the time we were here I was your best friend. Why, you even threw your brassiere at me.'

My face flooded with embarrassment. 'Coffee, please,' I said. 'For the love of God, coffee.'

'Black, I take it?' said Ralph, handing over a cup. 'Yes, I had a lovely night on your settee there. In fact, I think you may be sitting on my scarf. If you wouldn't mind. Silk does crease so dreadfully.'

I made another discovery. 'You're wearing evening dress,' I said.

'I don't yet have a selection of clothes available for me at your apartment.'

I held out my cup for a refill.

'What, no fiery response? You must be feeling rough.'

I gulped down the rest of the coffee. 'I think I'm in deep trouble. It's almost luncheon time.'

Ralph nodded. 'I thought of that. If you speak French I have a way round it. Please say you do, or I've put both our heads in a noose.'

'Like a native,' I said. 'Coffee!'

'Oh, thank the gods,' said Ralph. 'Right, I'm off to get into uniform. You need a bath. I take it you have a clean uniform?'

I nodded. He was filling up my coffee cup, so I was inclined to listen.

He checked his watch. 'Can you be ready in thirty minutes?'

I nodded again, between slurps.

'You should also try eating something. Even cleaned up you're going to look bloody awful.'

'Nice of you to say so. What exactly are you proposing?' I enquired.

'I believe I have a way to get us both out of this. Follow my lead.' He leaned over to whisk his scarf from beside me, and popped his hat on his head. 'Right, remember what I said. See you in half an hour.' Then he was gone before I could process any more questions. I stared at the door for a few moments feeling rather hard done by. Who was he to order me about? And what the hell was going on? The only thing he was right about was that I needed a bath.

As it ran I attempted the breakfast. I started off with the dry toast, but by the time the bath had run I had consumed a couple of eggs and two rashers of bacon. Then I splashed around getting clean, and trying to rid myself of that nasty sweaty drunk odour. My hair was short enough that I could dunk it, but if I didn't get it dry before I went out I'd end up with a mass of curls.

I was standing in front of the mirror trying to detangle my hair when I heard the doorbell go. Ralph brushed past me and into the flat. I closed the door behind him. He wore army uniform and a captain's rank. 'Captain?' I asked. I still didn't feel up to full sentences.

'I am. Yours?'

I peered down at my shoulder as if I'd never seen it before. 'Second lieutenant.'

Ralph smiled, an easy and open smile. 'If they decide to take you, you'll fit right in with our lot. They're not too bothered about rank either, as long as you respect the chaps in charge.'

'Like you?'

'Heavens, no. I'm a mere cog in the grand machine. A very shiny, charming and talented cog, but a cog none the less. Shall we go?'

'To?'

'All I can tell you is this is a new operation, and that your ability to speak French and your training, or whatever gave you that security clearance, is enough to get you an interview. It'll be a darn sight more interesting than typing.'

I hesitated. I knew Fitzroy considered me under his command, but I'd heard nothing from him since White Orchards. He'd kept me totally in the dark over what he planned for me to do next, but then this might be the way he normally operated. I mean, when I'd landed in the auxies, had he known there was a traitor

71

there for me to find? Had it all been some kind of plan all along? With Fitzroy you never knew.

'Is there a problem?' asked Ralph. He was slightly up on his toes, eager to go.

'I do have a commanding officer. I'm wondering if I should speak with him.'

'Him? Not Dotty?'

I shook my head. 'Him,' I said, and sighed. This obviously conveyed something to Ralph because he grinned and said, 'I worked for a chap like that once. Nightmare. Do you want to contact him?'

I shook my head. 'How old are you?'

'Thirty-five,' he said, raising his eyebrows. 'Does it matter?'

'I was wondering—'

'About my experience? A few years,' he said.

I nodded, as if I was the same. I didn't see the point of telling him that I had a lifetime. For all I knew Fitzroy was pulling his strings, and this was all some kind of covert op inside another op. Fitzroy took a lot of interest in operations in Britain, and he seemed to like parcelling them up like Russian dolls.

'You're very quiet,' said Ralph when we were in his army car.

'I was thinking about the nature of war,' I said.

'Really, like Sun Tzu?'

'Hmm, *Book of Five Rings*? No. I was thinking how different this war will be to the Great War and how it will have to be fought differently.'

Ralph gave me a dazzling smile. 'That's a girl. I knew I'd picked a good 'un.' He pulled up outside a nondescript office building. I didn't wait for him to open my door as I would have done last night. Today, it would have been more appropriate for me to open his. I did hate the way war made us less civilised!

We went in and past an older man sitting at a desk. Ralph showed his pass, and asked me to sign a book. I then received a temporary pass. 'Don't lose it,' said the guard, 'or someone might shoot you.' I didn't laugh.

Ralph ignored a lift and started running up some stairs. I followed at his heels like an obedient puppy. By the time we'd gone up three flights I wanted to stop. I also hadn't liked the leery, albeit good-natured looks that passing officers gave Ralph and me. There were a couple of comments about him being 'late again' and 'a naughty boy'. Ralph laughed any comment off and didn't slow to allow me to catch up. The phrase 'puppet on a string' popped into my head.

Just when I was considering calling out, he turned onto the landing and I caught up beside him. 'It would have looked worse if we'd walked in shoulder to shoulder,' he said.

'Really, for who?' I snarled and then remembered to add, 'Sir.'

'Ah, Hope, don't be snarky. You know how these hierarchies work. You're going to thank me later.'

I might have asked him for what if I hadn't noticed a man in uniform coming along the corridor, who took one look at me and attempted to dive into a door. Only the door proved to be locked. He tugged furiously at the handle.

'Dean?' I called over Ralph's shoulder. 'Dean West? Is that you?'

Ralph twisted round. Dean seeing Ralph more clearly, or I suspected the captain's insignia, sighed, let his shoulders slump and turned round to face us. 'No one is meant to know I'm here, Hope,' he said.

Ralph looked between us. He raised his eyebrows.

'We trained together for a while,' I said. 'I had to leave in a hurry, so I never knew what—'

'Happened to any of us,' finished Dean for me. 'We were disbanded and we ended up all over the place. I landed here.'

I took in his small stocky frame, balding head and round spectacles. 'You haven't changed a bit,' I said.

'No,' said Dean sadly. 'I don't suppose I have. Still, Hope, I'm useful here, but no one's meant to know I'm going to be working with the SOE.' He clapped his hand over his mouth as soon as he said it and looked at Ralph. 'That's all right, isn't it, sir? I assume counter-intelligence know about us?'

'I don't think you should assume anything, Corporal. I don't know you from a hole in the ground, and you seem to be acting both furtively and rather mouthily.'

'Sorry, sir, I was coming to get an index I need and I was thinking about the cypher – then I saw Hope—'

'The second lieutenant,' injected Ralph.

'I never knew her rank.'

'It's useful then that she is wearing it, isn't it?'

I squirmed and tried to throw a discreet sympathetic look at Dean.

'You were acting for counter-intelligence? For whom?' asked Ralph.

'Can't say,' I said. Generally Fitzroy liked it being known that he had fingers in lots of pies. But I was getting the distinct impression that the SIS was fracturing into myriad pieces, all doing different things. He'd more or less told me that before, but I'd had other things on my mind. Right now, I was suspecting that caution was needed in all future exchanges.

'Hmm. You'd better come along with us, Corporal,' said Ralph and set off at a smart pace in the direction Dean had originally sprung from. He stopped outside an ordinary-looking door and knocked.

'Come in,' said a light male voice. It sounded familiar.

Ralph entered with Dean and I bringing up the rear. When we were inside, I found we were all shuffled up rather close together. I had to lean away smartly to avoid a black eye when Ralph saluted. A major rose from behind a small desk piled high with papers. He smiled at Ralph. He was below average height, but despite this he had a presence. The room was far too small, and his personality dominated it. From the way he stood to the way his intelligent eyes darted around, this was a man of inexhaustible energy, and from the smile hovering around his lips, good humour. His cap was on the desk, and his hair was slightly longer than regulations would have specified. He took no notice of the boxes stacked all around the room, which we were now crowded up against.

'I'd say take a seat, Captain, but as you can see we can barely swing a cat in here. Who have you got with you?'

Dean and I shuffled either side of Ralph so he could see us more clearly. 'Good grief,' said the major, 'it's the girl from the Tea Room at the Ritz.'

Chapter Ten

On Probation

'Sir,' I said, saluting.

'This is a dash sight too crowded,' said the major in an annoyed voice. 'Pop off, West, and see if you can find an empty meeting room, will you? I take it you've finished that cypher?'

Dean left quickly without answering.

'We found him wandering the corridors and the lieutenant mentioned they had trained together, but he mentioned the SOE.'

The major sat down. 'For such an intelligent man he can be remarkably stupid,' he said. 'I had hoped to send him out into the field, but it's a pure case of chance what secrets he blurts out. He doesn't seem to understand the concept of prevaricating. Or that anyone might be untrustworthy. Unlike you, hmm, Lieutenant. You were as quiet as a mouse about your connections with counter-intelligence when we last met. Or should I say counter-counter-intelligence? After all, it was us you were checking up on, wasn't it?'

'I was simply doing my duty, sir,' I said, trying to be enigmatic rather than give away I hadn't had a clue why I'd originally been posted with the auxies.

'And what do you want from me this time? Which woodpile should I be looking under?'

'Actually, sir, it was my idea,' said Ralph. 'I don't know about her last operation, but she's currently working in the fish tank. It seemed rather a waste of talent to me. Apparently, she speaks fluent French. Bilingual.'

'Hmm,' said the major, sounding unconvinced. 'So you think we should poach her?'

'As I understand it, the lieutenant has an exceptionally high security clearance. I thought she might help us set up some administrative stuff. I know you've got your secretary, but I thought someone . . .'

The major nodded. 'I get where you're coming from. Let's go and chivvy up West so we can have a proper chat.'

He got up, and I thought for a moment he was going to leap over the desk. So did Ralph, as he stepped back and onto my foot. I managed to open the door and we all went out like peas popping out of a pod. Dean was in the corridor, and it wasn't long before we were settled in a much bigger room round the end of a large table. It was like an office boardroom, and it may well once have been. The Army were requisitioning buildings left right and centre. The major sent Dean on a 'perilous mission to find drinkable tea' and settled back in what would have been the chairman's seat.

'So what do you know about the SOE, Hope?'

'Nothing, sir.'

The major put his hat and swagger stick on the table. 'Now, here's my problem with the department you're in – I don't know whether that's the truth or not. I don't mean you'd lie to me precisely, but you might not be able to be as free as one might hope – if you'll excuse the pun. I don't believe you can serve two masters, do you?'

Ralph coughed. 'I didn't ask the right questions. I apologise to you both. I thought she was an auxie volunteer.'

'I thought you understood no women were recruited for that? It was a suicide mission, and I . . . well. Never mind. You have to think of these things, Captain.'

'Yes, sir. She might look meek, but this is rather an extraordinary young women if half of what I hear about her is true.'

'I think it doesn't generally occur to anyone that I might be trained in espionage,' I said. 'It's one of my main advantages.'

'Yes,' said the major. 'That's something we've been thinking about. Women have always worked for the SIS, but generally as assets. Although you know there have been female agents,' he said, looking pointedly at me. 'You also know it's not the rule. I read the report over what happened. I'd say everyone except your commanding officer, and including myself, underestimated you. Shockingly underestimated you, in fact. Does that happen often?'

'Sometimes,' I said.

'You specialise in observation and evasion, I believe. Anything else?'

'I'm not a bad shot.'

'Handgun or sniper?' he said with a small laugh.

'Both,' I said seriously, and enjoyed seeing the smile disappear from his face.

'Did it again, didn't I?' he said ruefully. 'So why do you want to come and work for us?'

Dean appeared with the tea, and the major poured it for us without comment. I was so surprised I didn't even notice Dean slip away.

'I don't know anything about you,' I said. 'But a new operation has to be more interesting than working in the fish tank. I assume you can apply to my commanding officer to transfer me, and he can refuse if he needs me to stay in place. But this time, I do think I am in a holding space—'

'Awaiting developments?'

'Something like that, sir.'

'If it's the same man we're talking about, I can't see him being keen on you joining us. I mean, the survival odds would be better than the auxies, I hope! But it's still risky stuff.'

I thought about saying something trite about *isn't everything dangerous in war*? Instead I asked, 'Can you tell me something about the SOE? Are you the CO?'

The major shook his head. 'No, I'm not, but I am heavily involved in the operational side. As for telling you about it, that's a notion in progress. We're pretty sure we'll get the formal go-ahead soon, but some of the regular SIS men aren't too keen on us at all. I wouldn't be surprised if your CO disliked the whole idea, but that may be to your advantage.'

'You mean, he might like me being stationed inside and getting intel on what you're doing.'

'Precisely,' said the major. He looked at Ralph. 'She is exactly the kind of sharp mind we want, but she comes with complications.' He turned back to me. 'This is a bit personal, but . . . do you think your CO is affected by your relationship?'

I thought about this, and how I could express my feelings without betraying Fitzroy. 'If that's so, I don't think it's a deliberate decision. He isn't a sentimental man.'

'He's not known to be except—' He broke off and lowered his head to look at me meaningfully. Ralph, I could see, was growing tenser by the moment. He couldn't call the major out, but he'd gone from being the experienced spy, who was impressing a naive young woman, to a man totally out of his depth. It clearly didn't sit well with him.

'My family have had an association with espionage for a long time,' I said. 'I don't believe it was ever intended that I joined the Department, but rather I was trained in certain skills as I grew up. I don't have the full set by any means.'

The major nodded. 'They'd be afraid that someone would come after you to get at them. Did you ever do any hand-to-hand?'

'Yes, I studied ju-jitsu. As you know, it was favoured by the suffragettes.'

'I didn't,' said the major. 'But that's jolly interesting and useful to know.' He sipped his tea. 'By the gods, this is awful, and yet so much better than we normally get.' He looked up at me hopefully, 'You don't bake, do you?'

'I can cook,' I said, 'inside and outside, but I've never been much into baking biscuits or cakes, even if we could get the ingredients.'

The major shrugged. 'Can't have everything, can we?' He glanced at Ralph. 'You're looking a bit left out, Captain?'

'Feeling it, sir.'

'You've stumbled across a rare individual in Hope here. It does mean your eye for spotting talent is excellent. I take it you haven't known each other long?'

'We met last night,' said Ralph.

'Jolly quick off the mark too, then. All things considered, I think we could use you, Hope, and not just to do a bit of typing. There are certain things about you that are – unique – and that we could use. Possibly not how you might expect.' He gave me a rather charming smile. 'However, we're already upsetting a lot of apple carts. I'm going to send a request to your CO for you to come and do some work with us. This may well include clerical work, but it will be a lot more than that. Of course, I need to pass it by my CO too. Sometimes it's a wonder anything gets done in the Army. If the stars align I'll get the captain here to explain what it is we do, and how you can help. Easy steps, in your case, are our best way forward. That sound all right to you?'

'Of course, sir,' I said. 'Any way I can help.'

'That's the spirit. I'd better get back to my forms, and you had better get back to the fish tank. As for you,' he said, looking at Ralph, 'I'd like a written report on how you intend to move forward in recruiting. Can't depend on striking it lucky at family dinner parties all the time, can you?' He stood up and so did we.

'No, sir,' said Ralph, slightly red in the face.

'Dismissed,' said the major, and I swear I saw a flicker of a wink in his left eye.

Ralph walked me wordlessly to the stairs. I nodded goodbye and went to hand my pass in and leave. 'Didn't get shot today,' I said to the old man behind the desk. 'Maybe tomorrow?' His laugh verged on the edge of bronchial cough.

'This lot's mad, you know,' he said in farewell.

I smiled and left.

I caught a cab to the fish tank. While London went past, I wondered what on earth I would say to Cerberus, but more importantly, what was the SOE and what the hell had I got myself into this time?

Chapter Eleven

Secrets and Lies

When I got to the fish tank Dotty waved me through without a word. She even smiled. I assumed that the major, whose name I still didn't know, had telephoned through and excused me from being late to the typing pool.

The girls all looked up when I came in. 'Sorry,' I said to them, 'had an interview somewhere else.'

'Where?' asked Flossie at once.

'Can't say,' I said.

'Oh, go on,' she said, 'we're all top-top hush-hush in here anyway.'

I shook my head.

'You shouldn't push her,' said Red. This was the longest sentence I'd ever heard her say. It seemed the same for the others too, as they turned to stare at her. Red turned her attention back to her machine and carried on typing.

'Well I never,' said Flossie.

'Break in ten minutes, ladies,' said Sammi. 'Let's get on with our work until then. The nation is counting on us.'

'Of course it is,' said Flossie under her breath. 'I mean, how would anyone manage without the menus for this banquet being typed up.'

Sammi pretended not to hear. I picked up a handful of papers and got to work. Flossie wasn't that far wrong. We were typing up the details of a departmental shindig of some kind. Lots of top brass would be present and the security arrangements were both highly classified and highly complex. I began to understand why when I came across a reference that could be a pseudonym for the king. Of course, even our clearance didn't go that high. But this wasn't what made me take a sharp intake of breath. I was halfway down the security arrangements for the arrival of some bigwigs and their wives, when I saw Bernie and her husband's name.

'Don't suppose you can tell us why you made that funny noise either, can you?' said Flossie.

'Break time, ladies,' said Sammi.

Having just drunk tea I didn't feel much like another cup. With some manoeuvring of the biscuit plate to get Flossie out of the way, and waiting till the twins were in their corner, I managed to get Sammi alone.

'I wanted to thank you for last night,' I said quietly. 'It was very kind of you to invite me out.'

'Yes, well, the food is never up to much, but . . .' she trailed off. She wasn't looking me in the eye.

'Is something wrong?' I asked.

'Well, no . . . I mean . . . I never took you for a man-eater,' she said in a rush.

'I don't know what you mean,' I said, bristling.

Sammi drew me over so we were as far away from the others as possible. 'Isn't it enough that you make sheep's eyes at my fiancé all night, but then you go off in a cab with Uncle Ralph. Well, we all know what he's like. It took my father six weeks to convince my mother to invite him round after the last dinner party he came to.'

'Why?' I asked, diverted from the insult.

'He brought a showgirl with him.'

'A what?' I said.

'An actress!' said Sammi, pursing her mouth as if she was spitting poison. 'You should have seen the way she dressed! Definitely skimping on her outfit.'

'There is a stocking shortage,' I said.

Sammi shook her head, and bent her mouth close to my ear. 'I don't believe she was wearing underwear.'

I could tell from her tone that she was as thrilled as she was appalled by this. I gave her a tiny grin. 'How naughty,' I said, lowering my voice as if we were sharing a confidence. 'But I can assure you that not only was I wearing everything appropriate for the evening, I did not go on a date with your uncle. He wanted to talk to me about something war related – and I'm sorry I can't say more than that.'

'Hmm,' said Sammi. 'I've always thought he was involved in hush-hush stuff. Even before the war. Doesn't change the fact he's a bit of a Romeo.'

I nodded. 'I got that impression. But to answer your other point, I was not making sheep's eyes at Wilfred. Idiotic expression anyway. Why would looking like a sheep help anyone further an acquaintance?'

Sammi pressed her lips together. I could tell she was trying not to be amused. She had little original wit herself, but a lively sense of humour, and tended to value others who could make her smile.

'I simply thought he was a nice man and easy to chat to. With respect, you can't say your father is the garrulous type.'

'But most people don't pay Wilfred much attention, especially women.'

'Because of the way he looks? Then they're fools. Break time must be almost over, and I need to catch up for this morning.'

I went off to my desk without allowing her to reply. Giving her time to think about what I had said I was certain would do the trick. I thought it sweet that seeing another women talking with Wilfred had awoken her ire. There was obviously more to Sammi than met the eye.

After a few days of interminable typing, yawn-making break times and long, long evenings, the phone in my flat rang at seven a.m. Unfortunately this was the morning after I'd decided to fill my evenings with indoor exercise, as I thought I was putting on weight, despite my limited diet. I rolled out of bed and crawled to the phone, discovering as I did so that I was full of aches, and even bits I didn't think could ache, did.

'Hello,' I said. 'This is Hope.' The line had been installed for me, and Fitzroy, as ever, had done his thing and made it a secure line. All the same I never answered it with my full name.

'Hello, don't say I woke you,' said the major. 'Young thing like you, you should be up with the lark.'

'Oh, good morning, sir,' I said.

'It is. A lovely, bright and sunny morning. You should take advantage of days like this. I've already been for a swim and a run, and I'm eons older than you.'

'Gosh,' I said, unable to think of anything further to say without either being scathing or too informal. He was definitely, I decided, a man who liked to flirt. What was it about these men in espionage?

'So aren't you going to ask me why I called?' he said.

'When it comes to senior officers, sir, I've been trained not to ask questions.'

'Well, that's rubbish. Useless way to behave. If you ask and I can't tell you, then I'll say so. No hard feelings. I'd much rather have the honest opinions and questions of those that work for me. As long as they are reasonably respectful when on duty!'

'You mean work for you?'

'Exactly, young Hope. I do. In fact I've been thinking of a name for you. I can't go on calling you lieutenant, and I certainly can't keep your records up to date without calling you something, so I've decided, you're to be Sunflower.'

'Sunflower!' I gasped.

'Yes, do you like it? It's a play on your name. You struck me as a happy sort of girl, willing to give most things a try, so I thought of a sunflower — always facing towards the sun no matter where it's planted.'

'Thank you, sir,' I said, carefully modulating my voice. It was fortunate we were on the telephone, so he couldn't see my face.

'Right. I'm sending Leo to bring you over. We've moved again.

You'll know him when you see him. Oh, better come in mufti. Neat and smart. Nothing showy or too inviting.' He rang off.

He had given me no idea of when Leo would appear. Let alone who Leo was. I got dressed quickly in a neat navy-blue outfit I had. I put on some make-up and did my best to contain my hair. It was at the in between long and short stage, when it was more thick than it was biddable. I'd barely brushed my teeth – and hadn't had either breakfast or coffee – when the doorbell rang.

When I opened the door Ralph stood there. I gaped at him like a fish, not sure whether he knew what was going on or not. As usual he brushed past me into the flat. He had a way of twisting his shoulders that got him past people without major impact. I shut the door. 'I'm waiting for someone,' I said.

'I know, Sunflower,' he said, an enormous grin on his face. 'Sunflower, I take it that was the boss's idea and not yours.' He began to peer around the flat.

'Yes,' I said, trying not to give him any more information. He laughed. 'And you're Leo, I take it?'

'I did suggest "bounder" or "cad", but they weren't having any of it.'

'Didn't want to flatter your ego,' I said.

He stopped snooping. 'Ah, now, that is pretty much how it was explained to me, but you remember that little thing about me being a captain and you being a lieutenant? And us being on duty? You know as well as I, or at least I hope you do, that uniform is not the definition of being on duty in SIS.'

'But you were teasing me,' I said.

'Privilege of rank,' he said.

'I see, sir. How far does privilege of rank take you? Just so I know, sir?'

He walked over to me and put a finger under my chin. I quelled a strong impulse to break it. I stood very still, but I didn't smile.

'I'll have to see,' he said. Then he stepped back and took his hand away. 'Seriously, I have no objection to the odd bit of banter

85

between us, but not, absolutely not, when any other ranks are around. Understood? I mean, we met as social equals and that makes it a bit difficult. Generally the people I recruit don't go on to have ranks. You're rather an exception, and I'm still working out how to handle you.'

He was trying to make me uncomfortable. I wasn't sure why, so I kept my eyes open and slightly vapid. He frowned and continued.

'I've been given the impression by the major that you are well connected in the espionage department of this fair country. I'll warn you now that he's torn between liking you and worrying you're a spoilt princess. Protected by your connections.'

'You mean like Sammi and her grandfather?'

He shook his head. 'All that meant was she was given an extra level of trust, and in reality it was more down to being my niece. I vouched for her ability to keep her mouth shut.'

'But she doesn't know?'

'She might suspect, but she doesn't know what I do. She also always has the good sense not to ask. My big brother, on the other hand, thinks I'm some kind of a wastrel.' I pressed my lips shut. 'Please, no comment. Thank you. Do you intend to keep in contact with her?'

'Is that a problem? I'm out on a limb a bit at the moment.'

'You do appear to be oddly isolated. The major said you were operating alone during your last operation, but your CO actually flew in at the end. Did I get that right?'

I nodded. I failed to suppress a shudder at the memory. 'Worst bit of the whole operation. He's a terrible pilot,' I explained.

'And you've told him that?'

'In a way. I'm not the only one who he works with who thinks so.'

'Sounds like a very odd department. Should I know about it?'

'Not unless my CO wanted you to. Flying is the only thing he does badly. He's brilliant, ruthless and makes Machiavelli look like a petulant toddler. I like him a lot.' The words were barely out of my mouth before I realised that sounded as if I was laying it on too thick.

'He's not allowed to have a relationship with a junior rank.'

I laughed. 'He doesn't tend to let inconvenient rules bother him.'

'I hope that's not true,' said Leo scowling.

My puzzlement turned to embarrassment as I understood he thought I was talking about myself. 'Me? God no! That would never happen.'

He raised a quizzical eyebrow. 'We should go.'

He led the way out to the waiting car with me following in his wake. I had the sinking feeling I was starting this new posting all wrong.

Besides, Sunflower. I mean, Sunflower?

Chapter Twelve

Sunflower

The driver stopped outside an ordinary-looking office building. Leo got out and opened the car door for me. I assumed he wanted me, for some reason, to act like a civilian, so I did. I even shortened my steps to a more ladylike totter as opposed to the normal stride I used. I also waited for him to open the entrance door to the building. He rolled his eyes at me, but did so. Once we were inside, he said, 'Well played. We want it to be seen that civilians regularly come into this building. We're a new bureaucratic department.' I clocked the Cerberus immediately. It was an older woman with thick-rimmed glasses.

'This is Rebecca, or Mrs Goldring to you. She'll give you your pass. This is Sunflower, Rebecca, security level W.'

Mrs Goldring looked me up and down. Then she sniffed. 'You're young for that kind of clearance.'

I smiled. 'Thank you,' I said sweetly.

She sniffed again and handed me the pass. I clipped it to my jacket lapel. 'You hand this to me before you leave the building. If you require any kind of outside authorisation that has to be made up specially. You'd need the major's authorisation at least.'

'I don't anticipate needing any, Mrs Goldring. However, if I do I will ensure you receive the correct authorisation.' I gave a small nod. Although inside I was repressing a desire to curtsey. What was it with these Cerberuses the SIS found? None of them seemed anything but ordinary, but they had this way of making everyone feel like naughty children. The armed guards helped. In this case they were badly concealed behind two screens. 'By the way, I can see two pairs of army boots and one of your guards has his stock on the ground.' I kept my voice low, but even and clear.

Beside me Leo gave a sharp intake of breath. Mrs Goldring bent to pick up a pencil and notepad, and in doing so allowed her eyes to run over the concealed guard posts. She wrote a note, folded it and passed it to me. I thanked her and put it in my pocket. Then she went back to her files.

Leo waited a moment and then took me past the guards and up the stairs. 'It's secure now,' he said. 'What did she give you?'

I opened the note and laughed. I passed it to him. The note read: *Well done, my dear. I'll have words. You can call me Rebecca. He can call me Mrs Goldring.*

Leo scrunched up the note and put it in his pocket. 'She loves me really,' he said.

'Of course, sir,' I said, as if butter wouldn't melt in my mouth.

Leo cast me an askance glance. 'I can't make up my mind about you,' he said. 'We should let the major know you're here. He'll want to say a few words. Then I'm to brief you, and after that show you your desk. Do you know shorthand?'

'Yes,' I said.

'I mean, can you really do it? Not just a few scribbles for show?'

'Yes, sir. Among other things I am a fully trained secretary.'

'You're not a medic as well, are you?'

I shook my head. 'Field-level triage only.'

Leo frowned, but didn't comment. He knocked on an office door and the major's voice told us to enter. This office was more than four times as large as the cupboard he had previously inhabited. However, the boxes remained. Only this time most of them were open, revealing file after file encased in army manila.

The major looked up from an open file on his desk. He closed it and lay his pen across the top. 'Ah, Sunflower, as you see we're in the middle of moving in. Still low on staff. I'm afraid we'll be using you in clerical for a while. Just while we get to know you.'

'Sir, may I ask if you have been in contact directly with my CO?'

The major ran his index finger along the bridge of his nose. 'Hmmm, I don't think one could call it contact precisely. Interesting man. I made some enquiries. Most discreet. Rather – er – ghost-like, one might say. But yes, he has given permission for you to work with us for now. However, he did place limits. Something to discuss in future if we come to that bridge, hmm? You did say you were competent in French?'

'I'm bilingual, sir,' I said.

'Hmm,' he said, his brow furrowed and his mouth skewed off to the side. Then he smiled. 'Right-o, Leo. Take her off and show her the works. Good to have you on board, Sunflower.'

I saluted him. 'Glad to be on board, Major Gubbins.' This earned me a surprised grin and a salute in return. It had been pure chance I had come across the papers in the fish tank that let me work out who he was, but he didn't need to know that.

Leo led me down a corridor, explaining as we went the rough layout of the building. It was all right angled and easy to navigate. 'So that's photography, clerical investigation, languages, let's just call that bit creatives, don't go down there ever, spot of wardrobe – more of a cupboard, general clerical. You're going to be there for a while, and this,' he threw open a door, 'is my office.' It was a small and untidy room, with a desk and chairs, and various boxes, books, maps and outdoor coats scattered around the room. Newspapers were folded and stuffed everywhere from the small set of shelves behind the desk to the seat in front of the desk. Leo brushed these onto the floor and told me to sit down. Then he fumbled under the pile of papers on his desk and found an ashtray. He took a cigarette case from his pocket and lit one. Then he reached them out to me. I shook my head.

'Everyone smokes,' he said, confused.

'Never wanted to,' I replied, trying hard not to cough at the smoke filling the room. At least it wasn't a pipe. I spotted a coat stand hidden at the back with a straw boater on the top and a pair of wellingtons stuck upside down on the other two hat hooks. It reminded me of the rooms I had seen when I was at university.

He must have been watching me looking. 'Homely, isn't it?'

'I'm getting the impression, sir, you're waiting on your clerical allocation?'

'And cleaners,' he said. 'Don't worry, you won't be expected to clean up my office. The clerical work you're to be assigned to is rather different. We're about to open a programme here recruiting civilians. I suppose we might get some people from the services, but mainly not. We're looking for a particular kind of person. The first stage is the interviews down here, and if we decide they might be right for the job then it's a trip to Scotland for some special training before deployment.' He paused, then shook his head. 'Can't accustom myself to you being quiet and attentive. Seems unnatural.'

I didn't rise to the bait, but waited.

'Anyway, your job will be to take notes at these interviews. You won't be asking questions, but we want you to observe them and give your impressions in a report. I think it's likely you'll be invited to join the selection committee too – as a member, not a scribe. It all depends on how good your reports are. But your friends in the auxies seem to think you're something special.'

'I wasn't with them very long, sir,' I said.

'I know. Says even more that you made an impression. Other than that you seem to have worked solo. Is that correct?'

'I had assets in play,' I said.

'That you were running?'

I nodded. 'Under supervision.'

'What happened to them?'

'One of them married and the other, well, returned to a life of crime, I believe.'

'Do you still have contacts for that one? Sounds like the kind of person we're looking for.'

'I'd need to check with my CO. He moved into his orbit.'

'Which is why you said you were alone?'

'I think my phrase was out on a limb, sir.'

'You don't make friends easily, do you?'

I winced.

'Oh, not my opinion. It's in the section of your file we were allowed to see. Still rankles, with Gubbins, that. Part of your file is redacted.' He stopped and considered me. 'You don't look surprised. I presume this is the Machiavellian CO you mentioned?'

'I wouldn't know, sir.'

'I've met the type. Old school. Don't even tell their left hand what their right hand is doing.'

I stayed silent. I wasn't stupid enough to criticise my CO to another officer, and besides, I wanted to punch him in the face for what he'd said about my godfather. I wanted to say, he knows more about espionage than you've drunk glasses of Scotch – which I presumed was a lot. But instead, I sat there with my hands neatly folded in my lap.

'Unnerving,' said Leo, standing up. 'Anyway, if you mention any of this to anyone, including your CO, you'll be shot for breaking the Official Secrets Act. I assume you've signed it?'

I made a non-committal noise he took as agreement. I could hardly tell him that Fitzroy had thought the idea of signing it ludicrous. 'It's in your blood,' he'd said. 'Besides, I've no inclination to draw further attention to you than your mother, simply by being your mother, has.' As far as he was concerned my loyalty to him was absolute and that was all that mattered. I tended to agree. But then, this was back when none of my family had ever thought I would be an active agent. That changed matters. I wondered if Fitzroy had simply forgotten or he had a reason for my not signing.

'So we're the department of "ungentlemanly warfare".' Leo said this rather dramatically. There was a pause that went on too long during which his open face became increasingly furrowed. Eventually I broke the impasse.

'Isn't that espionage in general?' I said.

'Hardly,' said Leo. 'It's more likely to be referred to as the Great Game, harkening back to the Great War. Played by the rules of cricket and all that.'

I had no idea if Fitzroy even knew how to play cricket. He certainly didn't generally allow himself to be hampered by rules.

'I thought those days were past,' I said.

'You'd be surprised,' said Leo. 'Some of those old duffers from the Great War clog the whole thing up with their Queensbury rules.'

'I think that's boxing,' I said and added as politely as I could, 'I hate to bring this up, but what will I actually be doing?'

'You mean in a day-to-day sort of way?'

I nodded. 'You made it sound as if the interviews were something for the future.'

'Exactly. At the moment people like me are out and about searching for suitable candidates and in the usual way of things when we find someone we write a report. Which you type, and then as I said, it gets discussed. I've got a couple here to get you started.' He passed across a sheaf of papers.

'Was this what you were doing when you brought me in?'

'You mean, was I hunting? Yes. But I seem to have found a lot more than I bargained for.' He waited for a response, which I didn't give. 'Anyway,' he finally said, 'I shouldn't imagine that sort of thing will happen again. Just regular candidates.'

I nodded, waiting for further instructions. Although I wanted to ask him about how he chose people. Nightclubs, flirting and surprising women in taxis didn't seem to be a great way to find new agents.

'I haven't quite decided where to put you. Obviously we can't have anyone reading over your shoulder, but most of the stuff here is exceptionally hush-hush, so I suppose it doesn't matter terribly. I could put you outside and you could take my messages. Sort of a secretarial role for now. How does that sound?'

I reminded myself that this was the Army and not a civilian operation. I wasn't being asked if I wanted to do this. 'Whatever you need,' I said.

'Very diplomatic,' said Leo. 'I get the impression you'd rather strangle me with my socks than be at my beck and call?'

'Do you wear very long socks, sir?' I kept my face deadpan.

He grinned. 'No, but I dare say you could tie the two together and form a kind of garrotte with the knot going over my wind-pipe.' I must have looked slightly impressed, because he said, 'I'm not the man about town my family think me. I can put on a show when required. Anyway, they should have installed a desk and typewriter outside by now. You don't get your own phone, but you do get a key to this office, and in an emergency you can use mine.'

I stood up. 'I'll get started then.' He nodded and turned his attention to the mess on his desk.

Outside there was a desk with a typewriter waiting. It was an ordinary, scuffed sort of desk. The chair backed against the wall, and although I was more or less in the corridor no one would be able to get behind me. I opened the main drawer intending to put the papers inside, and I found it already set up with 'in' and 'out' trays. These were empty save for a set of keys. One locked the main drawer and the other I assumed was an office key. I took these out and put them in my pocket. The side drawers were filled with blank paper and a selection of manila folders. Tucked into a discreet pencil ledge were pencils and a pen. I put paper in the typewriter and took out the first page of notes to transcribe.

<u>Marie–Ann</u>

Born London: mother French, father English
Middle-class upbringing, grammar school, teaching college
Languages: French, conversational German
Position: Teacher: school mostly evacuated
Age 24
Physical attributes: attractive, good health, goes on bicycling
    holidays, nice teeth
Manner: friendly, engaging, confident
Compliance under torture: Unknown. Life so far has been
    unchallenging

*Marital status: engaged to junior officer in the Navy, since before
the war*
*Attitude to Germany: Complete hatred. Beloved grandfather came
back from the last war having been gassed and suffered long
illness before eventually dying. Affected whole family*
*Attitude to war: Keen to do her bit. Feels accompanying children
to country pointless. Feels under current circumstances that they
will be unwilling and unable to learn*
*Capability to kill: Under direct provocation or if hatred for
Germans stoked*
Ability to keep secrets: Unknown
Other notes: Suspect brave. Very protective of children
Family: Fiancé, mother, father, younger sister (school age)
Recommendation: Interview

I put the completed page back in the 'out' tray. I flicked
through the papers I'd taken. Another seven candidates were analysed. I took out the next one. I was enjoying this. It was not only
interesting, but it gave me an insight in how Leo viewed people,
or at least how he viewed them professionally. It also told me a lot
about the kind of people they were seeking. I was particularly
curious to see what got a candidate recommended. I had to wait
until the fifth person to find out.

<u>John A</u>

Born Hampshire
*Working class: family works as travelling hop-pickers during the
summer, otherwise takes on odd jobs in the city*
Languages: English, Cockney
Age 27
*Physical Attributes: Undernourishment as a child has led to
shorter stature, but sturdy frame and muscular*
Reason not enlisted: Heart ailment (verified)
Manner: Cocky, friendly, cheerful

Compliance under torture: Due to heart liable to die under interrogation (plus)

Marital status: widower, wife died in childbirth. His mother is raising the girl (3ish)

Attitude to Germany: Inclined not to blame the ordinary people, but rather the ones at the top. Reckons most of them not unlike us (negative)

Capability to kill: Has been in his fair share of fights. Would not need much more training (plus)

Ability to keep secrets: Suspected by police of stealing to order during blackouts. Lifted more than once. Has never implicated himself nor others (plus and negative)

Other notes: Curious nature. Focuses on the nature of the individual rather than consigning people to groups. Fair. Happy to steal from upper classes only (Robin Hood self portrayal?)

Family: Large: parents, brothers, sisters, in-laws and daughter (most adults of age already enlisted)

Other notes: Keen to help, but not, I think, willing to kill for his country if he can avoid it. Sees only senior personnel as true enemy of GB (negative)

Recommendation: Pass this time. May be of more use to home-based SIS

I had typed the last sentence on my seventh candidate when Leo came out of his office. 'Lunch?' he said.

'Are you telling me to go for luncheon, sir?'

He nodded. 'With me. Lock your desk.'

I looked up midway through doing this. He gave a slight shrug of apology. 'It's easy to forget,' he said.

'Where are we going? Is there a canteen?'

'Not yet. Still in the works. We're going somewhere busy.'

Chapter Thirteen

A Nice Pot of Tea

I thought I knew London well by now, but as Leo led me through a labyrinth of side streets, I began to appreciate I had barely scratched the surface. We emerged onto a large street, with the biggest Lyons teahouse I had ever seen.

'Not a bad shortcut, that,' said Leo. 'Think you can remember it? It's good not to be seen going in and out of the building that often. Probably means we'll have to bring our own lunch in for a while.' He frowned.

'I can cook,' I said. 'I'll happily bring sandwiches or pies for luncheon, if you occasionally bring me here. You don't even need to stay. I'm afraid I have a unique sense of direction.'

'Which means?'

'It's permanently off. I can read a compass and orientate myself that way, but it looks a bit odd when you do it on a city street.'

'God, that's another thing to figure in. But yes, happy to swap. Four days in and one day out suit you? Not sure about the pies though. Can't be certain what's in them nowadays.'

'I said I can cook. I can make a decent pie and be certain what's in it. I'm not as good as my flatmate was. She is, was, brilliant, but I'm competent.'

'Oh, well, let's try that then. Do you want any money or coupons upfront?'

I shook my head. 'Luncheon at Lyons will do.'

'Hmm, maybe we should make it three to two days? Unless you're independently wealthy?'

'Just trying to be fair,' I said. The truth was that investments set up for me by Fitzroy meant I was comfortably well off.

Leo opened the door for me. 'It's lunch, Hope. Luncheon is what the upper class eat. You even find some of our lot call it dinner. Try not to flinch openly if they do!'

We sat down at a table at the back of the loud and crowded room. There must have been near a hundred people in. By the look of them it was mostly local shopworkers and men in the lower end of the reserved occupations. Whoever they all were they talked a lot. We weren't going to be overheard in here.

A waitress came immediately and handed us the menus. 'Start off with a nice pot of tea?' she said and disappeared before we could reply.

'You don't have a title, do you?' said Leo suddenly.

'Would it matter if I did?'

'If you were in double digits in line for the throne, perhaps.'

'No, no title,' I said. I could have mentioned my uncle the earl or my grandmother married to a prince of the church, but I didn't see any reason why I should. It was his job to vet me, not mine to disclose personal details. Being discreet was a core tenet of my job. I had no idea if he was still trying to test me, but I couldn't resist a shot across his bows. I said, 'I think my skill set is more limited than other people in my department, but I am good at what I do, and my CO is fair in reports. If you can get to read them.'

The teapot arrived, a pale green one with matching cups and saucers.

'Are you listening, Hope? I said that the paperwork came through this morning to assign you permanently to SOE. Whoever he was he's not your CO any more.'

I jerked my attention back to Leo. 'That can't be right. He'd never give me up.' I could have kicked myself for blurting that out.

'I hate to break it to you, Hope. Everyone is replaceable now.'

I shook my head. Was this another plan within a plan of

Fitzroy's. He must be making it look as if he was giving me up. How did he want me to react? Without any briefing from my godfather the only thing I could do was convert some of my shock. The waitress came over and I ordered without thinking. When the waitress had gone I said to Leo, 'Yes, I am aware of that. But I don't believe he'd transfer me without telling me himself.'

'So you were having an affair,' said Leo. Before I could stab him in the hand with my fork, which was my immediate reaction, my egg and chipped potatoes arrived with a side plate of bread and butter. Carefully, with my knife and fork I transferred some of the chipped potatoes between two slices of bread, and then I began to neatly cut it up. 'No, we weren't,' I said calmly. 'It's more a family thing. I don't think I should explain further – unless you already know who he is?'

Leo shook his head. 'Gubbins didn't share a name.'

'My father loved these,' I said, trying to divert him. 'He said he'd known a gamekeeper whose wife made them these for luncheon. I mean lunch. He said the man called them chip butties. We decided we liked them a lot, so it was a naughty late-night snack when Mother was away.'

'I've seen them before,' said Leo, 'just never being eaten with a knife and fork.' He started in on his gammon steak with a pineapple ring and chipped potatoes. 'So what did you think of what you were reading, in general terms.'

'It's interesting,' I said. 'Do you pick people and then research them, or does someone else hand you names?'

'A bit of both. Although sometimes I change my mind about someone I've chosen once I look into them a bit further.'

'I think I'm beginning to get the idea of the kind of person you're looking for, only it's not fully fleshed out yet, is it?'

'As I think I said before, a work in progress.'

I poured us both more tea. Neither of us had remembered to take the leaves out, and it had gone from a light brown to a septic-tank sort of colour. I took a cautious sip and felt the fur sprout on my teeth.

'It must be trying to think of the necessary skills that's worse. I mean, you realised your people would need to have a sense of direction when I made my confession.'

'To be fair, Hope, most people do have a working sense of direction.'

'How do you know that?' I asked. 'You probably know a lot of military people. People who need a sense of direction. When you're talking about the average member of the public, how do you know what's normal? Has anyone checked?'

'Touché,' said Leo. 'What skills do you think I'm primarily looking for?'

'I can tell you what I think you need. People who can live with having killed someone or caused someone to be killed. Acts of sabotage beget acts of revenge, and the Germans seem to prefer taking that revenge out on the most innocent if they can't catch the actual perpetrators. It was something I felt they never covered properly in the auxies. I think if you want your people to keep working long term in the field, you need to be honest with them, and let them know what's liable to happen.'

'Like reprisals?'

'Like if they're caught they'll be shot or hanged. They may also be tortured. The enemy will class them as spies, so they won't be taken to prisoner-of-war camps.'

He nodded. 'That's something we've been trying to get around. Men can be given officer ranks, so they have a chance of talking their way out, but at the moment we think the best we can do for the women is make them part of the fannies.'

'The Princess Royal's Volunteer Corps?'

'Not a lot, is it? I think the major and others are hoping the Germans will treat women well. I mean, it's not usual to see a woman bear arms or fight behind enemy lines.'

'No,' I said, 'but they have and they do. Extraordinary women for the most part, but they've been around for a while. I don't know much about the current German High Command. My briefing on them is limited. As you know, my last mission was distinctly home affairs. But I think it would be a mistake to think any military, with perhaps the exception of the British Army, would treat women differently in war.'

'That's a rather dark outlook, but I fear you're right. What else do we need from these people?'

'They have to walk that fine line between not having a death wish, but being willing to die for their country – or in this case, to win the war. I believe it's not going as swimmingly as the newspapers might have us believe, so they will also need to be optimistic – or perhaps misguided enough to think God is on our side.'

'Isn't He?'

'If He exists I don't imagine He would condone war.'

Leo scrunched up his eyes as if considering something. 'We need to get you a better briefing on what's going on in Europe,' he said.

'You also need people who don't panic easily, and who can act on their own initiative, but still respect authority, and orders that you have no ability to make them carry out. If these are all non-military people you need them to continue to obey a ranking structure of some kind even under the most brutal and trying of circumstances. That's a big ask even for a services officer. If you know your friend and comrade is being tortured – possibly raped if she's a woman – nearby, but you know that any attempt to rescue them will blow your operation, can you go on? How do you prepare someone for that?'

'I don't know if you can,' said Leo. 'You have a dark mind, do you know that?'

'I'm attempting to be pragmatic. The normal preparation for such an event is time-enforcing duty, the concept that the mission takes priority in all circumstances – and to be honest, I think you only learn that by watching people die in the field. There's a sense of this must be done to honour all those we've lost. A duty to the good of the whole, rather than selfish affection for one. It's horrible stuff. But then nothing about war is good.'

'You speak like someone who is much older, much more seasoned,' said Leo.

'It's the company I've kept,' I said.

'Upper class?'

I smiled. 'In my experience debs are rarely as lovely as they appear.'

'I wouldn't know.'

'But you're Sammi's uncle. I would have thought—'

Leo shook his head. 'I'm solidly middle class. My elder brother married up. It's my sister-in-law who comes from the upper class.'

I bent my head to hide my smile.

'I see your eagle eyes have noticed that she doesn't like me much. I'm a black sheep. The youngest of seven and totally spoilt.'

'You were the baby of the family?'

'At this point I feel I need to remind you of our difference in rank,' said Leo, but he smiled as he said it. 'I can't be your friend. We'll be comrades in arms at best.'

'I did have one good friend,' I said reflectively, 'but she got married. Her husband is in naval intelligence. Fairly high up, I think.'

'Is she good at keeping things to herself?'

'Not in the slightest,' I said, chuckling. 'Mouth as wide as the Channel. I miss her.'

'It's good for this job not to have friends. I'd also advise not getting close to the people we recruit.'

'You mean because you think their life expectancy will be short.'

Leo sighed and wiped a hand across his forehead. For a moment I glimpsed the tiredness and worry that lay concealed behind his confident demeanour. 'I hope we'll be able to give them decent skills. It depends on how fast we go into operation. I suspect it will be faster than any of us want. But no, I don't intend to send people off to die. The risks will be high, but we—'

'I get it. You want to give people the best chance, but you're working against the odds.'

'If this is to work we need people in the field yesterday. We can't let emotion get in the way.'

'I see that.'

'It's more than that. Should they succeed, these people will be changed beyond recognition. Unless you've been through what they will go through, you won't be able to relate to them.'

'Believe me, I know all about being different.' I wanted to say more about my upbringing, and how I'd been raised in what I now knew was, if not exactly isolation, at least in a very limited circle of people.

'Because you're a spy?'

'In a way, but I'm also an only child.'

'I can't imagine that,' said Leo.

I gave him a big grin. 'If I'm telling the truth, of course. Now, what is it you've been testing me for?'

Leo stood up. 'You still have to do the typing, but you're definitely on the selection committee.'

I swallowed my last sip of tea. 'Your treat?' I said.

He nodded. 'You get to make sandwiches tomorrow.'

When we emerged, the sun was bright in the sky, and the idea of war felt far away. Leo touched my arm. 'You're not going to thank me for this,' he said. 'People will be hostile because of your age.'

I shrugged. 'I can survive disapproval.' I didn't add that I'd been educated in Fitzroy's school of disdain.

Leo held on to my arm. 'That's not all. It's a huge responsibility, and you will have to live with the results.'

'You mean I will be party to sending people off on life-threatening missions?'

He nodded.

'But they will have volunteered. I assume you will tell them the odds.'

'At the interview,' said Leo.

'That's a mistake,' I said. 'Tell them at the end of training. They will be more invested, and will have learned that they have attained skills they previously hadn't thought possible. There will also be an element of peer morale that will make them want to stay in it together.'

Leo stopped mid-shortcut. We were in a small alley. I became curious as to what he might do next. I surreptitiously stretched my shoulders to check for the degree of movement this suit gave me should he attack. It didn't seem likely that he would, but he was giving me the oddest look. My body-language-reading skills are good, but other than a certain sense he was closing down on me, I couldn't understand what he was thinking.

Finally he said, 'You're clearly an intelligent woman. Very intelligent, and you've been trained by someone extremely competent, it seems. But you're very cold-hearted for your age. I haven't seen this kind of chilly detachment in anyone below the rank of major. And you're in mourning. Remarkable. Remarkable.' He repeated the word, his head tilted slightly to one side, and his eyes narrowed. I realised he had become, if not exactly frightened, wary of me.

I shrugged and walked on ahead, so he wouldn't see he had upset me. Had Fitzroy really abandoned me to people who would never see life as he and I did? In the middle of London I had never felt so alone.

Chapter Fourteen

Selection

I left several messages for Bernie with her housekeeper. She didn't call back. I held out hope she would come back to collect the last of her things from the flat. She'd left her favourite fox fur (which I found creepy as its eyes always seemed to follow me) and a string of real pearls, which lay discarded on her dressing table along with a pair of pearl and sapphire earrings. Some of the night clothes draped across the wardrobe door looked like they might be silk. Who knew what else was in there?

If it had been me I would have returned for things half as good as these. It's not easy shopping for quality items in the Fens, and I had learned to value my possessions. But then her new husband was meant to be important in the Navy, maybe he was rich too. Her wedding might have been a bit of a blinder for relations with the United States (she was the daughter of the previous American ambassador), but Bernie had all but disappeared. Both my mother and Fitzroy had advised against the marriage, encouraging me to prevent it. I had failed to do so. Then shortly before I went into the auxies Bernie suffered an injury that I felt certain her husband had caused. However, he moved her into the family home to convalesce and I hadn't been able to gain access. Harvey, my other erstwhile asset and supposedly ex-con man, had tried too and also failed.

I didn't know where Harvey had been sent after the auxies folded. He might have been sent back to prison. He'd been on his own for only a couple of weeks after our previous brush with

British-based Nazis and turned back to the black market. As I told Fitzroy, he had siblings and an invalid father to support. However, I had got the impression that my godfather had got a bit fed up with towing him out of trouble. He'd expunged his criminal record once, and I doubted he would do it again. In normal circumstances I'd have called Fitzroy and simply asked where Harvey was and could I have him back as my asset. But in the middle of a war it seemed a bit petty to phone my commanding officer, even if he was my godfather, and ask if he would let my friends come out and play with me.

I wanted to call because he and my mother were together. I'd expected to hear from her once I came to town, but there had been no contact. Now, I'd been told Fitzroy had handed me over lock, stock and barrel to the SOE. I didn't want to believe this, and last time he'd had me reassigned (to the auxies) it had all been a bluff to get me to root out a traitor. Of course, he hadn't told me this until afterwards. So he might not have abandoned me after all – despite our row. Not knowing was almost as painful as thinking he had written me off.

Night after night I hovered around the telephone at my flat thinking of calling the contact number. It was a secure line, I told myself. It couldn't go wrong. And yet I remained convinced that Fitzroy had not passed me on, but had a plan that meant we could not be in contact. This would mean, if it was about internal security issues, I couldn't even trust the department operator not to tell someone I had called him.

I hoped, I really hoped, that he wouldn't be so cruel as to leave me without instructions for much longer. When I was alone I still struggled with grief. I could bottle it up during the day, but when I was alone the sadness and feelings of abandonment grew larger as the shadows grew longer. I tried to tell myself I was being selfish, and that I should keep my chin up. However, I found I did not care to be alone. I began to appreciate how much Bernie's antics at university had stopped me being homesick. That and my godfather turning up unexpectedly and frequently to take me out to luncheon or tea, and to talk to me about the lectures I'd attended. He'd never been that interested in my mathematics degree, but he frequently urged me to go and sit in the lectures of other professors at any of the colleges, who he felt were thinkers of their day.

In the middle of the night, I thought how halcyon it had all been, and how very lucky I had been without even knowing it.

Leo was due to take me to lunch at a Lyons tomorrow, having expressed himself more than happy with the picnic-style luncheons I had been providing for us both. He'd been impressed at the pies I'd made, not realising that I often cooked long into the night due to my insomnia.

And then there was that other thing. I had a man in my flat. Except I didn't. It was like a waking nightmare. I struggled to find the words to explain even to myself what was happening – battle fatigue was all I could come up with and that wasn't right. I had never been in a battle.

Every now and then, when I thought he was banished from my mind, my phantom attacker would reveal himself. I would find myself on the floor or lying awkwardly across furniture from where I had flung myself or rolled to avoid the attack that would inevitably prove to be all in my mind. Once he appeared in the bathroom mirror and I knocked myself out on the side of the bath. I don't know how long I was unconscious, but I had to change the way I wore my hair for a week to hide the bruise on my temple. All this had been going on for three weeks.

I wasn't dealing with my life very well and I needed help, but I had no idea who to turn to. I quite liked Leo, but for all I knew he was the man Fitzroy wanted me to investigate. If so, the last thing I could show him was weakness – and that went for everyone else as well.

If it hadn't been for the intervention of Cole during the first very real attack, an old ally of my mother and of Fitzroy, then I might well have died. The man had tried to drown me in my bath, but I had been ready for that, and I'd fought my way out.

However, I suffered a head injury and got generally battered. I'm not sure I would have bested him in the end, but Cole made short work of the man. It only occurred to me then that among all the other things that had been happening I had never reported this incident to Fitzroy. Was my brain trying to tell me there was something important about the event that he needed to know? Or had I suffered a permanent brain injury? But with everything else going on I hadn't wanted to worry my mother, and then I was injured during the incident at the auxies. Really, I needed to be more careful. I must be underestimating my enemies. But until recently it hadn't occurred to me that I might have some. I'd thought, naively, only excellent spies like my godfather got enemies – as if they were some kind of merit badge.

With my mind circling in on itself I made a note to tell Fitzroy about the attack. I didn't think about writing it up here, because it wasn't that secure. Especially when I was in the office all day. What I needed to do was tell Fitzroy when I next saw him. Even if the worst had happened and he had relinquished his role as my CO I was bound to see him sooner or later, wasn't I? I went to bed and slept heavily. I awoke with a start as Fitzroy's face loomed over mine and said, 'You need to take more care in selecting your friends.'

'What?' I said, sitting up so smartly I would have head butted him. Fortunately, it was the tail end of a dream, and it fell to pieces like a dissolving cobweb, any importance it might have had driven out of my consciousness by the blast of sunlight as I opened the curtains.

I still wore my civilian outfit to work. Today, I had put on my striped cherry red and black blazer with the black pencil skirt. As I considered myself still in mourning I had tried to avoid bright colours, but today was the first day of the interviews, and I wanted to look smart, but friendly. A little bit of colour among all the dull khaki of army uniforms would be a good thing. It might subconsciously make the candidates warm to me. I hadn't been given permission to ask questions, but if they happened to talk to me before the interview started that would hardly be my fault. A smile from a reasonably pretty, and cheery young woman might make some of them open up. That, I felt, would be proving my use to the unit. Although I was taking notes today, I had been doing an awful lot of typing. Occasionally other members of staff had asked me if I had time to type things up for them. Clearly, it had quickly gone round that there was a girl with a very high security clearance and quick fingers sitting outside Leo's office. This was not how I wanted the Department to see me. But today I intended to change all that.

I tripped up the steps to the building, smiled at Cerberus, and walked as quickly as I could within the narrow confines of my skirt up the stairs. As I passed by the second level one of the boys who worked with post wolf-whistled me. I didn't acknowledge him as although I knew he was being inappropriate, I couldn't remember the last time a male had indicated they found me attractive. If I was ruthlessly honest with myself, despite the chauvinism of the action, it rather pepped me up.

I thus had a big grin on my face when I tapped on Leo's door, notepad in hand and ready to be escorted to the first interview. Leo's response should have alerted me that all wasn't well.

'Yes!' he barked.

I opened the door and said brightly, 'Good morning. Exciting day, isn't it?'

The Leo seated behind his desk was a more dishevelled version than I had seen before. 'Aren't you ready?' I persisted in my ignorance. 'Is something wrong?'

Leo hunted among the debris on his desk and pulled out a battered cigarette pack. He knocked one into his hand, and dropping the packet back into the mess, he took a trench lighter from his pocket and lit up. He took a couple of what I can only describe as savage puffs. He scowled up at me. He was unshaven and his hair tousled enough that he looked like an extremely grumpy barn owl. Common sense told me not to mention this.

'You're obviously amused by something. Care to let me in on the secret?'

I retreated half a step, signalling I knew he was angry. 'I'm excited to meet the new candidates,' I said. 'And I have a Lyons lunch to look forward to.'

'Oh, that. I'll give you something for the food you've made.' He pulled out some coins from his pocket, checked them over and pushed them across to me, creating a little valley between the paperwork on either side. A small notebook toppled over the edge of his desk. He ignored it.

'I don't want any money,' I said. 'If you're too busy today, we can go any other time.'

'Besides being a junior rank, you're really not my type.'

'With respect, sir, you're about as far from being my type as it is possible to be while still remaining human,' I fired back.

He blinked as if I had splashed water his face. 'Oh, I'm sorry, Hope. It's my damnable temper. When I'm in the weeds I tend to take it out on everyone else.'

'In the weeds?' I queried.

He gestured at me to sit. 'We won't be conducting any interviews today. To be honest I can't think of a thing I could usefully get you to do. It's all a bit rough at the moment.'

'Did they decide I was too inexperienced?' I said, trying not to show my disappointment.

'Only if they decided the same thing of me.' He stubbed out his cigarette, which was less than half done, and began to play with the trench lighter.

'I don't understand.' Sometimes when people aren't making sense I find the easiest and quickest way out of the situation is to tell them so. It's not always diplomatic, but it generally brings about a speedier resolution.

Leo raked one hand through his hair. 'The higher-ups have decided to start recruiting from among their own. It's all being conducted in a local gentlemen's club today. It's practically as old school as the current SIS. Not what I signed up to do at all. And certainly not what I put my candidates up for. Seems like the whole thing has been one big joke. My brother was right, I have been wasting my time. I am, and you are, surplus to requirements.'

I sat down in the seat opposite the desk. It was on the low side, and in my limited range of movement in my pencil skirt, it was not an easy feat. Especially if when I asked my next question he threw me out on my ear. Not that I thought he could, but he might try. Which would be embarrassing for him.

'Have you been drinking?' I asked in as non-confrontational a manner as I could. Being drunk on duty would get you into all kinds of trouble. I wasn't entirely sure what would happen to someone, but even Fitzroy took care never to drink when he was on a mission. 'Because I don't think you're meant to do that on duty,' I finished.

Leo looked at me from red-rimmed eyes. 'I may be slightly hung-over. Last night I went out and got spectacularly drunk, but I did not commence until I was off duty.'

'So what were you told last night?'

He slouched back in his chair. 'The first candidates are apparently the "right sort", no selection procedure required. Just a little chat over supper at the club.'

'Ah,' I said. 'Bit unoriginal. Pretty much how they used to recruit people back in the day. My godfather said he got tapped on the shoulder because his father had put him forward. Said they had no idea what to do with a younger son.'

'And did he jump at it?'

'I don't believe so. He agreed to go somewhere for them over the summer. He was meant to be observing only, but he said he found himself in the middle of a revolution. When he came back he walked out of college and took the job. He said what he had seen made him think that there was little point in studying languages at Oxford. There were other things that needed doing.'

'He's an idealist?'

'Very much so, but he'd deny it strenuously if you asked him.'

'Doesn't sound too bad. But then he's a younger son.'

111

'Did anyone tell you we weren't needed any more?'

'Not exactly,' said Leo, not meeting my eye.

'Is it possible you've jumped the gun, sir?'

He sank lower in his chair. 'Maybe,' he said.

'Possible that, with respect, sir, you have a bit of a thing about the upper classes?'

He shrugged. 'God, I could do with a strong cup of tea and a Chelsea bun.'

'I think you should go and get washed up somewhere and we should go out to lunch as planned.' I put up a hand to forestall any complaints. 'It's the quickest way to get you tea, sugar and starch, which is what you doubtless need. It will also give you time to sober up properly. You get sorted. I'll sit at my desk and repel boarders.' I hauled myself to my feet and left before he could offer more objections.

Half an hour later, Leo presented himself at my desk. He'd borrowed a razor and changed into a clean uniform. His eyes remained bloodshot, and my fingers itched to rearrange his hair. He looked like a hedgehog that had had an unfortunate encounter with an electrical circuit. He was hamming it up, pretending he was on parade. I gave him a friendly smile and got up. We walked together to the front door. Leo winced when we passed another typist. I realised he was reaching the stage where he had the most awful headache. I quickened my pace and exited the building. I marched swiftly off, only for Leo to catch me by the shoulders and turn me round.

Chapter Fifteen

The Mystery Man

'You really do have no sense of direction,' said Leo, facing me in the right direction.

'No, I don't. People think I'm joking, but that homing pigeon part of the brain most of humanity has was missed out in me. I doubtless have something more useful.'

But Leo wasn't up to further conversation. He hunched his shoulders, kept his head down and walked off. I followed. At Lyons I ordered my well-earned lunch, egg and chipped potatoes, bread and butter, and a slice of treacle tart. I thought how much my father would have loved it. I wasn't listening to Leo, but I did spot the surprise on the waitress's face. Leo put his elbows on the table and groaned. I poured him a cup of tea as soon as it arrived and put in the two lumps of sugar we'd been allotted. Leo took the cup and added in the other. I felt my eyes narrowing in annoyance.

'Like you said, I need it,' he said.

When the food came I saw the reason for the waitress's reaction. Leo had ordered himself five Chelsea buns. I had no idea how he had got around the waitress. He ate them fast, and with more efficiency than manners. Then he poured himself another cup of tea, leaned back in his chair and burped loudly. I focused on my plate, dreading to think if anyone else had heard.

'Do I owe you any ration coupons?' he asked. 'You can't have made everything just from your own.'

'I had some things I'd brought from home,' I said, 'but yes, I expect if I'm carrying on making sandwiches and pies I will need some.'

'If?'

'You seemed to think the Department would be reassigning us. Besides, I think we rather bumped up against the rank barrier today.'

'You have been very bossy,' said Leo, scratching his head with his large, bear-like paws.

I lowered my voice, 'You said we were surplus to requirements.'

'I meant on the selection process. There's still training to be sorted out. I had an early indication from the major that was one of the things I'd be doing.'

'So why are you so upset?' I asked.

'I spent ages rooting out people. Making a nuisance of myself. Devising ways to get to know them without letting on what I wanted. I mean, eventually I told them we wanted to interview them to do something with the war effort, but it took a lot of effort to get to that point.'

'You were diligent.'

'Yes, I bloody was. I thought on my feet. I checked out all of the people I put forward thoroughly and discreetly. It wasn't an easy job. Especially when your family think you're shirking your duty to your country.'

'What do they think you do?'

'Paper shuffling for the most part. I'm a bit of a joke. I've been with the Department from not long after I left school.'

'You mean college? University?'

'Not all of us are as privileged as you. My elder brother might have hooked himself an upper-class heiress, but the rest of us have to work for our living.'

He was beginning to sound belligerent, and I wondered how much of the alcohol those buns had really soaked up.

'We'd better go,' I said and stood up.

He did remember to pay the bill, but I seemed to have accidentally set him off on a diatribe about the out-datedness of the class system. I needed to get him into the alleyways before people took note of a serviceman who was coming damn close to suggesting we should be a republic! I wondered if he had hit his head when drunk? The Army swore allegiance to the crown, and speaking ill of the king during a war was tantamount to being a traitor.

At last we turned off the main street. Leo was gesticulating with increasing bravado. Rather than get into an argument I stopped listening, only acknowledging the odd word or phrase with a nod. The passageway narrowed. Technically it was a one-lane road, but I had never seen a car along here. Then I spotted a man ahead, and my gaze flicked to Leo. Was he looking where he was going enough to avoid collision? Should I say something? In this state would he even pay any attention. *He's not a toddler*, I told myself. *He's a grown man and he should be able to talk and walk down a street.*

As the man came closer I felt the hairs on the back of my neck stand up. He wasn't in uniform, and he looked like a perfectly ordinary young man. Of course, I had never seen the face of the man who broke into my flat, but I had no reason to think . . .

The man was now within a couple of yards of us. Leo was still spouting nonsense and waving his arms around to reinforce his points. I was going to have to say something. Then suddenly the stranger launched himself at Leo, striking him in the gut with his right fist. Involuntarily, I moved backwards. Leo doubled over under the force of the punch. The other man brought his right knee up to crash into Leo's jaw. Leo's arms flailed out of control as he flew backwards. His feet skittered as if he was dancing wildly as he fought to regain his balance. He failed and landed on his backside with a thud.

I didn't move. I couldn't move. I felt like one of those insects trapped in amber or a fly in the cocoon of a spider. Something was wrong with me. I neither moved to engage or turned to run for help. I stood stock still. I tried to shout, but my voice was as useless as my legs. The stranger advanced on Leo. It seemed like time was slowing. He reached out and grabbed Leo by the front of his collar, jerking his head upright and yelling into his face.

'Raised in the gutter, were you? Did no one tell you it's not nice to go after another's man girl? Or is that your thing? This one,' he gestured at me. 'Does she belong to some other poor sod?'

This was getting too ripe. I didn't belong to any man. A loud honk made all three of us start. I turned my head and saw a car almost on top of me. I had staggered back into the road and today of all days someone was trying to use the alleyway as a shortcut. The driver was an older man with a large grey moustache. He leaned out of his window and waved a silver-topped cane at me. He was yelling. I couldn't understand him, but it must be about my being in the way.

Spittle flew from his lips. He scowled furiously at me. His face grew redder and redder. He waved his cane at me as if he would strike.

His cane.

I grabbed it from his hands and in one smooth motion turned back to the fight. The stranger was still shouting at Leo. 'Stay away from Marie.' He raised his right hand again, clearly intent on landing Leo a facer.

The blow never landed. I swung the cane in a tight arc and the silver finial connected with the back of the man's skull. Fortunately I had hit him on the thickest part of his cranium. *He'll probably live*, I thought. The man remained standing, stilled for what seemed like a long moment, then he toppled forward, crashing to the pavement just to the left of Leo.

'Cracking shot, Hope,' said Leo in a slightly hollow voice. 'What the hell was that all about?'

'Hooligans!' shouted the man in the car. 'Give me back my cane this minute, young woman.'

I turned to pass the article back to the driver. 'He was attacking my colleague,' I said. 'I had to do something.'

'Colleague! Huh! Paramour more like. War always brings out

116

women like you.' He looked over at Leo. 'Now, both of you. Get in the back of the car, I'm taking you to the police station.'

Leo stumbled across towards me. He still held one arm protectively against his stomach. As he came beside me, he slipped his hand through mine. He brought his head close to my ear, and whispered, 'Run!'

Then tugging me behind him he took off. Leo, I immediately discovered, had very long legs and could cross a lot of distance very quickly. As well as being much shorter than him, I was wearing the damned skirt. I tottered so quickly I could feel friction between my stockings and the fabric of my skirt. My flesh burned with the heat.

'I can't do this!' I yelled at Leo. He didn't slow and he didn't let go of my hand. I felt myself teetering. I flailed my one free arm, but to no avail. I landed heavily on my knees. Leo stopped almost immediately and released my hand. I dropped to all fours, my eyes stinging with the shock of the impact. Leo looked down at me in astonishment.

Glancing over my shoulder I could see no sign of the car and its driver. 'He's gone,' I said.

'To the nearest police station,' said Leo. 'Get up!'

I sat up on one knee and did the only thing I could – I ripped my skirt to my thighs. Leo stood and stared at me, his mouth slightly agape. I was unsure if he was gazing at my knees, now trickling with blood, or the edge of my underwear I had now revealed. Fortunately it was one of my better pairs of knickers.

'Go on then!' I said snappily, as if this was all his fault. He ran off without taking my hand. I took off my shoes and went after him. Unencumbered by the trappings of female fashion, I kept pace with him easily enough. Running is far from being my favourite exercise, but the auxies had been frightfully keen on it.

Leo swerved from our normal route at the last minute and took me through a side door that I hadn't used before. It had an armed sentry and an old man in a box. Leo showed his ID card and I extricated mine from my handbag. The old man got us both to sign in and said, 'You'll need to write a report.'

'Who's on the incident desk?' asked Leo.

'Captain Green.'

Leo nodded and headed to the stairway. Under his breath, I heard him mutter, 'Grimers Green, that's all we need.'

Chapter Sixteen

Confessions

I thought he might detour via a first-aid room, but he went directly to his office, saying curtly, 'Come.'

I followed him in. 'Sit,' he said. He was bent over the open lower drawer of his desk, from which he produced a bottle of whisky. Then standing up to reach for a small first-aid box on the shelf behind him he came over and knelt in front of me.

'Sorry, no antiseptic,' he said, and poured whisky onto some cotton wool before he started cleaning my knee.

'I'm going to reek of whisky,' I protested. 'Wouldn't it be easier to go to the first-aid person or whatever we have here. And shouldn't you have told me about it? Ow! That stings.'

'Probably. We don't have time to go to the nurse. We need to talk things over before we have to make the incident report. Jolly good thing you got injured. Gives us a spot of leeway.'

I shook my head. 'What are you talking about?'

'Any run-in that leads to involvement with the civilian police has to be reported as soon as possible, so we can put a lid on it. There's no point in being a top-secret organisation if your people's doings are all across the press. So how did you know this man? Is he an ex-boyfriend?'

I pulled my leg away from him and took the cotton wool. 'Let me, you're making a mess. And no, I'd never seen that man before in my life.'

Leo sat back on his heels. 'Are you sure, Hope?'

'I have never seen his face before in my life.'

119

'He was yelling at me about his girlfriend. I thought he meant you. And you weren't exactly rushing to my rescue.' Leo frowned. 'I need you to tell me the truth. That's an order.'

I held out the cotton wool for some more whisky. Leo broke off another piece and gave it to me. He threw the used piece under the desk. I hoped there was a bin there. 'I have never seen that's man's face before. I don't have any ex-boyfriends. I do have some male friends, but he wasn't one of those either. I haven't the faintest clue who he is.'

'Are you expecting me to believe that a random man came up to me in the street and punched me in the stomach?'

'Maybe you reminded him of someone. It's not that bright with the high walls along there.'

'Lieutenant, what are you not telling me?'

I sighed. 'A while back someone attacked me in my flat. He came through the window. I was lucky, a friend came to my aide. But if he hadn't . . . I was in the bath and he held me under by my legs. I can only account for my freezing as some kind of after-effect. He got away. He could still be out there.' *I see him all the time. But he's never punched anyone before. He's only a shadow,* I added silently to myself.

Leo still looked at me suspiciously. 'You know if I find out something later you should have told me there will be all hell to pay.'

'I'm sure I'd feel right at home,' I said rudely, and handed him the last bit of cotton wool. 'Do you have a needle and thread. I'd rather not report to anyone showing my knickers.'

Leo flushed. 'No,' he said, standing up and looking away. 'I'll see if I can get a uniform brought over for you.'

He called wardrobe, and within a few minutes I had a reasonably sized uniform that even had the right rank. Leo left the office so I could change. Or at least I thought he did. Since I'd mentioned knickers, he had commenced addressing me only in grunts and mutters.

However, when he returned and I was suitably dressed, he reverted to normal. The flush had completely died away. Still, it told me it hadn't been my bloody knees he'd been looking at earlier.

Captain Green turned out to be a dour character, who expected the worst. When we entered his office, he glanced at Leo and said, 'Who have you killed now?'

'No one,' said Leo. 'We had a run-in with a civilian who attacked me on the way back from lunch. Sunflower, here, laid him out.'

Green raised one thin eyebrow. 'Did she indeed? You'd better sit down and tell me all about it.'

We did. Green made notes. 'Did you check his pulse?' he asked me.

I shook my head. 'I didn't have a chance to.'

'Ah, yes, the captain's sudden desire to flee the scene. Never looks good, a man in uniform running. Either the enemy is behind him or he's running away from something. Both very worrying to a member of the public.'

I was sitting close enough to Leo that I could hear him grinding his teeth.

'What would you have done?' I asked.

'Oh, I wouldn't have been taken by surprise,' said Green imperturbably. 'Never am. Always expect the worst.' He sat back gathering his notes together. 'So neither of you knew the attacker? I'll get right on to this. I'll be in touch.' He lowered his head to look at the papers on his desk. 'Goodbye.'

Leo looked at me and shook his head. He got up and we headed back to his office.

'I wish I hadn't wasted all that whisky on your knees,' he said, sitting back down behind the desk.

'You said you didn't drink on duty,' I said.

Leo fished two smeary-looking glasses out of his desk drawer and poured an inch of whisky into both. 'The whisky will kill the germs,' he said, and threw back the glass, swallowing his in one gulp.

I shrugged. 'I smell as if I've been drinking anyway,' I said, and drank mine in two swallows. It wasn't good whisky. It felt like someone had rubbed sandpaper all around the inside of my throat. Even Leo blinked a bit after swallowing it.

'Feeling more relaxed?' asked Leo as he poured himself a second measure. He hovered the bottle over my glass, but I shook my head. 'I think we have more to discuss. This man who nearly drowned you.'

'No, I got away from him.' I saw Leo's surprise. 'If someone ever does that to you, you have to do the opposite of what instinct tells you. Don't try and fight for air. Let yourself go under. Then you stand a chance of breaking his grip by twisting.'

Leo gave me a strange look. 'I'll remember that odd bit of advice. Now, I need to know what you weren't telling me earlier. I don't buy this incident in your flat causing you to freeze at the scene of more violence. You killed a man while you were in the auxies. No hesitation there.'

I'd been wondering if he would remember this. 'If you know about that, then you'll know he was attacking me at the time. Being attacked is very different from watching someone else be attacked.'

'It's a good line,' said Leo, 'and I might even buy it being true, but you've a tell when you're evading the truth.'

'I have not!'

'You have.'

'Then tell me what it is!'

Leo went round to the other side of the desk and sat back in his chair. 'No, I don't think I will.'

'But on a mission . . .'

He shook his head. 'If you need to know, I'll tell you. So, what is it that you're keeping from me?'

I lowered my head. 'I've seen my attacker again. More than once.'

'What?' said Leo. 'Is he blackmailing you?'

'He isn't real,' I said. 'Well, he was real, obviously. The damage he did to the flat was real. My friend evicting him – that was real. But the other times I've seen him he hasn't been. I mean, I thought he was at first. You should have seen me diving and rolling out the way.' I glanced up to give him a small smile, but his face was set and serious.

'But when he vanished on me for the third or fourth time it occurred to me – finally – that I was seeing shadows.'

'I see,' said Leo. 'And you were going to tell me when?'

'I thought the effect would fade. I didn't think I would be involved in hand-to-hand combat with anything other than a typewriter for the near future.'

'I presume you've noticed we're at war. As an ex-auxie with a commendation for hand-to-hand combat, I thought I could count on you for backup.'

'You mean, as if we were partners?' I asked.

'No, as if you were someone under my command,' said Leo.

'My mistake, sir. I didn't mean any disrespect. I didn't realise it would be part of my position.'

'You're in the Army not the typing pool,' said Leo.

I nodded. I couldn't think of anything to say that would make things better.

'Have you told anyone else?'

I shook my head.

'I think we had better keep it that way. Go home. I'll try and sort this mess out. I'll see you tomorrow.'

At home I tried to recall when I last saw my intruder. I searched for a diary and found one in Bernie's room, and tore out the used pages. I put these in one of her drawers, suppressing the surprisingly strong desire to read them. I went back through to the living area to put temptation out of my reach. Then I listed the times I had seen him. From now on I'd mark every incident with a little stick man. Who knew, perhaps I had seen the last of him?

I slept badly. Finally, I gave up and got up several hours before

I needed to. I paced around the flat. I understood Leo asking me not to tell anyone else about my hallucinations. It would reflect badly not only on me, but the new department of the SOE. But mostly, I guessed his fear was that as he'd recruited me, his commander might think his judgement too fallible and cast doubt on any other candidates he'd recruited.

I padded around my flat in my dressing gown making cup after cup of tea, letting them grow cold and then making another. It gave me something to do.

Dealing in secrets can be frustrating. So much of what you know must be kept in your head. You can't take the risk of writing anything down anywhere but in a secure building. This means all those good ideas you have during the evening, you must keep in your head till you're back at your desk. Worse yet, it means you can't use notes to work anything out. I wanted to sit down and draw myself a diagram of any connecting events recently, from Leo's attack, my attack, Bernie's attack (although I was fairly sure her attacker was her husband), the incident at the auxies, the people I'd met, and how some of them were attached to more than one recent episode. I felt if I could only see everything on paper then I might find a pattern to some of it.

But even if I waited until I went into the SOE this morning, I couldn't do what I wanted. I had suspicions and activities that I wanted to include that were very much part of Fitzroy's work. Whether or not I still worked for him was irrelevant. What I knew from one department I could not share with another.

My fifth cup of tea was going cold in my hands when I gave up my internal fight with the telephone. I had avoided phoning Fitzroy all the way through my last mission. However, my mother had also given me a code to reach her through the switchboard. It didn't take me long to reach the operator. I gave my name and code and my mother's. I asked for us to be connected. I'd barely finished speaking when the operator said, 'I'm sorry, agent. Agent Alice is unavailable. Is there anyone else you wish to contact?'

'Fitzroy,' I said. Thoughts were now racing through my mind of my mother ill or injured. That would explain why she hadn't been in contact, but why wouldn't he have told me?

The line whirred and clicked. Finally the operator came back. 'I'm sorry, agent, Fitzroy is not currently available, but you can leave a message. He will respond as soon as he is able.'

'Ask him to confirm the location and safety of Agent Alice,' I said, 'and to confirm my orders. Thank you.' I rang off.

I finished getting ready for work. In uniform, but this time I wore a skirt. It was a halfway step as I didn't know what would be needed of me today. Then I sat and waited for the telephone to ring.

It didn't.

I got into work in good time, but Leo was already sitting on my desk waiting for me. 'I owe you an apology,' he said. 'That attack was down to me. I'm just too damn attractive for my own good.'

'Girl problems, sir?' I said, taking my seat.

'Yes, but not mine. It turns out our attacker was the fiancé of Marie. He's a junior officer in the Navy, remember?'

I nodded. 'She was the first candidate I typed up.'

'I'd discounted her boyfriend as a possibility as he was meant to be at sea, but apparently he got last-minute leave, and on his way to see his girl, he saw me walking arm-in-arm with her towards the nearest decent watering hole, and jumped to entirely the wrong conclusion.'

'Oh,' I said, a wash of warm relief coursing through me. 'How unfortunate.' It was nothing to do with me or my attacker. It was a pity I'd mentioned anything about that to Leo, but I'd done what I thought was the right thing.

'Hope, are you listening to me?'

'Sorry, sir,' I said, forcibly pushing my cascading thoughts aside. 'I didn't hear what you said.'

'I was remarking on the man's injuries. Don't you want to know if you killed him or not?'

'Did I? I didn't mean to.'

'You don't look as if you would be very cut up about it,' said Leo frowning. 'But no, the man seems to have an abnormally thick skull. He's got concussion. He'll get a curt briefing from one of our mop-up people, but not many details, and be on his way back to sea in a few days.'

'Excellent,' I said. 'But it does sound like it would be a good idea for you to be less . . . er . . . charming with any other female candidates, with respect, sir.' I tagged on the last bit as I saw his frown deepen.

'I do seem not to have been on good form yesterday,' said Leo lightly. He stood up. 'As it happens there's an interview in ten minutes. They want you to take the notes. I'm escorting you to the room. Get what you need, and we'll set you up.'

Leo led me down the corridor he'd forbidden me to enter on my initial tour. I was disappointed to find that it was no different to any other parts of the building. Except as we went further along I saw the locks had been changed. After the halfway point there were a number of armed guards standing about with those steely-eyed expressions they think make them look mean, but really signals their intense boredom.

Leo stopped and rapped on one of the doors. A guard opened it and ushered me through to a room beyond the first. The room had been cleared. In it stood two comfortable armchairs, and against one wall a hard chair. I looked at it. 'That's mine?' I said to Leo. He nodded and left.

I made myself as comfortable as possible. Then I opened my notebook, got my pencil ready and waited. It wasn't long before an officer I hadn't seen before entered. He must have been in his mid-forties, slightly stocky and bald as an egg. 'You the steno?' he asked curtly.

'Yes, sir,' I said.

'Good God, a lieutenant!' he said, peering at me closer. 'How did you get to be an officer in typing, hmmm?'

I assumed this was a rhetorical question. He went over and

126

fussed with the chairs. Then he pulled at the curtains. 'Where's the damn table,' he said suddenly.

'Table, sir?'

'The one for our tea and bickies. Can't do this kind of interview without tea and bickies. Hop to it, girl, and get it sorted.'

Chapter Seventeen

Showing My Mettle

I found the nearest secretary and requested her help. Between us we found a small table, a kettle that had to go in the room with the armed guard, along with some tea and a tiny amount of sugar. The guard, whose name turned out to be Ernie, took it all as a big joke (even losing his steely-eyed look for a bit). He reckoned that the tea was the most valuable asset he guarded all week. However, biscuits were beyond us. The secretary bid me the best of luck in explaining this to the interviewing officer.

'I've managed to get tea set up next door,' I told him, 'but I'm afraid I can't find any biscuits.'

The man's jaw dropped. 'Good God,' he said, 'things must be getting bally serious if Jerry has stolen all the bickies. Never mind. Sit down and be quiet. Next to invisible.'

Shortly after this there was a tap at the door, and a young woman was shown in. She was neatly dressed in a two-piece suit. Her make-up and hairdo showed a woman who followed fashion, but in a quiet rather than a brash way. She was attractive in a girl-next-door sort of way. There was tension in every line of her body. She was putting on a brave face, but she was clearly miserable. I hoped the interviewer was the kind of man who noticed these things.

'Hello, me dear,' said the officer in an entirely different voice to the one he'd used to me. 'Come in and sit down. Nice of you to come in for a little chat. Get us both some tea, will you?'

I realised he was speaking to me. Of course, he was just the type to think I'd be able to take notes and make tea at the same time. Fortunately Ernie knew him better than I. As soon as I opened the inner door he passed me two fresh mugs of hot tea. He had his hard face on, but winked at me, which was somehow even scarier. I took the cups gratefully and presented them to the officer and the woman.

'I'm sure you've been told I can't tell you too much about anything until you agree to sign the Official Secrets Act.'

At this I was on the edge of my seat ready to be sent for a pen.

'But before we do anything hasty, let me ask you a question or two, if you don't mind? It is a very serious document.'

The woman nodded. Idiotic, I thought, as if she's going to say no after coming in here.

'I understand you're keen to do your bit?'

The woman nodded again.

'How do you feel about the Germans?'

'I hate them.'

'Jolly good,' said the officer. 'How do you feel you could best contribute to the war effort?'

The woman thought for a while. 'I could join one of the tea wagons at the railway station that gives tea to the troops. They always need more volunteers.'

'Anything else?'

'I did think about becoming an ARP warden. Everyone's talking about how London is going to be gassed and bombed. I also thought about trying to help out at the hospitals. But the thing is, I don't have any experience in either area. One doesn't want to make a fool of oneself, obviously, but worse than that one doesn't want to get in the way of someone else doing a decent job. I wouldn't want to mess anything up.' Her head lowered as she took a sip of her tea. It didn't come back up.

'Hmm, yes,' said the officer. 'I can see that. Want to do your bit, but not get in another fellow's way.' He referred to his notes. 'Says here you're a schoolteacher. Ever want to be anything else?'

The woman shook her head without lifting it to meet his gaze. 'I've always been fond of children.'

'No other hobbies?'

'Not really.'

My ears had pricked up at 'teacher'. I had no idea how many candidates they were interviewing, but I began to wonder.

'Anything else you'd like to say?'

'Not really,' said the young woman. 'I don't know what this is all about, but I'm happy to help the war effort in any way I can.'

The officer got up. 'And I'm sure you'd make a fine tea lady or ARP warden or volunteer nurse. I think I'd go for the latter. Pretty little thing like you would be bound to cheer them up on the wards.'

The woman got up, looking confused. 'I don't have to sign anything?'

'I don't think that will be necessary.' He was about to rule her out.

I coughed. They both looked round. 'Is your fiancé a junior officer in the Navy?' I asked.

Finally her face showed signs of animation. 'Yes, do you know him?'

'Not exactly, but I think I've met him. He was involved in an accident yesterday, wasn't he?'

'Lieutenant Stapleford!' barked the officer.

'Yes, he was,' said the girl. Her bottom lip trembled and she blinked back tears.

'Is he going to be all right?' I asked.

'They think he will make a full recovery.'

'Do you know what happened?' I asked carefully.

She shook her head. 'Someone in the street attacked him, but there were no witnesses.'

'What a despicable thing,' I said, 'to attack a member of our serving forces. I'm glad he is going to recover. I'm sure he wants to be back with his ship before it sails.'

She nodded. 'Do you think it could be anything to do with him being a Navy man?'

I sat down and she followed suit. The officer also sat, with a strange look on his face.

'I don't know,' I said, 'but we all have to be on the lookout for German agents, don't we? And, believe it or not, there are even British people who are so opposed to the war—'

'No!' said Marie, interrupting me. 'Don't they know what we're fighting for?'

'What do you think we're fighting for?' said the officer gently.

'Democracy, freedom and the abolition of fascism,' said Marie.

'What would you have done if you'd been there?' I asked.

The woman's voice lost some of its refinement. 'I'd have lamped the bastard!' She put her hand over her mouth and blushed.

'Would you have known how to?'

She shook her head. 'But they say in situations like that you can do a lot of things. Like mothers lifting cars off babies.'

I blinked. 'Sort of a surge of energy in a dire situation? Have you experienced that?'

'No, but my blood runs red hot when I think about what happened to Harold. Some German agent wants to get to one of my loved ones, then he goes through me first!' She gritted her teeth. 'I might only be a woman, but I'll fight to the last to protect my family and my home.'

'Good show!' I said, and looked at the officer. He gave me a slight smile.

'I think perhaps we might continue our conversation a little longer. Would you be willing to sign the Official Secrets Act?'

After that I was allowed to speak in any of the interviews if I thought I had something worth saying. The officer, a Captain Woodard, thought it was 'most amusing' that a girl like me could tease out the mettle of our possible candidates. Although, to be fair to the man, most men of his era would simply have banned me from the room. He might say he found it amusing, but he was enough of a decent soldier to use any useful resource, and that included me.

'Should have seen how she got under one chap's skin,' I over-heard him telling Leo. 'Thought I was going to have to step in before the chap punched her.'

Leo caught sight of me behind Woodard and said, 'Sunflower can be extremely irritating. I'm glad we've found a use for her skill.'

The days passed. We continued to interview people. Some were passed, some were not. None of them yet knew what exactly they were going to be asked to do or where or when they would be trained. However, although the pace of the interviews didn't change there was a sense of urgency in the air. In the first week people had occasionally passed by my desk. Now it was more like being seated on the edge of a busy road. There was a sense things were moving. I still typed up interviews, for Leo was churning them out thick and fast. He was often in late, and I wouldn't even see him before I went off for the first interview. On my return I would find a new stack of papers locked in my top drawer. Each sheet would be crammed with Leo's tiny spider-like writing.

The first time this happened, I knocked on the door and went in to check with him that I hadn't left the drawer open. He was sitting with his head in his hands.

'I'm sorry to bother you, sir,' I said. 'But I had to check I hadn't left the drawer open.'

Leo looked up at me through red-rimmed, blurry eyes. 'Do you not think I might have made a bit of a fuss if you had?'

'If you also had access to the drawer I thought you'd have told me you had a key, sir. I understand it's absolutely your right, sir, but there is a lot of – subversion abroad at the moment.'

Leo grunted and gave a nod. The nod made him wince.

'Are you a little the worse for wear?' I asked in tones of astonishment, and quickly added 'sir' again.

'It's all part of accessing people without arousing their suspicion,' said Leo. He blinked owlishly at me, as if proud of the long sentence he'd managed. Then he dropped his head back into his hands. 'Go away now, please.'

I closed the door quietly behind me and went to get my bag, having decided I'd go to buy some salts for Leo to help him recover. I wrote the time I'd be back on a piece on paper and left it tucked under the typewriter. I thought it unlikely Leo or anyone else would come to look for me, but it was better to let people know I would soon return. I signed myself out at Cerberus' desk.

My mission was easily accomplished and I was on my way back when it occurred to me how very confined I felt at the SOE. It was completely different to working for my godfather, where individual initiative was encouraged and prized. The SOE felt more like being a tiny cog in a big machine.

Back at the office I made up the salts and took them in to Leo. I also handed him a big packet of them. 'For the nights when work takes it out of you,' I said.

He drank the contents of the glass down quickly and pulled a face like a child taking cod liver oil. He gave me a small smile. 'Thank you, Hope,' he said, and for the first time I thought he actually meant it.

It turned out to be a bit of a seminal moment for Leo and me. Although he would remind me from time to time, in case I forgot, that he was my senior officer, we got on a lot better from then on. We managed two Friday luncheons at Lyons. I opted to remain respectful at all times. It was all very well for Leo to say he allowed a bit of banter with his men, but he could turn like lightning back into a scolding superior. He clearly had his own internal set of rules and I had yet to fathom them out.

Then one day when he remarked on how well I made the pies, I jokingly said that he should see how well I could do dinner sometime.

'How about Saturday?' he said.

'Of course, sir,' I replied automatically. He didn't refer to it again that week. I wasn't sure if he had been joking or not, so I got food supplies ready in case. I felt a bit of a fool doing so. I couldn't believe he would actually come, and I wasn't sure I wanted him to. I continued to find his moods too quixotic.

Despite being a reasonably good-looking man he held no attraction for me. Besides, I had no intention whatsoever of dating a senior officer.

Come Saturday evening the doorbell rang. He stood there, looking a bit awkward and holding a bunch of flowers 'I think the old man who owns my billet thinks I have a girlfriend.'

I laughed. It felt a little strange to be in his company off duty, but the flowers delighted me. 'It is so nice to have these,' I said, taking them and his coat. 'I've grown to like London, but I do miss the countryside at home. I'd have house plants, but I'm so bad at watering them they generally die.' I led him to a seat in the living area and offered him a drink.

'I've laid my hands on a bottle of wine to go with dinner,' I explained, 'but pre-dinner the best I can do is gin and lemon or whisky.'

'I'll have a whisky,' said Leo, 'with a dash of soda if you've got it.'

I froze momentarily on the way to the kitchen, but moved on quickly. I checked on the food, put the flowers in water, and poured the whisky. I went back to Leo and took the seat opposite. 'Believe me,' I said, handing him a glass of twelve-year-old Bowmore, 'you do not add soda to this.' I don't generally drink spirits so I'd only poured myself a half measure. I closed my eyes and took a sip. The warming, smooth, smoky liquid with just a touch of an earthy peaty note, slid down my throat. It immediately brought back memories of my godfather and him introducing me to whisky. I opened my eyes to see Leo's startled face. 'It's good, isn't it?'

'It's bloody marvellous. Please tell me you're not dealing with the black market?'

I shook my head. 'I've had this bottle a while. My godfather gave it to me. I don't often drink whisky.' I gave a laugh. 'Although when my flatmate was here she'd drink anything. I used to hide it in the cupboard where we kept the cleaning stuff. I knew she'd never look there.'

Leo was looking round curiously. 'This is a nice place. It can't be a billet.'

'No, I have a lease. I took it over shortly before the war. Bernie and I shared, but now it's just me.'

'Isn't that expensive?'

I shook my head. 'I've had many woes in my life, but money isn't generally one of them. I don't mean I'm terribly rich or anything,' I added hurriedly.

'Money, beauty and brains, and yet single. What's wrong with you?'

'A lot,' I said drily. 'I'd better check on the food.'

I got up and went through to the kitchen. It only occurred to me when my head was in the oven that Leo had called me beautiful.

Chapter Eighteen

Fitzroy

'Grub's up,' I said, putting the dishes out on the table. 'Sorry it's not anything more exciting.'

Leo smiled, his cheeks slightly flushed. 'It's a very long time since I had a home-cooked meal.'

'Don't you get food at your billet?'

'I'm not entirely sure that it's accurate to describe it as "food". Sustaining substance maybe?'

'Not vital victuals?' I said.

He laughed. We were both seated now. It felt very different dining alone with Leo to eating lunch together among a hundred or so others. I realised I'd forgotten the wine and shot up. Leo looked a bit startled, but when I returned from the kitchen with a bottle and glasses in hand, he didn't look disappointed.

'Another legacy from your godfather?'

I checked the label. 'Yes, this is one he gave me, so it should be good.' I poured us both a glass. I had let the wine breathe, but Fitzroy would have been annoyed, to put it mildly, that I hadn't decanted it.

Leo took a sip. 'Goodness,' he said, 'I don't think I knew wine could taste that good.'

I shrugged. 'My godfather is a bit of an oenophile.'

'What else did he teach you? How to buy a good racehorse?'

'Oh, the usual godfather to god-daughter kind of thing. How to build an outdoor fire. How to cook. Although I have to admit, he cooks far better than me. But I think I'm competent.'

'It could be the wine,' said Leo, 'but I am enjoying this very much.'

I got up and topped up his glass. 'It's good to do things like this once in a while, don't you think?' I said. 'Holding on to some sense of normality.'

He nodded, his face suddenly serious. 'It's one of the things I'm most worried about for our operatives. They will be in a foreign country that's under occupation, doing things they will never have dreamed they can do. Even if we have picked the best of the best, how do you stop that scenario from being overwhelming?'

'If you look at the way the people in London have adapted to the new norms, the air-raid drills, the shortages of food, the shelters springing up on street corners, and learning first aid, et cetera, not to mention most of their menfolk being called up, they do adjust remarkably quickly. When there are no other options human beings are good at making do.'

Leo shook his head and drank some more wine. We were going through the bottle fairly fast, but it was good. I'd been saving it for a while. 'But at home we still have familiar streets, familiar landmarks . . .'

'The BBC,' I said in an overly refined accent.

'Yes, that especially. All the markers of normalcy. I think it was Napoleon who said all civilisations are only three meals away from disintegration.'

'I see your point. There are still things for us to hold on to. Things bigger than us. In the field then I imagine your radio operative will play the main part in morale. They keep the group in contact with back home. "Back Home" becomes the equivalent of the BBC and cocoa and biscuits before bed all thrown into one.'

'I hate to ask,' said Leo, 'but do you have any more wine? I think this conversation will require it.'

I went and got another bottle. 'This isn't as good,' I said, 'but we don't have time to let a decent wine breathe.' I turned to get more glasses.

'I'm a barbarian, Hope. This will do,' said Leo, holding out his glass. I filled it up. 'The thing is,' he went on, 'the time we think a radio operative is able to evade capture is around two months.'

'Oh God,' I said.

'As they are not officer combatants they won't be sent to a POW camp.'

'No,' I said. 'They'll be shot.'

Leo was looking down into the depths of his glass as if he expected to find salvation there. We were both drinking more than we should. I felt a little light-headed.

'But we knew that from the start,' I said. 'We talked about how these people didn't have great survival possibilities.'

'Yes, well, there's a huge difference between theory and reality. You've been taught to kill, but if you are ever in the miserable position of taking another's life you'll see all too well what I mean.' He looked up from his glass. 'I hope you never have to kill,' he said.

'Too late,' I said.

'Hope! How could I forget the auxies report? I'm so sorry. It's not something a young woman should ever be asked to do!'

'I have only ever disposed of particularly nasty and dangerous individuals,' I said. 'I don't make it a habit.'

'More than once?' asked Leo.

I changed the subject. 'It must be hard getting to know the candidates as well as you have during pre-selection and then realising they don't stand that much chance of survival.'

'We're not sending them on suicide missions,' said Leo, with a touch of anger.

'We will be telling them during their final training about life expectancy,' I said. 'At least that's what I was told by Captain Woodard. Right until the last minute they have the option to back out.'

'I'm sure true-blue spirit and peer pressure will hold them back,' said Leo, and I could hear the sarcasm in his voice.

'I think it's very unlikely any of them will opt out as they wait for the plane to take them out. Although I expect all of them with any sense will want to do so. However, the training that's happening in Scotland – Woodard says I'm going up with them, so I assume you are too?'

'Yes.'

'Well, I think that's the time for them to be able to pull out if they wish. They'll be trained enough they could help with further training. There might even be a home with counterterrorism when they're trained. It won't be a disgrace to step out then. We both know that having someone in France who panics or freezes endangers not just them, but any Resistance they are working alongside. It's as much a matter of personal honour to be truly honest about your abilities as it is to go into the field. Not everyone will be cut out for this kind of work.'

'Do you think you are?'

'I don't know,' I said. 'I speak French fluently, but I don't know France. I'm self-reliant, but I don't know how well I would work with trained amateurs. I'm used to thinking on my feet, and knowing the likely intentions of those I'm with. I have worked with assets, and I've managed to keep them alive, but not safe. I think I'm more of a loner. If you dropped me in the French countryside I think I could do good work, yes.'

'You're speaking like a traditional SIS operative,' said Leo. 'The SIS in general aren't pleased that the SOE exist. They think we're going to blow their operations and put their agents in danger.'

'You might,' I said. 'It depends on the COs communicating across the departments.'

'Bugger,' said Leo.

'I'm hoping that in these extraordinary circumstances they will cross-communicate. I mean, there is the XX committee. That's a good start.'

'Jesus, Hope. You shouldn't know about that!'

I hung my head. 'You're right. Loose lips and all that.' I could feel myself blushing at the mention of lips. I really was drinking rather too much.

He caught my wrist. 'Are you cold enough that you don't mind that we're sending people we've hand-picked to their deaths.'

I realised he too had drunk more than he was used to. I refrained from saying he'd hand-picked them, not me.

'There's mothers and fathers across this country who are sending their children off to war not knowing if they will ever return. If they can be that strong for the sake of our country, I think feeling morally challenged over people who are getting to choose if they take on a dangerous mission is . . . well . . . self-indulgent.'

He didn't release my wrist. I thought about various ways I could make him do so. 'Look,' I said, 'any engagement with the enemy demands a pragmatic and stoical outlook that doesn't sit easy with this much wine.'

He looked away from me.

'Oh goodness, did you sleep with one of the women you recruited?'

He turned to face me again at that. 'No, I did not. That would be immoral on so many levels.'

I nodded. 'So why this emotionality?'

'Emotionality? Oh, for Heaven's sake, Hope,' he said, pulling me closer towards him. 'Can't you see I'm worried you're going to volunteer to go over there? It might be damned selfish, but I don't want you to go. You're an absolute brat, but I've grown rather fond of you. God help me. I don't want to see you hurt.'

He pulled me down onto his lap. I could have resisted, but I didn't. I rested my head on his shoulder. He smelt nice, of soap and decent cologne. 'You're my commanding officer,' I said quietly.

'Not tonight,' he said. 'Not tonight.'

I lifted my head to ask him what he meant and found myself gazing into his eyes. Our faces were so close. Our lips within an inch of each other. I had no idea what I wanted to do. He put a hand behind my head and gently pulled me towards him. Our lips touched.

The inner doorbell rang. We sprang apart like cousins caught kissing. I staggered slightly, regaining my balance. Leo stood to help me. I heard the sound of a key in the lock. The door opened. In the doorway, surveying the scene and missing no detail, stood a man.

Fitzroy.

Chapter Nineteen

Abduction – or Almost

'I rather thought you were expecting me,' drawled my godfather. He closed the door behind him and walked into the room. He was wearing his big driving coat, and underneath it a suit that would have cost the average man a month's salary. His gait still held the usual swagger, but his back was ramrod stiff. Despite the genial expression on his face I knew he was furious.

He held his hand out to Leo. 'You must be my god-daughter's commanding officer. They're calling you Leo, I believe.' There was just enough stress on the words 'commanding officer' to drain the blood from Leo's face.

'Yes, sir,' he stammered, shaking my godfather's hand. Fitzroy held on to his hand.

'Might I enquire what you are doing in the home of a junior officer at this time of night? Are you preparing for a mission?'

'Tomorrow we're taking the candidates up to Scotland for training,' I said. 'It's a big departure.'

'I know, and you're not,' said Fitzroy. He released Leo to go and look at the wine bottles on the table. He picked up the one he had given me. He raised an eyebrow, and put it back down. Leo and I were still standing awkwardly at the side of the table.

'Has something happened, sir?' asked Leo. 'Has there been a problem with the Scottish site?'

Fitzroy turned back to face him. 'I haven't the faintest idea. Hope, do you have your grab bag ready?'

'Yes,' I said.

142

'Get it and your coat, we're leaving.' He looked at Leo. 'I'm sure you can manage to close the door on your way out.'

'But—' I began.

'No buts, Hope. It's an order.'

'Excuse me, sir,' said Leo. 'I am Hope's commanding officer.'

'Your rank?' snapped Fitzroy.

'Captain,' said Leo. He was doing his best to stand up to Fitzroy. It didn't help that Fitzroy was wearing boots that gave him extra height. Leo, in civilian dress, without his jacket looked rather unimpressive. But I gave him kudos for trying.

'I'm a Lieutenant Colonel. You are insignificant to this conversation.' Without turning he added, 'Ready, Hope?'

I flew into my room and grabbed my bag. By the time he turned around I was struggling into my coat. He came over to help me. He looked into my eyes. 'You're drunk,' he said.

'I'm not on duty.'

'Your CO should not be getting you drunk.'

'I poured the wine,' I protested.

'Downstairs and into the car,' said Fitzroy. When I didn't immediately move, he barked, 'Now!'

I fled with a backward glance at Leo. I mouthed 'sorry'. As I left I heard Fitzroy saying, 'You may have heard of me. My name is Fitzroy.'

Outside I found Jack guarding the car. He jumped all over me in welcome. Once I was seated, he clambered onto my lap and gave my face a thorough wash. Between this, the cold of the night, and Jack's expression when he ate some of my lipstick, I quickly sobered up.

Fitzroy had walked in on what was not the way I should have been conducting myself. After the pass he'd made at me when he was 'Uncle Ralph', which was all part of his recruiting act, Leo had never given any sign he felt anything special for me. I should have known never to get involved with him – buying him hangover cures and going for lunch with him. I should have kept my

143

distance. Fitzroy had every right to be furious with me. I was allowing myself to be compromised. How far would I have gone if he hadn't turned up? I didn't think there was any malice in Leo, or heaven forbid that he was some kind of security risk. No, this had all been about our sending people we had come to know and like to their probable deaths. We had the most involvement with the recruits, and what we were doing, even for the best of reasons, felt bloody awful. It wasn't that much of a surprise we'd turned to each other for comfort. But could I get Fitzroy to see this?

For the first time I felt sorry for my mother when she was training with him. He must have been unbearable.

A combination of wine, the aftermath of stress and sheer fatigue had my eyes drooping long before Fitzroy bounced into the car. He leapt in with some aplomb, curtly told Jack to 'stay' when he showed signs of welcoming Fitzroy in the same saliva-laden way he had welcomed me, and then said, 'It is good to see you, Hope. How are you faring?'

Before I could answer he drove off. 'I'd be happier if I knew what was going on,' I said.

'That's a question for the lieutenant-colonel side of me and he's cross with you. I was asking as your godfather.'

'I'm grateful to my godfather for asking. I'm coping. I'm functioning well in work for the most part. I believe I have proved my worth to the SEO.' I changed the subject quickly when I caught a glimpse in the moonlight of him frowning. 'I still miss my father, but so far I've managed to keep those thoughts under control until I am on my own, after duty.'

Fitzroy reached out a hand and patted my leg. 'It will be hard,' he said. 'You loved your father dearly, and even though you had become more independent of late, you always had the security of knowing he was waiting for you back at White Orchards.'

I felt tears prickle the back of my eyes. I sniffed. 'Sorry,' I said at once.

'I'd pass you my handkerchief if I wasn't driving,' said Fitzroy.

'We'll stop somewhere for a spot of something. I'm terribly hungry.'

'Aren't you always – godfather,' I said.

Fitzroy snorted, 'You sound just like your mother.'

'How is she?'

'That's part of why I'm here,' said Fitzroy. 'To assure you that she is well. I've been trying to teach her German, but it would be easier to teach a cat to knit.' He glanced over at me. 'She wanted to come with me, but I'm doing a long round trip tonight. If she was with me, I'd feel I had to stop more often and I'd worry about her being cold.' His teeth glinted in the dark as he smiled. 'Even though she would tell me not to fuss.'

'She's lucky she has you,' I said.

The atmosphere changed suddenly. Fitzroy stiffened beside me. 'I'm glad you think so,' he said eventually. 'Do you think you could get your head down and sleep for a short while? We'll stop for a bite somewhere and talk about everything we need to talk about.'

'All right,' I said. 'But why did you say I was expecting you?'

'Gracious, Hope, you phoned, didn't you?'

I could have said that I called some time ago, but all I said was, 'Yes, of course.' I could almost sense the smugness in the air. My godfather considered he had won another round. Well, let him think it was all safe for now. We would certainly be having words when I woke up and I didn't think he would like all the ones I had for him – by far.

Chapter Twenty

Suppertime Conversation

I awoke when the thrum of the car ceased. 'Food stop,' said Fitzroy, getting out of the car. 'Come on, boy!'

The warmth on my lap disappeared as Jack leapt down to follow his master. 'Traitor,' I muttered under my breath. 'They probably don't even allow dogs in here.'

We were outside some small inn or hotel in the middle of nowhere. Exactly the kind of place my godfather would know about, and possibly own. He opened the door, and went in. Jack trotted at his ankles like the best-behaved dog in the world, which he wasn't. I followed them. We walked into an empty lobby, small and dark. There was one low light at the reception, and the windows were completely blacked out. I wondered if anyone was here. A moment later, a man in his early forties appeared. He wore a waiter's costume, and from his short dark hair, greying at the temples, to his well-polished shoes, he was the epitome of a waiter. But he was so utterly like a waiter that I was fairly sure he was another spy. He had an open, clean-shaven face that was devoid of anything possibly memorable. He showed us through to a small dining room. There was no one else there. We went directly to a table with three chairs. There were three places set and one had a dog bowl.

Jack jumped up onto his seat, which also had a cushion for added height, and put his paws on the edge of the table. 'No matter how many times we come here,' said Fitzroy, 'he will put his paws on the table. I'm sorry, Fred. He may be of good pedigree, but he has no manners. This, incidentally, is my god–daughter, who will be dining with me. I've allowed an hour to eat. Does that suit what you've rustled up?'

The waiter spoke in a quiet tone into his ear. Fitzroy smiled. I took off my coat and was startled by the waiter arriving noiselessly behind me to remove it. Definitely a spy.

Fitzroy and I joined Jack at the table.

'I do hope we're not all having the same,' I said once the waiter had left. Then Fitzroy took off his driving gloves and I forgot everything else I had to say.

He must have been talking for some while, but the first I knew was a sharp bark of my name. 'Have you heard a word I've said, young lady?'

'You're wearing a wedding ring,' I said. I tore my eyes away from his left hand and looked up into his face. 'Tell me it's part of some cover.'

'It isn't,' said Fitzroy. 'I am married.' He played with the ring in the dim light and regarded it with a slight lifting of the corners of his mouth. 'Interesting idea for the man to also wear a ring. It began in the Great War. Helped men remember their wives and families back home. Didn't stop them going to the foreign brothels when they were on leave, I suspect. But still they were thinking of their loved ones.'

'Since when?'

'Not that long ago,' said Fitzroy. He began to play idly with his fork.

I snatched it off him. 'Who did you marry?'

Fitzroy removed his fork from my clenched fist with gentle ease. 'Why, your mother, of course. I'm your stepfather now.'

I couldn't find any words. None at all. I just sat there agape. My father wasn't even cold in his grave . . .

Soup was brought to the table. It was red, and came with little white rolls. 'Eat up,' said Fitzroy. I ate mechanically. I didn't taste any of it. My new stepfather ordered some wine for himself and orange juice for me. I didn't object. I didn't say a word. Jack's bowl was filled with sliced, cooked steak. Jack pulled each piece daintily from the bowl, and onto his cushion. Then he lowered his head, and made noises like an angry lion while he ate it. Normally, this would have made me laugh.

After the soup there was a plate of meat and vegetables. Again I didn't taste a thing. When these plates had been removed and he'd asked for coffee, Fitzroy sat opposite me, wiping his mouth with his napkin. I knew he was watching me intently, waiting for a reaction, but I didn't have one to give.

'I seem to have you at a loss for words,' said Fitzroy calmly. 'I would have thought that when I removed your mother from White Orchards it would have been obvious to you that I intended to marry her. It's really not the thing to gallivant around openly with a lady. Besides, I wanted to take her to my home. It was the obvious and natural thing to do. Your father asked me once that if he predeceased her, I'd look after you both. This is what I intend to do. You've always known your mother and I were close, I don't understand your reaction.'

'Am I your daughter?' I blurted out.

'You're my step-daughter now, yes. Obviously, you are of age and free to do as you wish, outside the necessities of your military duty. However, I hope you consider yourself part of my family now. As well, of course, as remaining a Stapleford.'

'That's not what I meant,' I said, all my anger rushing up inside me. 'Am I your natural daughter? Were you having an affair with my mother?'

Fitzroy, who a moment before had been calm and relaxed, totally in charge of the situation, went white. All the colour washed out of him. I wondered if he was about to faint. Was he shocked I knew the truth? I felt my eyes fill up.

But I had misread him badly. He put his napkin down carefully on the table, and stood up. 'Jack and I are going for a walk outside. When we return I will pretend for both our sakes this conversation never happened.'

'But—' I said.

'No,' snarled Fitzroy. His eyes blazed. Finally I got a view of the part of him that he had always said was bad. The fury directed at me was white hot, like the centre of a furnace. I realised his reaction to Leo and me was like a taper flame compared to the volcano that now threatened to erupt.

'Anyone else, Hope. If anyone else spoke of your mother so disrespectfully, man or woman . . .' He didn't finish his sentence, but called sharply to his dog and left. He didn't even ask for his coat and left his gloves lying on the table. I couldn't remember ever seeing him so angry, and I didn't want to see it ever again.

To my embarrassment tears coursed down my face. I kept my head lowered and mopped at them with my napkin, but I didn't seem to be able to make them stop. The rational part of me knew that I was in shock. I was still grieving my father, and my other father figure turning on me was shattering. My stepfather. Cole had been so convincing. Did Fitzroy's anger mask the truth? From what I had just seen he would do anything to protect my mother. *Would he have done anything to be able to marry her?* whispered a little voice at the back of my mind.

Fitzroy and I had always been close. I looked up to him and trusted him completely. To suddenly find myself on the outside of his regard, alone in the world, was more than I could bear. I buried my head in my napkin and sobbed. What the waiter might think of my behaviour had become insignificant.

I don't know how long I cried. I hardly ever cry, and I flee from strong emotion. I needed to shut down what I was feeling. My mother and Fitzroy were together now, and unlike when my parents were together, I was not allowed within the charmed circle. Whether or not Cole was right, it was clear Fitzroy had attained his goal. He had what he wanted and no one was going to take it from him. I had never imagined that there could be a circumstance in which my godfather threatened me. But he just had.

I was only aware they had returned because Jack licked my elbow. Fitzroy, stealthy as ever, had slid into his seat. On his travels he had acquired a small glass of brandy, which he was now sipping. Jack returned to hopefully nuzzling his empty bowl. I had no mirror, but I tidied my face and hair as best I could, and put my handkerchief away.

'We need to leave soon,' said Fitzroy. 'I'm putting you on a train to Scotland. You will be the community liaison officer for one of our airbases.' He passed some paperwork across to me. I didn't look at it but put it directly in my bag. 'It's probably better if you avoid wearing uniform much of the time. I've left your rank as it is. Now, I'd be grateful for an oral report on what you learned of the SOE while you were there, and the roles you were asked to fulfil.'

I summed it up for him. I didn't mention names. He would have to ask me straight out for those. I did detail the procedures, the questions the assessments were based on, and the type of people who were recruited.

'So, your Leo was one of the ones assessing who should be given a tap on the shoulder?'

I nodded. 'We were both due to go to Scotland to be present during the training of the first cohort. However, I don't know how or if I would have been used, except as an observer.'

'So you weren't privy to any of the training plans, despite what was initially said?'

'No.'

Fitzroy sucked his tongue over his teeth. 'Interesting. Interesting, and while I see where they are coming from, I would expect most of the *agents* to die within a month, two at most. The other concern is that they might unwittingly interfere with a legitimate operation that's already on the ground. You won't be sorry to be out of there. There may be some small success, but in the main it will be tragedy upon tragedy. I am not as simple-minded as you think. I do realise it was shared guilt drawing you and that boy together. But the fact that even happened shows you are not fit for that work.'

I looked up at that, genuinely surprised.

'I do occasionally recognise emotions,' said my godfather, 'even if I don't have them myself.'

I tried a different tack. 'It's not only amateurs they are training to work with the Resistance. As I speak fluent French—'

'Come hell or high water you won't be joining them. In fact, I'll send a memorandum to them and attach it to your file. You are not being sent overseas.'

'But why? I'm good at what I do—'

'I will not have your mother distressed.'

'For God's sake, there's a war on. You can't hold me back through sentiment alone. Not even you have that much influence.'

Fitzroy raised an eyebrow. 'No?' he said calmly. 'How mistaken you are.' The words were said with a flat coldness. He certainly thought he could keep me tethered, and I saw no point arguing about it now. He was in one of his moods, and there would be no shifting him no matter how wrong he was.

'You should go and freshen up,' he said. 'We need to leave.'

I did as I was told. When I came out the dining room lay empty. I found him sitting in the car with the motor running. Jack had hunkered down in the back beside my kitbag. Fitzroy nodded as I climbed in. He'd left a blanket on my seat, but I had barely arranged it before we were away.

He drove fast and without lights. Jack snored loudly. Fitzroy seemed intent upon the road. I thought about all the things I would have liked to have done before I died in a road accident.

My sense of direction is never good, and with the countryside in total darkness, I had no idea where we were. It must have been about two hours later we drew up to an army checkpoint. Beyond this I could see the outline of a station house and platform. This was not a London line.

The soldiers took one look at his pass, saluted and let him past. We drove down to the very edge of the platform.

'Right. Out,' said Fitzroy. 'If I go any further I'll be on the damn tracks.'

I climbed out and opened the back door to get my bag then

came to stand by the passenger window. He wound the window down.

'That's your train there. They've held it for you. Don't cause any trouble. Goodbye, Hope.' Then, without even closing the window, he turned his eyes back to the windscreen and drove off.

I watched him go in bemusement. Never in my entire life had I heard Fitzroy say 'Goodbye' to anyone. He hated farewells and always avoided them. What did that farewell to me mean? Was he about to go into danger? Or was it the question I had asked meant he wanted little to do with me any more? Was it exactly as it sounded – 'Goodbye'.

152

Chapter Twenty-one

Taking the High Road

The train had many more carriages than I had expected. Fitzroy's car was barely out of the station, before a uniformed guard came over to me. 'ID card, ma'am?'

I pulled the sheaf of papers out of my bag and struggled through them to find the right one. I offered it to him. He had a small torch with a shaded light. He checked the pass and then shone the light in my face. He flicked the light back and forth. 'Welcome aboard, Lieutenant. You're one of the lucky ones. We've got a berth put aside for you. Sergeant will bring your tea at six a.m. Train to be evacuated by six thirty a.m. Should be someone at the station to meet you.'

He led me over to one of the cars and, proceeding me, walked along the corridor. On one side the windows were all blacked out. On the other was a row of doors. He opened one, and gestured to me to go in. 'Necessary is at the bottom end. It's shared between this carriage only.' He said the last bit as if it should mean something to me. I nodded and went in. I heard him turn the door latch with a click. A moment's reflection told me that I was not locked in. Rather that the door was latched against swinging open.

Groping around I found a tiny light. The window in here was also blacked out. There was a small washbasin, and what must have been a row of seats in its civilian days that had been made into a bed.

I took the papers out of my bag again and tried to read through them. The light was extremely weak, and I had to screw up my eyes to make out anything. In the end all I learned was that I was to be billeted at Mrs McKenzie's bed and breakfast house. I was also to report directly to Wing Commander Buchanan. I put the papers away and lay back down. There was no way I was going to be able to sleep with everything that had happened today.

The next thing I knew a portly sergeant barged his way in and dumped a cup of tea down beside me. ''Alf an 'our and oot,' he said. And it was only a cup of tea. No toast. No bacon. Not even a stale biscuit. I could well imagine how Fitzroy would respond to this kind of treatment. But then he'd undoubtedly have driven himself, and probably brought a Fortnum & Mason's hamper for breakfast. Even Jack had had actual steak last night. The man lived in a different world. And now so too, presumably, did my mother.

I drank my tea, which was surprisingly good – hot, sweet and strong – and struggled internally with my morals. With all the awful things that were happening, those living a life of privilege were overindulged, but I liked being overindulged. It might be wrong, but was it criminal in wartime? I finished packing everything, splashed my face in the basin, did my best with my hair, and wrapped up tight in my jacket. I'd pulled the jumper over my head rather than repack it. I'd always been told Scotland was cold, and before dawn there was even ice on the inside of the window.

I checked my watch. It would feel better if I could keep moving, but I had no mind to stand on a windy platform for half an hour. But my watch said time had moved on enough that I was prepared to get out.

The rest of the platform was empty. Either the others on the train weren't disembarking or they had already left. A nasty little breeze nipped at my nose and ankles. It reminded me fondly of Jack.

On all sides the imposing dark shadows of mountains rose above us. We had to be in some kind of dip or valley. I hadn't felt the train struggle up a steep incline, but then the recent emotional incidents had worn me out. I looked up and down for my guide.

A lone figure, in a blue uniform, stood at the other end of the platform. I walked towards him, my bag over my shoulder. As I came nearer I saw the flare of a red point of light and a trail of smoke. Not a sniper, I thought.

'Hello, miss,' said a jolly voice. 'Have you come to take me to my new home from home?' I closed the gap between us and his features became clearer. He was younger than me, and wore a junior insignia. He'd nicked his face in a couple of places. However, his skin glowed like that of a newborn baby. He had the obligatory tiny moustache on his upper lip, but it was so light it could have been the froth from a cup of milky coffee. He was blond, with short-cropped hair, and around average height.

'I'm afraid not,' I said. 'In fact I was looking for someone to take me to my billet.'

'Jolly-ho,' said my new friend. 'We can rout them out together.' He held out his hand. 'I'm Cadet Officer Simon Stewart. The lads make jokes about my being SS, but I don't think that's terribly funny, do you? Are you coming to work at the canteen? I've heard the Scottish bases have excellent scran.'

I shook his hand. 'I'm Hope Stapleford, the new community liaison officer. Lieutenant.'

'Oops, sorry, ma'am.' He leaned in slightly closer. 'You are my senior, aren't you? Once you go cross-services I get terrible confused. I usually call everyone who is an officer sir, sometimes the NCOs too if they look fierce enough.'

'That's a sound practice,' I said. 'Shall we go through the ticket gate and see if there's a welcoming committee? Do you know where you're being billeted?'

'Not a clue,' said Stewart brightly. 'Warm, wind- and rainproof will do. Oh, and—'

'Scran,' I said, anticipating him.

'Exactly. I can see we are going to get on famously, ma'am.' He chatted inconsequentially about his eagerness to get on with the job. I let him ramble, hoping to pick up useful information. At one point he said something about he'd heard why they needed a new community liaison officer. I shot him a look askance, and his normally happy face looked downcast. I decided on the spur of the moment not to enquire further, but let him go on without interruption. However, I noted it as something I needed to know.

The small rural station appeared deserted. Our footsteps rang as we walked through the ticket hall. The shutter was down on the kiosk. As we came out onto the roadside a sliver of gold was cresting the mountains ahead.

'Gosh,' said Stewart. 'What an amazing sky, and to think I'm going up among that soon. I'm ever so lucky.'

'How many hours do you have?' I asked.

'Oh, one hundred and thirty. Almost finished my training,' said Stewart cheerfully. 'I'm looking forward to it enormously. That and bagging some Jerry, ma'am. Oh, look, there's a donkey. You don't see many of them about nowadays.'

I followed the direction of his arm, and saw a rather fluffy grey donkey. At the donkey's head stood a man in an unusual hat. It was a cross between a squashed beret and a peaked cap. A dull green, it had the advantage of giving an overhang to the ears to protect them from rain. The man also wore a half-length coat and a kilt. I thought this more remarkable than the donkey. The donkey shifted slightly, and between the two of them I caught a glimpse of a cart.

'I rather think that donkey's our ride,' I said. I stepped off towards them. The road itself was clear and empty. Stewart made a rather confused noise in his throat, and then I heard him follow.

'Good morning,' I said to the donkey's handler, 'I'm the new community liaison officer up at the airbase. Are you by any chance waiting for me?'

I held my breath, fearing an outburst of raw Scottish dialect.

'Good morning, miss,' said the man in perfectly understandable English. 'I'm to take you to Ma McKenzie's. She's a bit ruffled having to take in services people for the bottom rate, but you won't go hungry and she keeps the place clean as can be.'

'Are you also here for me?' asked Stewart.

'I can take you on to the airbase after I've dropped the lady off, sir. I haven't been advised where you're billeted. More than likely you're with Ma, but they will tell up at the base.'

He took hold of the front of his cap, and gave a half nod, half tug. 'If you would like to ascend.'

The back panel of the little cart folded down and the man lowered a step. The cart was empty but for benches opposite one another. We climbed in. There was another bench at the front for the driver. However, our man avoided this, instead going to the donkey's head and taking hold of the side rein. ''Ere we go, Maud,' he said. The donkey lowered its head, swished its tail, and took a step forward. Then another, and another. It became clear within a few moments that the pace the animal set with the handler at its side was akin to my normal walking pace. I consoled myself with the thought that at least I didn't have to carry my case. Stewart did not accept the situation so easily. He was fidgeting in his seat and bobbing up every few moments to look out at the donkey. 'Is he not going to get into the driver's seat,' he said in a bad stage whisper to me.

I shrugged. 'Who knows?' I said quietly.

'All the bally people will be waking up soon, and they'll see us sitting up here like kids on a beach ride. It's embarrassing.'

'I suppose they may see you,' I said repressively. 'You are the taller of us, and you're wearing the RAF uniform. I expect there will be plenty of young lasses eager to see the men protecting our country.'

Stewart blushed a fiery red. 'This is not the way I want to be seen.' He shuffled to the end of his bench. 'Hey, you! Excuse me? Could you possibly drive the cart rather than walk the donkey? Or if you don't drive, I've a little experience. I could drive her for you.'

The reaction he got was not what he wanted. The man stopped the cart in the middle of the high street at one of the grey buildings with taped-up windows or shutters obscuring their business. Only one shop was open. A greengrocer, who, fresh from market, was putting out his wares. He stopped what he was doing, and leaned back against the shop door to watch.

Our guide, whose name I really should have asked for, said, 'Well, mayhap I did come up and sit in the cart, then poor Maud would have three bodies to pull as well as your luggage. I'm just as good walking. You and the lady need to rest yourself for your labours. I'm not the one doing the hard work.'

'The thing is,' said Stewart, leaning further across the front of the cart so he could lower his voice, 'the lady and I would like to get there quicker. Is the donkey weak?'

'Maud, oh no, sir. She's a refugee from the mines. Don't like the daylight much, but you two will be lighter than any of the mining carts she pulled.'

'Apart from you not wanting to burden your beast, is there any other reason we cannot go faster?'

'Well, there's the conversation.'

'The conversation?' repeated Stewart mystified.

'Aye, me and Maud, we have a conversation every morning around this time. She'd miss it bad if we didn't. She's just been telling me that her chestnuts hurt. I don't like to overwork her if that's the case.'

'Chestnuts! What on earth are you talking about, man? There's a war on, don't you know?'

'Stewart,' I said quietly, 'stand down.'

The cadet ignored me.

'I do, sir. I was in the last. Hell on earth, it was. Hell on earth. Didn't reckon like I'd ever see my missus again, I didn't.'

'I don't want to discuss history with you,' shouted Stewart. 'I want to get to the airbase in time for this one!'

'Stewart, enough!' There was no chance of him not hearing me.

The cadet continued to ignore me, stood, and rushed to the back of the cart, his face red with anger. I caught him before he got down and threw him down on the bench.

'If you do not start paying attention to me, Cadet, I will have you on report,' I snarled. 'Stay here!'

He looked so startled by my forceful handling of him, I thought him incapable of doing any more harm for the present. I jumped lightly down and went to greet the driver.

'I am so sorry, I never introduced myself or even asked your name. That was most remiss of me. I'm afraid I was thinking about other things, but it's no excuse for being rude. I'm Hope.'

The man's face – and I could see he was in his middle years now I was close enough and the sun was rising – lit up. 'That's very nice of you, miss. This is Maud.'

'How do you do, Maud?'

'Well, like I said, she has sore chestnuts.'

'And you are?'

He saluted me. 'Sergeant Brian McKenzie, ma'am.'

'It's good to meet you, Sergeant,' I said and saluted back. 'If we are to be formal I am Lieutenant Stapleford, but I don't think we need to be right now, do you? Let's have a look at Maud's chestnuts.' I bent down, stroking Maud carefully, and talking nonsense in a low voice. On the back of her front legs were the residual toes, often referred to as chestnuts. I straightened again.

'Does Maud have a sense of mischief?' I asked.

'Of a kind, ma'am.'

'Well, I know donkeys are very smart creatures,' I said. 'The thing is, I'm not a professional donkey handler like yourself – you handled them in the Great War, didn't you?'

The man nodded, and his eyes began to fill. I hurried on. 'Only Maud's chestnuts look perfectly fine to me. I think she's been pulling your leg.'

Brian checked the donkey's legs. 'I reckon you're right, ma'am. She's been a naughty one this morning.'

'Probably not that keen on leaving her stables so early. I assume you normally have your chat over breakfast.'

Brian smiled and nodded.

159

'Do you think we could perhaps go a bit faster? I'd like to see Maud doing her paces.'

'Up you hop, ma'am, and now I know she were being a rascal, I'll show you why I calls her Flying Maud.'

I got back on the cart, and the driver climbed to his perch. I wasn't expecting much, and almost fell over the side, catching myself at the last minute, as Maud showed us 'her paces'.

When we arrived, I got out and left Stewart to head up to the airbase on his own. He hadn't said anything to me since I'd pushed him over. Rather like a toddler, I thought, and left him without a backward glance.

The B & B was a typical grey, square house. It had a little bit of grass at the front, and a low wall that had probably once had railings. There were a few steps up to a large wooden door, and on the left side there was a painted sign that read 'The Manse, B & B, Proprietor McKenzie, Licensed'.

I rang the doorbell.

Chapter Twenty-two

The Manse

A middle-aged woman, wearing an apron and her hair done up in a cloth turban to keep it clean, opened the door. She peered slightly short-sightedly at me. 'Yes? I'm full with the services people. The airbase has me all taken over.' She had a slight Scottish burr to her voice.

'I'm the new community liaison officer,' I said. 'Hope Stapleford, Lieutenant. I think you were expecting me?'

'Don't say they put you on the cattle train?' I must have looked blank. 'The one that comes in before the dawn.'

'They did,' I said, smiling, 'but I was made a cup of tea before I disembarked, by a sergeant who knew his way around a teapot.'

'That's as might be, but you'll get the best tea you've ever had here. Although I say so, who shouldn't. It's the water, you see. Fresh Highland water. Best in the world. But I'm keeping you on the doorstep. Come away in. I take it you'll have had your breakfast?'

'Only the cup of tea, I'm afraid. But once I've put my things in my room, I'll be heading straight up to the airbase. I'm sure I can get something up there.'

'Oh no. I won't have anyone leaving my establishment hungry.' She led me in past some big rooms. 'Residents' lounge. I've a lot of young lads in right now. But if you have any trouble you come right to me. I won't have any of their mucking about.' Then, 'Dining room. I do luncheon if you tell me in time. I can also do a sandwich instead. You have your ration book? Dinner is

161

a serve yourself. I keep dishes out until eight o'clock. But like everyone I only have so much, so get there as early as you can. Doors open at six thirty.'

She made it sound like a theatre performance. The hall was long and broad. There were brown framed mirrors, what-nots, and even a grandfather clock, but we were moving at speed.

'This is the staircase you need to remember. There's three. Four if you count the old servants' one. But this is the one I put all my girls on.'

At the top of the stairs she led me through a small hallway and opened a white-painted door. 'This is you. Come down when you're ready. Just follow the stairs till they stop and you'll be in the kitchen. I don't normally allow guests in the kitchen, but the world's tipsy-turkey, and it'll be quicker if I don't have to open up the dining room.'

'Goodness, no,' I said. 'Don't open up the dining room for me.'

'Oh, I'd get a lot of takers if I did,' said Mrs McKenzie. 'Them who flies nights or works at odd times are always wanting their breakfast. See you shortly,' she said and retreated down the stairs.

That was the moment I realised her shoes made no sound. All the house was carpeted. A rare luxury. My room turned out to be neat, white, with a single bed, a lovely view of the mountains, and all the white-painted furniture I might need. Even the carpet was white with roses. I sat down on the bed and immediately took my shoes off. No one had ever entrusted me with a mostly white room before.

Downstairs I found a low passage that opened out into a large kitchen. Mrs McKenzie was busy at the range. She directed me to sit at a kitchen table that stood near the door. It bore many scratch marks but was, as Brian had said, spotless. Of course, I was glad for these signs of hygiene, but I couldn't help feeling I wasn't the kind of guest you had in a boarding house like this.

Fried eggs, a strip of bacon and toast were put in front of me. There was also a freshly made pot of tea.

Mrs McKenzie sat down on a chair beside me. 'Do you mind if I join you?' she said, already sitting. I shook my head. My mouth was full of egg. 'We keep our own chickens,' she said, 'so we can sometimes go a bit further than the rations. I grow a few things too, but it all depends on the weather and the season. The truth is, since the services booked me out I've barely had a moment to myself. Just before you arrived I was cleaning out the residents' lounge, setting up the breakfast table and giving the stairs a thorough brush down. I'm not as young as I was, and I'm fair tired out, and there's the breakfast to be doing.'

'Do you do this all alone?' I asked, surprised.

'I've two girls that come in from the village. Not that they likes working for the service people, but beggars can't be choosers. One that does the breakfast and one that does the dinners. If I'm lucky I get one or the other to help out with any lunches, but it depends. Some of the girls that stay here give me a hand from time to time.' She looked enquiringly at me.

'Well, I'm a good basic cook,' I said. 'If I have time I have no objection to giving you a hand now and again. But I have to report to my CO after this, and everything I do is down to him. I don't know how much leeway he'll give me.'

Mrs McKenzie made a quiet raspberry-like sound.

'You don't like the wing commander?' I said, lowering my voice conspiratorially, and I hoped invitingly.

'Oh, he's not a bad man,' said Mrs McKenzie, 'and at least he's one of our own. Born not ten miles from here. Kirk would have still had The Manse then. Married Margaret Sinclair that was. She's not local. Born in Sutherland. Comes from well-to-do folk. Funny how a wife can change a man. Tries to be a mother to all the lads, she does. You'll put her nose right out of joint. As far as she's concerned she is all the community liaison the base needs.'

'Oh dear,' I said. 'I don't want to tread on anyone's toes.'

'Oh, I'm not a one to gossip, but it's about time someone stood on those tippy toes of hers. Acting all high and mighty with the locals. There's some funny things been going on up there from what the lads tell me. But then we've always been a bit out of the way of things here. Gets lonely this far north. And then there's the planes, flying all times of the day and night. Not just ours. Theirs as well. For a place with hardly any people we're getting more than our fair share of action – or so it seems to me.'

'But you get on all right with the lads?' I asked.

'Aye, well, I have to be professional, don't I?' She poured herself another cup of tea and shot me a shrewd glance. 'It's delicate, the balance between an army base and a local town. Misunderstandings are all too easy. I'm not saying there's a mite of harm in any of them, but put them all together and things can get a wee bit difficult, if you see what I mean.'

I didn't, and I didn't think it would help to pretend I did. 'It's all new to me, I'm afraid. I was sent directly here from a different mission, so I need to learn about the place. Is Sergeant McKenzie your brother-in-law?'

Mrs McKenzie edged back in her seat and crossed her arms. 'What of it?'

'He was kind and welcoming,' I said. 'We had a chat about Maud. She was up to her tricks. Pretending she had sore legs when she didn't, but we straightened it all out.'

Mrs McKenzie unfolded her arms and half slumped over the table. 'I hope as he didn't put you out, miss. I weren't going to send him until eleven, but he was so sure you were coming in.' She gave me a small embarrassed smile. 'He just knows things sometimes. Since he came back.'

'From the Great War?'

'Well, yes and no. Look, I'm telling you this as the community liaison lady, so you can keep it confidential. I mean, everyone in the village knows, even some in the local town have heard the rumours. But they're thirty miles and more off. Not our folk.'

'What do they know?' I prompted. A quick glance at the kitchen clock showed me the wing commander was going to be wondering where I was.

'Like I said, Brian just knows things sometimes. Mary Benson, the young wife of our local farmer, she lost her wedding ring. And she's out and about and working all the hours God sends. She's even feeding a whole lot of land girls too. Her husband's not a bad man. Got a bit of a temper on him, and always on about how they struggle to make ends meet. Though not as much now, I'd have thought. She knew he'd be fair raging if he heard she'd lost the ring – it was his mother's, you see. So she comes and asks Brian, and he says how she took it off yesterday to do the washing-up, and it's been picked up by a magpie and put in his nest. Told her where the tree was and everything. Anyway, her being desperate as well as a bit of a game girl, she goes off and finds the blooming tree. Then she climbs the ruddy thing and lo and behold if there ain't her ring in a nest on the third branch up, just like Brian said.'

'Gosh! How does he know these things?' I was thinking that he sounded like a country man who knew the habits of magpies.

'I'm not sure. Maybe it's meant to make up for what was taken away in the war. You'll have noticed he's not right in the head. No harm in him. Wouldn't hurt a fly. Not ever. Probably why the war got to him so much. Seeing all those other dead fellows. He joined up with six of the lads from his school. All of them barely more than children. All died in the trenches. Brian still sees some of them and they tell him their stories. But then we've always had fey folk up around here. Just that most of them have the sense to keep these things to themselves. Brian, he'd tell anyone anything. Trust Judas Iscariot, that one.'

'He sounds like he has a heart of gold,' I said, and made a mental note never to even hint at anything important when Brian was around.

'That he has,' said Mrs McKenzie. 'He was still trying to dig them out when they found him. Bullet hole in his shoulder weeping blood like a stuck pig. No one knows how he kept at it. Didn't make no difference though. They'd all died when the trench came down on top of them. Inhaled earth as if it were air.'

'You must have married very young,' I said.

She smiled. 'Barely sixteen. He were Brian's twin. My Bob were one of them he was trying to dig out. You'll see why I'd forgive him anything.'

I didn't get a chance to reply. The back door opened and a young, plump girl with flaming hair clutching a basket of greens walked in.

'Heavens,' said Mrs McKenzie. 'If it isn't Jeanie, and I've not started the breakfast. You'll forgive me, Lieutenant Stapleford, I must be getting on. Leave your plate when you're done. Jeanie will see to it.' Jean cast me a foul look.

Mrs McKenzie scooted off out the back door with Jeanie at her heels. I heard, 'You do the hens, hen, and I'll deal with the goat. Oh, and Jeanie, get that wee bit of borage by . . .' before the door closed.

I washed up my own plate and cup and put them on the draining board. I still had little idea of how to get to the airbase, but there had to be someone from here going up. I decided I needed a proper wash and brush-up before I left, and I should change into my uniform to meet the wing commander. I was already late, and late and disordered would only make it worse. I located the shared bathroom, performed my ablutions in record time, and was closing my bedroom door behind me fifteen minutes later. A last look at my room showed my influence. Wet footprints all across the floor, and even though I hadn't slept in the bed the linen was in chaos. There was no lock, so I could only hope Mrs M didn't decide to check in on it while I was away.

I rushed down the stairs. I could hear the sounds of men and women in the dining room. I wondered if there might be a useful noticeboard in the residents' lounge. I didn't fancy going into the dining room. It would look odd after I'd been fed a special breakfast. Maybe I should just go outside and see if I could find a friendly local.

With all these thoughts rushing through my head I wasn't paying that much attention to where I was going. I ran into a man, and bounced off him like I'd hit a wall. I would have fallen heavily on my butt, but a paw-like hand, large and with the back covered in hair, grabbed me and steadied me. I looked up, ready to apologise, but no words came. He was dressed in black casual clothes, clean shaven and wearing a strong cologne. Neater and more civilian-like than I had ever seen him. But he was unmistakable.

'Hello, Hope,' said Cole.

Chapter Twenty-three

The Airbase

When you see something or someone in the wrong place, it's confusing. I know this. I've used it to misdirect other people before. However, I was completely flabbergasted to see Cole. I was torn between angrily demanding to know what he meant by his comments about Fitzroy being my father, and throwing myself on his broad chest and crying. God help me, but at this moment he was the nearest I had to a father figure in my life. As it was, I stood there open mouthed. I heard further footsteps, and Cole put his arm around my shoulders and turned me towards them.

'Why, Mr Cole!' said Mrs McKenzie. The cloth was gone from her head, and she sported some fine victory rolls. She had also removed her apron to reveal a smart day dress. Her eyes narrowed with suspicion.

'The way things work out, Mrs McKenzie,' said Cole. 'Would you believe this is my niece, Hope Stapleford. I had no idea she was being posted to the area.'

Mrs McKenzie's face softened and her eyes were restored to their normal size. 'Ah, isn't that nice. It's moments like this when one has to make the most of family. No wonder the poor wee mite looked shocked.'

I realised I was the poor wee mite. 'Yes, I haven't seen my uncle for months,' I said. 'We had no idea where he was.'

'Well, that's not a surprise with his work, is it? Though I shouldn't say so.'

'Indeed,' said Cole, his voice tinged with ice.

'Oh, now, don't be scolding me, Mr Cole.' She actually dabbed a handkerchief to her eyes. 'I'll make a cake for your tea. I've a couple of eggs put by. Although I'm not too sure about this new substitute for flour.'

'Very kind,' said Cole. 'I should take my niece to the airbase. I don't want her to be late on her first day.'

'Oh no,' said Mrs McKenzie, 'but then she's only been communitising and that's her job after all.'

As we exited The Manse, Cole said under his breath, 'You'd get more sense out of that donkey.'

Despite everything, I found myself smiling.

'I don't have a car up here, Hope. Are you all right on the back of a motorbike? I assume you are going to the airbase?'

'Yes, and I've never been on one,' I said, secretly rather excited at the thought.

'Well, hold on tight, and lean as I lean. Have you got something to tie your hair up with?' I nodded. 'Ponytail. Roll it up and it might keep the helmet above your eyes.'

We walked along the path at the front of The Manse. 'I take it you've parked it out of sight because it has petrol in it?'

Cole gave a grunt. The further we went from other people the more he retreated into himself. He had been almost chatty with Mrs McKenzie, but in all the time he'd trained me at the farmhouse we'd barely exchanged more than a few words. But I felt safer with him around. He'd rescued me from the attack in my flat, and I remained grateful to him. He was also rather large and solid. Comforting in the way a solid bookshelf is.

We turned a corner and came onto a small lane. One side was hedged, but the other side was a row of shed-like lock-ups. They looked out of place. I imagined that before the war this had been the kind of place where people left their front doors unlocked.

'Cole,' I said abruptly. 'Did you ever find out who the man was who attacked me in the flat?'

'Yes. He won't trouble you again.'

Or anyone else, by the sound of it, I thought. My insides wobbled a bit. The idea that Cole had killed someone for trying to hurt me was confusing. I had been responsible for loss of life before, but I had been the one who took action. Not someone else on my behalf. I had a sudden impression of Cole as some kind of half-tamed animal, who you might befriend but could never control. He would always be a wild animal at heart.

'I did something a little unwise. I asked Fitzroy if he was my father.'

Cole stopped in front of a lock-up. He was fishing for a key in his jacket pocket. He paused for a moment. 'No, that wasn't wise. What did he say?'

'He denied it. I've never seen him so angry.'

Cole shrugged. 'Even Alice said he had a filthy temper, and she was always the one to cut him the most slack.'

He produced a key and undid the padlock.

'But you said—'

'Hope, we can discuss this later. Now is not the time.' He went in and I heard him starting the motorbike. Then he came out with a helmet. I'd tied my hair back and he pushed it up inside the back of the helmet. Being a regulation issue for a man, it was slightly too large for me even so. He tied the strap under my chin, then stepped back and looked down at me. He gave a slight smile.

I had never seen Cole smile. It was like seeing a shark sneeze, somehow sweet and yet still menacing. 'I'll drop you a little way from the base, so you can straighten yourself out.'

Then without another word, he went back and came out on the bike. He waited while I figured out how to climb on the back. The seat had no back. I knew motorbike passenger seats had no back, but climbing onto the running bike I felt certain that whoever designed these machines had a sick sense of humour. How on earth was I to stay on?

Cole reached behind and taking one of my hands pulled it

around his waist. He let go, and I put my arms around him. I could feel myself blushing. I was close up against him. It felt odd, but nice at the same time. It was the latter that was embarrassing me. He kicked the bike into gear and drove off. Immediately my shy hold around him tightened like a vice. I clung on for dear life.

Once I accepted that I wasn't going to fall off, I opened my eyes. I didn't have goggles, so I kept my face shielded against him. If I thought the speed from my little car thrilling, this was beyond amazing. In fact, when he opened up the throttle on an empty lane, I may have inadvertently whooped aloud.

We stopped by a tall hedgerow. I got off and Cole kicked down the stand. My legs shook slightly. I missed the hum of the engine vibrating through my body. Being back on firm ground with stationary scenery was disconcerting. Cole turned me towards him and undid the strap beneath my chin. I pulled the helmet off and took out the ponytail and ran my fingers through my hair. My fingers met a mass of knots.

Cole produced a comb from his back pocket and made a motion for me to turn round. He began to deal with the knots. As he ran it through my hair, teasing some part gently apart with his fingers, it felt strangely intimate.

'I'm not going to ask you if you liked the ride,' he said. 'That much was obvious.'

'Will you teach me to ride it?'

'I don't know if I'll be around long enough. You'll find a leaflet somewhere knocking around the base that tells you the basics. Find, read and digest one of those and if I have time I'll try. You can already drive, so you only need to learn the hand–eye coordination. You've already got the balance.' He paused, dealing with a particularly bad knot. 'You'll have to be less reckless than usual. Motorbikes are unforgiving heavy machines that will easily crush someone as small as you to a pulp.'

This was the second time in an hour that someone had commented on my fragility. However, there were things I wanted from Cole, and I knew better than to push him.

'Mrs McKenzie thinks she knows what I'm doing up here. She doesn't. I'd be grateful if you didn't mention I gave you a lift up. Let's not make our connection known to anyone if we can.'

'Yes, Uncle Cole,' I said. He'd finished with my hair, and I turned and gave him a cheeky grin. I wanted to see how much I could get away with. Whatever our connection, it felt different to the one at the farmhouse. But then we were both out in the field, even if we weren't working together.

He flicked me under the chin with a careless finger. 'Mrs McKenzie won't say anything, and don't you.'

I nodded. My throat had gone dry, and my words stuck in my throat. That careless gesture of his made me feel as if a man-eating tiger had given me a lick. Was it being friendly or washing its dinner?

'Walk on this way for a quarter of a mile, take the first turning on the right, and you'll see the guard post.'

He climbed back on the motorbike, gave me a mock salute and roared off. I was seeing a very different side to Instructor Cole and I rather liked it.

Cole's directions were precise. I found the checkpoint easily enough and handed over my pass to a very bored-looking young man in his little box. There was a bar across the road, but either side of the road were hedgerow and fields. It wouldn't be that difficult to bypass it.

The boy looked at my pass and looked at me. Then he did the same again. By now I was hot, tired and in dire need of a cup of tea. I'd also been racking my brains to explain how I had got here and how I was going to get back to the billet.

'Where'd you come from?' asked the man-child suddenly.

'London,' I said without thinking. 'Before that Norfolk. Why?'

'You ain't got no luggage.'

'I left it at The Manse, my billet. I'm afraid I'm already late. If you could—?'

'Nah,' said the boy. 'Don't be in such a rush. There's nothing up the hill that's going anywhere for a while. Who did you say you were seeing?'

'I didn't. I'm to report to the wing commander.'

'What's his name?'

'I can't remember. Burton? Something like that.' I could feel my temper rising. I spied a field telephone in the box. 'Perhaps you could get on the telephone and confirm that I'm due? I have a valid pass, ID and I am in uniform.'

He took a step back at that. 'How did you know I had a telephone? No one knows I have a telephone.' He placed a hand inside the box and on his rifle.

'I can see it,' I said as calmly as I could.

He wrapped his hand around his rifle and dragged it back with him into the box. 'You stay there,' he said. He picked up the receiver and called through. Once he was on the line I was disappointed to see him raise the rifle in my direction.

I doubted he was much of a shot and that by dropping to the ground I could avoid the worst of it, but I didn't want to be shot by someone this stupid. I didn't want to be shot at all, but being shot by this country bumpkin would be a severe embarrassment. Then I heard him say as he raised his voice, 'She appeared out of nowhere, I'm telling you. Says she's a lieutenant. She's a German spy, no doubt about it. Even her hair is messed up. Like she came down out of a plane.'

Clearly Cole hadn't done as good a job as I'd thought. I considered protesting, but on the off-chance he'd taken the safety off his gun I decided to stay silent. Presumably the people he worked with knew what he was like. Unless, of course, they were all like him. There had to be no way that Fitzroy would send me to deal with that kind of a problem.

I shook my head to clear it of ridiculous thoughts. The gun twitched. I went back to being motionless. I could hear a faint murmur at the other end of the telephone line. Finally, the telephone call ended.

'They're sending someone to bring you in,' said my guard. 'I'm to watch you till then, so no funny stuff.'

'I'll stand here,' I promised.

'No, stand there. You might want to stand over there for a reason.'

I moved to where he indicated with a waggle of the gun. He frowned, and I could see him double-guessing himself. Fortunately I could also hear the roar of a Land Rover. It came into view, dust flying from its wheels as it squealed to a halt less than a yard from the box. The driver, a squadron leader, who had to be not much older than me, jumped down in a manner that suggested he wished the height was higher. As it was, he did it with a certain amount of panache, flinging open the door, with its open window and using it as a springboard as he pushed out with one hand. He was dark haired with a thin black moustache that reminded me of a London spiv. He had a cocksure air about him that suggested a mischievous nature.

'Jamie not shot you yet?'

The guard turned quickly on his heel and saluted the senior officer, and in so doing dropped the gun. As it hit the ground, a sudden bang showed that, as I had feared, Jamie did not believe in having the safety on. Fortunately the bullet lodged in a tree.

'Good God, man! Remember the bloody safety!' said the squadron leader. 'Or I'll see your access to ammo is removed.' Jamie scurried to pick up his gun. The squadron leader walked over to me. I saluted.

'Lieutenant Hope Stapleford, sir,' I said. 'The new community liaison officer.'

'I know,' he said. 'Cadet Stewart said he met you off the cattle train. We were wondering if you'd got lost.' He returned my salute. 'Squadron Leader Hamish Abercrombie. Bit of a mouthful, I know. We'd normally have you walk up to the old HQ, more a shed really, but the commander didn't want Jamie to shoot you.

174

Luckily this time only a tree seems to have been a casualty.' He gestured towards the car and we walked over to it. I got into the passenger side.

'Does Jamie often shoot people?'

'Oh, not really. I mean, the vicar had a nice big Bible that stopped most of the damage. Bit of a flesh wound. But if a man of God can't forgive you, who can?'

'I see.'

Abercrombie laughed. 'No, you don't. You're wondering why he wasn't pulled from duty. Part of it is he's a local man, and we don't need relations with the locals to get any worse. Then, there's quite a few of the men who get jittery out on their own. Jamie Spey doesn't have the imagination for that. Helps keep the rumours at bay.'

'I'm afraid I'm not following you,' I said. 'Why is the relationship with the local people bad? What rumours?'

'Don't tell me they sent you into this without explaining the situation?'

I shrugged. 'I wouldn't ask if I knew anything, sir.'

Abercrombie raised his eyebrows. 'I hope you're good at what you do, because this place has a lot of problems.'

We'd driven up the track and I could see the hangars and the airstrip ahead. A number of planes were out on the field. The base seemed to be a rattle–gaggle assortment of prefab buildings. All the buildings were painted green, and around the airfield lay open fields that ended in a treeline on two sides, and in a copse on the other. The land looked more suitable for a cricket field than an airbase.

We were now well into mid-morning, and the day was both brighter and warmer than I had expected. The land here was on a rise, and as Abercrombie pulled up sharply outside one outbuilding, I had a view over the countryside that between the mountains seemed to stretch for ever. I got out of the car and got a whiff of clean air. I never noticed how dirty the air in London was until I left.

Abercrombie bounded out of his side, like a Labrador let off the leash. 'I suppose I should at least give you a hint before you see the old man,' he said. 'We, my dear Lieutenant, are an airbase that is bewitched. We have gnomes in our hangars, and imps in our kitchens. The locals hate us because they believe we have disturbed a faery mound or some such thing, and loosed the malicious and mischievous fey on the general locale. Your job as community liaison is to put these faeries back where they came from.'

Chapter Twenty-four

Away With the Faeries

Abercrombie set a smart pace towards the nearest prefab. I followed, looking around me as I went. As far as I could see it looked like a normal, if hastily erected, airbase. I certainly didn't see the remotest sign of anything arcane. But would I know it if I saw it? I was still unsure if I was being teased by Abercrombie. He struck me as that kind of man. If they had village dances I was sure he would be popular. Playful and dangerous is how I rated him. Not dangerous to me, of course. From what Fitzroy had told me, the fly boys did next to no hand-to-hand training. After all, that wasn't much use mid-air. However, as we passed the fighter planes currently out, I reflected that a good pilot probably did live life fast on the ground. From flying with Fitzroy I had learned the exhilaration (and frequently, terror) of being up in the air. But to be engaged in a dogfight with another pilot where only one of you would survive, and the other in all likelihood would die or be burned alive; to know every time you went up the odds of you coming down safely decreased, then yes, I thought you were not only astoundingly courageous, but would also attempt to live life at top speed. The wing commander must have his hands full with his cadre of pilots. I didn't envy him.

I stopped mid-stride. 'Come on, Stapleford. No time for dawdling,' said Abercrombie, although his light tone made this less of a reprimand.

'What's that over there?' I pointed at a fenced-off area by one treeline. It looked like a prime place for a runway. Very even. In fact, through the fences I was sure I saw what looked like the glint of tar rather than grass.

'Oh that,' said Abercrombie, 'that's not something we talk about.' He kept his tone light, but there was a rigidness around his mouth that belied his levity. 'And I was being serious about hurrying up. The old man's having luncheon with his wife today, and we'll all have hell to pay if he isn't ready for her in time.'

When we reached the prefab, Abercrombie went straight in. A pretty secretary with red curls and blue eyes smiled up at him. 'You're expected, Squadron Leader. Go right in.'

Her voice was professional, but the look on her face was of blatant adoration. She was younger than both of us, and had an ivory skin and a sense of innocence about her. Which meant, in my experience, either she took the local Sunday school or was a hell-cat when off duty.

'Thanks, Sue,' said Abercrombie and he winked at her. Being a redhead, the poor girl turned crimson. Sunday school teacher, I thought.

The squadron leader tapped on a nearby door and walked in on the echo. He stopped in front of a worn desk that looked like it had been an old schoolteacher's desk and saluted smartly. I did the same.

The man behind the desk didn't rise, but he returned our salute. He was middle-aged, grey-haired, and older than I had expected. His face showed signs of the sag and flab of the well-fed middle class he surely belonged to.

'So this is our missing lady? Well done for retrieving her, Abercrombie. Dismissed. Come in and sit down, Miss Stapleford.'

Abercrombie gave me a sly wink as he left. I didn't blush.

'So, Miss Stapleford. You've come to jolly things up around here as I understand it. Put us all into the way of being friends again. Not entirely sure why they sent you. My wife's been doing the old memsahib bit, and she's jolly good at it. Grew up around here myself. They're a curmudgeonly lot, but hard working. But there's a lot of coming and going on the base. Obviously led to a touch of pilfering. Can't expect my wife to involve herself with criminals, so I'm afraid that's down to you. Not too hopeful myself. Still, try your best. It's a nice country up here, and while we do send our boys out from time to time, so far we've not had to do more than see Jerry off. No bombings in this area. Pretty safe. We finish off teaching boys how to fly, and we go into action more than enough, but our civilians are in no danger. So that's about it. Ask my secretary, Susan, to show you about a bit. Young girls like to have fun, but she's a level-headed little thing.' He stood up. 'So that's the low-down on the situation. I'm sure you're eager to get off and look around.' He held out his hand. 'We don't ask civilians to salute.'

I didn't get up. 'With respect, sir, I'm not a civilian.'

He stayed standing. 'A cadet? I suppose we need all hands to the wheel.'

'I'm a lieutenant, sir. This isn't my first assignment.' I wanted to say quite a bit more about my capabilities. I recognised that was my ego pushing. The wing commander, who hadn't even bothered to give me his name, had put my hackles up. He was a bombastic, patronising chauvinist. But working with Fitzroy it was easy to forget that most men were. However, I calmed my temper enough to realise it might be worth it to get everyone underrating me.

'I'm Army, sir,' I said. 'Seconded to you for the present. From my orders I understood there was such a significant degree of unrest here that London felt you needed help.' I left the words *that you couldn't manage* floating in the ether.

He finally sat down. It might be more accurate to say it was a controlled crumple. 'How extraordinary. I suppose London command know what they are doing,' he said. I didn't answer. 'Well, I suppose, to be fair, things have been a little frosty with the locals . . . There's been a couple of incidents.' He waved his left hand as if batting a fly away. 'All in the past now. Left a bit of a sour taste, I expect. But keep going forward, only thing to do. Margaret, my wife, is well in with the WI, and I've always said control the wives and girlfriends and you've got the community. She's doing a grand job. Everyone loves her.'

'I appreciate that you don't want to open old wounds, sir, but—'

'Exactly. Exactly. Knew you'd understand. Smart girl.'

'I do think—' I tried again.

'It's the pilfering that really troubles me. Tools mainly. A wrench here. A hammer there. Fortunately we keep a tight control on any ordinance, but all the same, to think that one of our lot is stealing from an airbase in time of war . . . I mean, that's not on. It's treason. If it's a serviceman I'll probably have to shoot the blighter, and if it's a civilian he'll be sent off for trial, but might still get the same fate. Very nasty business. And for what? For things you could get at an ironmonger's for less than one pound sterling. All I can think is it is malicious. The ground boys, the mechanics say, it's always the tool they need the most that's missing. It's messing up operational times. So far we've always been able to get in the air when we've been needed, but we've cut it close.'

'Do you fly, sir?'

'Me, goodness no! Used to in the last bash, but not now. Oh, you mean how am I wing commander when I don't go up? Well, I was a flyer and I did lead chaps up. Now, it's all different. I hear they're talking about creating a "Wing", that being a chap that commands three squadrons. But anyway, chaps here call me by my rank from the last war. HQ do the same. I've never queried it. But I can see how it might be confusing to a newcomer.'

'So it's Squadron Leader Abercrombie that takes the lead in the air?'

'Exactly. Damned fine pilot. Ever fancy going up, he's the man for you. Might help you understand our perspective.'

'My godfather flies,' I said. 'I've been up with him a few times.'

'Goodness, unusual. Good pilot, is he?'

'Terrible,' I said. 'But he always says any landing you walk away from is a good one.'

The wing commander roared with laughter. 'Sounds like a card. I expect I'd like him.'

'Most people do,' I said, smiling. While he was in a brighter mood I chanced my hand. 'On the way here – well, is the squadron leader a bit of a joker, sir?'

Immediately I saw his shoulders stiffen. 'He can be. Especially where there's a pretty girl involved.' He gave a rather forced laugh that sounded like a crow coughing.

'Only he said that the local people thought that the airbase had caused some kind of disturbance. Unearthed something? I couldn't quite follow.'

The wing commander wilted under my gaze. 'Those bloody faeries!'

'Faeries? Did I hear you right, sir?'

'Of course there are no bleedin' faeries on site,' he said. 'It's local superstition and ruddy Brian McKenzie and his wittering. I'm sorry for my language, Lieutenant, but you're going to hear far worse from the boys if you're around when they come back from an op.'

'People do seem to set a value on Brian McKenzie. They seem to think he has some fortune-telling ability, isn't it? Mrs McKenzie at The Manse said he helped people find lost things. She never said anything about faeries.'

'Brian McKenzie is a brave man who fought in the last war and came back with his brains addled from what he'd seen. A lot of chaps did. Poor buggers. But as far as I'm concerned neither before nor after the war has he possessed any supernatural abilities.'

'So what do the locals think?'

The wing commander sighed. He seemed to have aged ten years since our conversation started. 'They think the airbase was put on the site of a faery knoll or some such thing. There's a local legend. I knew it as a boy growing up here, but I never paid it any mind. People round here are used to getting food from the hedgerows, but even my own mother wouldn't pick the mushrooms that grew up on these fields. Always left as wild grazing. Which is why the RAF moved in on them. Least local disturbance.'

I made a jump of logic. 'Does this mean things are also happening in the local villages?'

'Oh, every jug of milk that turns sour is our fault,' said the wing commander bitterly. 'Every dog bite due to a faery poking it with a pin in the backside.'

'Oh dear,' I said. 'That is awkward.'

'Oh, I could put up with that if it wasn't for the fact that flyers are so damn superstitious.'

'You're afraid it's going to affect their flying?'

'Their chances of survival, to be blunt.' He checked his watch. 'Look, it doesn't matter what I think, it's what the chaps on the base think.'

'I've only met the guard and—'

'Oh, Jamie Spey, more sense in a bowl of fruit, but sounds like Abercrombie's already told you a lot. Spey's the only one who doesn't mind being out at the guard point on his own. No sense. No imagination. Right, I think that's all I've got for you for now. Base is open to you. Abercrombie can either point things out to you, or hand you over to someone who can help if he's busy. Susan can help out with any files you need to see. How about we reconvene in a week? Nine hundred hours? You might have had it all sorted by then.' He checked his watch again and frowned.

The intercom on his desk buzzed. A female voice I recognised as the receptionist said quietly, 'Incoming! Incoming!'

Chapter Twenty-five

Meeting the Men

Immediately I looked out of the window expecting to see enemy planes. The wing commander had gone white at the hissed announcement. All I saw were the calm blue skies. I looked back at the wing commander. He was fiddling with one of his cuffs. The next moment the door opened and a middle-aged woman, clutching a large handbag, with neatly curled hair and a taut smile on her face marched into the room. She stopped as if pole-axed a few inches from me. Clearly she had set course for the wing commander and only just managed to pull up short when she saw me. Her face realigned itself into the rigid disapproval of a vicar who has found a burlesque act being conducted in his crypt.

'Ah, Margaret. This is Hope Stapleford. Lieutenant. New community officer I mentioned,' said the wing commander. His tone lacked the dismissive authority he had used with me. I realised I was seeing the reason for his wariness of women.

I reached out a hand. 'Delighted to meet you, ma'am,' I said. 'I understand you have done a great deal of good work with the community.'

She ignored me. 'Don't be silly, Edwin. There is no such rank as lieutenant in the RAF. Unless she's supposed to be a flight lieutenant. Someone is having you on. Really, you are so gullible! Next thing they will have us dancing round a circle of mush-rooms to appease the faeries.' She turned her attention to me. She had the steely grey eyes of a warrior set in a face filled out with cake and cream puffs. 'Run along now, dear. You've had your fun. Tell Abercrombie I will have words with him.'

I didn't move. She pursed her lips. As she took a breath I spoke up. 'I'm Army, ma'am. Seconded here to help with your local issues.' I kept my tone polite, but steady. Behind his desk I swear the wing commander stifled a nervous giggle.

'Then you'll have papers to prove your identity.'

'Indeed, ma'am.'

She waited for me to produce them. I didn't. She held out her hand.

'I'm not at liberty to show my documentation to a civilian, ma'am,' I said.

'Don't be ridiculous! I'm the wing commander's wife!'

'I'm aware of that, ma'am. You have no jurisdiction over me. I would be grateful to have your input over the community issues, but I am not working for you. In fact, technically, I'm not even working for your husband.'

'Not even working for . . . Edwin! Say something!' From the frustration in her voice I gathered that referring to her husband was a last resort.

'She's absolutely in the right of it, Maggie. Sorry.'

'It was stupid of me to think there was any point to us talking,' said Margaret and slammed out of the room.

The wing commander, who still hadn't stood up, sighed. 'Bit of a matrimonial tiff going,' he said. 'We spent some time in India, you know. Wives have much more power there. She's not adjusted well. And then with everything else . . . Had some bad times. Not a happy woman, my wife. Worst of it she means well. Terribly keen on community relationship and looking after the boys. Storms around like a rhino, but has a soft heart.'

I wondered how far his wilful self-deception went, but all I said was, 'I'll be respectful, sir, but I can't give her access—'

'No. No. Of course you can't. Don't do it myself. Hence the strife. I think a lot of people avoid her. Pity, she was quite a

184

heroine over . . . well, never mind that. I'd better go after her. Till death us do part and all that.'

'I'll get started, sir,' I said, and saluted him. I left him at his desk still fiddling with his cufflinks.

I walked around the base again to get a feel of the place. I saw men on duty lounging on deckchairs by their planes in case they were called. I found the mess hall. At least, I smelt the chipped potatoes, and heard the voices. It reminded me that it was almost luncheon time. I passed by the hangars, and saw the various pilots and mechanics going about their business. Overall, the place impressed me as well run. Occasionally there was a shout of amusement from the on-duty pilots, and the mess hall seemed full and riotous in an acceptable way. Morale was not an obvious problem, except with the wing commander.

I caught the smell of gravy. My stomach muttered beneath my skirt. It didn't seem likely the unhappy couple would have gone there for luncheon. If I had to, I could always sit with the cadets. I opened the door and was hit in the face by a warm fug of cooking smells and cigarette smoke.

Smoking always catches me by surprise. Bernie smokes, but no one else I know does. The idea that people smoke over food makes me slightly nauseous. I think about all that ash and the component aerial parts falling into what I'm eating. I am aware I am unusual in this.

I walked up to the serving counter. For all I knew there was also an officers' mess, but I could already hear Abercrombie's voice telling some ridiculous tale.

'Hello, hen. What can I get you?'

The middle-aged woman, white hairnet, scarlet lipstick, but thankfully with no cigarette, hovered a ladle over a couple of trays. 'Haggis, neeps and tatties; steak and kidney pie – no' so heavy on the steak if I'm an honest woman, which I am – and standard cottage pie?'

185

'Cottage pie, please,' I said.

'With chips?'

'Oh yes,' I said. 'That would be great.'

The woman gave me a big grin and piled up a plate. 'Good to see a lassie that likes her food. That Susan, I'm lucky if I get her to eat a thimbleful of peas. So concerned about her figure. A man likes a woman with some meat on her bones, I say. Something that won't feel all sharp and bony when he gives her a cuddle.'

I smiled. 'I don't think I'm made to be that thin,' I said.

'Och, hen. You are as the good Lord made you, and that's good enough. Condiments on the table. And watch out for that Mr Abercrombie, he's after all the girls.'

'I'm the new community liaison officer,' I said. 'So I'm probably safe.'

'Oh, are you, hen? That's nice. Tell you something, it would be lovely to have another fete. The WI used to be so good at them. I won prizes for my custard. Course it all stopped after the stushie about—'

'Hey, Morag, some of us are dying of hunger back here.'

I looked over my shoulder and saw that a line had formed. Near the end of it stood Harvey, my erstwhile ex-con asset and fellow auxie. My stomach felt like it jumped up and lightly punched my brain. But I managed to keep my face poker straight. 'I'd better move,' I said. 'I'll catch you later?'

'Aye, on you go. Come on then, boys. I've got three trays of spotted dick for those that want.' There was a chorus of ribald laughter.

I picked up some cutlery from a basket and surveyed the room. I saw a group of men stand up at Abercrombie's table, leaving him alone. I went over. 'Can I join you?' I asked him.

'Of course,' he said, leaning back in his chair. On his plate was the remainder of the steak and kidney pudding. It didn't look as if he'd eaten a lot.

'Not up to your usual standard?' I asked.

'Ssh, Morag's a fiery woman. No, I don't have much of an appetite in general. It's why I have such a trim figure.' He ran his hand down over his flat stomach. 'No paunch lets me get the ladies closer.' He held out his arms as if he was dancing for a moment.

I picked out a long green blade of something. Abercrombie slid forward in his chair, took it off me and popped it in his mouth. 'Wild garlic,' he said. 'You're among country people now. They're always picking something off the hedgerows to put in the food.'

'You are very outspoken when you're off duty, aren't you?' I said.

'Unless it's about the food or the wing commander.'

'Seems about right.'

He propped his elbows on the table and considered me closely. 'Have you worked on an airbase before, Lieutenant?'

I shook my head.

'From what I can gather, I'm far too young to have been there, but in the Great War just before they went over the top, they'd be laughing and joking, and in high spirits until the last hour or so, when things would go solemn. Flyers tend to lark around on the ground. It's the same kind of thing. Frivolity and japes until we're up in the air. We get cut a lot of slack as most of us don't last long. I'm overdue by three weeks.'

'Overdue?'

'Being dead.'

'Does that mean the men see you as lucky?'

He nodded.

'I've been told you're a superstitious lot,' I said.

'So he told you about the faeries.'

'Eventually,' I said.

'You must be better than you look. I heard you met Mrs Wing Co too. Made quite an impression. Maybe I should teach you to fly. We need pilots with confidence and aggression.'

'It's a shame you don't mean that,' I said. 'I'd like to learn to fly. I've been up in a small plane a few times. With a relative, who must be one of the worst living pilots. He's not in the R.A.F.'

'Really? And what did you think about being up among the clouds?'

'I liked it. Different perspective. Quiet, too, when I wasn't convinced we were going to crash. Wonderfully calm and quiet.'

'I'm impressed. Fighting this war in the air flips between enjoying an angel's view of the world and fighting for your life. It's a contrast of opposites. If I was more inclined to believe in the best of humanity, I would have said anyone who experiences the peace up in the clouds would seek to emulate it on the ground. Only Jerry doesn't seem to feel like that at all.'

'Can you ever see the pilot's face?'

'In a dogfight? Often,' said Abercrombie. 'They're not much different to us. Most of them are boys barely out of school. Some of them look fierce and you can see them mouthing curses. The worst are the ones that look panicked or are crying. Always takes me a couple of drinks to get over those when I come down. I'm long in the tooth by most standards. Can feel like killing children.' He looked down soberly at his plate. The other diners were making enough noise to drown our conversation out.

'Our bombers will be doing exactly that. Mothers, children and old people in German towns.'

'Not the kind of talk to be encouraged, Lieutenant.'

'Between you and me, sir,' I said. 'Letting you know even if I'm not doing the shooting, I do think about what we ask our people to do. It's part of my role.'

'Wait until you end someone else's life.'

'I have,' I said. 'It changes you.'

'What the hell kind of community liaison do you usually do, Stapleford?'

I'd said too much. I laughed. 'I did say I was seconded,' I said, trying to cover my tracks. 'Will you take me up?'

'I might.'

'What happened here? I mean, I look around and everything looks fine. People keep talking about stushies and incidents, but they don't ever seem to want to get into specifics.'

'If you ask me—'

'And I am,' I said.

'Behind all the fuss there's some serious things happening. When Collins went down, it was a tragedy, but these things happen. Only with all the thefts and other malarkey people start wondering if there's anti-government agents around. Enemy agents parachuted in. All nonsense, of course. It's stress, all of it. Waking up every day wondering if this is to be your last takes it out of people.' He gave a sigh. 'Look, I'm expecting we'll be going up tonight. There's news some of Jerry's lot will be flying out of Norway, and we might need to edge them offshore. Can't have them dropping uninvited visitors, can we? Anyway, my thoughts are everywhere. Talk to me when I come back. I'm always more grounded when I've come off a mission.' He gave me a cheeky grin. 'Sometimes literally.'

He excused himself and left. Out of the corner of my eye I saw Harvey get up. He caught my gaze. I waited until he was near the door then I got up myself. I hadn't eaten all my chips, but talking to Harvey had to be more important than chips. With a last regretful glance at my plate, I followed him out.

Chapter Twenty-six

Harvey

Harvey strolled ahead of me, heading towards the hangar where they worked on the airplanes. At the last minute he swerved aside and took a narrow track that wound down along the treeline. When I caught up with him, he was leaning against a tree and smoking a cigarette.

'I didn't know you smoked,' I said.

'It's nice to see you too, Hope. How's tricks?'

'Considering I work for my godfather, as tricksy as ever,' I said. 'What have you got to tell me?'

'You mean other than him towing me out of the nick again and giving me a severe bollocking? He's a mean one when he tries.' He placed a hand melodramatically over his heart. 'His words cut me to the quick. He said—'

I cut him off. 'Oh, Harvey, that's twice he's cleared your slate.'

'Yeah, well, you try providing for your old pa and your hundred and one siblings on what I could make as an honest man.'

'I thought you'd got them apprenticeships – and not a hundred at all.'

'I've four siblings, and none of them are earning enough to support themselves. Then there's Pa. Veteran of the last war, bloody hero. You should see his medals. But his army pension barely pays his rent.' He looked me up and down. 'You ain't got no bloody idea what that's like. And Charlie, he's sixteen, he keeps trying to sign up, pretending he's older. Do my head in, the

190

lot of them. And now, I'm stuck up in bloody Scotland with no way of reaching them.'

'Fitzroy has a reputation for taking care of his people,' I said. 'He'll see they're all right. In his own way.'

'Yeah, right, muttered something about getting Pa down on his country estate like it was all some ruddy joke.'

'Well, he does have at least one,' I said. 'He's rather rich.'

This did not go down in the way I had hoped. Harvey grew more and more angry, and ranted for a while. He sounded a lot like Leo. I didn't interrupt. Partly because I thought he had a point, and partly because he didn't want me to put him right, or persuade him that everything would be all right. He clearly needed to let off steam. When he took more than a breath, I broke in. 'Is it very stressful working on the planes?'

Harvey ground out his cigarette under his heel. 'It's just like you to see through me,' he said. 'I mean, everything's true, but yeah, getting the planes ready for those men to fly them is a big responsibility. Your man, Fitzroy, sent me on a short course, and apparently I showed up here, knowing more than most of them they get sent, which is terrifying. Those poor blokes are risking their necks against Jerry, let alone defying the laws of bloody gravity, the least they should be able to rely on is their ground crew.'

'Are they not up to par?'

'Nah,' he said, taking another cigarette from a packet and lighting it. 'They're a good lot. I've always got someone senior checking my work, and I check a junior's. But the fact I'm already above some of the lads shows you how much training we're getting. Still a hell of a lot more than those pilots.' He sighed. 'No big hiccups yet, but before I got here something happened. I don't know much because they don't talk about it. Some of them were even transferred out because of the bad feelings. But it's to do with that fenced-off bit of tarmac.'

'Yes, I'm curious about that.'

'Yeah, well, that's for later. You need to find out what's scoring holes in these planes while they're in the air. What's stealing the very wrench you need practically out of your hands. I'm not superstitious, but there's something wrong and creepy about this place.'

He dropped the half-smoked cigarette. 'You're looking all right, Hope. Not at your brightest, but better than Bernie when I last saw her. Have you heard anything from the girl?'

I shook my head. 'When I was in London, I rang, wrote, and even turned up on the doorstep.'

'Her bloody husband. I don't like it one bit. I don't trust the blighter.'

'Neither do I, Harvey, but she chose this. We have to respect her choice.'

'Do we?' said Harvey. He ground his cigarette out. 'I need to get back. How we going to work this?'

'I've only just got on the ground,' I said. 'Any chance I could meet you up at the hangar later tonight and see what you're talking about?'

'Not tonight, but tomorrow night – there's a dance at the village hall. Say twenty-three hundred hours? Here. If it's clear I'll bring you in.'

I nodded. He strode off. I waited for a while then made my way back to the base.

I was going to need a flashlight. Preferably a covert one. Next time I'd put one in my grab bag. I had lock pics, but aside from the ammo, which I hoped would be decently protected, a pair of scissors would get me into any of the buildings.

I fancied chatting with more of the pilots, but I suspected that joining in with the boys waiting for the call without a specific invitation was not the thing to do. I guessed that they spent their time before a mission convincing each other they weren't afraid. Sometimes to become a thing, you have to act as if you are that thing already.

I resolved on returning to The Manse and taking the afternoon to think through what I had learned, and to work out who

I needed to talk to. It might look suspiciously as if I was having a nap, but then until I could come up with some kind of code to use that no one else could read, I wouldn't be able to make notes.

I dropped in to see Susan and ask her how I might get a lift back.

She checked her watch. 'You've just missed one lot going back. There's a turn-about at fourteen thirty, and you can catch a lift easily then.'

'When's the next change?' I asked.

Susan pulled a face. 'Twenty hundred,' she said.

'Damn,' I said. 'I'm guessing that there's no getting my own vehicle while I'm here, is there? I can drive a car.'

She laughed. 'No way there's a spare car going.'

I must have looked especially crestfallen.

'Gosh, you do look a bit ragged. I have an idea. Hang on a mo.'

She picked up her telephone and put a local call through. 'Hello, Mike. It's Susan. Have you done the post pickup today?'

She listened at length. She rolled her eyes at me, and held the phone out from her ear. Eventually when the voice on the other end died down she said, 'Mike, I know you work harder than a donkey with eight legs. I've got the new community liaison officer here. She's been up since the crack of dawn and needs a lift back to The Manse. I thought you might be able to help her out and get a moment away from the base. Things should be easing a bit, shouldn't they, with the dance tomorrow night?'

The voice went off again. Susan held the telephone away again and waited. When the volume of the speaker had diminished she put it against her ear again.

'Yes . . . Yes . . . I am going . . . I might . . . See you in ten?'

She put the receiver down. 'You'd better be coming to the dance tomorrow night. I'm going to need your help with Mike. He's fine when he's sober, but when he isn't you need to beat him off with a stick.'

'You owe him a favour now on my account?'

Susan wrinkled her nose. 'Not exactly. He often leaves picking up the mail, and as my grandfather keeps saying, it's the mail from home that keeps morale up. I mean, a number of the men here are local, but most of our pilots aren't – and they're the ones who need keeping cheerful, poor sods.'

'I'll certainly come and help you beat back Mike,' I said. 'I'm grateful. Besides, going to the dance will count as working for me.'

'If you were anywhere else I'd say you have a grand job,' said Susan. 'But heaven help you with this community. Granny says she's not speaking to Granddad, but she gave him a lot of words.'

'About what?' I asked as casually as I could.

'I don't listen,' said Susan. 'I let it all wash over me. I don't want to take sides.'

'Very wise,' I said.

The door opened and a young man in overalls came in. Despite his attire he looked as if he had just walked off a film set. He must have been one of the most handsome men I had ever seen. Dark, tall, lantern-jawed and with a set expression most girls would take for enigma or maturity, but I saw as barely concealed petulance. Most lovely-looking people don't have good manners. They don't need them.

'You the one needing a ride?' he said, ignoring Susan.

'I'm Lieutenant Stapleford, yes.'

Immediately his manner changed and he saluted me. 'Sorry, ma'am. Army, are you?'

I nodded. 'Seconded for a while. I would be very grateful for a lift back to The Manse. I will have to look into arranging transport of my own, but I understand that's far from easy.'

''Fraid so, ma'am. I'm the quartermaster, and I can tell you to a drop how much petrol we have on site. It isn't enough. Even if we had an extra vehicle.'

I thought of Fitzroy blithely driving around the country as if petrol came down with the rain. All I could think was, some people must owe him some very big favours.

Mike had a small army car. He drove steadily and smoothly.

'You were a chauffeur before the war, were you?' I asked.

He jumped slightly. 'Correct, ma'am.'

'You drive very well, and these roads are far from the best I'm sure Scotland has to offer.'

'Be better driving through a riverbed than going along some of them, ma'am. Thank you for the compliment.'

'Do you have information on bikes – motorbikes – at the base?'

'Funny you should ask,' said Mike. 'I was looking into them today. There's a possibility of getting a couple for urgent messages. If you search in the side pocket there you'll find some leaflets.'

I picked them up and looked through them as he drove. I finally came across one on the basics of driving and maintaining. 'Can I take this?' I asked.

'You can borrow it, ma'am. I only have the two.'

'I'll bring it back to you when I come in tomorrow,' I said. 'That suit?'

He nodded. 'You interested in them, ma'am?'

'Well, I can drive a car. However, I suspect that learning to drive something that uses less petrol might be useful. I'm often having to get around various parts of the country. Liaison work and all that.'

'If we get them, ma'am, I'm happy to give you a few hours tuition. If you know about cars then there's not much more you need to know. More practice than anything.'

'That's kind. I'll think about it.'

'And if you happen to know anyone who could put a word in to make sure we get them?'

I shouldn't have, but I laughed. 'I can see you make a good quartermaster,' I said. 'I take it you rode a bike as well as being a chauffeur?'

'Me and engines, ma'am. Can't leave them alone.'

Chapter Twenty-seven

Bernie

The Manse was quiet when I got back. In the hall there was a notice that said, 'Please remove your shoes. People on night duty are trying to sleep.' Underneath was another one that said, 'Keep Mrs McKenzie's carpets clean. Hitler hates a clean carpet.'

I took my shoes off and spotted another notice. 'Eat your spotted dick. No waste, less want.' Someone had written in pencil along the bottom: 'Keep up your sausage intake for the boys.'

I sniggered quietly at that one. Fitzroy would be horrified I understood the double entendre, but then I had shared both college rooms and a flat with Bernie. I might have written some of her essays for her, but when it came to the social side of things she was distinctly more advanced than me. I doubted Mrs McKenzie understood the comment, or maybe she pretended not to. The young men and women under her care were risking their lives and I suspected a bit of high spirits would be overlooked even by our prim landlady. That is, as long as the boys used one stair and the girls the other, as she had decreed. It would be interesting to see how they got around that on dance night. Those pilots who knew they had a short life expectancy might smile and seem content to be treated like schoolboys, but when you knew you might die any day it changed the way you saw rules. Waiting for the right girl, a nice little wedding and two kids asleep upstairs might be what they had once aspired to, but the war had put that in jeopardy for everyone.

Seeing Harvey had made me start asking myself questions about Bernie all over again. The world had been opening up to the kind of permissiveness she had always seemed to hunger after. Why choose this time to tie herself down with an older man, one who Harvey and I thought overly controlling? Or was it simpler than that? Might she have wanted someone strong and commanding to make her feel safe? She'd never been close to her mother, and her father's return to the States had left a big hole in her life. But at least he was still alive.

I took off my outer clothes and hung them up. Then I had a quick sponge wash to get rid of the grime from the train. I lay down on my bed and began to go through the people I'd met and the rumours I'd heard. I tried to match them together, but in the middle of the odd realisation that a bear had wandered into the base I fell fast asleep.

I was awoken by a tap on the door. I quickly pulled on a robe and answered. Mrs McKenzie stood there. There was a telegram in her hand. 'A boy brought this up for you from the post office. I like to get these to people as soon as I can.' I took it from her. 'I hope it's not bad news, dear,' she said. She patted me on the shoulder and turned and walked quickly away. No one wanted to stay near anyone else opening one of these. They almost always meant bad news. It was as if people feared it was contagious.

Slowly I shut the door. I sat down on the edge of my bed and turned the telegram over in my hands. I knew there wouldn't be any clue on the outside, but I couldn't help looking. Eventually I had no option but to open it.

THOUGHT YOU WOULD RATHER HEAR THIS FROM ME THAN READ ABOUT IT STOP BERNIE KILLED IN EXPLOSION STOP WOULD HAVE BEEN INSTANTANEOUS STOP VERY SORRY STOP LOVE FITZROY

The telegram fell from my numb fingers. I looked at it lying on the floor for a long time. Then I lay back on the bed and waited to wake up.

Bernie was gone.

A few months ago, I would have denied the truth of such a missive. Before my father's demise no close death had touched me. Then the long-expected end of my father's life had occurred. Even that I might not have believed, had I not seen him. I had to admit finally that death could reach in and pluck away any of my family. Love did not save lives. I read the telegram again, and registered that Fitzroy had signed it will love. It was most unlike him to ever make such a public declaration. It didn't make things better, but it gave me enough strength to get up off the bed.

I folded up the telegram and tucked it into the mirror. I went along to the bathroom and washed my face. I came back, combed my hair and put on make-up. All the while watching the actions of the figure in the mirror who seemed to exist without any will on my part. I dressed in trousers and a blouse. I tied a heavy jumper across my shoulders. It was blue and went well with my eyes. I looked nice. Some might even think pretty. I looked calm. I looked in control. That was the best I could do.

I checked my watch. I still had time before the dining room opened. I sat looking at myself in the mirror and wondered if I was going to cry. Someone tapped at my door. I didn't answer. I didn't move. I sat there watching myself in the mirror. I only turned when I saw Cole in the reflection.

'Mrs McKenzie doesn't let men on this floor,' I said.

Cole shrugged and sat down on the end of my bed. 'What's she going to do to me?'

'Throw you out.'

'I'd like to see her try,' he said and flashed me his teeth in a cold smile. 'Besides, it was her idea I came to talk to you. She said you had a telegram. Who died, Hope? Not your mother?' His voice went rough with sympathy.

I turned my stool round to face him. I shook my head. 'Bernie.

A friend from college. An asset. Someone I cared about. Blown up. Gone. Like my father. Only he just fell asleep. Didn't wake up. Didn't wait for me. Both gone.' With an effort I stopped my mouth moving. 'Sorry,' I said.

'May I see?'

I passed him the telegram.

'Love Fitzroy? He is worried about you.'

'It's a family thing, I expect. He married my mother.'

I heard a sharp intake of breath from Cole. 'That was quick,' he said in a tone that wasn't quite level.

'They left together after my father's funeral service. Before he was even buried. I had to stay behind and make sure everything ran well at the wake. That the chauffeur drove people home safely in my father's car. Fitzroy took mine. We'd arrived by plane.' I could hear myself chattering on, but it was as if someone else, someone polite and distant, was speaking.

'That would have been an unwelcome excitement,' said Cole.

'I think they – my mother and Fitzroy – were trying to get me there before my father died. This time they failed to achieve their mission.' I looked down. Tears burned hot at the back of my eyes. One drop splashed into my lap.

'It was inevitable those two would marry,' said Cole gently. 'Fitzroy would never leave your mother alone to grieve. He wouldn't have wanted to compromise her reputation any further. He had no choice but to marry her. Besides, I think he'd wanted to do so for a long time. Personally, I would have arranged a speedy exit for my rival, but he respected your father.'

I nodded. 'They had an odd relationship.'

'Yes,' said Cole. 'But now Fitzroy has claimed his title, most things will be forgiven him and his wife.'

'Title? I never knew—'

'No, well, he wasn't meant to inherit. He's a duke.'

'A duke?' I said startled. 'But . . .'

'Attrition. All other male siblings lost to war or illness. Much the same way as your uncle Joe became an earl. The wars have decimated the aristocracy. As usual, everything has come up roses for your godfather.'

'You're bitter.'

'When around Fitzroy, it's hard not to be bitter from time to time. Eventually everything comes to him. He has the luck of the devil.'

'Bernie didn't have much luck. I always thought she did.'

'Don't think about it, Hope. She's gone. Sometimes the brightest ones burn out the quickest. Having friends is a luxury in our profession. That you had one for a while is a blessing. During your career you will see a lot more death. It actually gets easier once those you care for are gone.'

I looked up at that. 'What a horrible thought.'

'But true. Come on. We had better go down and grab some food. Mrs McKenzie still has that cake she made for us.'

'I can't.'

'You don't have a choice, Hope. Consider this a lesson in carrying on. Regard my advice as the orders of a senior officer. I'm doing no more than Fitzroy would do if he were here.'

'No, no, you're not,' I said, as hot tears ran down my face. 'He would be kinder to me. He loves me.'

'Your godfather does – your stepfather might – but your commanding officer would tell you to pull yourself together. Crying is what you do on your own time, not when you're on a mission.'

He was right, of course. So I smothered my tears, wiped my face and followed him downstairs.

200

Chapter Twenty-eight

On the Beach

Somehow I choked down toad-in-the-hole, onion gravy and the potatoes and peas Cole put on my plate. Then Mrs McKenzie gave us each a piece of cake. It tasted odd as she'd used ground nuts mixed with semolina for flour. We thanked her. She told me I was so brave when Cole told her what my telegram said. I answered mechanically, but politely.

'There's something you need to tell me,' he said, when we got away from the landlady. 'Go and fetch that riding jacket I lent you.'

It was getting dark as we roared off along the road. This time Cole went in the opposite direction. After a while I could smell the salt of sea. He stopped beside a rocky outcrop. I got off and took off my helmet. He tied it to the bike, picked up the panniers, and led the way towards a path that descended into the dark. The sky above was velvet black, littered with more stars than you will ever see in a city, and the air from the sea rushed over us smelling of brine and reminding us we were out of the city.

We were at the top of some steps. Cole's covert torch shone a discreet pool of light. Without it we might well have tumbled to our deaths. The steps were uneven, rough cut and old. As we went down they became wet with spray. But I barely noticed. Below us the lacy sea breaking on the sands glowed a faint luminous green.

When we got to the bottom, Cole led the way to a small, sheltered cove, from where we could watch the sea, but not be seen.

He started a pit fire, and produced a blanket that he put around both our shoulders. I looked up to see a star shoot across the sky.

'What's here?' I asked when Cole finally settled beside me.

'Us,' he said. 'Only us.'

'Did you want to talk to me about something?'

'I'd like to know what you learned at the base. Whatever you can share with me. But we're also watching out to see if any U-boats try to make land here.'

'That's what you're doing?'

'Among other things I'm keeping an eye on the coast. I don't think anyone will land or I wouldn't have brought you. But I need to be sure.'

'Is it something the Germans are trying?'

'We expect them to try,' said Cole. 'We're doing our damnedest to see they don't succeed. I know Fitzroy doesn't concern himself much with the Navy, but keeping the sea routes open is vital if Britain is to win the war. We're even taking things over the top now.' The fire had taken hold and threw flickering light across our faces. It gave out little heat, but the smoke rising against the night sky was as thin as a gossamer ribbon. No one would see it. 'The Pole, Hope, across the top. Using ice breakers. It will be hell.'

'Are you going?'

He shook his head. 'I wouldn't be any more use than your competent merchant seaman. But here, I can wait and see if anyone comes ashore from a submarine. Catch them, question them, and kill them without anyone ever knowing I was here.' He smiled, his face cast demon-like in the red flame. 'That's my area of expertise.'

'Why am I here?'

'Tell me how you're coping after the attack. Did you tell Fitzroy about it?'

'No,' I said.

'Have you told him about our training?'

I shook my head. 'I suppose I should have done, but—'

202

'You've got the right instincts,' said Cole, his lips curving in almost a smile. 'Don't ever offer information. Even to those you work with. Now, you've had a hat-trick of horrors – your bereavement, your attack and now your friend. How are you holding up? This is a professional question,' he added as I opened my mouth to say I was fine.

I hesitated for only a moment. This was Cole, who had not only come to my rescue on numerous occasions, but used to work closely with Fitzroy and my mother. He was an old friend. They were no longer in the same section, but Cole had heavily implied they kept in touch. Then I told him about the shadow man. When I'd finished, he nodded.

'That's stress, Hope. It can really mess with your mind.'

'I'm not going mad?'

'With your upbringing, I highly doubt it. Your mind is too strong. It'll pass. Use it to make yourself more observant. Your shadow man won't affect the real world like an actual attacker would. Note the details.' He patted me roughly on the shoulder. 'Now tell me about the airbase here. What have you learned?'

Cole had just warned me about offering information, and yet I did exactly that.

'There are a number of things that feel very wrong,' I said. 'There's the walled-off piece of airstrip no one wants to talk about. The wing commander and his wife are at odds, and somehow in people's minds this seems to sum up the differences between the community and the people on the base. Then the ground crew are finding weird things on returning planes – marks of some kind. I've arranged to see them tomorrow night. There also seems to be pilfering going on, but nothing serious. Then there's everyone's growing superstition. I'm not saying they all believe in faeries, but there's something disturbing them. Something they can't put their finger on.'

Cole grunted. 'Sounds like the start of one of the old witch trials. Old Granny Harris looked at my cow wrong and now it won't give milk.'

I smiled. 'They're not rural bumpkins.'

Cole frowned. 'Two things, Hope. One, everyone becomes a rural bumpkin subject to fear when the lights go out – except for people like you and me. The witch trials came about because ordinary people were scared. Don't minimise how primitive humans can become when they feel their sense of safety is failing. War knocks aside the rule of law and order. It shows us what we truly are, and for most that is a terrifying thing. Most people believe in order. They can't comprehend that civilisation is only the thinnest of veils over the chaos that is everything. You and I know the limits of our control. They are small. Few can face that. Look into the void, if you like. Assassins like us are different.'

I didn't think of myself as an assassin, but Cole had been too good to me for me to quarrel over labels. Essentially, I felt we saw things the same. 'What would you suggest I do?'

'Are you here to fix things or merely to observe?'

'As usual I don't have any standing orders,' I said bitterly.

'That means that Fitzroy trusts you to establish what needs to be done and to do it. Whether that be taking it upon yourself or calling for backup.'

'I can call for backup?'

'You can always call for backup. Even I have called for backup once or twice.'

'Even you?' I said with a grin.

He was about to say something, when there was a sound from the direction of the sea. It was no more than a soft splash. Cole put his finger to his lips and opened one of his bags. He took out and began to assemble his sniper rifle. He did it quickly, and without looking at his hands. He barely made a sound. Then he rolled onto his front and positioned the rifle so he could see out of the cove. He beckoned me over. I copied his position. He handed me the rifle, so I could look through the scope. He moved above me, his hands still in contact with the gun.

Automatically, I put my finger close to the trigger. I looked through the scope and there, slogging his way out of the water, was a figure, weighed down by a heavy wetsuit and carrying a pack on his back. Cole's head came down next to mine. 'That's not one of ours,' he said. 'Take the shot.'

'What?' I said, starting with the shock, but Cole pressed down on my back.

'I said take the shot. He's not ours.'

'But—'

'Look through the scope and breathe like I taught you.'

I looked through the scope hoping more than anything that I would see some kind of British insignia on the person in my sights. Nothing. Cole's hand wrapped over mine on the gun.

'Inhale. Breathe partly out. Hold your breath. Squeeze the trigger.'

I did the first part of what he told me without thinking. But it was his fingers over mine that squeezed the trigger. The rifle fired. The shot echoed in the silence, like a sharp hiss. Nothing more. Sniper rifles don't make loud noises. They were less powerful than many other guns. You had to be precise.

The man stayed upright for a moment, before swaying and then falling. As he collapsed onto the sand I saw the hole in the centre of his forehead.

'Good shot,' said Cole.

'It was both of us,' I said. I felt numb. I had had few reasons to kill, and all the times I had it had been in self defence. My enemy had fought me hand to hand. This was the first time I'd killed at a distance.

'Can you disassemble this?'

I nodded. Mechanically I began to disassemble the gun. Cole had taught me to do it blindfolded. This meant I could watch him run towards the body. My eyes were well adjusted to the night now and with the light from the moon and stars, I saw him bend over the man. Without the scope I couldn't see exactly what he was doing. I heard the sound of stone hitting stone and decided I didn't want to see this. I turned my attention back to the rifle and packed it away. I was nowhere near as fast as he was. Besides, my hands had started to shake. I'd felt nothing when I saw the man fall. It had been so unlike any fight I'd ever been in. So far away. But gradually the realisation that I had shot a man was beginning to register with me. I struggled to close the case and I had barely finished before Cole returned.

He came back into the little cove and sat down. He had the intruder's bag in one hand. Both his gloves were covered in blood. He stripped them off and threw them in the fire. They caught light easily. There was an odd smell as the material burned, coupled with a faint whiff that reminded me of steak cooking. Bile came up in my throat, but I managed to swallow it.

Cole rolled the bag in the sand to remove any traces.

'The body?' I asked.

'I've put it where it will be hidden until the tide turns. It will go out to sea again. I removed the wetsuit, and filled it with stones to make it sink. The man had no papers on him. I had to obscure your handiwork, I'm afraid.'

I went cold as I realised what the sound was. 'You bludgeoned his head in with a rock?'

'I needed to get the bullet out.' He pulled it from his pocket, a squashed, flat piece of lead. It looked like nothing, and yet it had taken a man's life. He must have washed it in the sea. 'Want it as a memento?'

'Yes,' I said and took it from him. I put it in my pocket. I had to face what I'd done. At this moment I wanted to pretend it was a bad dream. I was with Cole. This was sanctioned. If I wanted to forget it I could, but I knew I mustn't. I had often been called cold, but if I allowed myself to detach myself from this then I was on the way to becoming someone I did not want to be.

'Good girl,' he said. 'You've packed the rifle well. I didn't think you'd want to see your handiwork close up this first time.'

'Why not?' I said. Cole seemed pleased with me. It was easiest not to let him know how revolted I felt.

'Bludgeoning a dead man's head in isn't most people's idea of a good time.'

I shrugged. 'He was dead, wasn't he? It's unlikely a corpse would complain.'

'Most people don't want to be reminded they are made of meat,' said Cole.

'I don't think that matters when you're dead,' I said.

'Your attitude is better than I expected,' said Cole. 'I'm pleased. Next time I won't have to help you take the shot, will I?'

'No,' I said. 'You won't.' Silently I thought, *Because there will never be a next time.*

Chapter Twenty-nine

Aftermath

Conversation on a motorbike is not possible. When we reached The Manse, Cole sent me in first. 'As quiet as you can, please,' he said. I didn't argue. I wanted very much to see what was in the bag we'd taken from the dead man, but if Cole didn't want to show me then he wouldn't. Nothing I could say would make any difference. He was a man of absolutes and closed to persuasion.

I entered The Manse as soundlessly as I could. Removing my shoes, I tiptoed to my room. I met no one. I waited for a while to see if Cole would come to talk to me, but after fifteen minutes I got into bed. I was bone weary and more shaken than I had ever been. I couldn't sleep. I played what had happened over and over in my head. I went back through every encounter I had ever had with Cole and finally, slowly, inevitably the pieces fell into place.

I knew now that Cole had been lying to me all along. There was no way Fitzroy would have put me in that position. He took life as a last resort, and if he'd had to kill that man, he would have either done it alone, or explained it to me. He would never have helped me take the shot and given me the bullet as a prize. I had known that Cole went to much darker places than Fitzroy, but I had not realised the extent of it. It seemed, for his own reasons, he had taken to me. He had made himself my part-time protector. Now, I saw what I should have seen all along: he wanted to cast me in his image. The question remained as to why he wished to do this. I had come to the conclusion he was more of a rival to Fitzroy than a friend. Could it be, that for reasons I didn't yet understand, I was some kind of trophy both men were fighting to win? Or was it worse than that?

Cole was a brilliant assassin. A genius level of intelligence without, it appeared, a modicum of morality. Was he entirely a psychopath? Or did he have his own code? He'd shown emotion in my presence on a number of occasions. Had that been real or an act?

What worried me most was the possibility he was replaying some kind of obsession he had had about my mother. In his undoubtedly twisted mind was he playing some kind of rerun of a competition he'd had with Fitzroy to win her affection? And this time, was I the prize?

If I wanted to survive I had to ensure he didn't know that I suspected he wasn't all he made out to be. Oh, God, if only Bernie was here. She'd say something sassy and inappropriate and then everything would seem, not better, but something we could fight – together.

Then I remembered she was dead. It was all too much. I closed my eyes and willed myself into oblivion.

The moment I entered the breakfast room I was under fire. Two bread rolls on intercepting courses came towards my head. I ducked and they bounced off each other in a small shower of flour. 'Sorry,' called someone.

'Simon, you have the luck of the devil,' shouted a youth in a flight cadet's uniform.

I felt like saying, 'It's sorry, ma'am,' but I smiled through gritted teeth and went to help myself to some eggs from the buffet on the sideboard. I might be living in a nightmare, but my stomach wanted food. Two girls were standing there chattering by the eggs on the best way to curl hair and what they might use instead of lipstick. When I came over they said 'good morning' politely and moved quickly away. I must look as much like a storm cloud as I felt.

I piled my plate high with eggs, some bacon and a roll that had yet to become ammunition. Then turning I surveyed the long tables packed full of near-riotous young people. Three things occurred to me. Tonight was the village dance and must surely be the cause of all the excitement. Secondly, there had to be thirty people at least here, and bearing in mind senior officers would be billeted elsewhere, could they possibly all work at the airbase? It didn't seem likely. Thirdly, on average they were probably around my age, but this morning I felt like Methuselah. But then, killing someone during a nice evening outing to a beach will do that to you.

I knew that I should mingle, but I couldn't face that this morning. However, despite being fresh from the kill and learning my best friend was dead, my stomach continued to operate at normal capacity. I finished my plate, got myself black coffee from the urn and helped myself to some toast. I didn't see any butter, but I didn't much care. I wanted fuel more than I wanted taste.

Various people smiled nervously at me as they passed by. I wasn't in uniform, but either my reputation was preceding me or I had the innate dour look that seniority brings. The pilots, of course, most of whom would automatically outrank me, ignored me, and continued to lob rolls at each other and general rag. Mrs McKenzie came in a couple of times to replenish the food and surprised me by taking a roll to the head in good humour.

I finished breakfast and decided I would take a few minutes to think in my room before I left. Although I had mostly been left alone, the noise in the dining room had hindered me from deciding exactly what I should do next. It felt like everything was slipping from my grasp. I had a meeting with Harvey set up, but little else. It was hard to see how to move forward. There were enough rumours on base for me to ascertain that something was wrong, but I still had no idea if I was looking for enemy agents — and the man on the beach lent credence to that — or if the discontent was rooted deeper in the community. For now, I could conclude the pilfering was an exercise in annoyance. Nothing had been seriously disturbed, but might it go further? Was this the extent of someone's plans or was it a dry run for something more sinister? If I had to write a report now, I could use lots of words, but at the end any fool would be able to see that I didn't know a thing other than the wing commander had matrimonial issues and some of his guards were, by his own admission, less intelligent than items normally sold in a grocery store. What I wouldn't be including was my outing with Cole. Until I understood what it was about, who we had shot, I had no intention of mentioning this to anyone. In the pit of my stomach was the unspoken fear that Cole might be a double agent.

I opened the door to my room and found a folded piece of paper on the floor. I picked it up and closed the door. For a moment I held my breath. Could it be another message? An urgent note taken by phone from Fitzroy telling me that Bernie's death had been inaccurate? That she'd turned up at some damn awful nightclub, coughing her heart out on late-night cigarettes, lurching from too much gin, and looking down at her bombed home, asking, 'Who's dead?' It would be such a Bernie thing to do that I couldn't dismiss the hope.

I opened the sheet of paper. The lettering was printed by hand in capitals.

OFF NOW. WILL CATCH YOU WHEN I CAN. ASK ABOUT COLLINS. GOOD TO SEE YOU. UNCLE C

Although it was from Cole it was a very Fitzroy kind of a note. I wondered if they taught them all how to write largely unhelpful and enigmatically patronising notes in regular spy school. I'd simply been taught not to leave notes. It was odd of Cole to leave me this. I sat down on the bed. Clearly he thought I wasn't on to him. He would assume I would destroy it like a good little spy. I got down on my hands and knees and began to examine the floor.

Eventually I found what I could use. A loose piece of skirting board would have been nice, but instead I found that the far corner of the carpet under my bed wasn't nailed down properly. It was an obvious place for a trained operative to look, but so far I'd had no indication that anyone other than your standard nosy parker would be rummaging around my room. I stuck the paper under it and was in the process of crawling out when there was a knock at my door. Like a startled dog I lifted my head and banged it on the bed.

'Miss Stapleford,' said Mrs McKenzie's voice, 'I'm off to the WI's coffee morning in about twenty minutes. Would you like to come with me?'

I managed to turn around on the floor, so I was facing the right way. 'Yes, that would be perfect, Mrs McKenzie,' I said. 'Shall I meet you downstairs?'

'Bring a brolly, it's liable to be wet.'

I heard the sound of her footsteps going away. Brolly, I thought. No one puts a brolly in a grab bag. But then who in their right mind would come to Scotland without a brolly?

I quickly sorted through my belongings, looking for anything waterproof. My best option was to go in uniform. I'd look official, but better that than looking like a drowned rat. At least I could put my hair under my hat.

Mrs McKenzie's eyes opened rather wide when she saw me in an officer's uniform, and in trousers too. I suspected such advanced notions had yet to make it this far north. 'It's just a wee coffee morning,' she said. 'Nothing official.'

'These are the best wet-weather clothes I have with me,' I explained.

'Didn't you ken where you were being posted?'

I smiled thinly. 'I'm afraid I can't answer that.'

'Och, men,' she said. 'It would be a man what gave you the posting. For all they're keen on the airmen not losing their boots, they haven't a thought in their head for proper clothing. People are always leaving things here. I'll have a wee scout around when we get back and see what I can dig up for you. Might not be the best of the best, but I can certainly find something to keep you a wee bit warmer and a sight less wet.' She opened the door. 'Pah! Men! If it weren't for that damn fool Adolf and his nasty wee cronies, we wouldn't be in this mess.' I followed her out and closed the door. She looked back at me. 'Now, if women were left to run things there'd be no war, all the meals would be on time and the kettle would always be on the hob, ready for a nice wee cuppa.'

'Sounds like a perfect world,' I said, this time with a genuine smile.

'Right, let's crack on. I'll have to set a wee bit of a pace, but a young 'un like you shouldn't mind.'

She started off down the lane Cole and I had first driven along at a good clip. She walked in the middle of the road. It was yet to rain although the sky was the colour of gunmetal. Mrs McKenzie carried her umbrella in a grip that suggested should she meet anything else on the road it would be the worse for them. I followed slightly behind, my eyes and ears open for the sound of any traffic.

'It'll take us about ten minutes,' she said. 'As long as Agnes hasn't taken it into her head to go out.'

'Where is the meeting?' I asked.

'Oh, the town hall. They'll be wanting our help putting up the bunting for tonight's dance. I expect there would have been some sugar smuggling too, but not with you looking like that.'

'Sugar smuggling?'

'Och, we just do a wee bit of a swap around. Especially if there's a gathering on. You ken how it is, swapping a few eggs for a cup of sugar, or lending someone some milk for a touch of flour. But there you go . . . oh, blow and blast it, here's Agnes.'

I could immediately see why Agnes might be a problem. She was a large female of the black and white variety. She stood in the middle of the road, completely blocking it. Her head was turned towards us. She was chewing cud and looking belligerent. Anyone who has lived in the countryside knows that when a cow takes it into its head to be – well – a cow, it's a very large lump of flesh and even if it does no more than stand on your foot, that's quite enough.

'What does she do?' I asked.

'She's a cow. She makes milk,' said Mrs McKenzie. 'Did you grow up in the city?'

'I meant, what nastiness does she do when you move her on?'

'Oh, she bites and kicks a bit. The worse bit is, we'll need to get back to the farm. Can't very well leave her out and about.'

'First person who sees her?' I asked.

'First person who sees her and admits it,' said Mrs McKenzie scowling.

'Ah,' I said. 'Village bus and base traffic?'

Mrs McKenzie grunted.

I went over to a hedgerow and broke off a long stick. 'Where does she have to go?'

'Not far if she were any other cow. Just a paddock down the way.'

I approached Agnes with a firm expression on my face. She looked at me belligerently. I produced my stick. Agnes continued chewing her cud, but there was an angry glint in her eye. 'Shhh! Skkk!' I said warningly and brought my stick down hard enough that she felt the downward motion of the air, but that it did not touch her.

In reality, a cow's hide is tough, and I doubt I could have injured her. But I don't like the idea of harming an animal in any way. Agnes didn't know this, and once I repeated the action she set off at a fair gallop, heading straight for home, and Mrs McKenzie shut the gate behind her.

'I thought you were going to get yourself stampeded.'

A little breathlessly, for I had to run to keep up with Agnes's pace, I said, 'I thought if Agnes was so bad tempered no one would ever have threatened her with a stick for fear she'd bite. She wouldn't have run if I had hit her – which I wouldn't have done. But the threat of being struck made her run.'

Mrs McKenzie eyed me with her head tilted. 'I'm thinking there's a kind of wisdom in that.' I smiled. 'Or,' she continued, 'you've something loose up top like my brother-in-law.'

Then she gave a small chuckle. 'The look on that cow's face.

214

She could nae believe it. Like a queen being chased off her throne by a goat.'

'Indeed,' I said, not much liking my role as the goat.

'Aye well, we need to get a shift on or all the biscuits will be gone.'

The town hall proved to be much as one would expect in the countryside. A solid building with a kitchen, a loo, a wooden dance floor, small platform come stage and a room for the committee. The latter, Mrs M informed me, was used for coats and boots during the dances. 'Surprising how hot it gets in there with everyone flinging themselves about. If you've come out in a storm you want to be leaving your outer things away somewhere. Would nae want anyone to fall over them. Whole village could go down like a pack of dominoes. Only they'd be all those arms and legs and other things all tangled up.' She tsked at the thought and shook her head, though whether she found the image amusing or scandalous I couldn't tell. If they ever learned to play poker in the village, she would no doubt clean them all out.

She led me through the green double doors and into the small hallway. Immediately I smelt disinfectant and wax polish. It was strong enough to be quite a heady mixture. In front of us a small pair of double doors with glass insets opened into the main hall. Mrs M turned left through a smaller single door. The air changed immediately. Now I was near overwhelmed with the smell of face powder, violet scent and a musky undertone. Loud chattering stopped in a heartbeat, as the ladies seated around a table, which contained a teapot and various treats the like of which I hadn't seen since before the war, looked up open-mouthed at Mrs McKenzie. Or rather at me.

'Her uniform's the warmest thing the girl's got,' said Mrs McKenzie, sounding her most prickly. 'This is the new community liaison officer, Hope Stapleford. She's staying with me.' Then she plumped herself down in a spare seat and gestured for me to do the same.

I did so and smiled round at the other women. I recognised

Margaret Buchanan. If anything the victory rolls in her hair had got bigger. She had one hand proprietarily on the teapot.

'Why don't we all introduce ourselves,' said Mrs M. 'I'm Senja McKenzie and I run The Manse B & B, currently converted as a services billet.'

'We've met before,' said Margaret Buchanan. She was wearing an expensive-looking silk scarf and a glossy rose lipstick. The colour didn't suit her complexion but I doubted anyone here would dare tell her.

A brown-haired young plump woman spoke up. 'Vicky Malone. Both me and my husband are Irish. He's a flyer. I do the cakes.' This heralded a flood of introductions. For a small village there seemed to be a lot of women present. I did my best to remember all the names, but I kept thinking about last night. It was as if I had a movie reel playing over and over in my brain. There was some poor girl with German grandparents, who seemed terrified of me, a large young woman with a large laugh who was doubtless a terror on the hockey fields at school, the archetypal vicar's wife who was into flower-arranging, and the wife of one of the mechanics.

The last member of the committee was a grey-haired woman, whose bone structure was excellent. In her youth she would have put all the others in the shade. She was knitting. When the others had finished, she took her eyes off her stitches for a moment and said, 'Bridget Fraser. Nice to meet you,' and went back to her knitting.

'I'm Hope Stapleford. I was born in the Fens, and I'm here to help in any way I can,' I said with yet another smile. My cheeks were beginning to ache. I couldn't remember ever smiling so much. I'd instinctively liked a woman called Ursula until I realised she reminded me of Bernie. I still liked her best of the lot of them, but I was heart-sore.

'Please don't let me interrupt your meeting,' I said. 'Pretend I'm not here. If anyone has any questions, feel free to ask.'

'Very kind of you,' said Margaret glacially. I noticed her victory rolls quivered when she was annoyed.

'Hope moved Agnes on,' said Mrs M. 'Did it right well. But if you're from the Fens you must be a country girl?'

I nodded. 'Very much so.' I noticed the atmosphere in the room lighten. Vicky, the Irish one, pushed a plate of Empire biscuits towards me. 'Do have one,' she said. 'We all save up for today, so there's plenty to go round.'

I took one. 'I'll ask Mrs M to put some of my ration towards your next meeting,' I said.

'Oh no, you mustn't do that,' said Marie, the vicar's wife. 'You're our guest.'

'I insist,' I said, catching Margaret's eye just as her victory rolls began to wobble. 'There's a war on and we must all play a part.'

'Speaking of which, do you think you could convince the wing commander to let my husband take a service on the base? I think it would bring us all together so much more.'

It was an odd request from a vicar's wife. 'There will be a chaplain attached to the base,' I said carefully. 'It's not usual to have civilian priests on a military base.' I saw her face fall and wondered why it was so important. 'I could suggest to the wing commander that the officers make a particular effort to attend a community liaison service in the local church. It would be his call, but if he was willing it would be something, wouldn't it?'

'Yes, it would,' said Marie and I could see there were tears in her eyes.

I moved on quickly. 'I'm afraid I'm rather a plain cook or I'd offer to help.'

'Surely you're here to do your duty rather than fuss about in a kitchen,' said Margaret.

I took a breath. 'I can see what you mean. It's an honour to serve, of course, and my role is a fluid one requiring odd hours, but I do still get a little time to myself. It would be my personal time I would use should I be able to help out.'

'It's a social role, isn't it?' said Mrs Hardcastle. 'A bit like mine. It's about being available and mending fences where you can.'

I nodded. 'Very much so.' Considering I hadn't the faintest

clue what community liaison officers did, and was making it up as I went along, I thought I was doing rather well. Mrs Wing Co didn't agree.

'It's a talking shop role,' she said. 'That's why they've given it to a woman. Goodness knows we were doing well enough ourselves. If only the RAF would be a bit more flexible everything would be tickerty-boo. Why, when I was in India, I looked after the staff at home and at the base. Got to know them all rather well. I even held tea receptions for the wives. Helped them out with the etiquette for the officers' balls. My open suppers for the junior ranks were legendary. We used to set up cricket on the back lawn. Nothing like a friendly game of cricket to get everyone together.'

'Aye, well, it'd be shinty, up here,' said Bridget Fraser. Margaret frowned, so Bridget continued, 'That's like your hockey, but with nae rules and you can lift your stick as high as you like.'

'Gosh,' said Ursula. 'Sounds fabby! I take it it's mostly the chaps that play. Are there many injuries?'

'A few broken heads among new players is not uncommon. The more established ones tend to keep themselves out of harm's way.'

'Ooh, sounds very manly. I love seeing men do manly things, don't you, Hope?'

This time I tried not to smile. 'It certainly sounds interesting, but I think the chaps at the base are in enough danger.'

'You can say that again,' said Vicky. 'Why, my Fergal had hardly any time in the air before they sent him here as a full-blown pilot. I'm just grateful I found a way to come along.'

'Squadron Leader Abercrombie struck me as a good officer. I'm sure he does his best for his men.'

'Oh aye,' said Bridget. 'He's a good man. Does his best to bring them hame.'

'I suppose I shouldn't be surprised you know Abercrombie. You're not married, are you, Miss Stapleford?' said Margaret.

'It's Lieutenant Stapleford,' I said, deliberately not answering her question. I thought I saw a sly smile on Bridget's face, and her knitting missed a beat. Ursula, on the other hand, grinned widely.

'Are you coming to the dance tonight?' she asked.

'Susan talked me into it,' I said. 'But yes, it will be a nice way to meet more people.'

'And what are you going do when you're there?' Bridget again.

'Talk to people,' I said. 'You know, set up shop.'

Angelic little Marie looked away in embarrassment. Bridget kept knitting and Mrs M nodded her approval. Goodness, I thought, I've already nailed my colours to the mast here. But if the WI were this divided among themselves, I didn't hold out much hope for the wider community.

Chapter Thirty

Don't Ask About Collins

I stayed on at the coffee morning and helped decorate the hall with paper chains and vases of wild flowers. I learned that both Mrs McKenzie and Margaret Buchanan had gone for chair of the local WI. Margaret had been a newcomer then. Although they all knew her husband, this was the first time they'd met the exotic wife, who according to her husband had enthralled the good and wise of all India.

'We know now,' said Ursula to me as she scrambled up on a table to tack up a chain, 'that she's no more than a bully. Wants things her way, and won't listen to a word of criticism.' She climbed down, to my relief, and as we unknotted a chain together said, 'Only little Marie would put herself forward to be secretary. She thinks everything can be mended. I didn't think it possible, but she's almost as innocent as she looks. I imagine she and her husband use the sweetest pet names for each other. Ugh!'

'What do you call yours?' I asked.

Ursula stopped and pretended to think. '"Oi, you! Yer crumpet!" and "lover" when I want a new hat. What about you?'

'I'm not married.'

'But you must have a sweetheart. You're bright and lovely. Don't tell me you've not met someone?'

'Well,' I said, 'there was someone I thought might be a possibility, but I got posted elsewhere.'

'With this dammed war going on you have to grab every moment. I'm lucky. I get to see my Jimmy. They've not sent him anywhere, and God willing they won't. Tomorrow we're going to dance our socks off. I'm going to drink all the punch – he's on duty tomorrow. I'll find you someone. Only, I'd suggest *not* Abercrombie.'

'I've heard he's a bit of a man about town.'

'He's a pilot. They die young. It's not talked about. Abercrombie's fast, but he's not a heartbreaker. He knows his days are numbered.'

'Is it that dangerous? He's made it to squadron leader.'

'Dead men's shoes,' said Ursula, keeping her voice low. 'I'll allow he's a better pilot than most, but you haven't been here long enough. They die all the time. The pilots. It's not worth being fond of one. Breaks your heart, it does.'

'You two seem to be getting along rather nicely,' said Margaret. 'I suppose youth calls to youth.'

'Just doing our bit,' said Ursula in a cheery voice.

Margaret frowned. 'Of course,' she said. 'Found anything useful out yet, Miss Stapleford? Have a campaign of action to put us all to rights?'

I smiled and turned back to the chains.

'I asked you a question, Miss Stapleford!'

I stopped and turned to face her straight on. 'I'm a lieutenant, ma'am. I am confident you understand that I am not here to institute plans. I am here to help facilitate a positive change in the relationship between the RAF personnel and the local people.'

'With what, three weeks, training under your belt? What do you know about facilitating community?'

Several retorts came to mind. I took another deep breath. 'If you have an issue with my conduct you can take it up with my superiors. I believe your husband will be able to forward a complaint.'

'You are not answering my questions.' I swear the woman almost stamped her foot.

'With respect, I do not report to you, ma'am.'

'But you report to my husband. He tells me everything. There is no difference between answering me and him.'

I had heard the description 'jaw-dropping', but I really did feel my chin wobble.

'Oh, Margaret, really. You'd have to be a fool to believe that,' said Ursula. 'Besides, the whole village knows you and Edwin are at odds.'

The older woman went scarlet. I looked away, so she could imagine I hadn't noticed. I fiddled with the chains. 'I don't know who told you I am under your husband's command, ma'am, but I'm not. I am in a different chain of command.'

'Ridiculous!' she said and stormed off through the doors.

'Well, that's one enemy for life you've made there,' said Ursula. 'It took us a couple of months to get on the wrong side of her. You're a quick worker. Fancy a cuppa?'

'Thank you, no. If you can manage without me I should move on.' A thought struck me. 'Unless you know something about someone called Collins?'

Ursula's face went blank. She grabbed me hard by the elbow and hustled me out of the same door that Margaret had just gone through. The hallway was empty.

'Ow,' I said. 'That pinches.'

'What do you expect, bringing up something like that? Do I know about Collins? There isn't a soul for twenty miles who doesn't know about Collins.'

'Well, I don't!' I said. 'I'm sorry if I've upset you, but all I have to go on is the name.' I didn't like being held, but I had no desire either to show how easily I could escape. Instead I wrenched my arm free with a girlish show of exasperation.

'Ask to see the records. And if they let you, you can tell us what really happened. None of them ever liked him.' With this extra-ordinary comment she returned to the hall without a backward glance.

This time, at least, I knew my way back. Mrs M had left before the decoration started in earnest, pleading luncheon preparations. I was almost disappointed not to meet Agnes again on her wan-derings. By comparison with the women of the WI she seemed positively friendly. The threatened rain had passed, but the lane was one of those that stayed muddy. Cattle driven back and forth left permanent ruts. The mud had dried during the morning, and I had to pick my way carefully between the raised honeycomb-like structure that passed as the lane. It was as well Cole had left. The bike would have found this lane impassable. But then Cole would have probably taken it across the fields.

Thinking about this brought back a lot of thoughts I had been doing my best to push to the back of my mind. As part of my training, although I didn't realise it at the time, Fitzroy had taught me to compartmentalise my thoughts and emotions. Two of the top agents of SIS trained me in observation and evasion, but as far as I was concerned we were playing games, and it wasn't until I was an adult I began to understand what they had been doing. Fitzroy spent a lot of time and energy getting me to control my emotions. His reasoning was that in a crisis emotion was a handicap. Clear, quick thinking was needed. So instead he taught me a variety of exercises to put emotions to the side. I tried one now.

As I walked back, I could hear little but the occasional bird, cattle lowing in the fields and the wind in the branches, flicking the leaves back and forth, as if nature herself was bored by the quiet of today. I thought about my feelings at the WI. I imagined it in colours to try and pick out what had made me so uneasy. It wasn't anything anyone had specifically said or done. I saw it was red, white and blue. Hardly surprising. But with undertones of an unpleasant green. An almost infection-like colour. Worse yet, in my mind's eye, it was flecked with a dull red, reminiscent of tiny scabs. There had been an undercurrent of unpleasantness, competitiveness – which was maybe allowable given the number of cake and jam contests they doubtless held – but now I thought about the colours, there was a great deal of spite. Not what I expected to find in a group of women who were determined to 'do their bit'. I arrived back at The Manse in better time than I'd hoped. I would be able to eat before I headed back to the base. I was going to need to find a lift again. I needed transport. Either that or I would have to borrow Mr McKenzie's donkey.

'Maud likes you well enough, but she wants to stay with me,' said a voice from the bushes by The Manse's front door.

Brian McKenzie appeared from behind the hedge. I wondered what he had been doing there, but I was wary of asking. 'Baby hedgehog got separated from its mother,' said Brian. 'Cos it probably had fleas and now Senja will be on at me. I'll stay well away from folks till I've defleaed myself, but they don't half hop.'

I wondered how he defleaed, but again didn't want to ask.

'Strip down and jump in the faery pool. Rub myself all over with the right leaves and they're gone in a trice.'

I could only assume that my poker face, of which I had been proud, was easily readable by this man. 'What do you know about the fey folk, Mr McKenzie?' I asked.

'More than I could tell you in a day, Miss Hope. They're real, all right, and they talks to me.' He rubbed the side of his left temple. 'I got awful banged up in the war. Senja's probably told you I'm a bit daft.' He smiled and his face lit up. Suddenly I could see the handsome young man he must have once been. 'Don't think I was that bright before I went to war, to be honest with you. Thinking about it, if any of us had been bright enough none of us would have gone. Not like this one. All about greed and politics that one was. Now, this one's a fight against evil. I keep telling the faeries that. That we have to make a stand and they'll get their land back when it's over, but they don't care much for the affairs of mortal men. Living so much longer than us. I reckon they see us rather like that hedgehog thinks about its fleas. Parasites that annoy. Have to say, a lot of the time I think they have a point.'

'You're right though, Mr McKenzie. This is a different war to the last one. My parents and my godfather were involved last time. They think this is a very different affair.'

Brian leaned towards me. I had to grit my teeth to stay still. I'd caught fleas once as a child and it had not been a pleasant experience. I also didn't fancy stripping down with Brian in his faery pool. 'They were spies, weren't they?' he said. 'You've got that look about you too. Secrets. You hold secrets inside like a chest of jewels. All bright and shiny. The faery folk, they can see things like that. They'll be interested in you.'

I did my best to cover my shock. 'That's good, isn't it? They might listen.'

He shook his head. 'Nah. Not at all, Miss Hope. You've heard the expression "away with the faeries"? It's not a good thing to be. They can torment a soul something rotten. That's what's up with the wing commander. He's fair tormented, and his men. Sticking little tiny swords in his ears while he sleeps, they are. They done wrong, they did. You didn't do no wrong. They won't harm you. Too scared they are. They say you have the darkness about you. But then there's no knowing what scares a faerie. Them not being that helpful during their chat. They don't care much for us, but they enjoy tormenting. And then there's the ones that muck about with the livestock and the vegetables. Them's right little b—'

The front door of The Manse opened. Mrs McKenzie appeared carrying a broom. 'Brian McKenzie, what are you doing hanging around the bushes and accosting my guests!'

'I'd stay back, Senja,' he said as she took a step towards him. 'I've been helping the hedgehogs again. Poor little mite. Lost its mum.'

Mrs M raised the broom and swatted at him. I could see she meant to miss. 'Away with you. I'll not be having fleas in my good house. Away with you, you fool.'

'I'm going, Senja. I'm going. I was having a chat with the young lass here. She's one of the good ones, Senja. Although she ain't no happier than me at the moment. That's why I had to . . .'

What he had to do I never learned as Mrs M barrelled down the steps waving her broom and Brian wisely fled.

Chapter Thirty-one

Highland Dancing and Kilts, Especially Kilts

Luncheon was good, hearty and filling. I didn't remember a mouthful. I had a feeling that Brian had accidently told me something useful, but I couldn't pick out the truth from the nonsense, try as I might. His conversation was worse than some of the cyphers I'd been trained in.

I went back up to my room after I ate to freshen up and consider my options. I found another note under the door. I opened it with slightly shaky hands only to discover that is was a telephone message from Susan to say she'd pick me up at seven thirty from The Manse, and if I'd decided against going could I please call her back.

I searched through my things to see what I could come up with. Mrs M had mentioned finding me clothes that had been left behind, but I imagined that would be more jumpers and boots than concert dresses. I remembered what Cole had said about asking for things. He seemed to regard the Department as a treasury of things for him to plunder. Maybe I should take a leaf out of his book?

I only brought him to mind for a moment, and suddenly in front of my mind's eye I saw him bending over the dead man on the beach. This time I felt a tingling of excitement, horror and awe at having taken a life flood through me. I sat down heavily on the bed and inhaled deeply. My head spun as I finally digested that I had in part enjoyed taking that shot. The success of it had excited me. The power of it. But in equal part I had wanted to vomit, and I was relieved to feel I retained that revulsion. That this put me square in the middle of internal conflict was unfortunate, but at least it meant I knew I wasn't a psychopath. Well, not entirely psychopathic anyway. I knew I was building up an emotional debt that I would need to attend to in the near future.

I stood up, straightened my jacket, and went downstairs to the phone in the hall. This was in all likelihood not a secure line, so I would have to be circumspect. I dialled the code for contacting the Department rather than my direct line to Fitzroy. I found at present I didn't want to speak to him. It was unlikely he was in the office, but I didn't want to take that chance. I knew that the sound of his voice would unleash a whole flood of emotions. Part of me would want to tell him everything and part of me would want to shout at him for marrying my mother, for abandoning me and throwing me into this situation without backup. Especially as he knew what had happened to Bernie. Bereavement was becoming a common thing, but I doubted Fitzroy understood the pain of losing a friend. It appeared the only person he had ever cared about was my mother and now she was his.

Even thinking about him made me scowl. I picked up the receiver and asked the operator to connect me. When I finally got through, I said, 'I have a shopping list.'

'Can I take the items?'

'When is delivery?'

'Late afternoon or tomorrow.'

'Dress suitable for a dance, an umbrella, casual clothing, walking boots, transport, and reading material.'

'Transport, ma'am?'

'Transport. I need to be able to get around independently.'

'I'll pass the list to Father,' she said and rang off. Then, as I had nothing else to do and no way to get to the base, I went and offered my services to Mrs M in the kitchen. I had hoped to learn more village gossip, but in the end all I came away with was an excellent recipe for oat shortbread.

Someone had left a parcel outside my room. I assumed things

227

were left in the hallway to explicitly demonstrate that although there were no locks no one would enter another's room without permission. Inside was a blue dress that went well with my eyes. It wasn't an evening dress, but a full-skirted, knee-length one. It would have to do. It came with matching shoes, which even had overshoes, and a waterproof jacket with a hood. This wasn't something picked out by wardrobe, from my notes. This was clearly something chosen by someone who had met me, who knew me to a significant degree.

However, other than that, there was nothing in the parcel. I didn't think it likely I had been sent any transport. If I was lucky someone might drop off an ordinary bicycle at the railway station tomorrow or the day after. I'd at least be able to use whatever route the buses took with one of those.

Supper was only sandwiches and tea. There would be refreshments at the dance. As I'd been one of the ones cutting the sandwiches, I'd taken some for myself. If I was quick, perhaps I could take a bath while the others were in the dining hall.

I didn't tend to spend much time in bathrooms since the attack, but one needed to be clean. I ran a regulation two-inch bath, and enjoyed the warmth of being the first one to attack the boiler.

After that I went back to my room, ate my picnic supper, got ready, and then, although I had forgotten walking boots, I had packed a couple of novels I'd been meaning to read, so I lay down on the bed to surrender myself to a murder mystery.

I lost myself in it. The whole scenario was quite ridiculous. It was like reading a mystery written by a mathematician who had never met a real person. Indeed, I reflected, some of my tutors at college had been like that. I wondered if the name on the cover was actually a pen name and if it could be my algebra lecturer, who only left his rooms when he needed more tea leaves.

At seven o'clock I went down to the hall to wait for Susan. I saw from the staircase she was ahead of me, dressed in a polka dot dress with an equally full skirt. I supposed the lanes were muddy enough that no one would wear proper evening wear. I didn't normally care about such things, but considering my role I was happier to think that my outfit would fit in with others'.

'Oh, there you are,' said Susan. 'I'm a bit early. Mrs McKenzie said I could go up, but I didn't want to chase you. I'm so glad you decided to go. I hear it's going to be lots of fun.'

Her cheeks were flushed pink, and at first I thought she'd been drinking. But her breath didn't smell of either alcohol or of mints. Her eyes darted around the hallway. As I got near, she leaned in and whispered, 'I hear some of the men might be wearing kilts. What a hoot! I wonder if they're going to be traditional about it?'

'You mean wearing the right clan tartans?' I said. 'Is that important? Are people concerned about that?'

'Well, yes, but anyone can wear the Black Watch. But no, silly. A proper Scotsman goes in full regalia.' She hissed the last two words and stared me straight in the eyes. Then to my astonishment winked.

I shook my head. 'I don't get it,' I said.

Susan hooked her arm through mine and led me outside. 'Honestly, do you need me to spell it out?'

'Looks like it,' I said.

'Real Scotsmen don't wear anything under a kilt.'

'You mean . . .'

Susan nodded.

'But it's not like we're going to look,' I said uneasily.

'No, of course not,' said Susan. 'But it's the knowing that counts. Doesn't it make you feel all tingly?'

'It's going to make me feel embarrassed,' I said. 'I'll be looking at their faces, but wondering . . .'

Susan nodded enthusiastically. 'Exactly. I'm so hoping Abercrombie will wear a kilt. I bet he's got smashing knees.'

The night was less dark than I imagined it would be, the sky more of a brilliant navy than black. A slight breeze, like tender fingers on your face, wafted by. All along the lane we saw spots of bright light bobbing as people with lanterns and torches made their way to the dance. I couldn't help thinking this was a bad idea. Weren't we meant to be in blackout? But then a cynical part of me wondered if anything that might divert the enemy away from the airfield would be welcome. I had no authority to do anything about this anyway, and no desire to make myself unpopular. I would, however, keep my ears open for the sound of aircraft. If the village hall wasn't in blackout, I wouldn't be staying. I'd take the risk of walking along the lane, but I wasn't staying for hours in a place that shone a definite light in the dark.

An owl hooted somewhere, and I wondered if it was alarmed at the sudden traffic through its usually quiet territory. 'I hear he's a bit of a heartbreaker,' I said, returning to what I suspected was going to be Susan's favourite and particularly tedious part of the night's conversation.

'He's a fly boy,' said Susan dismissively. 'They're all that. It's not like you can blame them. Facing death daily in the air. They have to live for the now. And as long as you're careful, what's the harm? No one knows which way this war is going. We all have to grab what we can when we can.'

I almost said something about kilts making that easier, but decided not to.

Suddenly a terrible noise broke out. I threw myself back against a hedge, and looked from side to side. Susan bent over double. Then I realised she was laughing.

'What the hell was that?' I said.

'The skirl of the pipes, you ninny,' said Susan. 'Och, I'm laughing so much I'm crying. I'll ruin my mascara. They're just tuning up. You do know tonight is a ceilidh?'

'No, I hadn't thought,' I said, feeling sheepish. Of course a village dance in Scotland would be a ceilidh. 'I don't know any of the dances,' I said. 'Only English country dances.'

'I expect they won't be that much different. Besides, they always have a caller and it's not like most of the airmen have any idea. Half the fun is everyone getting it all wrong.'

I was far from convinced. However, when we got to the hall I noticed that the walkers extinguished their lights and the hall itself had all its blackout curtains in place. In the entrance hall there was a great deal of excited chatter and foot tapping. It certainly looked like if I slipped away with Harvey, no one would notice us leaving. I could only hope he'd been luckier with transport than me. There was no way we could walk to the base and back.

We queued up to hand in our coats and overshoes to the makeshift cloakroom. Already the hall was becoming extremely hot with all the bodies inside. Susan and I squished our way through to the main hall and found some seats at the edge. 'Keep the seats,' said Susan. 'I'll get us some drinks.'

She returned shortly clutching two glasses. 'It's meant to be fruit punch.' She giggled and passed one drink to me. It looked like watery lemonade. A solitary piece of orange fruit, not readily identifiable, floated in the middle.

'Cheerio!' said Susan, saluting me with her drink. 'I'm going in. First dance will be soon. I'm hoping for a Gay Gordon. That's my favourite. Gets everyone on their feet, and there's no figure of eights or whirling bits. You have to watch out for a couple of the whirlers when they've got a drink in them. The mechanics are the worst. Last time Marie Hardcastle was being spun so fast she got frightened and let go. Don't know what the lad was thinking not keeping a good enough grip, but she flew across the room and out the double doors. Landed in a heap in the entrance. Only bruises, and of course Marie would never make a fuss. She went home early that night.'

'This is sounding dangerous,' I said.

'Oh, you'll be fine. I've heard Senja is very taken with you. Anyone she likes must have a bit of backbone. She's not one for the spineless.' Susan ground her toe against the floor. 'Typical boarding-house landlady, if you show fear she'll have you. Like a Rottweiler, she is. Only don't tell her I said that.'

There might not have been anything in the punch, but I was beginning to think there might already be something in Susan.

231

'But she's kind,' I said. 'She took her brother-in-law in.'

'Brian?' Susan's eyes were scanning the room. 'He's harmless. Of course it was him that stirred up all the stuff about the faeries. So not entirely harmless. Granddad thinks he should keep his mouth shut, but Granny wants to get him put into an institution. She thinks he's a menace to society. But it's really because he said that she wasn't so much descended from a Scottish earl as an earl's by-blow. Of course, he's right enough, but how he knew, goodness knows. Granny does get her knickers in a twist about her station. To hear Granddad talk she was practically a marjarinee in India. Marjarinee, is that right? It sounds like something you spread on bread, but it's like a princess or a queen, I think.'

Susan shifted forward on her seat and quivered like one of my father's gun dogs scenting game. I followed her gaze and saw Squadron Leader Abercrombie making his way across the dance-floor. He was wearing a green tartan, and even I had to admit his knees weren't bad. I then of course wondered if he was wearing the kilt traditionally, and felt the blood rush into my cheeks. Damn Susan for telling me that! I wouldn't be able to look a single man in the eye tonight.

'Susan,' I said, figuring she was now at her most distracted. 'I keep hearing a name, but no one will tell me who this person is or what they did. It's Collins. Do you know?'

Susan tore her gaze away from Abercrombie. 'Has someone been talking to you?'

'No,' I said, 'that's rather my point.'

She picked up her glass from the windowsill, where she'd hidden it behind the curtain. She downed it in one. 'Rats,' she said. 'I'd forgotten there was nothing in these yet. I'd rather not. Not tonight. I want a break from the war. I'll tell you what you need to know if I must – but later. Although I do think for once Granddad is right. Least said, soonest mended.'

'Abercrombie's coming this way,' I said. I didn't want to push her for more information now. I'd wait until she was tipsy, and see what I could get then. I already knew far more than I had this morning.

Abercrombie wandered over to us. Susan moved to the edge of her seat. Her back was at a forty-five degree angle as she leaned forward. Her arms were clenched tightly into her sides, so she made the best of her figure. The collar of her dress opened in a slight 'V'. I wouldn't have said she had her charms in the shop window, so to speak, but she was offering a glimpse of her wares to anyone who wanted to sneak a look.

Abercrombie looked her directly in the face, and nodded. 'Susan,' he said. 'You're looking pretty tonight.'

Susan edged slightly further forward. I worried she was about to fall off her seat and land at his feet. 'The kilt suits you, Hamish,' said Susan. 'You were clearly born to wear it.'

Abercrombie addressed me, 'Lieutenant Stapleford, joining in with the locals, I see.'

'I've even been to a WI meeting,' I said. 'It's my job. And please, for tonight at least, call me Hope.'

'And, although I have barely a drop of Scottish blood in me, call me Hamish,' he said, offering me his hand.

I laughed. 'Really, with a name like yours and you're not Scottish?' I took his hand, unsure if I was meant to shake it.

He pulled me to my feet. 'If you'll give me the pleasure of the first dance, Hope. It's a Gay Gordon, I believe.'

I heard a tiny whimper behind me. 'I don't know any of the Scottish dances,' I said. 'And it's so crowded I'm sure I'd get in everyone's way.'

If Susan had had a tail I was sure it would be wagging now.

'Rubbish,' said Abercrombie. 'They'll all move to the side to allow for the circle to form when we start. If you can waltz you'll have no trouble. There's a caller and I'll be leading! If I can lead a squadron across the skies I can lead a female army officer around a dance hall.'

He hadn't let go of my hand. 'Don't say I didn't warn you,' I said.

'Right, the first thing you need to know is we start holding hands like this. One hand behind your head and one behind your back. Looks a bit strange, but it gets fun once we start going backwards.'

'Backwards!' I exclaimed.

'Ladies and gentlemen,' rang out a voice, 'If you will take your places for our first dance – the Gay Gordon.'

Chapter Thirty-two

Hamish

It wasn't until halfway through the dance I got the hang of it. However, everyone, including Hamish, was extremely good-natured about it. I realised quickly that this ceilidh was about having fun and getting your hands on your partner. Hamish did manage to keep me mostly right by guiding me, almost forcibly at times – especially when I forgot to go backwards and almost ploughed into an octogenarian couple, who looked so wrinkled and ancient that a puff of wind would have taken them out. I found, to my surprise, I didn't mind him manhandling me. He kept his hands in appropriate places and it was rather nice for once to let someone else take control. By the end of the dance we were both laughing and breathless. I had almost forgotten about the man on the beach. Almost.

'I don't know when I had such fun,' I said.

'For our next dance, once someone has brought me a pint, we have the Dashing White Sergeant,' said the caller, who had been frantically issuing instructions. The room buzzed with excitement. I looked up at Hamish. He took my hand. 'I think we might catch a breath before we unleash you on that. Let's have a cigarette.'

He led me out of the room. I could feel Susan's eyes on my back. I was going to have to do some pretty heavy fence-mending there. 'Susan likes you,' I said as we emerged into the hall.

'I know,' said Hamish. 'She was practically half out of her dress by the time I'd got across the dancefloor.' Still holding my hand, he pushed the outer door open, and pulled me through the black-out curtain into the street outside. I inhaled the cool night air. I hadn't realised how hot I'd got. 'You looked like you enjoyed that,' he said and twirled me round as he had done in the dance and into his arms.

'There's no music to waltz to,' I said lightly.

'Oh, Hope, there's always music,' he said. There was enough starlight that I could see the planes of his face, but not enough for me to see what he was thinking. I realised this was not the moment to ask him about Collins. Although I did consider it until his next words emptied my mind of thought.

'Kiss me, Hope.' He pulled me close against him. It gave me a better idea of his musculature and which would be the best way to break his hold or his arm. It also outlined the intensity of his interest.

'Um, I don't really know you that well,' I said. 'We're both officers. Besides, aren't you technically my—'

He pulled me close. 'Right now, we are a man and a woman standing together in the night – not knowing if we will live to see tomorrow.' His voice was breathy with passion.

'I think we will see tomorrow. Barring some kind of natural disaster,' I said. 'Do these lines really work on some women?'

'I think my moustache comes into it, and being a daredevil of a pilot,' he said, but his tone had changed entirely. 'I should have known it wouldn't work on you. You're no more a community liaison officer than I'm an albatross.' He loosened his grip on me, but didn't entirely let go.

'That explains why you're so good at flying,' I said. 'Good evening, Mr Albatross.'

This time he laughed properly. 'Fine,' he said. 'You're imper-vious to my charms. The night's young.'

'And there's always Susan,' I said, putting in a word for my new friend.

'Her grandfather would skin me alive,' he said.

'Really, even though you're his best pilot?'

'Well, he'd beat the soles of my feet with bamboo or some other Indian punishment.'

'I don't think that's Indian,' I said. 'But poor Susan has it bad for you.'

'She hasn't the faintest idea who I am,' he said. He released his hold on my waist, and went to sit down on a bench by the wall. I joined him.

'You could let her get to know you,' I said. 'Less the dashing pilot and more of the man behind him.'

'Could we stop talking about Susan? She's a child.'

'Some of your pilots are her age,' I said.

'And they were children when they first went up, but none of them are any more. You know what I mean. I saw it on you the first time you came to camp.'

'What?' I said. I tried to think of something to make a joke about, but the atmosphere between us had changed.

'You've had to kill, haven't you? It changes a person. And if you did that being a community liaison officer, then you're damn bad at your job!'

I didn't laugh. 'I've taken more than one life,' I said. 'Only when I had to. And I wish that I had never had to . . .'

'It gets easier, I know. Even exciting. But don't worry, that's only for a while. Then you get sick of it. Sick of everything.'

This time it was me that took his hand. 'Hamish, I can't imagine what it's like to do what you do, but I don't think you're a bad man.' Was I talking to him or myself? I didn't know . . .

'I'd find it easier if I was.'

'Everyone is a victim in war,' I said. 'In any violence. Even if you win you're—'

'Made the lesser by it,' he finished for me. 'I did wonder if you might understand.'

'I don't think I can – not entirely.'

'More than a lot of people. At least you haven't told me to buck up and get on with it.'

'The wing commander?'

'I told him I was struggling. You'd think after everything this base has been through he'd be more sympathetic, but it seems a few years in India grinding down the natives makes you a bit of an insensitive arse.'

I squeezed his hand.

He lowered his voice further. 'Sometimes, Hope . . . It just struck me, you're *Hope*.'

'Last of the spirits to be let out of the box, and set to fight all the monsters before me,' I said lightly.

'Well, I hope, Hope, that you've seen your lot of monsters and the demons war makes of men. I hope they put you in a little typing pool underground somewhere to keep you safe during the rest of this ruddy war.'

'They tried!' I said, almost crying with laughter. 'I fought hammer and tongs to get out! It was awful.'

'And this isn't? You know sometimes when I'm speaking to the lads and giving them the talk about how we are the defenders of the air, that we are the sole defence against invasion, how history will call us heroes . . . sometimes I wish I could tell them all to go home. Let someone else fight this war. We've done our bit. Only that's not going to happen, is it?'

'No, it's not. I expect you are more fully briefed, but even I know that the battle for air superiority won't be won by next week.' I waited, sensing he had something to tell me. When he did nothing but stare into the night for several minutes I eventually asked, 'What will you do?'

'Hope that it's quick. A shot through the cockpit that takes me out before I go down in flames is my favoured plan. That's what I want, you know. That next time I go up I don't want to come back. What do you think of your dashing hero now?'

I turned to face him on the bench and freeing my hands lifted them to his face. Then gently I tilted down towards him. The kiss was gentle at first, but as it deepened it wasn't lust I felt surging inside me. Or perhaps it was a little. But mostly it felt that for a moment, as our mouths and tongues touched, our two souls intertwined. When our lips parted, he traced a finger down my cheek. 'You are amazing,' he said gently. 'I hope you find someone who appreciates you, Hope.' He got up and offered me a hand. 'The next time I go up I'll remember that kiss.' I got up. 'And now, my lady, may I escort you back indoors?' he said. 'There's bound to be an eightsome reel by the end of the night, and you will be able to create absolute havoc in that.'

I tucked my hand in his elbow. He opened the door.

'Lieutenant,' said a man's voice behind us.

I pulled my hand free. 'I have to go,' I said quietly so only Abercrombie could hear. 'This isn't an assignation, although some people might think that. I've work to do. You were quite right about me. I do have demons to punish.' I kissed him quickly on the cheek and stepped back into the darkness. Abercrombie went back inside without looking back.

'So I see you've been enjoying the dance,' said Harvey, his voice heavy with sarcasm. 'Or is this the way you intend to get to know the locals. And I thought Bernie could be fast. They say the war changes everyone.'

Harvey couldn't see me pale and then blush. I made my voice cold. 'It wasn't clever of you to announce yourself.'

'Oh, Abercrombie obviously already has an idea of what kind of a girl you are. He's a gent though. Won't say a word.'

'Right, we need to move. Have you got transport?'

'Yeah, I brought one of the base motorcycles down. Think you can stay on the back?'

'It won't be my first time,' I said.

'Yeah, I guessed that,' said Harvey.

Chapter Thirty-three

Teeth and Claws

I had intended to hold on to Harvey lightly, but his style of driving required me to take a firmer hold. As the wind tore at my face, tangling my hair, despite my having tied it back, the air choked all words. This gave me the chance to reflect on what I was about to do. I wasn't proud of what I must do to Harvey, and I doubted he would forgive me. If he didn't know Bernie was dead – and surely he would have mentioned it – I wasn't going to tell him until after this mission was over.

I had never quite understood Harvey's relationship with my best friend. He had offered to run away and marry her to prevent her marriage. This plan had been conducted via letters and, when he told me about it, I recognised it immediately as a 'Bernie plan'. These were grand plans she made, but knew in her heart would never happen. I'd been fooled by more than one when I first met her, so I had every sympathy for Harvey. However, during that discussion I didn't get the sense that Harvey truly loved her, but rather he was trying to do something he thought any decent man would do – rescue the damsel in distress by any means. As I had written in my report for Fitzroy when Harvey first became an asset:

> *Despite his more unsavoury contacts and methods of acquiring money, Harvey is driven not by greed but by a desire to support his father and many siblings. He has an innate sense of right and wrong, and chooses to fleece only those who can withstand the loss*

240

of fortune. He is intelligent, but overly eager to assume the burdens of others.

I hadn't known how accurate that was at the time. Part of the difficulty of my relationship with him was that while I had needed him operationally, I had repeatedly shown I could shoulder my own burdens. At least up until now. Something I think Harvey both respected and found unladylike. I confused him.

I also knew that while Bernie might have had a fondness for him in a sibling-like manner, she had never loved him, though he clearly felt more for her. I would eventually have to tell him of her death, but I didn't know how to tell him in a way that I could subsequently still handle him as an asset. I also feared that discussing, accepting openly, her death would make me emotionally fragile. Something I could not afford to be on a mission.

I had no real way of telling where we were as Harvey drove without lights. When he unexpectedly came to a skidding halt some time later, I could barely unclench my fingers from his jacket.

'G–g–goodness,' I stuttered, 'I think even my bones have turned to ice.' With stiff legs I climbed off and stumbled slightly.

Harvey flicked down the stand and took off his jacket. 'Here,' he said roughly, 'it's still warm from me. I should have thought to bring you a jacket. Or you should have done.'

'I d–d–didn't even know you could ride a motorbike,' I said, snuggling into the jacket as if it was the last warm place on earth. 'I thought we might steal a car.'

'Do you know how to do that?'

'No,' I said. 'Not really. But you're the mechanic now.' As I began to thaw I got more of a sense of our surroundings. I didn't know the airbase well. There were still buildings I hadn't explored. Largely because I had no right to go into them. Harvey had brought us round the back of the aircraft workshop. We were out of sight of most of the camp. 'Won't they have heard us?' I asked.

241

I could only see Harvey's outline against the night sky. He shook his head. 'There are bikes coming and going all the time. Everyone will presume it's a message for someone else. Either that or they'll think it's someone trying to impress a girl from the dance. I wouldn't say that discipline here is exactly rigid.'

'More Fitzroy-like?' I asked. 'You do your job and he doesn't ask many questions?'

Harvey shook his head again. 'No, even your godfather wouldn't put up with this.'

That was interesting. I said without much thought, 'He's my stepfather now. He married my mother.'

'You lot do like to keep it in the family, don't you? Hang on, what about your father? Oh, Hope, I'm—'

I cut him off. He sounded suddenly so kind and caring, I thought I might cry. 'We'd all expected it. He'd lived much longer than his doctors predicted, but we all saw how he had declined since Dunkirk. He went out there, you know. On one of his old friend's ships. Rescued people until the ship was sunk beneath them. Then he went on to another boat to help them.'

'A hero at the end,' said Harvey. 'I would have liked to meet him.'

I shrugged. Although I secretly thought that my father would have liked to meet Harvey too. My father had always been happy interacting with all sorts of people, and he would have been fascinated to learn about Harvey's more criminal activities. But if I revealed any of this now I knew my emotions would override me. This was not like me and I didn't like it. So perhaps I was more brutal with him than usual. 'Look, I need to get back to the dance before I'm missed. What did you want to show me?'

'Yeah, right,' said Harvey, reverting back to his earlier tone. 'Back door is this way. Shouldn't be anyone around in this bit, but we'll have to be quiet.'

'What aircraft do we have on the base?'

I couldn't see his face, but from the start he gave I realised I'd asked the wrong question.

'You don't know what aircraft we have? An airbase is what craft it has.'

'I would have thought the personnel came into it,' I snapped back.

'We have two "wooden wonders" – de Havilland Mosquitoes to you. The squad flies Hasker Hurricanes and we've two North American Harvards for training alongside the blue boxes on site. I've heard we used to have three Harvards, but whenever I ask what happened to the third they all shut up. Other stuff passes through, but that's what we run.'

'Have you heard people talking about Collins?'

'Only that whatever happens you shouldn't know about him.'

I gave Harvey a hard stare. 'This isn't funny.'

'No joke, Hope. I overheard a couple of the mechanics talking about the new liaison, and how the story had to be kept from you. They shut up the moment I came fully into the hangar.'

'Great,' I said. 'More bloody mystery. Shall we get on?'

Harvey opened a door that had been hidden by the darkness, and a low light crept out. He hustled me through as quickly as possible. Inside the workshop it was intimidatingly huge. I knew some of the aircraft were out ready to fly quickly, and some of the others would be in a separate hangar, but still the space here was filled with the shadows of sharp angles and giant shapes thrown on the wall. I felt like a tiny Alice in Wonderland creeping through dangerous territory. I had always hated that book. Alice has so little control of her environment and no way to know what surreal nightmare she is about to encounter next. The fact she isn't a screaming mess by the end of it has always confused me.

Harvey made his way carefully through to one side of the hangar. I realised, with relief, that the doors were closed, so not only were we still in blackout but hopefully no one would notice our presence. But then why was there a light on? Had Harvey left it on for us? I took a breath. If I continued like this I was going to be completely paranoid. It was always an issue when you worked in espionage – that you lost your sense of perspective and suspected everyone. I needed to remind myself that Harvey had been through a tough time. His hostility towards me was nothing personal.

When we got over to the wall, he turned over a section of panelling.

'Is that part of a plane?' I said, crouching down to see it properly.

'One of the Hurricanes. From the fuselage.'

There were broad stripes across the metal.

'Touch it, but be careful,' said Harvey.

I reached out tentative fingers and touched the metal. Cold, smooth, and then the stripe, the edge of it was sharp. It sliced into me. I pulled my hand back quickly, and sucked my finger.

'I warned you!'

'Next time be more specific,' I said. My authoritative tone was compromised by the finger in my mouth. I peered closer, keeping my hands well away. There were five parallel marks. 'It's like something clawed the panel,' I said. 'I've been told Scottish wild-cats are tough, but . . .' I stood up. 'So you think someone is sabotaging the planes?'

'I worked on this plane before its last flight. I checked it over. These marks weren't on it.'

'So it's someone on the base? Or do you think the local people are involved? How tight is the security here?'

'No, you don't understand,' said Harvey. 'These marks appeared mid-flight.'

'That's not possible,' I said.

'No, it isn't,' said Harvey. 'But it did.'

'What does the pilot say?'

'He's in hospital. Shell shock or some such thing. Anyway, it's over fifty miles away. I thought that might have been arranged by your godfather – sorry, stepfather.'

'Why? I don't believe he has anything to do with medical relief.'

'Because the pilot, a Flight Lieutenant David Wallis, was tell-ing everyone that a faery tore up his plane. An ugly, green, warty faery with claws and gleaming fangs.'

244

'Poor chap,' I said. 'I can't imagine what they go through.'

'Yeah,' said Harvey. 'Me neither. But look at the frigging panel, Hope. Something or someone tore through the side of that panel as if it was made of butter.'

'You're sure it wasn't gunfire? Even gunfire from the ground?'

'Absolutely. Whatever did that was sharp, like a knife. You can see where the metal has curled up. I have no idea what did it, but I have to say that claws, really, really strong claws would fit the bill.'

'Did he talk about it? This David Wallis, before he was taken away? Did anyone on the base or even, heaven forbid, any civilians hear about it?'

'He was screaming his head off when we got him out of the cockpit. I reckon more than half the country heard his shouting. But yes, it's still a favourite topic of debate in the local pub.'

'Damn,' I said. 'What do the locals say about it?'

'Oh, they agree Wallis is off his head. But they think the faeries did it. Same faeries as carved up the side of his plane. I've got to say if I looked out along my wing and saw some airborne critter taking my craft apart I'd start losing it too.'

'You cannot possibly believe this was done by a faery.'

'You're thinking of the Victorian idea of cherubs,' said Harvey. 'Up here they remember the old fey, believe in them still, and those creatures are ancient and malicious. Brian McKenzie saying how the fey are angry the airbase is on their hill hasn't helped matters.'

'But Brian's harmless,' I said. 'He's a nice bloke. Bit odd, but—'

'I'm not saying an eight-year-old couldn't beat him at arm wrestling, but he's a local legend round here. When it comes to the odd, the lost and the supernatural, his word is gospel to the local people.'

Chapter Thirty-four

Susan Confesses

Breakfast at The Manse the next morning proved to be a quiet event. At each of the long tables many chairs stayed unoccupied, and those who did come down for breakfast had grey faces and handled their heads with great care. I let my saucer clatter experimentally, and every other face winced in pain.

Harvey had taken me back to the dance. We'd arrived to see Abercrombie and Susan emerge from round the back of the hall. I went inside with them, and Harvey headed off. Hamish gave me a slightly sheepish nod, and headed back to the dancefloor. Susan came with me to put my hair to rights, and at the same time gave me a far too detailed synopsis of what she and Hamish had been up to. In the end I knew enough that if I was ever caught by her grandfather and interrogated, I could say that Susan now knew an awful lot more about male anatomy, but that her virtue remained intact. It seemed that without the buffer of my presence, Abercrombie had disregarded her relatives and accepted her flirtatious invitations.

I saw him later in the night, drinking and smoking with some of the other pilots. He held himself well, but he was to my eyes very drunk. At this point I assumed the pilots were passing whisky around among themselves. Hamish had a kind of desperate cheerfulness about him. I managed to dance close enough to hear him telling some of the crudest jokes I had ever heard, worse than anything I'd heard in the auxies – and they really were training to be a suicide squad. The crudity didn't sit well with him. I had

246

become increasingly aware that how men behaved around women they liked and how they behaved with their own kind was quite different. But Abercrombie rattled me.

He wasn't at breakfast. In fact no one I had got to know well was. Susan was upstairs asleep on my floor. She'd been sick three times before we left the village hall. I'd taken one sniff of the punch and gone to the loo for a drink of water when I was thirsty. I didn't know if spiking the drink was the villagers' idea or some-one else's.

I finished up my unusually large and satisfying breakfast – so much food on the side lay untouched that for once I hadn't wor-ried about taking more than my fair share. I took two pieces of cold toast and a cup of weak tea and headed back up to see Susan.

She made a revolted face at the toast, but disentangled herself from my spare blankets to sit up and drink the tea. Her face, smeared with last night's make-up, still had a slight green tinge and her hair hung lankly with grease.

'I'm ever so grateful to you for letting me sleep here,' she said. 'I'm going to get a rocket when I get home. I'm staying with my grandparents.'

'I know,' I said, 'you told me last night. I rang them and said you were staying with me as the heel had come off your shoe and we couldn't find anyone we thought sober enough to drive you back. I'm afraid you will have to sacrifice your shoes.' I picked up one of the pretty pink strappy things and broke off the heel with a loud snap. 'Mrs M will have a pair of boots in the downstairs cupboard you can borrow. You can say we only found them this morning. We might even be able to find you a change of cloth-ing, but you need to wash your face and hair at least.'

She sprang up at that and putting her tea on my dressing table, flung her arms briefly around me. 'Oh, Hope, you are a brick,' she said.

'You need to hurry,' I said. 'Your grandfather is sending a car for you in forty-five minutes, and I'm coming back to the base with you.'

By now Susan had seen her reflection in the mirror. 'Oh no,' she said. 'Oh no. I had this dream about being at the dance – but it wasn't a dream, was it? I really was that bad.'

I nodded.

'Oh, God,' she said. 'Did I really go out the back with Hamish?' I nodded again.

'What if I'm pregnant!' she said.

'I don't believe you can get pregnant with what you did. You told me all the gory details.'

'I don't remember a thing! How will I ever face him?'

'He's ten years older than you if he's a day. He hasn't exactly covered himself in glory. But I do think he's a decent bloke. He won't talk about it – and not only because he's scared of the Wing Co.'

'Just my luck, I misbehave for once and can't remember a thing.'

'I'll keep your secret,' I said. 'Now hurry up and get ready.'

While she made herself smart I tidied up the room. Then I went downstairs and found some clean clothes from the ubiquitous 'lost items' hamper that stood in the hall: a blouse, slacks, jumper and some undersized men's loafers. She wouldn't look glamorous, but she'd be warm enough and smart enough for work. In the end she was ready ten minutes before the car was due. She gave me a glowing smile. 'You've been the very best pal a girl could have, Hope,' she said. 'I don't know how I will ever make it up to you.'

I took a deep breath and looked her straight in the eyes. Sometimes I hated my job. 'There is something you can do for me,' I said. 'You can meet me at luncheon and tell me about Collins.'

She went a little paler. 'I don't know anything about that,' she said.

'I think you do,' I said. 'I think you do because everything official goes through you. You've got one of the highest security clearances on the base. Which considering the state you got yourself into last night is a bit of a concern.'

'You're going to speak to grandfather!' Her hand flew to her mouth.

I shook my head. 'I really, really don't want to do that. I need you to promise me that you'll be more careful – drink less punch.' I smiled. She didn't.

'I thought you were my friend.'

'I am,' I said. 'You know, normally people your age are expected to mess up. I was at university with a great pal, Bernie. She was crazy. Utterly boy mad and related to someone important. The scrapes I got her out of would make your hair curl. But I've come to realise that it's normal for young people to mess up – and that includes me. Only the thing is, we're at war now, and we simply can't mess up. Other people's lives are on the line. We have to be prepared to stand by whatever we do – so if someone asked you to show them a file or they'd tell the wing commander about what you did at some party – you need to tell them to go right ahead and shout it out to the world. If you want to continue what you're doing then you have to be blackmail-proof. You know too much.'

I expected her to hang her head in shame, but she scowled. 'I never wanted this job,' she said. 'A nice cosy office experience that would stand me in good stead after the war,' she said the words with bitterness. 'I wanted to be a nurse, but neither Papa nor Grandfather thought it was a job for a nice girl. My mother kept going on about how I'd be expected to wash men's personals. I thought she meant underwear.'

I laughed out loud. 'But she meant something more firmly attached,' I said. 'I've done some nursing and if you're in an army hospital there are male orderlies for that kind of thing. How about I talk to the wing commander about this for you? I can tell him what it's really like in a military hospital.' I was lying, of course. I would be drawing from the stories my mother had told me of the time she went undercover as a nurse.

'Would you?' said Susan.

I nodded. 'I'm sorry I need to ask you about Collins, but I do really want to help you.'

Susan sat down on my bed. 'The driver can wait a few minutes,' she said. 'I need to get something straight. You're here to investigate what happened with Collins, aren't you? Granddad repeatedly asked for someone to investigate even though he thought he'd be blamed. You know that, don't you? He's trying to be a good officer, but he's — he's old and this lot aren't like he was as a young man. I don't think he understands them. They don't—'

'Susan, I can't tell you what I think you're asking.'

'You don't have to. When you said you'd been a nurse I knew I was right. You're an official investigator. You don't have to say anything. I'll tell you about Collins — everything I know and everything I've read, but you have to promise to put in a good word for Granddad. They should have left him in retirement.'

'I'll certainly do what I can for him.'

'I'm only glad we're finally getting an official investigation. There's been so much bad feeling. It will be a relief to talk to someone. I was there, you know. I heard it all.'

I neither confirmed or denied a thing. The driver outside hooted his horn impatiently. We got our things together and went downstairs. Susan walked with a light step, confident I would set everything to rights. I felt like a bit of a cad, but then as Fitzroy would say, that's the job.

Chapter Thirty-five

The Morning After

At the base the driver let us off and Susan disappeared into the wing commander's office. I didn't have much interest in seeing him, so I decided to walk around the base. I met Abercrombie as he came out of the mess hall.

'Busy?' I asked.

'I can make time, if you need it, Lieutenant.'

I smiled wryly. 'Thank you, Squadron Leader,' I said. 'Now, do you want me to do the embarrassing part first, or—'

He stopped and took me over to the side of one of the buildings. 'Hope, we're on duty. I can't talk about . . . I've been made aware I behaved badly last night. You disappeared and I thought—'

'I was still on duty,' I said. He gave me an odd look. 'Look, it's not personal, Hamish. I can't imagine the pressure you're under, but what you did with Susan . . .'

He groaned and put his hand over his face. 'She told you?'

I couldn't resist. 'In great descriptive detail.'

'I'll be court-martialled,' he said.

'She doesn't remember a thing this morning,' I said. 'She has a vague idea that you and she got up to something, and is desperate that no one else finds out. She was so drunk she blacked out when she got to The Manse. Was it one of your men that spiked the punch?'

'No, they were on strict orders to leave the punch alone. We had some whisky we were passing around, but Susan's not the only young woman who would have been drinking the punch. I come down hard on my men. I don't let them take advantage of the girls here.'

'So you and Susan?'

'She was fine when we . . . I swear, Hope. I'm not that kind of man.'

'I didn't think you were,' I said. 'Anyway, all I'm trying to say is she's forgotten it happened, and I suggest you do the same. I don't think you'll find she's trying to flirt with you at the village dance again. I'm more concerned with who spiked the punch and if they were genuinely trying to do harm. I assume pilots don't fly drunk?'

'Drinking on duty is a court-martial offence.'

'How about being hung-over?'

'I see your point,' said Hamish. 'You think someone might have been trying to put the pilots at a disadvantage. But how would they know we'd be going into action today.'

I tilted my head on one side and sighed.

'Oh God, you think we might have traitors, enemy agents here?'

'Or it could simply be a local with a heavy hand and a large bottle,' I said. 'But I have to consider possibilities. I also suggest that in future you have someone sober watching any shared drinks at one of your dances.'

Hamish nodded. 'I agree completely. And, Hope, I am so sorry about my behaviour. I'll make it up to you, I swear.'

I felt a bit sick inside. Hamish was nice enough, but I didn't have any particular feelings for him. How did you say that to a chap who went off to risk his life in the air almost every night?

Hating myself every moment, I put my hand briefly and lightly on his arm. 'Hamish, don't. It's fine. I'll forget it too. As you say, we are on duty. Can I ask you something? Something official?'

He frowned, but nodded.

'One of the mechanics showed me a piece of metal with what looked like claw marks. I wondered why you hadn't got rid of it. I mean, it's only adding fuel to the ridiculous fire about the fae-ries,' I said.

252

'The most straightforward answer is that we are short on supplies. Hence the wooden wonders. The Air Force is criminally undersupplied. But there is more to it. Have a drink with me tonight? The local pub has some quieter corners. It's not only that I have a lot to do this morning, and I feel like a three-day-old cabbage, but I'd rather not risk being overheard.'

'All right, a drink it is,' I said.

'I'll pick you up at The Manse after dinner?' He bent down and brushed his lips briefly against my cheek. 'You're a bit of a marvel, Lieutenant Stapleford, you know that?' Then he walked quickly away.

And I thought I couldn't feel any worse when I was blackmailing Susan into talking to me. All I needed now was for Harvey to think I'd betrayed him in some awful way, and I'd have a hat-trick.

I walked over to the first-aid centre. No one had said if they had a medic here or simply a box with bandages, and I didn't like to bet on the odds with either. I opened the door to the small shed that seemed to be used as a triage centre. 'Is anyone here?' I said.

Mike, the quartermaster, who'd given me a lift on my first day, appeared in the doorway. 'Good morning, Lieutenant. You lost or looking for another lift?'

'I'm looking for the airbase medic,' I said. 'I'm not hurt. I just want a chat.'

'Well, that would be me. Basic combat medic training. Anything more serious and we ship them off to hospital. For the most part it's my job to keep them alive until they see a real doctor. Come into my office and have a cuppa? We got off on the wrong foot, I think. I was in a foul mood when we met. A quartermaster's lot is not a happy one.'

He opened the door wider and I saw that as well as some cupboards there were two seats and an electric ring with a kettle sitting on it. 'That would be wonderful,' I said and came inside. He filled the kettle from a large canteen of water and set it to boil. He spooned tea into a large brown teapot, and set out a couple of mugs. He even had a small jug of milk.

'I might even have a bit of a sugar lump if you want,' he said. 'I keep a bit by in case anyone needs some strong sweet tea. The ladies on the base can find some things disturbing. Although I'd say that by now most of us have hardened up a fair bit.'

'Do you see a lot of injuries?' I asked.

'It's most often the mechanics. Bruises, trapped fingers, that kind of thing. Sometimes I open the bar and administer a drop of brandy to the lads if they've had a bad sortie. But that's about it. And to be honest, the lads are usually more interested in a cup of tea or getting to their beds. When they're out over the sea looking for the U-boats it seems to really wear on them. Don't know if it's battling the wind we get up here, or the tedium of it. As far as I know they've not spotted one yet.' He picked up the kettle and paused, mid pour. 'Not sure I should have told you that.'

'I didn't hear a thing,' I said with a smile. Then I fell into a serious expression. 'But it's different for the Hurricanes, isn't it? They regularly see action, don't they? It feels horrid to ask, but have you lost many pilots since the base opened?'

'I'm sure it's all in the files,' he said, and handed me a cup of tea. 'I don't know that we've lost more than anyone else.'

'It must affect morale,' I said. 'I imagine there's a strong camaraderie on the base, and even more between the flyers.'

'Yeah, some of them do bond, the lads. But between you and me, it's an odd friendship. Most of the time I think they're pretending to each other how brave they are. Generally they're scared – except maybe Abercrombie. He's odder still or maybe it's a command thing. Nothing much seems to rattle him.'

'They are all so terribly young,' I said. 'We ask so much of them.'

'You're not much older, with respect, Lieutenant.'

'I'm not flying into a hail of bullets,' I said.

The quartermaster settled himself more snugly in his seat. 'One of the cats that hangs around the base is pregnant,' he said, 'and I've been told by Mrs Wing Co that I'm to look after Mitzi during her "lying-in". From what I've read, cats go off and do it all by themselves, and that's what I'm hoping for. Too much gore

254

in that for me. But I've pulled a body from a burning plane and not turned a hair. I've laid out the dead and burned for the ambulance to take away. I felt sad, mind, but I always felt that was a last respectful thing I could do for them. Other men vomit at the sight of a clean corpse, let alone one burned to hell. But the point is this, what scares one person is meaningless to another. There was one pilot we had, who was scared of wee bugs, but once he was in the air nothing phased him. We've all got our demons.'

'What about your faeries?'

'Oh, them yon buggers!' He gave a deep sigh. 'I'm not saying as I believe in them, but I can't explain how hammers, wrenches, even the wing commander's rubbish bucket somehow disappear overnight. We've security, and I keep everything under lock and key.'

'No missing ordinance, then?'

'No, thank the gods. Whoever is taking stuff is making sure they take stuff that causes daily strife, but—'

'Is never important enough to get a whole load of servicemen on a search,' I said thoughtfully. 'So it's about inconvenience rather than direct malevolence.'

'I don't know about that, ma'am, but it could cost me my sergeant's stripes if it goes on much longer. The roast potatoes went missing just before mess on Sunday, and the wing commander was beside himself. Insists we have a proper Sunday meal if we're on base on a Sunday. I'm not sure what they're using for the beef now, and to be honest I don't want to ask.'

'I'll do what I can,' I said. 'The faeries are clearly part of the community here too.'

'That's right, ma'am,' said the quartermaster, downing the last of his tea, 'you have a bit of a parley with them and then read 'em the riot act. Otherwise I'll be all for driving iron posts down into the hill.'

I handed him back my empty mug and smiled. I had a vague memory of reading in some folk tale that faeries didn't like iron, but it was the seriousness of the way he said it that surprised me.

He gave a sudden little laugh, as if it was all a joke, but when he'd spoken of driving in iron posts there had been an echo of the unpleasant person I had first met in the quartermaster.

I left the shed and walked at random along one of the paths that wound through the base. The whole thing was set on a hill, but the size of the hill coupled with the sprawling nature of the base tricked your eye into thinking it was set among the paddocks below us. The base around the dome was wide and gentle in slope. The top of it easily accommodated the landing strips for the Hurricanes. If the 'wooden wonders', as Harvey had called them, were going up then it looked to me as if the rest of the planes needed to be cleared to one side or to be already in flight. Then there were the odd chunky yellow Harvards. There were two out of the hangars today, but these were well away from the Hurricanes. The Harvards took up two pilots and they didn't look anything like the Hurricanes. I wished I had some time to do some more research on military aircraft. Even reading up on the RAF in general would have been helpful. Fitzroy might be intelligence now, but he was army through and through. Generally his operations involved army personnel. I'd certainly never met any Navy men through the Department and there was a rumour I'd picked up that he loathed the Navy. He'd told me he'd kept up his pilot's licence in such a back-handed manner, as if it was of no real import, and indeed he flew so very badly, that I suspected he thought the RAF was actually a poor subset of the proper service – that is the Army and Military Intelligence.

I stopped, suddenly brought up short by a fence. My wandering had brought me to the taped-off area that had previously intrigued me.

I looked around. I could see no one nearby. I began to walk the perimeter. I looked about me again. I couldn't see a soul. Usually I would have planned this, but sometimes you have to act on the spur of the moment. I set one foot on the bottom ledge of the fence and began to climb.

The fence was a mixture of panelling and wire roll. Both

seemed integral to keeping the other upright. I reckoned it reached about twelve feet up. Certainly no pedestrian could see inside, but planes would fly across it every day. Whatever was in there all the pilots knew about it. I was about halfway up, and had caught sight of something yellow through a gap in the wood, when there was a sharp tug on my right ankle. I twisted, locking my right arm through a hole in the fence, and kicked out hard with my left leg. A man's voice uttered an oath. I swung on my arm, attempting to turn round, and if possible drop directly down on my attacker. But before I could manage this I felt the strength of a man applied to each of my legs. A sharp forceful tug, and my arm unlocked. My shoulder flamed raw with pain, and my vision blurred. I felt myself falling, out of control. I curled as best I could, and hoped to land on something soft. Preferably a vulnerable part of one of my attackers.

Chapter Thirty-six

And Then There Were Three

'Crikey,' said Harvey's voice. 'It's Hope!'

I opened my eyes. 'My head!' I groaned. 'Why does it always have to be my head?' A face leaned over mine. It had blurry edges, but I didn't think it was Harvey. 'Who's you?' I asked. My words sounded a bit slurred. 'I've only had tea,' I managed to say.

'How many fingers am I holding up?' asked a second voice.

'I can't even see your face properly,' I said. Then I added, 'Twit,' for good measure. It didn't make my head less sore, but it felt good. 'Why'd you pull me off?' I asked. 'Twits,' I added for clarity.

'We didn't realise who you were,' said the big blobby face above me.

'So if you see someone climbing you go ahead and pull them down if you don't know who they are?' I asked, still keeping my eyes shut.

'It's a restricted area,' said the second voice, sounding slightly apologetic.

I opened my eyes at that. The features of the face resolved this time. 'Leo!' I said. 'What the blithering whatsit are you doing here?'

'I'm your transport,' said Leo. 'I came with a motorbike.'

'And I've been telling him I have a motorbike,' said Harvey, sounding cross.

'Yes, but you're meant to be undercover,' I said. 'Harvey – Leo. Leo – Harvey.' I closed my eyes again. 'I thought Fitzroy had chewed you up and spat you out,' I said.

Leo grunted. 'Your godfather is . . . well . . . he's Fitzroy. That was a bit of a shock.'

'Stepfather now,' I said. 'Did someone turn the sun up?'

'You should sit up,' said Harvey.

'No,' I said. 'I don't want to.'

'But I thought your father had only . . .' said Leo. 'He shouldn't have sent you on a mission. He had a go at me about you being vulnerable because of your father and your friend – and then . . . You should have stayed with us.'

I struggled to sit up. 'Did I seem to have much of a choice to you? Besides, you don't look as if you're still with them.'

'Seconded,' said Leo.

'That's how it always starts,' said Harvey darkly. 'What friend?'

'Hang on, wait. He didn't tell me till much later – and my telegram. You mean he knew all along? You mean he could have told me in person?'

Leo shrugged. 'Are you ready to stand yet?'

'What friend?' asked Harvey again.

'Her best friend,' said Leo. 'What was her name – Amy? No, it began with a B.'

'Bernie?' said Harvey, going sheet white. 'Hope, what's happened to Bernie?'

At this point it seemed my best option was to pass out, so I did.

I came to lying on a makeshift bed in the medical shed. 'If you wanted another cuppa you only had to ask, ma'am,' said the quartermaster. 'It would have been no trouble.'

'How is she?' asked Leo.

'I'd prefer it if she went into the hospital,' said Mike. 'It's not like I can look inside her head and see what's going on.'

'But you're confident she doesn't have any fractures, skull or otherwise?'

'Not as far as I can tell,' said Mike. 'Is anything hurting really bad, ma'am?'

'My head,' I said. 'All over. I've had concussion before. This hurts but no more than usual.'

'You've the start of a mighty big bruise on the back of your head. I'm still not entirely sure how you tripped and landed on your back,' said Mike. 'But that's a thick part of the skull. Rest is what she needs. You want to help me get her back to The Manse? I can rig up a bed in the jeep, but I'll need someone to stay beside her over the bumps.' He looked at me. 'Are you sure you'd rather not go to the hospital?'

'Is it a military hospital?' asked Leo.

'We've had plenty of military folk go through it,' said Mike, 'but no, not as such.'

'Then she can't go. I'll call it in, and perhaps you can get the local doctor to drop by. As long as she's chaperoned that should be all right.'

'Och, I see,' said Mike. 'She's been privy to something secret? Our folk at the hospital are good people.'

'I'm sure,' said Leo, 'but I'm not allowed to let her go there.' He loomed over me. 'I'm pulling rank here, Hope.'

'Fine,' I said, closing my eyes again. 'I need to talk to Susan. We were meeting for luncheon. Where's Harvey? Could he ask her to come and see me later?'

'Harvey's in a bit of a pet,' said Leo. 'Seems you forgot to tell him his lady love was dead.'

'Ah,' I said.

'I understand,' said Leo in a voice that meant he did. 'Rest for now, Hope. You're no use to anyone like this.'

'But why is it always my head?' I said. Then I passed out.

When I came round I was lying on my bed back at The Manse. Leo was sitting in a chair beside my bed. 'How on earth did you get around Mrs M?' I asked.

'Oh, I said I was your husband,' said Leo. 'Sorry, I didn't think anything else would cut it. Do you remember the doctor coming by?'

I shook my head and immediately regretted it.

'He thinks you were jolly lucky. Said something about you having a stronger skull than most. Kind of an inbuilt crash helmet. He said it ran in families and asked if anyone in your family often bumped their heads or some such rot. You didn't seem to understand as you kept repeating that your stepfather did. I think the doctor thought you were rather a fool.'

I raised a hand to my forehead. 'It's going to get worse. I've got a date tonight, and you've just told everyone you're my husband.'

'I told your landlady,' said Leo. 'I needed to be with you, and check what you said. You know that.'

'About what's going on here? Really? I barely have a clue.'

'No, Hope, about what we were working on together before you were pulled back to your department.'

'Oh,' I said. 'You mean—'

'Exactly.'

'Damn it. I'm not going to come out of this well, and I'd only just got close enough to Abercrombie to get him to talk. Damn. Damn. Damn.'

'You mean it wasn't an actual date?' said Leo.

'You sound relieved?'

'Makes it less complicated,' said Leo. 'If this guy is an officer we can maybe tell him the truth about you being here undercover. He doesn't need to know that it's stuff from my department I'm worried about you spilling.'

'Won't work,' I said. 'He's one of the people who might have the info I need. I can't tell him.'

'I suppose you could be a bit of a floozy?'

'If it didn't hurt to sit up I'd throw something at you.'

'No you wouldn't,' said Leo. 'I outrank you, remember.'

'So? My stepfather regularly punches people above his rank.'

'But you're not him,' said Leo. 'At least not yet, thankfully.' He sighed. 'I suppose you could make me the rotter. I've run off with my secretary or something before the war started, but I'm back because I heard you were hurt and I feel remorseful.'

'I like that,' I said. 'He'll probably punch you.'

'Yes, I missed you too,' said Leo. He leaned over me. His forehead was furrowed with worry. 'Are you sure we shouldn't get you to a hospital?'

'You said the local one wasn't secure?'

'It's not, but I could manage something.'

'Ah,' I said, 'they have a facility up here? Did Fitzroy nab you at my flat or later?'

'Later. I was working up here with the – you know.'

'Is it going well?'

Leo nodded. He sat back down. 'The people are extraordinary. I'll tell you what I can when we're somewhere more secure.'

I sat up. My vision swam, but nowhere near as badly as before. 'More secure than a boarding house full of servicemen and women.'

'And gabby staff,' said Leo. 'What is up with this place? It feels . . .' he searched for a word, 'off.'

I tried to pile up some cushions behind me. I was making a right mess of it, so Leo took over. It felt strangely intimate to be with him like this in my room. However, I was fighting a battle not to vomit so kissing was out of the question. Not that I was thinking about kissing Leo. It was simply that he was big, and solid and decent. I had an urge after everything that had happened to collapse into his arms. He was a huge improvement on Cole for company.

'Right, I should explain what I know – and it's only bits and pieces. The wing commander is from the Great War. He doesn't fly. He was in India too, and his wife, the current head of the Women's Institute, thinks she can order the whole community around, as she presumably did overseas. The funny thing is although in lots of ways the locals resent her, they still let her be in charge of the WI and she appears to champion them. Even when she's up against her own husband. I'm beginning to suspect he might not be up to the job. He's a local man, and I think they thought he would garner goodwill.'

'If he's not up to it he has to be replaced. You have no idea how crucial the war in the air is now, Hope. We have to gain air superiority if we are to prevent invasion.'

'I know. There's more,' I said. 'There was a submarine at the beach two nights ago.'

Leo shot up.

'It's all right,' I said quickly. 'This isn't part of my mission. I met up with a senior officer. He told me about the sub. He said the danger was over, but I'm wary.'

'Where is he?'

'I couldn't tell you, even if I wanted to,' I said. 'Besides, it's not as if I was there.' The lie came out all too easily. I wanted to erase what had happened, and while I couldn't turn back time, I could rewrite this bit of history. I had a sense that Cole would keep me out of his report.

'I shouldn't have told you,' I said. 'But it's part of the picture. Please don't repeat it, even to Fitzroy.'

'That's a big ask,' said Leo.

'I never saw it. Perhaps I misunderstood,' I said. 'Perhaps I even dreamed it because my head hurts?'

'I'll make you a deal,' said Leo. 'We scout this beach for a couple of nights. I know there are patrols to check for subs. But if something is getting through – I don't think you realise how serious this is.'

'And then there's the faeries,' I said. 'The locals believe the base has been set on a faery mound, and that it brings ill luck. Stuff keeps going missing too. Not ordinance, thank goodness, but small things, tools, rubbish bins, food trays with the food in it. I think a lot of the servicemen are most upset about that.'

'And they believe the faeries are doing this? Do you?'

'No, I think it's someone unhappy about the base being there and using the folk tales to express their discontent.'

'That sounds possible. Do you know who?'

'No, and it means the base isn't secure.'

Leo nodded. 'That's a worry.'

'Something happened to someone called Collins. He's a pilot. Whatever that was it either started the rot or pushed things on a lot. I thought the fenced area might be something to do with what happened.'

'Harvey climbed over after we left. He'll have a report for me later.'

'Good,' I said. 'I take it you're heading up this op now?'

Leo shook his head. 'No, I can overrule you if I think you're being reckless – your stepfather's words, not mine – but it's your command.'

'He said that?'

'He's worried about your recent bereavements – and he said other stresses you've faced?'

I shrugged carefully. 'So subs, missing equipment, bad feelings, possibly bad commander, faeries, the mystery of Collins, and sabotage.'

'I thought you said the faeries didn't do any real harm?'

'I'm talking about something clawing through a plane's fuselage mid flight. That's what my date with Hamish Abercrombie is all about. He'd said he'd talk to me about that.'

'I see. And why is Susan coming to see you? She is, by the way, as soon as I let her.'

'Oh, she behaved a bit inappropriately at the dance. I said I'd forget it and cover for her if she'd talk to me about Collins.'

'I don't know whether to be impressed or appalled, Stapleford. I suspect your stepfather would approve.'

There was a sudden rap on the door, and Harvey strode in. I looked at Leo. 'Who is he meant to be, my brother?' I said.

'I think we'd established you don't have a scrap of reputation left,' said Leo.

I poked my tongue out at him.

'I'm glad to see despite everything your sense of humour is intact,' said Harvey in a tone that suggested exactly the opposite. He went and leaned against the far wall. He folded his arms and regarded us much as one might something one has found on the bottom of their shoe. He had mud on his face and over some of his clothing.

'I thought we had cleared this up,' said Leo. 'You know why she didn't tell you mid-mission. Hell, her CO didn't even tell her until his hand was forced.'

'Forced?' I said.

'He clearly had no intention of telling you when I met him. I have to assume an event precipitated his change of heart.'

'Ha! Heart,' said Harvey. 'That man has no heart.' He looked pointedly at me as if to say he thought I was going the same way.

'I'm desperately sad Bernie is dead,' I said. 'It's worse that she wasn't happy, and that I can see no point in her death.'

'Hope,' said Leo under his breath, 'you're not helping.'

I could see that Harvey's brow was growing more furrowed. He'd crossed his arms, and I could see his knuckles going white as he gripped his own upper arms. One of the abiding memories I had of Bernie was of her teasing Harvey at a picnic we'd had on the way to Brighton. The war hadn't begun, and it had been a glorious day. She'd been on top form and poor Harvey was dazzled and bemused by her.

'She was my friend long before she met you, and she was crazy and silly, and scatty, and beautiful and naughty in many ways, but she was fun. She brought a bright light into what was my rather dull world at that time. I miss her every day.' I could feel a tear sliding down my face. 'And if you think for one minute she'd want me to mourn and mope and give myself over to grief, then you never knew her at all. She might have been half American, but she was also proud to be British, and when life became serious, she could be serious too – for a short while at least – and she'd want me to fight tooth and nail to get rid of Hitler. She'd expect me to single-handedly end the war, knowing her. Buck up, Hope, she'd say. This is what you do. Go and give those bad guys hell. And that's what I'm going to do, and every day I do it, I'll be remembering her. I can't bring her back, but I can honour her memory.' I sniffed. 'And will you both please get out now!'

I turned my face to the wall. The tears were coming thick and fast. I could manage to keep my sobs silent for only so long.

'Hope,' said Leo, 'we need to—'

'I'll be out in a moment,' I said. I could feel my shoulders shaking. I waited until I heard the door close, before I threw myself down on my pillow and cried my eyes out.

Chapter Thirty-seven

Collins' Legacy

I don't know how long I cried for. Grief washed over me like a tidal wave and I all but vanished beneath it for a short while. When I thought I might come apart and dissolve I pushed back against my sadness. I thought how Bernie would have wanted – unlike I had told Harvey – me to have a jolly good cry about her. She knew that I loved her and I believe she loved me. If this bloody war hadn't divided us, I would have expected her to continue getting me into trouble well into my eighties. Indeed, I'd rather relied on it. We'd talked about the fact that our husbands would have to be best friends, so they could console each other when we disappeared off on wild adventures. All this was, of course, long before I became an agent. Back when we had both looked at the open space of our lives ahead with some misgiving. I wished I'd forced my way into her husband's house. I wished I had thrown the blighter up against the wall and asked him what the hell was going on. I wished Bernie had trusted me enough to tell me what was happening inside her marriage. But it was all past. All over.

So I took my best memories of Bernie, my love and affection for her, and I folded them up very tightly and tucked them secure into my heart. Our friendship had changed me for ever and I would never forget her. Then I submerged my mind into cold rationality. I needed to figure out what the hell was going on here before someone got seriously hurt.

I got up and using the jug of water and basin that had been left in my room this morning, I thoroughly washed my face. I got into more casual clothes suitable for meeting Hamish later in case I didn't get time to change. I chose trousers and a jumper that brought out the colour of my eyes. I brushed my hair out and, for now, tied it firmly back. I could let it out later.

I opened the door. There was no sign of Leo or Harvey. I peered over the banister and saw the pair of them in the hall. Harvey had draped his lanky form over a chair. He looked like a balloon all the air had gone out of. Leo, in contrast, was pacing back and forth. Impatience radiated from him. I came quickly down the stairs. I walked past Harvey, and went up to Leo. 'What's wrong?' I said quietly. 'What's happened?'

'Not here,' said Leo, and taking my arm, he tugged me outside. Harvey followed.

We walked in silence until Leo found somewhere he thought was unobserved and where we could still see if anyone came close to us. The ground was damp, and the sky a dull, dirty cream colour.

'I told you Harvey climbed that fence. He said there's a crashed-up North American Harvard in there. It's been covered by branches, and even a tarpaulin, but he had a decent look.'

'What are they used for?' I asked.

'Advanced training,' said Leo. 'I didn't think this base was a training field.'

'It must be. I met someone off the train who was a flight cadet. Simon Stewart,' I said. 'He only had a hundred and thirty hours. That's not enough, is it? It's a hundred and fifty, I think.'

'That's odd,' said Leo. 'I got a chance to read up on some of the details about flight training. It didn't mention this as either an elementary training school or an advanced one. Besides, isn't it too small?'

Harvey coughed. When he spoke his voice was raspy, as if he was forcing himself to talk. 'They do train pilots here. Only a few at a time from what I can make out. This base is a bit of an odds and sods affair. Makeshift in more ways than one.'

'I suppose it's not impossible,' said Leo. 'We don't have enough pilots, enough ammo, enough planes, enough anything.'

'Tell me about it,' said Harvey gruffly. He still hadn't looked me in the eye. 'Half the time we're patching them up with string, waxed paper, a hope and a prayer. But you're missing out the important bit.'

'I can't believe you were right about that, Harvey. I don't mean to be rude but there is no way they would have left—'

'And I'm telling you there's a bloody body in it.'

'Collins,' I said.

'Unless anyone else is missing, that's what I think,' said Harvey. He was now looking at the ground rather than me.

'Could they be treating the plane like a grave in itself?' I asked.

Leo shook his head. 'Harvey's right about the trouble they have patching planes up. Even if this plane wasn't going to fly again it would be salvaged for parts.'

'You can't cover up losing a plane and a pilot,' I said. 'One or the other perhaps, but not both.'

'They stuck a fence around,' said Harvey.

'Hidden in plain sight,' said Leo. He considered this and then shook his head. 'No, I don't believe it. What I do think is possible is that something happened and that craft has been left there for an investigator to look at. That might be why you've had some hostility, Hope. Some people might think you're here to investigate and are being underhand about it.'

I pulled my most innocent expression. Leo rightly ignored me.

'But to leave a body in it,' said Harvey, 'that's wrong, immoral.'

'You have to be mistaken,' said Leo. 'Hope, I think you need to meet with Susan. She sent a message saying she'll see you whenever you wanted. Why don't I hop on the bike and go and get her. You convince your landlady to give you a private corner and a pot of tea.'

'What am I meant to do?' said Harvey. 'Pour the blimmin' tea?'

'I was under the impression you were acting as a mechanic,' said Leo coldly. 'You'll come up with me, and when I've dropped

Susan off, you can show me these damaged panels that have been clawed by a dragon or whatever.'

Harvey grunted a response. Then he said, 'You in charge now?'

'No,' said Leo. 'I'm here to help Hope, but she's still running the mission. I do outrank her, but from what I can gather, in your department that doesn't count for much.'

'Do I have a rank?' Harvey asked me suddenly.

'I don't know,' I said frankly. 'Fitzroy can't even remember if he made me a first or second lieutenant. He says promotion is rapid during a war, so it doesn't matter much.' Leo looked astonished. 'I know. He's not your usual type of commander.'

'Yes, I'm beginning to see that.'

'I think you remain a civilian asset, Harvey. He hasn't said anything to the contrary to me. Besides, you've not taken any oaths, have you?'

'No,' said Harvey. 'So I could enlist, if I wanted? He couldn't stop me?'

'I thought your limp did that,' I said. 'Sorry to be blunt.'

'I'm thinking that in the air my limp doesn't matter.' He addressed Leo. 'The lads let me use the blue box and I think I've an aptitude.'

My heart sank. Leo looked at me, and I saw my worry reflected on his face. 'To be honest, Harvey,' he said. 'I think as a civilian asset that you can withdraw your services from any section of the SIS at any time. At least that's the theory. From what I've seen of Fitzroy he tends to get his own way. I'd speak to him or ask Hope to do so after this mission. His or even her goodwill wouldn't go amiss. And if I may,' he glanced over at me again, 'I wouldn't make any sudden decisions.'

'You mean do I want to throw my life away now I've learned Bernie is dead?' said Harvey. 'I don't, but I do want to do my bit.' There was that phrase again. 'And I can't help but feel I would be more use shooting these blighters out of the air,' finished Harvey.

'Then ask Fitzroy to put you up for selection,' said Leo. 'It's a

270

fair process. If you have talent they will be more than happy to take you.'

'Thanks,' said Harvey. 'First time I've known where I stand.'

The two of them left to go up to the base, and I went downstairs to beard Mrs M in her den and beg for some tea and a quiet space. The first thing she said to me was not auspicious. 'So it's a husband you'll be having now?'

She was up to her elbows in flour, making pastry, presumably for tonight's tea. I decided it was time to throw Leo to the wolves.

'I haven't seen hide nor hair of him for the past three years,' I said. 'He normally works in banking, and he had a very pretty secretary. However, it seems his commanding officer told him to get himself straightened out, so he appeared on our doorstep.'

'He's a handsome man,' said Mrs M.

'He is,' I said, 'but handsome is as handsome does. I rather thought we were heading for the divorce courts, but obviously the war and my service must take priority. I've not been living as a single woman—'

'It's not my business how you live,' broke in Mrs M.

'I have my reputation to think about,' I said. 'Hamish Abercrombie has developed a tender for me. Quite unexpectedly and I need to deal with it carefully. He's also, it seems to me, somewhat involved with young Susan. I'm not after the man, or any man, for what it's worth. But Hamish is a flyer, and under a lot of stress. I want to handle the situation carefully.'

Mrs M had her hands on her hips. 'Men,' she said suddenly. 'They cause so much trouble.'

'Indeed,' I said. 'But it's different in war, isn't it? We can't go letting our private feelings crash over our duty. I've got Susan coming here. I want to see her and talk things out. If she's in love with Hamish and he with her, I'll not stand in their way.'

'Hamish Abercrombie wants all and every girl. I've seen his like before. Not content unless he has a lot of hearts on a string.'

'And in normal times I'd give him a piece of my mind, but he's up there fighting for our freedom.'

'Aye, well, that shouldn't let him get away with whatever he wants. There's standards. We can't let everything go, can we?'

'No, indeed,' I said, hoping she wouldn't spot I was changing tack. 'And it's about that I wanted to have a wee chat with Susan.'

'Och no, what has the silly young lass done now?'

'Nothing too bad, but I thought a word in her ear from me might help. Do you think it would be possible to find a quiet corner and a pot of tea? She's coming down to see me. I wouldn't ask if I hadn't got this bang on the head. We were meant to be having lunch at the mess, but I'm not up to bumping across to the base at present.'

'Och, of course, your poor wee head. Are you feeling better now, hen?'

'I'm on the mend,' I said, and gave what I hoped was a brave smile.

'How did it happen again?' she asked.

'I'm afraid that's classified,' I said and then laughed. She joined in, but looked confused. 'Where could I meet with Susan?'

'You might as well use the dining room,' said Mrs M. 'The tables are all set up and it's not like you two girls will leave a mess.'

'I'll do the washing-up myself,' I said.

'No, you will not. Not with your head. Susan can do some. It's about time she learned. Have you seen how she treats the wing commander's cups? A wee bit of a rinse, that's all. I had to take them home and scrub them with bicarbonate myself. It's not like Margaret would have known what to do.'

'Indeed not,' I said. 'She seems to like being the one giving orders?'

'I couldn't say,' said Mrs M, but her mouth broke into a smile. 'I'll get your tea now.' She nudged me on her way out. 'Susan's lucky to have you around. You've got your head screwed on right, young lady. Good to have someone around who sees things as they are.'

I went through to the dining room to wait for Susan. I had

intended to hang around the hall, but even standing for this brief time had made me feel dizzy. If this bump on the head was anything like the ones I'd previously suffered, I should be fine by tomorrow. I sat down at a table and rested my head on my arms. I supposed if I must fall prey so frequently to misadventure it was good fortune I had such a tough head. I only wished it wouldn't ache quite so much.

I must have fallen asleep, as I jolted up when someone touched my arm. I was on my feet and ready to defend myself, before I realised it was only Susan. Susan looking a bit alarmed. She was wearing a cherry-coloured wool coat and matching tam-o'-shanter

'Oh, sorry,' I said. Then I kissed her on the cheek like I would have done with Bernie or one of her classier friends. I hoped it changed the meeting from military to informal. Susan blinked a bit, but my greeting embrace didn't appear unwelcome.

I invited her to sit down. There was a pot of tea on the table and a plate of biscuits. I lifted the tea cosy and touched the side of the pot. 'Nice and hot,' I said. 'Thank you for coming all the way down here to see me.'

'Leo sent a message saying you'd been in an accident, but still wanted to see me. Are you all right?'

'I'm still recovering,' I said. 'My head aches a bit, but I'll be fine in a day or so. Thank you for making the time to come and see me. I do need to know what you know about Collins.'

'And you'll put in a good word for Granddad?'

'I'll certainly do what I can,' I said.

'For all I know, Brian McKenzie is right. The faeries murdered him.'

Chapter Thirty-eight

The Truth, or Part of It

Susan picked up a biscuit. She considered it. 'Do you think it's true that Mrs M puts horse oats in these?'

'Murdered by the faeries?' I said. Biscuits might be important, but I felt murder had a higher priority.

'I'm not mad. But I need to tell you the whole thing,' said Susan. 'You see, at the end Hamish and I were convinced there was something in the cockpit with him. It's the only explanation. I liked Collins. I think a lot of people did. Do you know what a blue box is?'

I shook my head gently. At least I'd learned something. I did remember Harvey mentioning it, but I hadn't had the chance to ask him what it was.

'It's a box the shape of a plane. Inside it are a mock-up of all the controls you'd find in a plane. There are also pedals and stuff linked to mock-up flaps. It's used to help train pilots. Granddad says originally it would take three hundred hours of flying before you were allowed to go solo. That's on top of all the lectures about weather, wind, and that sort of thing. Nowadays the boys are lucky if they get one hundred and fifty hours' training. Half the original time. That's where the blue boxes come in. Spending hours in one isn't the same as being aloft, but it helps the boys familiarise themselves with the plane and how it works. It even has a canopy that goes over the top so they can practise flying blind.'

So that's what Harvey meant, I thought. 'Is it easy to get to use a blue box?'

Susan shook her head. 'No, the hours are strictly regulated. All the pilots have to keep track of their time. Being allowed to fly solo isn't the end of training. All the different planes need you to do different stuff – oh, I don't know much, but I know it isn't easy. I used to work on radio. You know, talking to the planes when they're going in or out. It was such a small base to start with. I couldn't do it after Collins. I mean, I just choked. Hamish was with me when it happened. I thought it made a kind of bond between us, but it's all hot or cold with him. Nothing in between. I never know where I stand.'

She reached for her teacup and added more sugar. I thought this was a bit stiff as a guest. 'Do you mean you were on the radio talking to Collins when he crashed?'

She swallowed a sip of tea and put the cup down with hands that weren't quite steady. 'Yes,' she said. 'The dreams have mostly stopped now, but I used to have nightmares for weeks afterwards where I heard his screams. I didn't hear him die. Hamish turned off the radio. He said it wasn't respectful. There was nothing we could do, so we should leave him with some dignity. That surprised me. It wasn't as if he and Collins ever got on. In fact, I thought until that moment they hated each other.'

'You said someone was with him?'

'Before he lost control of the plane he was yelling at someone to get out. To leave him alone. There's room in the plane he'd taken for two, but he hadn't listed anywhere that he had a passenger, and we never found another body. Besides, why would you tell someone to get out of a plane mid-flight?'

'You wouldn't,' I said. 'So you and Hamish presumed it was a what? A winged being?'

Susan clasped her hands together tightly in front of her. 'Sorry, it's difficult to talk about. I'd never heard a man scream before.'

'Take your time,' I said.

She looked at me with wide eyes. 'I know how silly this sounds, but I can't think of another explanation. There was no one else there. Not that it was going to be an easy landing anyway.'

275

'Why?'

'Fog. We had low-lying fog. It had come in swiftly. The day had been as bright as anything when he went up.'

'Who first came up with the idea of faeries?' I asked.

'Brian.'

'Brian was in the radio tower with you and Abercrombie?'

'No, that was later. When Hamish brought me back here. He didn't want me on the base. When they were . . . when they were dealing with the plane and the body. With Collins.'

'But how did Brian hear about it?'

'It was my fault. I was in a right state. He and Mrs M were making me hot tea and sugar. Brian knew about dealing with shock because he'd been in the Great War. He was helping out. If he hadn't been here I don't think Hamish would have left me. Anyway, it all came spilling out of me. Everything that had happened. I was crying, sobbing and words kept coming and coming.'

Looks like I'll never be recruiting you, I thought. 'So what happened to the plane and body?' Of course I knew where they were, but I wanted to hear what Susan thought had happened.

'Oh, in the end they got the fire out. Collins had done something, a spin, I think, to put the fire out, so when the plane came down it was barely alight. Granddad said there needed to be an inquiry. I rather think he wanted to resign on the spot, but Hamish talked him out of it. He said he didn't have the experience to run the base, and there was no one who could take over his role.'

'You're saying your grandfather felt responsible?'

'Of course,' said Susan. 'If he'd stepped in and stopped the others from being mean to Collins none of it need have happened.'

'Who was being mean to Collins?'

'All the men on the base detested him.'

'Why?'

'I'm not entirely sure. I asked Granddad once and he said that Collins was the direct opposite of a ladies' man and that he should never have been let in the RAF.'

'Oh,' I said. 'Did something happen that made him think that?'

Susan shrugged. 'I don't know. I didn't understand. The WI was all over him. He was forever coming along to the village hall when he wasn't on duty, or he dropped by to chat to Mrs M. She liked him a lot. So why Granddad said he wasn't a ladies' man, when it was only among us that he seemed comfortable . . . You see, he'd come from a very poor background. Could I get some more tea, please?' She held out her cup. 'My mouth is getting very dry. Talking about it . . .'

'Brings it all back?' I said.

'It makes it real again,' she said. 'I coped before, by pretending it wasn't real.' She dipped her head. 'I know that isn't a nice thing. To pretend someone who died never existed, but I was on the radio. I should have said something. Done something. Helped him.'

'I'm sorry I have to ask you, but I need to know. Tell me more about Collins himself. How did the other servicemen treat him?'

'That's the problem. They were bullying him. They'd cut him out of the time on the blue box. He'd find things dropped in his food. They'd leave him messages sending him to places he wasn't meant to be.'

'And neither your grandfather nor Abercrombie, as squadron leader, did anything about this?'

Susan shook her head. She put the half-eaten biscuit down on the table. 'No, Granddad didn't like him at all. He didn't like that Collins hadn't done a full three hundred hours. He thought he was a liability. And Hamish, Hamish was new. I think he didn't so much dislike Collins as he wanted to curry favour with Granddad. He's not the easiest person to get on with. Disliking Collins was an easy way to get on his side.'

'Are you saying Abercrombie encouraged the others to be unkind to Collins?'

'No, neither he nor Granddad did.' She paused. 'But they didn't do anything to stop it either.'

'I'm surprised at Abercrombie,' I said. 'I thought he was more team-orientated.' Then I stopped and thought about it. How better to bond a team than to give them a common enemy. It was a scenario playing out again and again in this war. 'Was Collins a bad pilot?' I asked.

'Not at all. He was a natural. Even Abercrombie admitted that. It was like a cockpit was where he belonged. He didn't get the highest scores in the classroom stuff, but in the air I don't think anyone else was as good. I never understood why that didn't make him popular. I thought they would admire him, but they seemed to hate him even more because he was so good.'

'Hmm,' I said. 'That must have upset Collins. Not being seen for what he could do.'

'Yes, I think it did,' said Susan slowly. 'I hadn't thought of it like that before. I thought he had a chip on his shoulder because he came from a lower-class background, and all of the officers – the pilots – don't. He continually tried to prove he was the best, but it only made things worse for him.'

My head had began to throb again. I felt myself growing angry at the way this man had been treated and why.

'Why did he go up that day?'

'He'd had an argument with Abercrombie and another of the pilots. I'm not sure what it was about, but it had something to do with his ability to fly, I think. He wasn't cleared to go up. That was why Abercrombie joined me in the radio tower. He wanted to talk him down. You can be court-martialled for taking a plane without permission. If we didn't get him down quickly he could have ended up being shot.'

'But he would have known that, wouldn't he?'

'Thinking about it now I think something snapped inside him. Whatever had happened he couldn't bear being on the ground any more. He needed to be up in the clouds.'

'Do you think he meant to crash?' I asked.

Susan bit her lip. 'It has occurred to me that he might have meant to . . .'

'Kill himself? He was that unhappy?'

'But then there was something in there with him. Hamish and

278

I both clearly heard him yelling at someone.' She stopped. I poured her another cup of tea, and added a lot of sugar.

'Thank you,' I said. 'You've helped me a lot.'

'You are here to investigate his death, aren't you?'

'I can't tell you,' I said. 'I'm sorry.'

Susan stood up and put her coat back on. 'I hope you feel better soon,' she said.

'How are you getting back?' I asked.

'Granddad has given me the rest of the day off. I'm heading home. It's not too far. I might get Brian to give me a lift.'

I nodded. 'Perhaps don't tell him what we talked about? I don't want to add fuel to the faery fire.' I smiled to show I didn't blame her for starting that ball rolling. In reality, I did, but I couldn't see the point in throwing blame around – yet. 'Did you tell your grandfather what we were going to talk about?'

Susan shook her head. 'I didn't even say I was coming here. Just that I was feeling a bit peaky.' She turned to go as I wondered how well Fitzroy would take it if I told him I was feeling a bit peaky and needed some time off. On the whole I thought it would be better never to find out.

Susan stopped at the doorway. 'Who attacked you?' she asked.

'No one attacked me,' I said. 'It was a silly accident. I was clumsy.' Clumsy in the way I hadn't heard the other two sneaking up on me.

Susan gave me an odd look. 'No,' I said firmly. 'It was not the faeries.'

'Of course not,' said Susan. Something about the way she quickly turned her face away from me made me think that this was exactly what she thought.

Despite my headache, I seriously considered banging my head on the table. These people were impossible.

Chapter Thirty-nine

Heads Together

'So either he was a homosexual or they all thought he was,' I said as I finished explaining what I had learned to Leo and Harvey back up in my room.

By some previously unknown persuasive ability, one of them had convinced Mrs M to not only allow us to take fresh tea upstairs, but we also had a plate of freshly cooked raisin scones. I took one and proceeded to wrap myself around it while they thought over what I'd said.

Leo's cheeks were slightly tinged with red. I met Harvey's eyes over his head. As usual he had refused to sit down and was leaning against the wall. 'Hope is quite worldly wise,' said Harvey. 'She might not look it, but that godfather of hers clued her in on things most parents wouldn't dream of telling their children, especially their daughters.'

'I should have known it would be down to Fitzroy,' said Leo, glowering.

'I wouldn't be much use as a spy,' I said thickly through the scone, 'if I didn't know how the world worked.'

'I only hope he didn't go into details,' said Leo. His comment made his face go even redder. I looked down at my plate to hide my smile. Leo might say he wasn't a gentleman, but he had some pretty upper-crust ideas of what ladies should do, say and know.

'So who was in the cockpit with him?' said Harvey.

'I have to say, having heard what evidence we have—' began Leo.

'Oh, no, don't tell me you believe in faeries,' I said.

'Of course not,' said Leo. 'It sounds to me as if the man had some kind of mental episode. Doubtless brought on by the systemic bullying of the servicemen here. Whatever you might have promised Susan, I would say her grandfather is for the high jump.'

'Oh, I agree,' I said. 'I didn't promise anything. I said I'd do what I could and I don't think there is anything I can do for him.' I knew all too well that stress could make you imagine seeing people who weren't there.

'Typical spy's promise,' muttered Harvey.

I ignored him. 'It's unconscionable that he allowed a man under his command to be treated so badly by his peers. If he thought the man was a homosexual then he should have reported him and had him arrested. That he didn't suggests either he wasn't sure or he was being cowardly and didn't want to face his men.'

'Hang on a minute,' said Harvey. 'People can't help the way they're made.'

'Yes,' I said. 'I don't mean he should have done that. Collins was prepared to risk his life for his country. Frankly, what he wanted to do between the sheets is of no relevance to his flying ability.' I paused to slap Leo on the back. 'Don't inhale crumbs,' I said. 'It's bad for you.' He regarded me from watery eyes with an unusual degree of malevolence. 'It's not my fault,' I told him, 'that you're used to gently bred women. I only hope the women you tapped on the shoulder were made of stronger stuff than you generally . . .' I stopped as Leo scowled furiously at me, and then flashed a glance at Harvey.

'I'm not blind,' said Harvey. 'I get you two were working on something before but can't tell me about it. Let's move on. Leo thinks Collins went off his rocker. What do you think, Hope?'

'I think he was probably talking about himself,' I said.

'That's clever,' said Leo in an unflatteringly surprised voice. 'He was saying that he had to get out, but the two of them misinterpreted it. Had there already been noises about faeries before the crash?'

'I think so,' I said.

'I can see how with the marks appearing on the planes more susceptible people might have thought this added to the faery story.'

'Apart from imperilling the base I can't see what anyone might gain from promoting the idea about faeries,' I said.

'You've answered your own question,' said Leo. 'It's most likely a German sympathiser who is damaging the planes and promoting the story. Lowering morale alone can have a significant effect on performance. Why, just look at Collins himself!'

'Look, I don't believe in faeries any more than the next sensible bloke,' said Harvey, 'but I saw the damage. I saw the planes before they went up and when they came down. Whatever caused those markings I showed you today, it happened when the plane was in flight.'

'Could it be some kind of stress on the plane?' I asked. 'You said that everything is overused and on the verge of wearing out.'

'It's not like anything I've ever seen,' said Harvey.

'And you've been a mechanic for how long?' asked Leo.

I checked my watch. 'Abercrombie is due to turn up here in less than an hour. I think he wants to tell me more about what's happening with the planes.'

'You're not bringing him up here, are you?' Harvey stopped leaning on the wall and stood up straight with his arms folded.

'No,' I said. 'We're walking down to the local public house.'

'Well, I'm going with you,' he said.

'That would hardly be helpful,' I said.

Leo bit into another scone, and then leaned back in his chair. 'Harvey, how long have you worked with the lieutenant? Only you don't seem to have much of a belief in her abilities.'

'The lieutenant? Oh, you mean Hope. Well, we were sort of friends first. It wasn't until I met—'

'Fitzroy that you realised what she was?' Leo finished.

'Not even then really,' said Harvey. 'I mean, I've only learned she was a lieutenant since I've been here.' He turned to me. 'I mean, are you really? Or is that part of your cover?'

'I'm an army officer working in SIS,' I said. 'That's all I can confirm to you. Obviously that is not for general knowledge.' I didn't add that this was about as much as I knew. Fitzroy had never been good at handing out details, or in telling one anything he didn't feel it was vital for one to know. He preferred to hold all the cards.

'So in general you can be assured that she can handle herself,' said Leo. 'Also, as the mission commander, you're meant to be following her orders. Or didn't Fitzroy tell you this?'

I wasn't sure how I felt about Leo defending me. Firstly I shouldn't need him to defend me, and secondly I hadn't been as subordinate as I should have been to him. But from Harvey's deepening frown I could tell he wasn't happy.

'I've known Hope longer than you. Plus I'm a civilian and I don't like being patronised.'

Any moment the pair of them would face off to fight. I did the only thing I could think of. 'I'm going to have a bath,' I said. 'So right now I'm going to get into my dressing gown and that means . . .' The door banged behind them. 'I need to undress,' I said to the empty air. 'Honestly,' I said to myself, 'it's not as if they would go blind at the sight of a woman undressing.'

Chapter Forty

A Proposition Under the Stars

Abercrombie arrived exactly on time. He was out of uniform and wearing his kilt again. 'Are you sure you're not Scottish?' I asked him as we walked out into the mild autumn evening.

'I presume that somewhere back in the annals of time someone in my family was and that's why I'm named Hamish.' He held out his arm for me to take. I had yet to fully recover, and it was rather nice to have someone tall and broad that I was allowed to lean on. Neither Harvey nor Leo counted as I wasn't meant to be familiar with people I was serving alongside. How I dealt with Fitzroy now he was my stepfather, I had no idea. Doubtless he wouldn't be bothered by it one bit.

'Hope, are you sure you're well enough to go out?' Abercrombie's voice was silky with concern.

I turned to smile up at him. 'Sorry, I was wool-gathering. My mother has recently remarried and I'm trying to get accustomed to my new stepfather.'

'Goodness,' said Abercrombie. 'Is he a monster?'

I laughed. 'Not at all. I've known him all my life. He was my godfather, and he's an old friend of my family. It's that I am not used to thinking of him as a stepfather.'

'I like that little tam-o'-shanter you're wearing, by the way. I think it's the angle. Makes you look rather charming.'

I'd raided the lost box again, and while I did rather like the look of the cape and cap I'd borrowed I had done it to make myself feel better rather than please my prospective date. Or so I told myself. The truth was that a date with a handsome man was a nice break from everything else I was meant to be thinking about. For the length of the walk to the public house, I determined to enjoy myself as an ordinary woman.

'Thank you,' I said. 'I think the kilt looks rather good on you. All the ladies at the dance were whispering about how nice your knees were.'

Abercrombie gave a low chuckle. 'I don't mind the ladies of the village wondering about my knees.'

He said this with an emphasis on the last word, and I was glad the twilight hid my face. I could feel my cheeks surging with heat. 'Indeed,' I managed to choke out.

'With most of the local men away,' he said. 'I think it is our obligation as servicemen to provide – shall we say, a change of scenery. But as far as I am concerned, it is definitely window shopping only.'

'I thought you and Susan were close?'

'No,' he said, directing our footsteps down a lane I hadn't entered before. There was a row of farmworkers' cottages, four of them joined together, on one side. Low dwellings of only one storey, and with only one window looking out on the world, they were nevertheless in good order. Each of them had a small fenced-off front area that had been dug up to plant vegetables. Outside one of the houses a lone doll lay forgotten on a tiny bench. The bench rested right against the wall, and I could imagine an old man sitting on it and smoking a pipe while the sun set. Two of the houses had a flowering plant growing along the eves. I didn't recognise it. A faint smell of vegetable soup hung in the air. Abercrombie saw me looking. 'They look quaint, don't they? There'll be a woman and at least three children in each. They have little outcrops of these cottages all over the county. Some of the men stayed here to farm, but most of them joined up, even though they didn't have to. I wonder if it's something to do with the life here. It's hardly arable land and crofting of any kind is a hard way to live.'

'Have you tried it?' I asked.

'No, but my people have tenant farmers, and our land is much better for growing, and they struggle. All the more for the men being at war.'

'Do you have land girls?' I asked.

'I believe some are joining there soon.'

'Hmm,' I said. I wondered if I should talk to my factor and see if we could get some help that way. This being away on missions made it very difficult to keep an eye on other obligations.

'Hope? You've drifted away again. I had hoped I wasn't that boring.'

I stopped and turned to look at him. I put my other hand on his arm. 'You're not. I'm well enough to be up and about, but I'm not at my brightest. Besides, I think seeing all this farming land is making me homesick. I can see that you're right and the living is hard here, but it's still beautiful, isn't it?'

He put a gentle hand under my chin and tilted my face up to his. 'Yes,' he said quietly. 'Very beautiful.'

And then before I knew what was happening he put his lips against mine and we were kissing again. This time there was no one to see. I surrendered myself to the experience. His arms came round me and I melted against him. The kiss was gentle at first, but by mutual silent consent it became deeper and increasingly passionate. He pulled away before me.

'Hope,' he sounded breathless. 'If we don't stop now I will cease to be a gentleman.'

I frowned.

He put a hand against my face. 'I mean, my darling, that I will pick you up and lie us both down under the stars. And then, my very beautiful lieutenant, I will make love to you long into the night.'

'The nights here are cold,' I said.

Abercrombie sighed, and loosened his embrace slightly. 'I could say something corny like I would keep you warm but, looking at what I can see of the clouds, I think it will rain soon.'

It was on the tip of my tongue to say, we could find a barn, but I didn't. The truth was I was with a handsome man under a blanket of galaxies whirling through a palate of blues and black that took my breath away.

'This is very romantic,' I said. 'But I am a serving officer, who doesn't have time for a child.'

'If that is your only concern,' said Abercrombie, his eyes shining in the moonlight, 'I can take care of that.'

I rested my head on his shoulder. If he started kissing me again I wasn't sure I would want to stop. 'I admit it is my main concern, but I also have a mission to complete.'

'Community liaison or something more?' he asked. 'Whatever it is, we can be discreet.'

I won't say I wasn't tempted. Not to have a tumble in the field with him there and then, but to make more appropriate arrangements.

'I can't,' I said, but even to my own ears I didn't sound convincing. 'Besides, we hardly know each other.'

'Haven't you found since we've been at war that everything is sharper and brighter?' said Abercrombie. 'That you're living more by what your gut tells you than your head? I want you. I have no doubts.'

At least, I thought, *he hasn't said we might be dead tomorrow.* Then I heard a rustle from behind us. Oh, good grief, were Harvey or Leo following us? Or was it someone more threatening?

'Is there something you're not telling me?'

I looked up at him with a puzzled frown. 'Not that I can think of.'

'You are here for community liaison, aren't you?'

'What else would I be doing? I can't fly a plane and I'm not an especially good cook. I can't even ride a motorbike.' I was aware my reply sounded a little tart. His arms around me slackened further. I stepped back and out of them. 'Let's get inside before it rains,' I said. 'We have at least this evening.' I hoped this would

287

be a vague enough suggestion for him to agree, and yet not a
promise of further intimacy.

'As you want,' he said. I couldn't interpret the odd note in his
voice. However, he took my hand and I let him. We walked on
in silence. I was now convinced at least one person was following us.

Chapter Forty-one

The Public House

Despite my concerns we arrived at the public house without being accosted. It was an old stone house; whether it had always been a public house it was hard to say. The door to the main room was so low even I had to duck slightly to enter. Inside the vault-like arches contained a number of small booths. That might sound like it was rather elegant, and if it had been in London it might have been. Here it looked like it was only yesterday that cattle had sheltered here during the winter storms. The floor was packed earth, and there were candles on the rough, worn tables. Any windows there were must be already shuttered closed. There was a warm smell of hops, suggesting that home brewing might feature on the drinks menu, and two old wheels hung above the bar that had been converted into makeshift candelabras. There was darkness and discretion enough for secret meetings or trysts, but in its own way it was also welcoming. At the far back of the room was a small coal fire that added to the fug of the room, and cast shadows of what might be a staircase leading upstairs.

'It's not called The Byre for nothing,' said Abercrombie, watching me take in my surroundings.

'I like it,' I said. 'It feels safe. Almost like a shelter.'

He took me over to a small vaulted section and rather like a conjuring magician produced a small cushion for me to use on the wooden bench. 'If I was out when an air-raid siren sounded I think I'd happily use this,' he said. 'But as you will have noticed, the only exits are out the door we came in or up the stairs at the back. In the usual way of things, there's a small kitchen up there. Soups made from local vegetables and home-made bread. It sometimes runs still, but it depends on if they know there are enough folk coming to make it worthwhile and if they have the food. Very thrifty, our barkeep here.'

'Not a bad thing during a war,' I said.

Abercrombie bent lower and whispered in my ear, 'I suspect he's always been like that.' He straightened slightly. 'Now, what will you have? They're not much into dainty drinks here.'

I smiled up at him. 'I don't mind a good old-fashioned half pint of something made from hops,' I said.

He smiled back at me and ran a finger down my left cheek. 'Good girl,' he said. I managed to neither flinch nor hit him. It wasn't the caress that bothered me as much as the implication that I could be addressed in the same way one might a dog. I have never been one for being patronised by men. Even handsome ones.

Abercrombie returned shortly carrying a pint and a half pint of some dark drink. 'It's strong,' he warned me. 'I'd take it slow.' He then proceeded to down half of his in one gulp.

I took a sip, and discovered it was rich and nutty. Not at all unpleasant. But still nothing in comparison to my favourite tipple, champagne. I would have no trouble drinking it slowly.

'So,' he said.

'So,' I replied.

He raised an eyebrow. The candlelight reflected off his face, and I saw the worry lines etched firmly across it. He was both younger than I had realised, and older in experience.

'I was under the impression I was here to be interviewed,' he said. 'Although I'm not entirely sure that you work for community liaison. Not many such officers automatically check for exits when they enter a new place.'

'Not that many people notice me doing so,' I said, and took another sip.

'If I had to bet, I'd say you're either in intelligence or in some department joined to it.'

'It's certainly true that the Army is bristling with departments at the present. I wouldn't know about the Air Force. But with things the way they are,' I lowered my voice, 'and you know as well as I how close we are to the cliff edge, all sorts of programmes and projects are being trialled. Anything to break out of our current situation.'

'You mean until we persuade the Americans to come to our rescue?'

'I couldn't tell you that, even if I wanted to. I don't know where we stand diplomatically at the minute. It's a changing situation. But I work on the premise that no help is coming, and if it does I will be delighted.'

'Hope for the best, prepare for the worst.'

'Something like that. But in community liaison, you will understand my role is to ensure that morale is kept up, both locally and nationally. It's a more vital component in this war than many people realise.'

'Such an impressive and evasive series of answers,' said Abercrombie, but he was smiling. 'You're very clever, aren't you?'

'I hope you don't mean for a woman, but I did read Maths at Oxford.' I didn't add that I had scraped through by the skin of my teeth.

'So what do you want to know?'

'I want to know what the pilots are seeing when they're flying. What is being talked about and not talked about. What the theories are for the damage to the planes.'

'I'm not sure how passing on officers' mess gossip is going to help.'

'There's an officers' mess? I saw some of you eating in the canteen.'

'Well, we do at times. There's also our own place. I'm afraid there was an unspoken agreement not to mention it to you. You're the only female officer on the base and the men value a place to let rip.'

'It's a shame no one bothered to tell me. I would have understood.'

Abercrombie gave an apologetic half-shrug and smile. 'We – I – didn't know you then.'

'So it was your idea?'

He shook his head. 'The wing commander's. And to be fair, I think he thought if it wasn't kept men-only his wife might find a way to get in.'

'They don't seem very happy,' I said.

'I think India was their heyday. Plus they have to worry about their sons. He doesn't discuss any of this with me, but I work more closely with Buchanan than anyone. He's aged drastically over the last few months. He wasn't young when they hauled him in to run the base, but it's like the life has leaked out of him.'

'Would you like his position?'

'No.'

'That's rather a blunt answer,' I said.

'Well, it's true. I told you I struggle enough with the young men I shoot down myself. I'm responsible for our lads, but not directly responsible for their kills – at least in my mind. The wing commander is responsible for everything. I don't think I could bear it.' He hunched over his pint. 'If you're here to see if I'm up to the job, I'm not. I'm not even sure I should be squadron leader any more. Only there's no one else.'

'When did you last have any leave?' I asked.

'I can't remember, but Susan keeps on top of all that. She'd prod the wing commander if I hadn't had my share. When you're flying days and nights time gets all twisted up. In the air time can vanish or it can stretch and slow down to nothing. Sometimes you're so involved in fighting the other chap that although you're thinking at a hundred miles an hour, and you're firing and flying and manoeuvring and acting on instinct, all at the same time, it's almost as if time stops. You're so intensely aware of every moment that actions that last a few minutes feel like hours. Then there are other times when the action is over before you're even aware it started, and you're watching some poor sod disappearing down towards the ground with a black plume like a flare following him. As long as that smoke is there you know there's a chance he might bail. But mostly it ends in an orange burst beneath you as he explodes. They hardly ever bail. I don't know if pilots are afraid of parachutes, always think they will be able to land, or simply fear that they will be shot out of the air.'

'We do that?' I asked. 'Shoot men out of the sky?'

'I don't. Not any more. But yes, both sides do. What's the difference between killing a man inside his plane or outside? If you're thinking that one isn't cricket, then welcome to the war.'

'I hope that even in war we continue to embody some sense of humanity.'

Abercrombie laughed, but it was a dry crack of a laugh.

'You think I'm naive?' I asked.

'I think you are, Hope,' he said. 'I like that. Maybe your name is part of the reason I like you so much. We all need hope. The world is a dark place and it's only going to get worse.'

'Are the other men struggling as much as you?' I asked.

He shook his head. 'They're scared. But they still get that euphoric feeling when they land back at base. You can see it even in the way they walk – as if they are gods ten feet tall. That's what it's like until you start to feel responsible for the people you're killing. I'm not going to turn pacifist. If I could undo what I've done I wouldn't. I did what was necessary. I think that's what makes it worse, not even being able to regret what you've done.' He looked down at his empty glass. 'I think I'll get another. Do you want one?'

'No, thanks. I'm a sipper,' I said. His morose mood was beginning to make me doubt the whole idea of coming out here with him. Unless, of course, it was a masterplan to manipulate me into bed. I confess I was feeling bad enough for him that it almost felt like my civic duty to cheer up one of our brave lads.

Almost.

On the other hand, I thought, if this was how he truly felt he wouldn't last much longer. Either he'd be called out by the wing commander or he'd lose a battle in the air. It might be an idea to whisper in someone's ear that the chaps here needed a break. Although I suspected the answer would be all the chaps everywhere did. However, if I could get a note through to the air marshal's desk that some of the best men might be debilitatingly battle-tired, there might be some kind of result. Of course, I wouldn't be able to do that myself, but I could chuck it up the ranks and see if anyone was willing to throw it higher up.

Abercrombie came back with his second pint. 'Don't worry, this is my last. I'm not going to get drunk on you. Apart from being embarrassing for me tomorrow, I also have to fly. Can't afford hangovers. And I've got to try and get some maths into the idiot head of Stewart. Apparently, he has an instinct for flying. I don't know about that but he sure as hell doesn't have an instinct for numbers. You'd probably be better.'

'Undoubtedly,' I said.

'Answered with a cool assuredness that I lost long ago. How long have you been involved in the Army, Hope?'

'Since before the war,' I said.

'Even then the Army did community liaison?'

'All right, let's say you're right and I'm from a different department. I've come here posing as community liaison because it gets me where I need to be. Lets me hear what I need to hear. How likely am I to reveal that to you? Regardless of how much you flirt with me?'

'I flirt with you, Hope, because you're fun, and you're smart and you're beautiful. At another time I'd be taking you home to meet Mother. You'd get to see the estate.'

'Rather than being propositioned in a field?'

This drew a swift smile. 'Exactly, I'd proposition you in my ancestral halls.' He took my hand for a moment. 'Seriously, Hope. Please forgive me for that. Life is so unsure now that it's hard to keep within what used to be the lines.'

'I do understand that. If it helps,' I said, 'I was tempted. It rather shocked me.'

He looked more cheerful than he had all evening. 'So then there is hope for me?'

'Ah, there might be a problem. I have an estate of my own, and my stepfather has a huge estate, so yours would have to be something special,' I said teasingly, trying to make light of things.

'So you're an heiress? Better and better.'

'I've inherited,' I said. 'I'm a landowner. My factor is looking after things.'

'Surely you could stay at home if you turn some of it over to farmland.'

'I already have,' I said. 'But my factor does an excellent job. We stay in contact, and I take my leave at home. Couldn't you turn your place into arable farming?'

'My father has,' he said. 'And he's made it very clear there is no need for me to petition for reserved occupation. Before the war, I might have spent rather too much of his money in various London nightclubs.'

'I'm surprised we never met,' I said. 'I did the last season with my best friend. Her idea, but it wasn't as bad as I'd thought.'

'But you said—'

'I became involved with my department during that time.'

'You were hunting German sympathisers?'

He was getting far too close to home. 'Let's talk about you,' I said. 'After all, that's why I'm here.'

'Is your friend as beautiful as you?'

'She was. Life and soul of a party kind of girl.'

'Was?'

'As I said, let's talk about you.'

'I'm sorry,' he said.

'Everyone will lose someone by the end of this,' I said. 'My loss is no more or less than anyone else's.'

'I hope you stay strong, Hope,' he said.

'About what you saw,' I said again.

'Right, the gossip in the mess is that some of the men have seen small creatures on the wings, tearing at the metal.'

He must have seen the shock on my face.

'Yes, exactly. I've put it down to stress and high altitude. I suspect there are strains or sags within the fuselage that we're not being told about. When you're screaming down towards an enemy one minute and the next you're rolling or pulling yourself almost vertical, it's going to put a hell of a stress on the body of the aircraft. I'd never seen metal split like this before, but then we've never asked our planes to do what they are doing day in and day out.'

'What do these creatures supposedly look like?'

'Small, humanoid, warty faces. Some of them are described as having claws that tear up the wings. Others say they have pointed faces and are biting into the craft.'

'Dressed or undressed?' I asked.

'I don't remember anyone ever mentioning that. Usually the stories are they look out at the side and the creature is suddenly there. As if it popped into existence. It does – or tries to do – some damage and then it's gone before the pilot has completely understood what he's seen.'

'Do they ever get in the cockpit?'

Abercrombie paused. 'I've only ever heard one person suggest that – and I don't know if that was true. All the other stories are about the creatures being outside, on the wings usually.'

'But that's not what you saw?'

'No, I've never seen anything like that. I'd be checking myself into the nearest hospital if I had. It has to be related to oxygen starvation or having some kind of brainstorm.'

'So what did you see?'

'I don't know if I did.' He shook his head as if scattering stray thought. 'I was on my way back. I hadn't shot anyone down and I hadn't lost any of mine. It was the best kind of mission. I was looking over at one of the planes that had taken some flack, trying to figure out what manoeuvre he could have used to avoid it, when out of the corner of my eye I saw something move. I mean, I jerked my head round at once. We were all accounted for so if there was something up there with us it was one of theirs.' He took a pull from his pint. Then he set it down and spread his hands out on the table, palms down, as if he was readying himself for something. He bowed his head for a moment, then took a deep breath and turned to me. 'It was a ball of light. About the size of a tennis ball, I think. I can't be sure because it moved at amazing speed. It zig-zagged in a way that no craft we have could do. I had the feeling it was inspecting me, because it flew – I say flew, but more like darted – all around me. One side, then the other. As if I was getting a full mid-air inspection. It was the craziest thing. I found myself trying to avoid it, to get away, but it kept up with me effortlessly. There was chatter on the radio by then asking me what was happening. I kept blinking, thinking it must be something in my eye or on my goggles. But it wasn't. It was real. It was solid. I've gone over it again and again. I am convinced I saw something. I'd swear on my life, but I haven't the faintest idea what it could have been. It wasn't some gnome or goblin, but it was alive. It behaved as if it was thinking, exploring, curious. But it was just an orb.'

He finished and picked up his pint glass only to discover it was empty. I pushed my half-full glass towards him and he downed it in one. 'I understand you might not believe me . . .'

'Did you report it?'

'No. I hadn't long been appointed squadron leader. I didn't want everyone to think I was crazy. I was as mad on flying as the lads are now. I didn't want to be grounded.'

'Whereas now, you wouldn't mind. You might even want that.'

'Do you think I'm lying?'

I had been watching him closely; how he breathed, how his eyes moved, whether he sweated or not, and as much as I could note in the gloom of the public house. 'No,' I said. 'I think you believe what you're telling me. You saw something. What it was I don't think either of us can tell.'

'It wasn't a bloody faery with wings,' said Abercrombie. 'I asked myself again and again, could it have been someone messing about with a mirror either from the ground or even one of the other pilots. And I can't see it. I saw it as close to me as you are now, and in much better light. I saw the size of it and the shape of it. It wasn't a beam of light.'

'And you think it was alive?'

Abercrombie nodded. He was staring fixedly ahead of him at a horizon I couldn't see.

'Do you think it was what was in the cockpit with Collins?' I asked.

Even in the dim light I saw his colour bleach. 'What?' His voice was low and raspy.

'I spoke to Susan today. She told me about what you both heard in the radio tower when Collins crashed.'

Abercrombie glared at me. I could see him physically shaking. 'It has nothing to do with that at all.' He spoke through gritted teeth. 'The ball, whatever it was, was real. Collins was off his head. It's not the same.'

I edged back from him. 'You're angry,' I said. 'Why?'

'Furious,' said Abercrombie. 'I thought . . .' Words seemed to fail him. His fingers were gripping the edge of the table, the knuckles white. His whole body was taut with the kind of fury that possesses a man whole. If he didn't get himself under control I was in a lot of trouble.

'You,' he said and his voice was laced with hatred, 'I trusted you.' He rose to his feet.

Chapter Forty-two

When We Three Met Again

I stood up quickly. He had the advantage of height on me, but better to be on my feet. Would he actually hit a woman? The real problem with rage is it makes a man unpredictable – and there was an awful lot of well-muscled Abercrombie that was about to become unpredictable. I didn't dare take my eyes off him. My mind ran through all kinds of moves I could use. Even though I knew that my only saviour was reaction and muscle memory. No one ever thought their way out of a rage-fuelled fight.

'Hamish,' I said carefully. 'I don't think you are lying. I do want to help you. Don't do anything that makes that impossible.'

'Do you think I would hurt you? I know what I am,' he said. 'I kill young German men – boys – but I have never ever harmed a hair on the head of a woman.'

'Then let's sit down again,' I said, putting a hand out in front of me, palm down, and slowly lowering it. I sat as I did so, and so, thankfully, did he. I saw his eyes were brimming with tears. I felt a strong urge to put my arms round him and comfort him like I might a child. But before I could move there was the sound of male voices and the public house door opened and then banged shut.

What might have happened next but for this, and how it might have changed things, I will never know. I will always wish I had had more time alone with Hamish. If I had been able to get him to open up then, to tell me everything, it might all have ended so very differently.

*

'Hey, Hope,' called Harvey, waving from the entrance. 'Thought we might find you here.' He turned to his companion. 'Told you, Leo.' They both walked over to our table. I managed to fleetingly touch Abercrombie's hand under the table, willing him to understand my sympathy and concern, but then both of my co-workers in espionage were upon us, and playing out what they clearly thought was a clever bit of improvisation. I cringed. Abercrombie seemed to be in shock, so perhaps he wouldn't notice their ridiculous banter as they spoke about how they'd both gone looking for me, and that after a lengthy and ridiculous exploration, one of Mrs M's girls had said she'd seen me go off with Abercrombie.

'So we thought "public house" and here we are,' finished Harvey proudly.

'Why were you looking for me?' I asked.

In another situation the brief look of panic they shared would have made me laugh out loud.

'Captain, will you see Hope back?' asked Abercrombie of Leo. 'I'm afraid I don't feel myself. I'm flying tomorrow so I can't be ill.'

'Of course,' said Leo.

He turned to me and clasped both my hands. 'Another time?' he asked.

'Yes,' I said.

He nodded, released my hands and was gone in no time at all.

'Goodness,' said Leo. 'What did you do to the man? He looks completely wrung out. Harvey here was all for storming in here to protect your virtue.' He glanced around. 'I mean, it's quiet, but it's not like it's a deserted island.'

'Was it you following me?'

Leo looked at me blankly. 'I only came back to the boarding house a short while ago. Harvey wasn't around so I asked if anyone knew where you were. I'd forgotten your plans to deal with Abercrombie. One of the girls told me they'd seen you walk in this direction. I met Harvey on the way. He must have set off before me with the same idea.'

'The idea being?'

'Oh,' said Leo, 'I want to go down to the beach to watch for submarines. I've sandwiches in my bag and a thermos of tea.'

'You just suddenly decided?' I asked.

'Well, no, I er . . . well, I'm following something up,' said Leo, fidgeting slightly and avoiding my gaze. With Harvey present I didn't press him.

'But you were following me,' I said to Harvey.

He scowled at me. 'I've already lost one friend,' he said. 'I should have done more for her. I don't care if you shout at me or get angry. I was damned if I was going to lose you too.'

A large lump appeared in my throat. I swallowed and looked at the table. 'Fine,' I said. 'I appreciate your concern.' I looked up at him. 'But you have to trust me to manage the risks I take. It's the only way we can work. We can talk about it more later, all right?'

Harvey nodded. 'Fair enough.' That was too easy. He too was now avoiding my gaze. 'What did Abercrombie tell you?' he asked.

'If we're going to stay here you should go and buy a round. Otherwise we'll attract attention,' I said. I tried to lighten the mood. 'Rarely anything more suspicious than a group of people in a pub who don't drink.'

'I'll go,' said Harvey. 'Pint, Leo? Hope?'

'A half pint,' I said, 'but one of you will have to drink it.'

'Make it three pints,' said Leo, 'we can split Hope's.'

Harvey went off to the bar.

'So?' said Leo.

'Have you ever noticed it's the men with the least money who are most eager to get a round?'

Leo grunted. 'Harvey does have a bit of a chip on his shoulder, but from the little Fitzroy gave me to read about you, he's thought of you as a friend rather than an officer.' He paused. 'I presume I'm not wrong when I say you can look after yourself?'

'I have already killed a man in this war in hand-to-hand combat,' I said. 'I'm not over confident. Aggressors are normally bigger and stronger than me, but even before my army training I

301

had gained mastery of one martial art. My weapon, of course, is that people constantly underestimate me.'

'There's not many women who would be proud of killing someone.'

'I'm not proud, Leo. I've never wanted to kill anyone. It was a classic him or me situation. I'm trying to make you aware of what I'm capable of doing if I must. Fitzroy wouldn't have let you read my file.'

'No, he didn't. I suspect it's marked for his eyes only. He's a very – well, not protective precisely – what? Jealous stepfather?'

'He was the same as my godfather. It's probably as much about me being used as possible leverage against him as it is about me. He's allowed very few people in his life for that reason. He's very much old school when it comes to espionage.'

Harvey returned with the drinks. 'So have you told him what Abercrombie said?'

'I was waiting for you,' I said. 'You're the best person to pass comment working on the planes. I assume the pilots also talk more to you than other servicemen. Their lives are in your hands – literally.'

'I thought it would be all top-secret stuff,' said Harvey.

'Spill,' said Leo. 'We need to be set up on the beach in an hour.'

'Right, I'm not going to say whether I believe any or this or not. I do believe that Abercrombie is telling the truth as far as he is concerned.' I recapped the stories of the faeries on the wings.

'At least he doesn't believe in those,' said Leo. 'That's clearly a case of stress and fatigue. The hallucinations are being affected by the prevalence of local folklore – and as the topic of conversation in most of the villages around here is all about angry faeries, I'm hardly surprised.'

'The lads are overstretched,' said Harvey. 'For such a tiny base we're asked to do a lot.'

'How many of them do you think are seeing things?' Leo asked Harvey.

'No one had told me directly, but from what I'm picking up I think most of them have seen something or other.'

'And, of course, the gossip only strengthens the likelihood of pilots seeing things when they are fatigued or oxygen deprived. The brain might be a complex organ, but it is extremely subject to influence,' said Leo.

'Hang on a minute,' I said. 'I've got more to tell you about what Abercrombie did see, and it doesn't fit in with any faeries I've ever heard about. There's also a link to Collins. Did he think there was a faery in the cockpit with him? If he did, is there a case to answer for whoever is spreading these rumours. Is it a form of treasonous propaganda? Is it being done deliberately?'

'It's a bit advanced for what – brainwashing? Seems too much effort to waste on a little base like this.'

'Unless this was a test site?' suggested Harvey.

'I can't see the RAF being brought to a halt nationwide because of a united belief in faeries,' I said.

'Hitler's lot are into all kinds of mythological nonsense,' said Leo. 'Some of the reports I've read are hard to believe.'

'But there's still the damage to the planes, who is doing that?' I said, trying to cut through the discussion.

'Local sabotage?' asked Leo.

'I doubt it,' said Harvey. 'I've staked out the hangars and repair shed on several occasions. Nothing. I could have been unlucky, but I did it over random periods.'

'So we're left with what?' I said. 'Undue stress and strain on the aircraft?'

'More likely than flying metal-eating bogeymen,' said Leo.

'What did Abercrombie see?' asked Harvey.

'I was getting to that,' I said, and told them about Abercrombie's flying balls of light. 'Only about the size of a tennis ball, he said, and he was convinced they were physically present. Not beams of light. Nothing a mirror could throw up. He also stressed that these things were investigating. He said they didn't move like anything he had ever seen, but he felt as if he was being inspected.'

'Just like any night at the village dance,' said Harvey snarkily.

'Yes, I can see how he might easily recognise the feeling of being looked over,' I said. 'He's the most handsome man on the base, and on the whole he's a pretty decent chap.'

Harvey uttered a low growling sound, almost worthy of Fitzroy, and buried his face in his pint glass.

'Leaving that aside,' said Leo and giving me a warning look, 'it's interesting that he's also subject to these hallucinations. He strikes me as a man with a reasonable hold over his imagination.'

'As in he hasn't got one,' said Harvey, softly enough for us to pretend we hadn't heard.

'It is worrying, isn't it?' I said. 'Do you think this could be some kind of poisoning? They're all being given something that makes them hallucinate, but what they see is a reflection of internal fears, outside influence or something of that ilk?'

'It's worth looking into,' said Leo. 'Have you talked to any of the catering staff?'

'Only briefly,' I said. 'I haven't been here that long. But I've only recently been told there's a separate officers' mess. That's where I'd look when it comes to deliberately contaminating food. It only seems to be affecting pilots. I wonder if the wing commander has ever said anything odd? He must eat there.'

'If he did I doubt he'd tell his granddaughter,' said Leo, 'if you're thinking of asking Susan.'

'I was thinking, what if he had ever been affected at the base. He'd retreat to his office, but Susan might notice something.'

'She's young and not terribly bright,' said Leo scathingly. 'She mostly notices men – available men.'

'There's no harm in her,' said Harvey. 'She's just young. Listening to Collins' crash must have affected her. No doubt she's out to make hay while the sun shines.' He shrugged. 'It's one reaction to death. Give me laughter over tears any day.'

'I think we must also consider whether or not these lights might be some kind of enemy weapon,' said Leo.

'How would that work?' said Harvey, frowning.

'I haven't the slightest idea, but I'm not a weapons expert. I don't think we can rule out sabotage here – whether it's by poisoning, mental propaganda or advanced weaponry. Likewise I think we have to take seriously Hope's idea that this might be a test site.'

'Or there could be something going on here we don't know about,' I said. 'I've been bemused from the start as to why Fitzroy was so interested in this place.'

Leo opened his mouth. I put up a hand to stop him. 'If you're thinking that Fitzroy would have given me some background or warning, I have to tell you my experience is he prefers to send his agents in with only vital information. I'm guessing he has some idea that information can muddy the water and make you jump to the wrong conclusions.'

Leo picked up his pint and cradled it. Eventually he said, 'Generally agents are given as much intelligence as possible. Briefing from my previous work has always been extensive and intensive.'

'And this time?'

'I was given access to a number of files and some individuals.' He looked up suddenly. 'I'm here to support you, Hope. But I've other irons in the fire.'

'What?' said Harvey.

'I'm afraid I can't tell you.'

'That's ridiculous,' said Harvey, preparing, I could tell, to get up quite a head of steam.

'It's normal,' I said. 'There are many divisions in SIS. Not all of us even communicate with each other.'

'That's ridiculous,' said Harvey again, only this time he sounded more perplexed than annoyed.

'I'm not of a high enough rank to disagree with you,' I said. 'Sometimes it all seems crazy to me.'

'A few agents are sent in without briefing in certain circumstances,' said Leo. 'But they have a particular kind of training.'

I stood up. 'If we're off to the beach any minute, I'm going to see if they offer facilities for ladies in this cow barn. Be back in a minute.'

I felt a tiny bit embarrassed saying that, but I had no doubt that if nature called either Leo or Harvey they would wander off slightly at the beach and deal with the problem. It transpired there was only one lavatory, and you had to wedge your foot against the door at the same time if you didn't want someone walking in. It was also of the same cleanliness as you would expect from a male-only area not run by servicemen. Two of the good things the Army teaches a man is how to iron his trousers and clean a toilet properly.

I came back to find the table cleared and the two of them waiting at the door.

Chapter Forty-three

Return to the Beach

I remembered the walk to the beach all too well. It had been dark and I had been on the back of a motorbike, but somehow it had imprinted itself on my memory. Everything about that night bothered me. I'd put it to one side – especially after Leo appeared – but I was still conflicted over Cole. I had finally decided he was a foe rather than a friend; that there was no way Fitzroy would countenance me being obliged to assassinate a man as a sniper. But then, this was wartime. Could it be that he had had someone other than himself do the dirty work? Would he not want me to see him as a killer?

The first thing Cole had said that I ever doubted was that Fitzroy was an assassin first and foremost – that this had been his initial training. The idea that he might have been my biological father had struck me as less problematic than his being an assassin. I tried to let that sink in. It wasn't that I didn't think my mother had not loved my father, but the more I had been about in the world the more I had learned that people's personal lives were often messy, and rarely ran as true to form as they might seem by reputation. My father was an invalid, and my mother was often alone with Fitzroy on dangerous and vital missions. I knew only too well how the clash of mortality, duty and desire could lead anyone astray.

If my mother and he had stolen a moment together – they were clearly deeply fond of one another – if they had taken a moment together when they needed comfort, when they felt all was lost, when it was so hard to go on, then I would never have blamed them. I don't think my father would either. He might have blamed Fitzroy, but he enjoyed blaming Fitzroy for many things, simply because he was an active, handsome and highly intelligent man – as my father had been before illness overtook him. Goodness only knew, right now, if I could find someone's arms to step into without consequence then I might. I'd been tempted twice recently – with Leo back at my flat in London, and then, astonishing as it was now to reflect upon, by Abercrombie in a Scottish field. That I had felt closer to him in the public house when he let me see how much of a toll this life was taking on him, made me realise I must not put myself in the position where he and I were alone somewhere we could make love. No matter how much I was drawn to him, there were far too many questions for him to answer.

As long as I stuck near Harvey, I reflected, I should be fine. He suspected everyone and was as fierce as a bulldog when it came to protecting me. Why, I had no real idea. We were friends, but it might be no more than he had originally said, and that losing Bernie meant he was determined not to lose anyone else. I must remember, I thought, to ask Fitzroy to team us up as often as possible. I liked Leo a bit too much. I hadn't fallen in love with him, but if Abercrombie attracted me to a certain degree, that attraction was doubled if not tripled with Leo. Although again I was unsure why. He was a decent man, if sometimes annoying, but I felt a desire and general tug towards him that mystified me.

'Hope, we're coming to the steps. Are you listening to me?'

'What? Yes,' I said, pausing at the top of the steps cut into the rock. 'I was thinking.'

'You've been thinking all the way here,' said Leo. 'Both Harvey and I tried talking to you more than once, but you either didn't reply or said something nonsensical.'

I shrugged. 'I can be like that when I'm puzzling out a problem,' I lied.

'Any conclusions?' asked Leo.

'I wish,' I said. 'I'm as confused about all this as ever.' Now that I was more fully aware of my surroundings, a chill seeped through my bones. My heart pounded in my ears as if I had been running for my life. I watched Harvey examining the stairs, wondering all the while if I would be able to make myself go down there.

'I reckon these are old steps,' said Harvey. 'Cut for smuggling. Local people might know about them, but otherwise they'd be a closely guarded secret. How did you two find them?'

Fortunately Leo appeared to want to be as evasive as me, and he urged us to lower our voices and follow him down. 'Better yet,' he said, 'don't speak unless your life depends on it.'

I hesitated at the top. Harvey put my hand on one of his shoulders, so I could balance myself on him. I didn't need to, but I let him think I did. I could barely feel the warmth of his body through his jacket, but even the rhythm of his movement helped me disconnect from my previous time here. I'm with Harvey, I told myself. Neither him nor Leo will ask me to shoot anyone. No one is carrying a sniper rifle. Sometimes it's reminding yourself of the simple things that brings you peace.

To my astonishment Leo led us to the very same tiny cove that Cole and I had sheltered in before. I waited there while Leo and Harvey searched for driftwood. I didn't care to think about what I was left to watch for, but I scanned the night and the inky black sea as much as my vision would let me.

Harvey and Leo returned with some driftwood. Leo proceeded to make the tiniest, most concealed fire I had ever seen. He had us wedged up together in the limited space, and before long I could feel actual heat. He'd dug down into the sand, so the fire disturbed our vision as little as possible, but of course it had an effect. Leo, sitting on the far edge of the group, was the least distracted by it.

We sat huddled together for a while. Harvey leaned heavily against me, and I realised he had fallen asleep. As no one had told him to do anything I did no more than shift his weight towards the rock and away from me. His body remained in contact with

309

mine, and I had no intention of losing either the warmth or the feeling of companionship that brought.

I must have been dozing myself, because it was the sudden shock of the cold on the other side of me that snapped me to full wakefulness. Leo was gone.

I knelt up to see the beach more clearly. I spotted him halfway down. He stood out in the open with no attempt to conceal himself, watching the dark water lap against the paleness of the sand. I checked Harvey. He remained fast asleep. I crept towards the entrance of the cove. I wanted to see, but I also wanted to intervene if necessary. I flexed my fingers, and began tightening and releasing my muscles, getting the blood flowing through them, so I could move if I had to. Right now, my limbs were leaden with cold, but even in this small space I could warm up and be ready to do whatever was needed.

I couldn't see Leo's face, but he stood facing the sea. His hands were in his pockets, and I wondered if he had a gun held in one. For a long time it seemed as if nothing was going to happen. Then there it was, a ripple in the water. Leo took one of his hands out of his pockets and threw something into the sea. Then he turned to his left. I looked past him and gradually I was able to make out a solitary figure who was making their way along the edge of the shore.

The person stood as tall as Leo, and wore a greatcoat. I couldn't see well enough to know if it resembled someone from our own services. From the silhouette I could only make out a peaked cap and that they wore heavy boots.

Leo took both his hands out of his pockets and waited for the other man to approach. He stopped a few feet from Leo and there must have been some kind of verbal exchange because as one they turned back and began walking along the beach away from me. The night air lay still and heavy. I couldn't hear a thing. The pair of them disappeared off into the darkness.

Leo hadn't asked me to follow him. He hadn't explained anything, but he had to have a reason for bringing us along. The moon shone too brightly for me to skulk along the shore. The tide had ebbed. Lacy fronds of darkness lapped the sand. It would be some time before the tide returned. Was this the reason the man had not come out of the sea like the one Cole and I had met? Did it mean there was a boat, possibly a boat that had brought someone from a submarine, nearby. It seemed too much of a coincidence for us to have come to the same beach to meet different factions.

I couldn't get to Leo without exposing my presence, so I decided to watch and wait. I didn't like this, but he'd given me no other option. Behind me Harvey gave a soft snore.

Eventually, after what seemed like hours Leo walked back alone into my line of sight. He beckoned me out. I walked out to meet him. The space between my shoulder blades itched. It wasn't that I didn't trust Leo. I didn't know yet how good he was at his job, and whether he might be unintentionally leading us both into a trap.

'Harvey asleep?' he asked in a quiet voice when I was close enough to hear.

I nodded. My eyes weren't on his face, but scanning the horizon. I turned to check behind us, and Leo caught my arm to prevent me.

'Don't,' he said. 'You needn't worry. They're ours, but a bit on the shy side.'

'What the hell have you got yourself involved with, Leo?'

'I'm not cleared to tell you all the details. I can tell you a British agent was killed on this beach within the last few days. From what we can tell it was a sniper, but unusually the sniper went to some rather gory lengths to retrieve the bullet.'

'Who was killed?' I asked.

'You're shivering,' said Leo. 'I'm sorry you had to wait so long. I didn't share my thermos with you because it was spiked. I needed Harvey to fall asleep. He can't know any of this.'

It wasn't cold that was making me shiver, but I had no intention of telling him this. 'What do you need me to do?'

'I need you to witness that I met someone on the beach tonight. If it comes to that. Nothing more. You're not cleared for the details of this operation, and before you even think it, this isn't one of your stepfather's projects. It is, however, the reason my bosses were happy to let him second me without protest. I'd like to tell you more but I can't. You need to know I have other interests here, and if things blow up later you can attest to what you've seen, heard and been told – no more and no less.'

'Can I tell Fitzroy about this?'

'A good question. He's your CO and protocol dictates that you brief him fully about anything he needs to know. It's your call. I'd rather he didn't kick up a stink about this. We're trying to draw as little attention to this operation as possible.'

'Then why bring me here?'

'I don't know if we will continue working together or not,' said Leo. 'It isn't my call, but I wanted you to understand I'm in an odd position. I'm trusting you as much as my masters are allowing me to. If I had my way I'd bring you further in, but I can't right now. This is my best display of confidence in you I can give. I also wanted you to come here in the unlikely case that you could throw any light on the death of our agent?'

I shook my head. I didn't trust my voice at that minute.

'I didn't think so,' said Leo. 'Let's go kick Harvey awake. I want to be back next to a roaring fire as soon as possible. Harvey can sleep on the floor of my room at The Manse. With luck we can persuade our delightful landlady to rustle up some soup or something that passes for it in these parts.'

I followed him back up the beach. We trudged back to The Manse in near silence. I had no energy to talk. My thoughts were entirely taken up by the realisation I'd killed a British agent. Cole had made me kill a British agent. Did he know? Was it a mistake? Was Cole a traitor? Had he made me a traitor? Or was I involved in a far deeper game than either I or even Fitzroy had realised? Was Cole about to attempt to blackmail me into becoming a double agent? Had he, for all the years Fitzroy and my mother had known him, been a traitor to the crown?

Chapter Forty-four

The Faeries Revealed

By the time we arrived at The Manse I was shivering with cold. Seeing this, Mrs M didn't protest at our late arrival but stoked up the fire in the residents' lounge and provided us with bowls of soup. She didn't say what it was and we didn't ask, we were simply grateful for the warmth it put inside us. On his second bowl, when she was out of the room, Harvey did venture to say, 'What flavour is this?'

'Red,' Leo decided.

'Warm,' I said.

'Good enough,' was Harvey's verdict. 'Anyone want this last slice of bread?'

We all reached for it at once. I fell backwards into my chair laughing. Before long we were all laughing like loons, the combination of fatigue and the stress of the last few hours breaking under the weight of laughter. Mrs M collected our bowls, but wisely didn't say a word. Later, when I was walking up to bed, I realised that she must be used by now to the almost maniacal relief that the servicemen and women showed when they came off duty.

I tumbled into bed, undressed, but without brushing my teeth or my hair. I found myself giggling, like a child, at the thought of what my mother would say if she knew. At the back of my mind I knew I was responding to my sudden acute awareness of my mortality and that of my friends and enemies. I was attempting to force back the panic I felt as I saw the world I had grown up in dissolve into chaos. I had had an odd childhood by anyone's reckoning. But still, despite the strangeness, there had been an order to it, a predictability and a sense of safety given by that. Losing one's father is enough to briefly overset the mind of child. Your authority figure, the North Star of your childhood days, is gone, impossibly gone for ever. Your whole world re-orientates until it lies at a strange tilted angle, and you find yourself in the next generation below death. Yet even in this there is an order, an acknowledgement of this is the way things are meant to be. But war. War smashes through everything. It breaks every law of nature and every commandment to be kind. Black becomes white and white becomes black. What was wrong, to kill, is right. What was right, to forgive, is wrong. Voices compete to tell you what you must do. You can either follow blindly, or force yourself to examine every moral choice. Only the bravest do the latter. We call them conscientious objectors and we put them in prison. I am not that brave.

I will kill to defend my own – but what if I had been tricked into murder and not the supposedly justifiable homicide of war?

It was with these thoughts that I fell asleep. It is perhaps no wonder then that I spent a restless night full of nightmares and terrors. In the throes of my dreams I stood near a window. I knew if I looked out I would see the worst of all creatures, the most terrifying enemy I would ever face. In the dream I decided to walk away, but as I tried I was pulled, against my raging will, towards the window. Where, of course, I discovered it was no window, but a mirror, and the face of evil was my own.

Morning took a long time to arrive, but when it did I found myself hung-over from the nightmares, foggy brained and slow of thought and movement. I had too much to think about, not least of which was that Cole might have made me a murderer. It did not concern me what a military court might think. Fitzroy would easily have it made a technicality as I was the junior rank. He would say that Cole had coerced me physically and mentally. That made no difference. I still had to live with what I had done.

Thus I was far from in the best frame of mind when Margaret Buchanan accosted me on the way to breakfast. 'I must speak with you now!' she demanded, appearing from beside the clock in the hall like some evil genie.

'Will someone die if you don't?' I asked coldly.

'Well – no, I don't think so,' she said, momentarily put on the back foot.

'Then whatever you have to say can wait until after I've had my breakfast.'

'I demand you speak with me now!'

'Mrs Buchanan,' I said, 'you are not a ranking officer, and while I may be a community liaison officer, I have had a difficult twenty-four hours and I do not judge myself to be in the best space to listen to whatever request you wish to put before me. I am therefore going to have my breakfast. You may wait for me if you wish or you may choose a time for me to call upon you – provided, that is, I can obtain transport.'

At this point, I turned and walked away without waiting for a reply. Fitzroy advocated that rather than argue a conversation was over, leaving it demonstrated the fact more effectively than any words. Usually I found this rude. This morning I agreed with him.

Mrs Buchanan made a noise like a squawking hen drowning in its own indignation. However, she didn't appear to be following. I heard a male voice murmur something vaguely behind me, but I ignored it. I was almost certain I could smell bacon, and if that was the case it would take the entire German Army to keep me from the breakfast buffet.

I had loaded my plate, found a mug for my coffee, and obtained a corner seat before Leo appeared opposite me. 'You know I have been standing here for almost a minute trying to get your attention, and before that I was waving discreetly at you from the doorway?'

'I'm hungry,' I said through a mouthful of egg. He looked vaguely disgusted. 'You were clearly too discreet,' I added.

'The wing commander's wife—'

'I know. She tried to grab me on my way in here.'

Leo smiled slightly. 'Very unwise. I've got her stashed in—well, I'm not sure what it is, it can't be more than the size of a cupboard and I think it probably was one once.'

'Did you lock her in?' I asked, my interest aroused.

'No,' said Leo. 'You need to come and speak with her. You can bring your breakfast. It's clear there is no way I can part you from it.'

'All right,' I agreed. 'But you can do the talking.'

'Thank you for trusting me that this is almost as important as your eggs.'

I picked up an extra bread roll on the way out.

Leo led me to what I had assumed was a cupboard under the stairs. Bereft of space, it seemed Mrs M had made this her office. It had a desk, two chairs, wedged in tight, and a bucket full of something or other that Leo graciously sat on. The wing commander's wife was sitting somewhat majestically at the desk.

'I'm afraid we will have to swap places,' I told her. 'I need to be able to put my plate down if you want me to listen.'

The look she gave me could have curdled milk, but fortunately I take my coffee black.

I sat down, placed my coffee and plate on the desk, cut myself a final piece of bacon, but spoke before putting the fork in my mouth. 'So what can I do for you, Mrs Buchanan?' I then proceeded to chew (and savour) the last piece of bacon. It lost all taste after her first words.

'I want to confess,' she said, gripping her handbag tightly on her lap. 'It was all my idea.'

I swallowed my mouthful barely chewed. 'What was?'

'The purloining of items from the base.'

'By items, you mean?' asked Leo gently.

'Wrenches, spanners, bits and pieces I thought liable to be needed. My elder son was a mechanic and I picked up some knowledge about what was most useful.'

'Why on earth would you do this?' asked Leo, who had missed the important part.

I pushed my plate away, and turned directly to focus on her.

'I wanted to create some disruption,' she said. 'Things need to be looked at here. The boys don't get enough training before they are in the air . . . and there's been . . . well, there's been bullying on the base. I don't like that. I don't like it at all.'

'You wanted to get someone's attention. Why not speak to your husband?' asked Leo, before I could get a word in.

'I am very sorry to say that I consider my husband as part of the problem,' she said. 'I know what they all think of me round here. A memsahib who wants to rule the roost, and I suppose that is the way I tend to go about things. In India, things are somewhat different. It's a different world and the young wives who came out there looked to me for guidance.'

'I didn't know we had significant airbases there,' said Leo.

She shook her head. 'We were out with the Army. Edwin hasn't flown in years. I told myself that's why he was getting it so wrong, but it isn't, of course. He's just had all the stuffing knocked out of him. Couldn't pick himself back up again. It's the shame – naturally. He's been a soldier of one sort or another all his life. He never understood Peter. I can't say that I did myself.' She paused and took a deep breath. 'I knew he was different from early on. I wasn't a very fashionable mother, I'm afraid. I spent a lot of time with my children before Edwin sent them off to school.'

'My parents never sent me off to school,' I said as gently as I could. 'I didn't leave home till I went to university.'

She looked up at me, her eyes bright with tears. 'Good for them,' she said. 'It's a rotten thing in my opinion to send boys away when they are so tiny. Moral character my foot. It simply makes some of them downright miserable.'

'Like Peter?'

'Oh, yes, he hated it, but Edwin made him stick it out, and he did well enough. He was a bright boy.'

317

I think it was around now that Leo caught up with what was happening. 'I'll get some tea,' he said quietly to me and slipped out.

I gave him an exasperated look.

Mrs Buchanan gave a watery laugh. 'Tea, the great British cure. I sometimes think that's why we are trying to hold on to India.' She turned to Leo. 'But I would very much appreciate one, Captain.'

Leo ducked out.

'When did Peter die?' I asked.

'Five and a half months ago. It feels longer. Time can drag when one least wants it to.'

'I'm very sorry,' I said. 'It's not the same as losing a child, but I've lost two people close to me recently. Grief is a terrible thing.'

She shook her head vigorously at that. 'Grief is missing love, and if you're grieving then you know you have lost something very special.'

'You were close to Peter?'

She nodded. She opened her handbag and took out a handkerchief. However, she didn't dab at her eyes, but rather wound it round and round her fingers. There was something else. 'You haven't asked how he died,' she said.

'How?'

'He killed himself.'

'I am so very, very sorry,' I said. 'Words don't seem adequate.' I reached out and touched her hand briefly.

She gave a slight smile. 'Obviously, we haven't told anyone. Edwin didn't want people to know. Not even that we'd lost him. I said we could tell people of our loss without . . . you know.'

'Yes, it's still a crime, isn't it?' I said. 'But actually, I've always thought that it must take an act of great courage to kill yourself. The ancient Romans believed that it was one of the most noble things a man could do.'

I watched carefully. Fitzroy and my parents, I knew, disagreed with this view. We'd argued about it when I was studying philosophy at home. They thought you should face things straight on.

318

I, however, for whatever reason, could imagine how going forward could be too much of a burden and that when there was no opportunity to be or to live as you wanted that one could come to the conclusion that there was no point in life. Then, to override one's natural instinct to survive would take much courage and much will. Naturally, I didn't want anyone to reach that point, but I knew now, more than ever, that the world can be a most unforgiving place.

I waited to see how Mrs Buchanan took my comment.

'It's a mortal sin, of course,' she said. 'As well as a crime. But I do hope that a kind God would understand, and not keep him too long in limbo, don't you?'

'I think a priest could answer that better than I,' I said. 'But I would hope so.'

She made a sudden hiccupping noise and tears dashed down her cheeks in a sudden torrent. 'You don't know how much it means to me to be able to tell someone about this,' she said.

'I'm so sorry I turned you away.'

She put up a hand in protest. 'You couldn't possibly have known what I was going to say.'

'It's a poor excuse,' I said. 'So was Peter bullied for being different? I'm imagining that he was probably a gentle soul and not that keen on fighting.'

'Oh, he considered being a conscientious objector, but then we started hearing things about what the Nazis believe and what they were doing. He agreed then that sometimes you have to fight – you have to fight evil. But it still troubled him that the people he was being asked to kill weren't the ones responsible. He'd have gone face to face with Hitler with only a fork if he'd been given the opportunity. He was brave. Very brave. He always wanted to do the right thing. He tried so hard to be what his father wanted him to be. But the other men . . .'

'Rather like a pack of animals sensing someone is different?' I asked.

'I mean, I suspected what his nature really was. Edwin must

have done too, but we never discussed it. As far as I know Peter never acted on it either. He was popular among the local girls, but not in the way Abercrombie is. Do you understand?'

'You're saying that Peter wasn't like most young men who want to chase girls,' I said, wondering how far I should go.

'I'm saying he was a homosexual,' she said bluntly. As soon as the words were out her hands flew to her mouth and her bag tumbled to the floor. The contents spilled out – lipstick, powder compact, purse and keys. I bent down to put them back in and handed her the bag. She had pulled herself back together by then.

'I mean that's what I suspect, and it's what the others thought. But I want you to understand there is no suggestion that Peter ever acted on his nature, that he ever committed that crime.'

I wanted to say I thought that rather a pity, and that I felt everyone was entitled to fall in love. However, I knew that my opinion was in part informed by Fitzroy. I remember him saying on more than one occasion, that 'people make far too much fuss about sex. It's only love that counts, and frankly, as long as it harms no one else, I think there can't be too much love in this world.' At the time I'd thought he was joking, it was so unlike his normal manner towards humanity. When I'd asked for a further explanation, he'd said, 'Look, Hope, sex is something human animals do for entertainment. Sometimes that's mutual entertainment, sometimes it isn't. The latter is unforgivable to my mind. But at the end of my life I won't be counting up how many sexual partners I've had or haven't had, I'll be thinking about who I love and who loves me. Yes, unbelievable as it seems, there are people who I love and who have loved even me.' At which point the serious conversation ended as I threw my arms around his neck and told him I loved him. I was twelve or so at the time.

'Was he bullied?' I asked.

'Yes, I think that's what drove him to ending his own life. The other men in his barracks . . . Of course, we'll never know, and it was all hushed up. For the Army's sake as much as for ours.'

'That must be hard. Not knowing what happened.'

A lone tear ran down her face. 'I keep thinking why didn't he come to me? Did he know how much I loved him? I would have done anything for that boy. Anything.'

'So when Collins arrived, he reminded you of him . . .' I said.

'I suppose so. I liked Collins. All the women did. But Edwin saw something quite different. He turned his back on him. Wouldn't get involved. So when Abercrombie didn't put a stop to the behaviour of the other men . . .'

'I don't believe Collins killed himself,' I said carefully. 'I don't know what happened yet, but I don't believe he took up that plane intending to die.'

'No?'

'No,' I said. 'But I will do everything in my power to find out what happened.'

'It . . . it would make a lot of difference to me to know he didn't take his own life. For lots of reasons. I tried to stop him going up that day. He'd been so miserable. I invited him over and made him a special soup, but he insisted on going back to the airfield. Maybe I should have tried harder to keep him back.' She gave a loud sniff. 'At least he had a good meal. My wild mushroom soup was well known in India.'

Mrs Buchanan blew her nose like a sailor on shore leave, rather than a lady. She pocketed her handkerchief and stood up. 'I can leave it with you?'

I nodded and also stood. 'The pilfering?'

'Will stop.'

'The damaging of the planes?'

'We never did anything like that,' she said. 'I was careful to ensure the girls never did anything that could harm a man once he was in the air.'

I nodded wordlessly. She opened the cupboard door and met Leo on the threshold. He was carrying a tray filled with tea things. 'I have to go, Captain,' she said. Leo stepped back and she left. He came into the cupboard.

'What did I miss?' he asked, and began pouring the tea.

'That Peter, her son, was a homosexual. From the little she said he sounded like a very decent man.' I said this slightly rebelliously to see how Leo took it, but he continued to focus his attention on pouring tea. 'He took his own life after being bullied about six months ago. It was all hushed up, but her husband wouldn't even discuss it with her. Then when Collins turned up and started being bullied too, she felt as if—'

'History was repeating itself,' said Leo, passing me a cup with three sugar lumps.

'I'm not sure from what she said, but around this time she started stealing things from the base. She was trying to get someone up here to investigate what was happening. I'm not sure if she started before the accident. Incidentally she thought Collins tried to kill himself, which I think helped a bit. But the thing that bothers me is that although she admits to the stealing, she's adamant that neither she nor anyone else caused any damage to the aircraft.'

'Who was helping her?'

'Oh, I don't think she'll give you names. But I imagine it's her friends in the WI.'

'We're not going to pursue them?' asked Leo.

'I can't see the point,' I said. 'They were well intentioned, not malicious. The most important part is it has stopped now.'

'Why did she come and speak to us now and not before?' asked Leo.

I frowned. 'That's been bothering me too. Something must have changed, but I have no idea what.'

'That's worrying,' said Leo, and took a biscuit. He bit into it. 'Very worrying,' he said crumbily. 'So what do we do now?'

Now that was a very good question.

Chapter Forty-five

Confrontation

'Not always fun being the one in command, is it?' said Leo with an irritatingly smug grin.

'As I am used to working solo, I am used to making my own decisions,' I said. 'The difficulty, as ever, is when other people are involved.'

'Touché,' said Leo. 'Although, seriously, Hope, I'm not sure what our next steps should be. Other than reporting the bullying that has been rife here. We've stopped the pilfering, and if there are faeries in the air I rather think that's out of our jurisdiction – or the Army's anyway.'

'We can also report that the men here are under enormous strain, but that's hardly different to anywhere else, I would have thought.'

Leo sighed. 'We can at least add our voices – or you can add your voice in your report – to say we don't think the chaps are getting enough training hours before they fly.'

'I suppose so. But whether or not we are finished all depends on whether or not you believe Collins took his own life.'

'You don't?' said Leo with a sudden frown. 'If you think there is foul play involved this is going to get a lot stickier. I don't believe for one moment the body is in the plane wreck. That was Harvey overreacting. There won't have been any particular attention paid to the body, and any clues, with the exception of the wreck, will be gone. Do you want to go clambering around inside a crashed plane that has been left out in all weathers – Scottish weathers – and is full of weeds, damp, earwigs and goodness knows what? I mean, if I thought there might be anything decisive in there I would, but you've got to see—'

'Oh, I don't want to inspect the wreck. If anyone does it will be Harvey. It will come to that if I go down the line of sabotage. But I'm not even there yet.' I sipped my tea. 'It's all about the people, Leo, and all of them are still here. If anyone is responsible for his death then they've been carrying that around with them for months. It will have changed them. All the clues we will ever need are in the behaviour of the people here.'

'That's not the kind of thing that stands up in military or even civilian court,' said Leo.

I shrugged. 'If you apply enough pressure to any closed environment eventually it will give and split. I would say the community and the base here both count as closed environments, wouldn't you?'

'So you're going to push these people? They're on active service, Hope!'

'If no one is guilty then any pressure I apply will be ignored. I might annoy one or two people, but then they will be happy to see me leave. I just have to be careful how I do this. I need to ensure only the guilty are – or may be – affected.'

'And how do you propose doing that?'

'I've been putting together the characters of the people here. It's like a jigsaw puzzle but with personality traits, ambitions, worries and fears.'

'I don't suppose you can summarise it for me?'

'Only partly. It's complicated.'

'And don't tell me,' said Leo. 'It's only in your head and not written down.'

'Of course not. Where on earth can I store papers here securely?'

'You can understand my concern that you're acting only on some hunches.'

'Hardly,' I said.

'Give me an example at least.'

324

'Well, the Buchanans' behaviour has changed due to their son's death.'

'Obviously.'

'Mrs Buchanan is filled with regret. Not enough to have saved Collins, but enough to feel guilty. She's loyal enough to her husband that she won't speak out against him, but by arranging for incidents to happen she has drawn official attention to the base, and hopes that others will sort out the mess. She's far from being all sweetness and light, but I get the impression that she liked Collins and genuinely grieves for him. There's also something about not being able to save either her son or Collins that's really cutting her up.'

'And him? It doesn't sound as if he wanted to help Collins.'

'Far from it,' I said. 'To him Collins is something between an unwanted reminder of the failure of his own son (as he sees it) and his failure as a parent to make his son into a proper man. I expect he has also cast some blame onto his wife – using words in his head like "mollycoddling".'

'Sort of ostrich in the sand kind of thing?'

I nodded. 'Or worse, in some perverse way not helping Collins gave him revenge on his own son for disappointing him – in his mind.'

'Or perhaps he is simply too old to care any more?' suggested Leo.

'Exactly, what we definitely know is that between these two incidents the Buchanans have become unstuck as a couple, and it seems to me that after a life in service, neither of them is at their best without the other. I expect, in different ways, they both want things resolved. They want to return, at heart, to the old status quo, but can't find how to do it.'

'Well, they can't,' said Leo. 'Their son is dead.'

'But I can use that desire for nostalgia,' I said. 'In fact the more I think about it, the more I like the idea of going to talk to the wing commander. He has lots of issues I can apply pressure to, and he is a source of information we have more or less disregarded, because he took himself out of the questioning.'

'Do you think he will talk?'

'I think we should go up to see him and say we have a verbal report to offer.'

'I'm not convinced,' said Leo. 'But I will back you up however I can.'

'Have you got a motorbike?'

Leo nodded. 'It's my excuse for being here.'

I got up. 'I don't suppose you've changed your mind about telling me the reason you met the man at the beach? It might tie in with all this.'

Leo shook his head. 'No, Hope. No deal, I'm afraid. I'm confident it doesn't overlap with your mission.'

'Would you tell me if it did?' I asked.

'I wouldn't tell you that it didn't if it did,' said Leo.

'All right,' I said. 'I'll accept that.'

'I like the way you make that sound like a condescension on your part, when you actually have no choice in the matter.'

'I was taught by a master,' I said.

Leo brought the motorbike round, while I rummaged for something that could resist the drizzling mist outside.

'Lovely day,' said Leo.

I climbed onto the back of the bike. 'One of Scotland's finest,' I said. 'For once the rain isn't driving full force into your face.'

'You're not frightened being on the back, are you?'

'Should I be? You can drive this thing, can't you?'

'Some girls get a bit upset at the speed,' said Leo. 'I mean, going fast without the enclosure of a car around you.'

'I'd like to learn,' I said. 'I find it exhilarating.'

'Why doesn't that surprise me,' said Leo. 'It will be all the more exciting on the way back. I think the mist is going to come down later. I've been told tales by the chaps at The Manse of the fogs being so heavy you can't see your hand in front of your face. But I don't suppose you're afraid of fog either?'

'I dislike it,' I said. 'It forces me to be cautious.'

He laughed and started the bike forward with a lunge. I had intended to hold on to the back, but ended up grabbing his waist. He didn't object. Leo drove more cautiously than Cole, but it was clear he knew what he was doing. Of all the rides I had had over the last few days this was by far the smoothest.

We arrived at the base and found it quieter than usual. We saw one man walking quickly between the mess tent and the instruction hall, but there were few servicemen about on the grounds. From the hangar where Harvey worked we heard the faint sound of metal hitting metal.

Leo parked and I got off. I rubbed the back of my neck. 'Hackles rising?' said Leo. 'I feel it too. There's something off. Maybe all those issues of yours are finally working their way out, like a splinter coming out of skin.'

'Time could be a sufficient pressure without my intervening,' I said. 'Or maybe they're all spooked because the faeries have stopped stealing. With this place nothing much would surprise me.'

Leo gave me an odd look.

We walked over to the wing commander's office and went in. Susan sat at the desk, fiddling with a pencil and staring into space. She jumped when we entered.

'Something wrong?' I asked.

'Just one of those funny days,' she said. 'You get an odd feeling before the boys go up.'

'They're going up in this?' asked Leo. 'Isn't it too misty?'

'Visibility higher up is fine,' said Susan. 'Or so the weather chaps say. We've had a sighting of fighters escorting at least one bomber north east from here over the sea. It's unexpected. Daylight isn't a preferred time for that kind of thing and we've never been much of a target. In Scotland the lads are normally looking for U-boats or watching out for our subs.'

'They fly further though, don't they?'

'You'd have to ask Abercrombie exactly how far they can go. I think it's five or six hundred miles. But we have a large fuel dump onsite. That's what the security is all about here. Protect the planes and protect the fuel. Everything else doesn't matter that much.'

'Where is the fuel kept?' I asked.

'Nearby,' said Susan, 'but the location is need to know.'

Leo whispered in my ear, 'Harvey will know, do we need to do this now?'

'Susan, we'd like to talk to your grandfather. Does he have anyone with him?'

'He's got a luncheon later . . .'

'Fine,' I said, and walked away. I knocked on the wing commander's door and walked in before he answered. Leo followed behind me.

Buchanan looked up surprised. He had, of all things, a stamp album open before him. He saw us, and closed it with a slam. His cheeks reddened and he scowled. 'I don't know what discipline is like where you normally work, but here we keep to regulations, respect, and politeness.'

I sat down in the chair opposite him without waiting for an invitation. Leo came and stood at my shoulder. Buchanan huffed through his moustache. I could practically hear the cogs of his mind trying to find a blistering reprimand that was also suitable for a lady's ears. I didn't let him speak.

'Really? That's interesting. Do you believe that Collins was dealt with with respect?'

'Collins? What's he got to do with anything? The man's dead.'

'Yes, he died in the crashed plane you have cordoned off. I presume you removed his body?'

'Naturally, he had a full Christian burial in the local church.'

'Did a lot of local people attend?' I asked. 'Only I hear he was quite popular.'

'He had a way of ingratiating himself down in the village.'

'But he wasn't popular on the base, was he?' I said.

'Are you implying something, Lieutenant? Because I'll have you know I am a firm advocate of spitting it out. No beating about the bush and whatnot.'

'I can be more blunt, if you wish,' I said.

He gave a false light laugh. 'Very well, lay on, MacDuff. Although I can't see how any of this comes under your duties. What say you, Captain?'

I felt Leo tense behind me, but his voice, when he spoke, suggested he was completely at ease. 'On this mission, the Lieutenant is in charge. I'm here to add . . . er . . . authority, if it's needed.'

'You're both army. I don't know what authority you can believe you have here. Unless of course you're not regular army at all.'

'I can confirm,' said Leo, 'we are both in the SIS.'

I could have kicked him. I knew Buchanan was suspicious, but I hadn't wanted to show our hand this early. However, I kept a straight face. It was important Buchanan thought we were united in our approach.

'I see,' he said, then stood up and went over to the door. For a moment I thought he was leaving, but he merely called out to his secretary. 'Susan, get Abercrombie in here.'

'He's on standby,' responded Susan.

'I don't bloody care!'

'We will wait under he arrives before we go any further,' the wing commander said as he sat down behind his desk. His eyes had gone a flint-like grey. I wondered if this was the look he had worn when he shot down enemies in the Great War.

'Are you certain that is what you want?' I said. 'I may mention certain circumstances you would not wish your junior officers to know.' I didn't like the man, but it wasn't my job to destroy his authority or even, possibly, his nerve.

He looked down his nose at me. This man I had thought of as a vague but avuncular gentleman when I first met him was becoming before my eyes the man who in his youth had shot other young men out of the air. It appeared he carried no regret with him.

Abercrombie burst into the room some minutes later. He was in full flying gear. He began to speak before he had noticed us. 'I do hope this is vital, sir. Only the way things are going we might be in the air any minute.'

'I trust you will be able to hear the siren from here,' said Buchanan.

'Of course, sir,' said Abercrombie, coming further into the room and acknowledging us both with a nod. He slowed his pace and his voice when he realised Buchanan was not alone. 'But it will take me longer to run to my plane. We both know those extra minutes can make all the difference.'

'Do you hear that, Miss Stapleford? Let's get this done.'

If Leo had been tense before, he must now be at breaking point. I could feel the strain of him behind me like heat on my back. It was as if he was on fire.

'I understand Collins was believed to be of a homosexual persuasion,' I said.

'Nonsense,' said Buchanan, brushing this aside. 'He would have been arrested and confined. It is a criminal offence.'

'To be accurate, sir, the act is criminal. A man may legally feel attracted towards other men, but if he does not act on his inclination then no crime is committed. For Collins to be arrested someone would have needed to accuse him or there would have needed to be physical proof of homosexual intercourse.'

'I say,' said Abercrombie in a breathy gasp.

Buchanan turned red and almost purple as he huffed at me. If he carried on this way he would have an apoplexy before the end of the interview. I wondered if I would call for help or if I and the others would be prepared to watch him die. At this moment I found myself caring less and less. I hit him with my next punch.

'I believe your son recently died,' I said.

I heard Abercrombie lean against the wall behind me. 'I'm sorry to hear that, sir. If you need time away, I would be happy to—'

Buchanan waved the issue away as if it was of no more interest than a passing fly. 'That was some months ago. Life goes on. I know my duty. I serve my King and Country.'

'Unlike your son. I understand he was by inclination a pacifist . . .'

330

'I am aware he was not eager to fight. It is a family shame, but what has this to do with Collins?'

Abercrombie made an uncomfortable noise in his throat, but said nothing.

'I have been made aware that although peaceful, your son had, after considerable thought, decided that the Nazis represented an evil that needed to be fought.'

'Nonsense. The boy was a coward. Tried my best to bring him up in the fighting spirit, but he was always a mummy's boy. Timid, afraid – read poetry, for goodness' sake. Terrible shame, but all families get them sometimes. Some kind of throwback or aberration.'

Leo spoke as if the words were forced from him. 'You're talk-ing about your own son, sir!'

'Indeed I am, Captain, and I am more than aware of his fail-ings. Why do you bring this matter to my squadron leader's attention. It has nothing to do with him. Abercrombie, you may go.'

'You may not,' I said, doing my best to put steel into my voice. I stood and turned to the side so that both of them were within my gaze. 'Were you aware of the wing commander's family history?'

Abercrombie hadn't moved from resting against the wall. It was a casual pose, almost aggressively so, but his face had gone expressionless, flat with no effect. There was white shading around his mouth, and his eyes had narrowed. He crossed his arms as he spoke. He was shutting not only me out, but the entire world.

'I was not.'

'With hindsight do you realise the significance?'

Abercrombie dropped his gaze, and I thought for a moment he might be able to appeal to me as Hope, the girl he claimed he wanted to take to meet his mother, but he did not. I wanted to tell him that I did not like what I had to do, but that was, obviously, impossible.

He gave a grunt of assent.

'What is the girl talking about?' Buchanan asked his senior officer.

Abercrombie looked up then, directly at his CO. 'She's talking, sir, about how I murdered Collins, and how you did nothing to stop me.'

Chapter Forty-six

Inside the Cockpit

The room became quiet as the countryside does after a sudden snowfall. But this was no cessation of hostilities, this was merely the eye of the storm.

'Nonsense, Abercrombie. Collins killed himself. At best it was gross mismanagement of the plane, but you and Susan heard his last messages. The man was clearly off his head.'

'Your son killed himself. Collins did not. Whether he was murdered will be up to a military court to decide.'

'I don't know who you've been speaking to, but this is utter nonsense. Captain, don't you have any control over your subordinate? The girl is talking nonsense.'

I glared at him and considered how to respond for only a moment, but Leo was already answering. 'Sir, with respect, you are addressing a lieutenant in the SIS, an experienced officer, and the one currently in charge of our mission. At this moment she holds not only your career, but the fate of most of the staff on this entire base, in her hands.'

'Impossible,' said Buchanan.

'He's perfectly correct,' I said. 'I report directly to my head of section. And before you ask, sir, he's a colonel.' Although for all I knew Fitzroy might have decided he was a brigadier today.

Buchanan sat down again, muttering, 'I don't know what this world is coming to.' Along with various other swipes at girls, the Army, and officers in above their heads. I chose to ignore him. Fitzroy, I knew, would have hauled him out of his seat and held him up against the wall, rather roughly shaking hands with his throat. This would be the only concession he would make to the man's age. I mean that he would have refrained from punching him in the mouth. This being his most usual response to rudeness and insubordination.

I beckoned Abercrombie forward, so I could sit and see both of them. I expected him to perch on the edge of the desk, but he preferred to lean against the back wall, a little to the left of Buchanan's desk.

'Squadron Leader, you were aware that Collins was different to his peers, were you not?'

'I suppose so,' Abercrombie said. 'He didn't fit in well with the other men. If I'm honest he became something of a butt of their jokes. It's not always the best of the male of the species that comes out in groups,' he said, and gave me an apologetic smile.

'How generous of you to admit that,' I said coldly. 'So you would say that Collins was a man without friends here?'

Abercrombie stopped slouching. 'I wouldn't have said that. He had a number of friends among the people from the village. He was good at hitting it off with a certain sort of person. He could display an engaging sense of humour.'

'I assume you mean that, when he wasn't feeling threatened, he could be cheerful,' I said.

Buchanan opened his mouth to speak.

'I suggest you think very carefully about what you say next,' I said to him. 'Either you need to acknowledge that there was a campaign of bullying happening at the base, led by Abercrombie, which you knew nothing about, or –' I paused for a moment, watching Abercrombie carefully. 'Or,' I repeated, 'you will need to admit that you turned a blind eye to what happened with Collins because he reminded you of your dead son, who you resent for bringing your family name into disrepute and alienating you from your wife.'

'The difference,' said Leo, surprising me, 'is between an honourable and a dishonourable discharge.'

'You mean my career is over,' said the wing commander. 'I doubt it. You might be working for some army colonel, but I was in the last show. I did my bit. I am remembered and well thought of by the top brass. Who are you, but a silly young girl who's got some crackpot ideas into her head. Doubtless, Captain, she has you controlled by what lies between your legs. If anyone's career is going down the drain today, it will be yours.'

Leo stepped forward. I caught his wrist. His hands were clenched by his sides. 'Don't,' I said.

'You do seem to have rather an effect on the men round here,' said Abercrombie. 'But you are a beautiful young woman, Hope. Even if you don't have your head on straight.'

I looked at him. 'I have eyewitness statements from both service personnel and civilians that you not only allowed the bullying of Collins, but you encouraged it.' Part of this was conjecture, but I knew I was right. The statements wouldn't be hard to find. When I saw him swallow I was even more sure I was right.

'Rubbish,' said Buchanan.

'Even your wife has confirmed this,' I said.

'All you've done is take advantage of a grieving mother,' he said. 'You'd have been better spending your time finding who is pilfering from the base.'

'That is over,' I said. 'Dealt with. It was the least of the problems here.' I looked over at Abercrombie again. 'I think Collins' death has been troubling you for a long time. I don't believe you ever intended it to go as far as it did. I certainly don't think you meant to be the instrument of his death, but you were.'

Abercrombie muttered a denial, but he wouldn't meet my gaze.

The wing commander turned to look at his senior officer. 'Tell her she's talking rubbish,' he said, 'and we'll have an end of this. I'll have them both transported off base.'

It was then, with immaculate timing, that the siren went off.

Abercrombie's attitude changed in a moment. He went from being casually insubordinate to alert in the blink of an eye. I wanted to stop him, but even I realised his duty took priority here. He was already moving, but I had to know one last thing before he went. 'You never expected him to make it to the cockpit, did you?' I said.

Abercrombie paused, his hand on the door. 'I didn't expect him to fly that day. My mistake.'

'You were at fault,' I said to him, 'but you're not a murderer.'

'That's where you're wrong, Hope,' he said, and then he was gone.

The exchange took seconds and felt as if it was over before it had begun. The pit of my stomach fell and my skin came out in goose pimples. I had a bad feeling. It must have shown on my face.

'What's wrong?' Leo asked me.

'I wish we'd had time to complete the conversation,' I said.

'Damn it, girl, you must know it's his duty to fly,' snapped Buchanan.

'Of course,' I said quietly. Buchanan eyed me warily. I expect to his eyes I looked defeated.

'Is this nonsense over?'

'Hardly, sir,' said Leo. 'You heard Abercrombie claim himself to be a murderer. The lieutenant can explain while we wait for them to come back.'

'The Hurricanes have a range of six hundred miles,' said Buchanan, smugly. 'It may be some time.'

'Abercrombie was new as a squadron leader when Collins came, wasn't he?' I said. 'For reasons we may never know, he didn't feel confident with being in charge of his pilots, so he did what so many men have done and gave them, or allowed them, a common enemy – Collins. Like the rest of them, he sensed Collins was different. He may not even have realised how, but he allowed the bullying to continue, and to some extent he joined in with it.'

'I won't believe that.'

'Collins was an intuitive pilot, of natural ability. That only made the other men dislike him more. It was also part of the reason he crashed that day. He relied more on his eyes than he did

336

on the dials. My stepfather is the same. He doesn't even recognise all the dials on the dash nowadays. He flies largely by sight – as did Collins. So coming in that day during the fog would not have been easy for him at the best of times. As he was frightened out of his wits, it was the last straw and he lost control of the plane.'

'We know this,' insisted Buchanan.

'But you don't know why,' I said.

'Damn fool thought there was someone in the plane with him. Gone off his head! Weak minded, that kind always are!'

'No, what he saw was very real. He saw the spider that Abercrombie had dropped down his neck earlier in the mess. He knew that Collins, although fearless in many ways, was terrified of spiders.'

'Nonsense!'

'Any of your men can verify this. Even your new mechanic mentioned it. Phobias, such as arachnophobia, are irrational fears. In the worst cases they make people lose control. That's what happened to Collins. He found a spider crawling in his cockpit and he panicked.'

'So that's why Abercrombie said he murdered him,' said Leo.

'I expected him to feel partly to blame for Collins' death,' I said, 'but I didn't expect him to feel as if he had murdered him. I am worried about Squadron Leader Abercrombie's state of mind.' I looked at Leo. 'Perhaps I should have stopped him.'

Leo shook his head. 'You didn't have the authority.'

I turned to Buchanan. 'Whatever happens this day I hold you largely responsible. You turned your back on Collins. Even your wife was worried about him, but you wouldn't listen to her. Instead you allowed a campaign of bullying and tormenting to go on among your officers and did nothing to stop it. My report will make your culpability clear.'

I got up and walked out. Leo caught up with me outside. We had to speak up as we could hear the planes taking off. 'What will happen to Abercrombie, do you think? Court martial? It seems like a waste of a good fighter pilot.'

'You mean we should let people do what they want as long as they are fighting for their country?'

'I'm saying could there be some latitude for the stress of being a fighter pilot? I doubt Abercrombie thought his joke would lead . . . like you said.'

'An officer is responsible for the men under his command. A good officer does his – or her – best to ensure that the personnel they command are in as good a state in body and mind as they can be. There is no excuse for undermining or intimidating someone you are in command of.'

'But it happens,' said Leo.

'Of course it does,' I said. 'It's happened to me.' I thought of Cole and Fitzroy, both constantly testing me, and now Cole had pushed me too far. 'Abercrombie's fault can't be excused, but neither can Buchanan's. He's taken next to no notice of his men, or he would know how much of a state Abercrombie is in.'

'What do you know, Hope?' asked Leo. The lines around his eyes showed, as he frowned. Perhaps winced would be a better term. He knew the reality as much as I did, but he didn't want to look at it.

'Abercrombie didn't flirt with me because he liked me. I think in the end he did like me, but at the beginning it was all about misdirection. He realised from the start that I was smart, and that in liaising with the community I might come across Collins' death and realise there was something odd about it. When he began to suspect I was more than liaison, he turned his charm on full blast.'

'I thought you were falling for him,' said Leo.

'Well, I wanted him to think that,' I said. 'Truthfully, I did find him attractive, but what he had done to Collins was—'

'Do you honestly believe that a flyer like Collins would panic and crash because he had a spider on board?' said Leo. 'I know phobias can be strong, but isn't the instinct to survive stronger?'

'He was yelling at it to get out of the plane,' I said. 'I don't think it can be clearer.'

'I don't know, Hope,' said Leo. 'You could be right and yet it doesn't quite fit.'

It was only at this moment that I remembered the wild garlic in my food. The propensity of the locals to forage for food. Mrs Buchanan's wild mushroom soup. Could she have made a mistake? Could there have been a very earthly reason for why Collins was hallucinating? Had I missed a vital part of the puzzle? Was Mrs Buchanan an accidental murderer?

'Leo,' I said. 'I've had another thought . . .' My voice was drowned out by the sound of the engines.

We turned to watch the last plane take off.

'Everyone makes mistakes,' I said, 'but some things are . . . not so much unforgivable as actions you cannot undo. Abercrombie would always have been the officer who allowed one of his men to be bullied, and whose practical joke drove him over the edge. That happened. It can't be changed. Before that I think I would probably have liked Abercrombie very much, but not after.' I sighed. 'In a way the fault is all with Buchanan. Abercrombie is another one who doesn't like killing. He's sick of shooting down young Germans. Sick of watching pilots die in the air. He told me about seeing a pilot he was about to shoot down crying. I've no idea if he could have seen that close into a cockpit, but it was clear he was finding it harder and harder to live with himself. He wasn't the kind of man to refuse his duty, but he loathed what his duty had made him into.'

'You keep talking about him as if he's dead,' said Leo.

'I know,' I said. 'I hope I'm wrong.'

And I really did. I had no doubt Abercrombie was culpable, but was he the only one? I thought of the man on the beach. What would be gained by investigating this further. The wing commander would be removed. What good would casting any more stones do?

Epilogue

Abercrombie did not return from that sortie. Stewart, the young officer I had met on my way to the base, wrote in his report that,

> I had an FW 190 on my tail I could not lose. Squadron Leader Abercrombie had ceased active engagement after reporting his gun had jammed. He had been issuing commands, but seeing that I was in strong danger of being shot down, and having no other means of preventing this, he sacrificed himself by flying straight into the enemy plane. There was a mid-air explosion and both planes plummeted to the ground.

Leo and I were on a train south. 'You think he did it deliberately, don't you?'

'I won't put it in my report. It's not a fact. I believe, however, that he had been planning to do something of the kind for a while.'

'Because of Collins?'

The train juddered to a halt. I looked out of the window at a grey landscape, rolling with mist. Beyond the railway lines, a herd of cows lay in the field opposite, stoically chewing cud while the drizzle permeated everything. It was a cold, lonely sort of day that lowered the spirit and made one long for soup and a log fire.

'Because of everything, both things said and unsaid.'

Leo gave me an odd look. The train gave another judder and began to move again.

'That was quick,' said Leo.

I shrugged. 'I believe the local duke has a bit of a thing about trains running on schedule. He'll want his dinner at the usual time.'

'Why does your stepfather want me with you?'

'No idea,' I said. 'I didn't think he liked you.'

It was Leo's turn to look away. 'That was certainly the impression he left me with.'

Griffin, my stepfather's major-domo, picked us up at the station in a large car. Jack sat in the front seat. 'Do be careful of the dog,' he said, as Jack leapt onto me in the back seat and began to wash my face. Tears rushed to my eyes as I hugged the little dog, but he was already squirming away from me.

I might have broken out in great sobs at the thought of almost being home, being safe, but Jack bit Leo and that made me laugh. I didn't mean to but the look on Leo's face was so comical.

We arrived with Leo cradling his bleeding hand at the entrance to a stately home that seemed much more castle-like than I had expected. The butler had scarcely opened the door to a rather grand stone hallway with a black and white chequered floor before my mother had engulfed me in a hug.

'Oh, my darling, it is so good to see you!' she said. She smelt of expensive scent and wore a black silk dress that had clearly been made for her, it fitted so well, and must have cost more than my entire wardrobe. Around her neck hung the Christmas Star, now with matching diamond earrings and a diamond bracelet. But most strikingly of all, she looked ten years younger than when I had last seen her. It took me a little while to realise that I was finally seeing her happy, radiantly happy.

My mother released me and held out her hand to Leo. 'Leo, isn't it? I've . . . oh, that wretched dog has bitten you. I told Eric not to send him in the car, but he would insist that Jack knew you were on your way and wanted to see you. I am so sorry.'

As she was saying this, Fitzroy arrived, walking into the hall as if he owned the place, which he did, and looking impossibly handsome in an evening suit. He also looked outrageously smug. He came up behind my mother, and put his arm casually around her waist.

'He's young yet. He'll improve with age,' said Fitzroy, looking over at Leo, and leaving it open as to whether he was speaking about the man or the dog.

'I have so much to tell you,' I blurted out.

'I've read your report,' said Fitzroy. 'You did well in an unfortunate circumstance. Your ability to unearth information is much improved.'

'I . . .' I began almost timidly. I wanted to talk to him about the man I had shot, about Cole, about what I might have missed, about a hundred and one other things that had both my mind and stomach constantly churning, but Fitzroy didn't notice me trying to address him.

'I have the most interesting news,' he said. 'My wife and I are going to Cairo at the end of the week. There's a chap there whose intelligence abilities are meant to rival my own, and we're off to investigate.' He pulled my mother even closer towards him, and looked down at her with open and deep affection. 'Just like old times, don't you think, my love?'

My mother looked up at him. 'Nonsense,' she said, 'no one could be as good as you.'

He bent down and kissed her on the forehead with a complete lack of embarrassment. 'I knew there was a reason I loved you,' he said. 'Now, will someone please summon the housekeeper, that young man is dripping blood on my floor.'